"With its lively prose, well-developed conflict and passionate characters, this enjoyable, poignant tale is certain to enchant."

—*Publishers Weekly* on *Halfway to Heaven* (starred review)

"With this final installment of Wiggs's Chicago Fire trilogy, she has created a quiet page-turner that will hold readers spellbound."

—*Publishers Weekly* on *The Firebrand*

"In poetic prose, Wiggs evocatively captures the Old South and creates an intense, believable relationship between the lovers."

—*Publishers Weekly* on *The Horsemaster's Daughter*

P9-DOH-604

"*The Charm School* draws readers in with delightful characters, engaging dialogue, humor, emotion and sizzling sensuality."

—*Costa Mesa Sunday Times* on *The Charm School*

Praise for the novels of

SUSAN WIGGS

HALFWAY TO HEAVEN

"Wiggs' writing shimmers…. Her flair for crafting intelligent characters and the sheer joy of the verbal sparring between them make for a delightful story you'll want to devour at once."

—*BookPage* on *Halfway to Heaven*

THE FIREBRAND

"With this final installment of Wiggs's Chicago Fire trilogy, she has created a quiet page-turner that will hold readers spellbound…."

—*Publishers Weekly*

THE MISTRESS

"Susan Wiggs delves deeply into her characters' hearts and motivations to touch our own."

—*Romantic Times*

THE HOSTAGE

"Once more, Ms. Wiggs demonstrates her ability to bring readers a story to savor that has them impatiently awaiting each new novel."

—*Romantic Times*

THE HORSEMASTER'S DAUGHTER

"In poetic prose, Wiggs evocatively captures the Old South and creates an intense, believable relationship between the lovers."

—*Publishers Weekly*

THE CHARM SCHOOL

"*The Charm School* draws readers in with delightful characters, engaging dialogue, humor, emotion and sizzling sensuality."

—*Costa Mesa Sunday Times*

Also available from MIRA Books and
SUSAN WIGGS

HALFWAY TO HEAVEN
THE FIREBRAND
THE MISTRESS
THE HOSTAGE
THE HORSEMASTER'S DAUGHTER
THE CHARM SCHOOL
THE DRIFTER
THE LIGHTKEEPER

Watch for Susan's newest novel
HOME BEFORE DARK
Available in hardcover April 2003

SUSAN WIGGS
ENCHANTED AFTERNOON

MIRA®

If you purchased this book without a cover you should be aware that this book is stolen property. It was reported as "unsold and destroyed" to the publisher, and neither the author nor the publisher has received any payment for this "stripped book."

ISBN 1-55166-938-2

ENCHANTED AFTERNOON

Copyright © 2002 by Susan Wiggs.

All rights reserved. Except for use in any review, the reproduction or utilization of this work in whole or in part in any form by any electronic, mechanical or other means, now known or hereafter invented, including xerography, photocopying and recording, or in any information storage or retrieval system, is forbidden without the written permission of the publisher, MIRA Books, 225 Duncan Mill Road, Don Mills, Ontario, Canada M3B 3K9.

All characters in this book have no existence outside the imagination of the author and have no relation whatsoever to anyone bearing the same name or names. They are not even distantly inspired by any individual known or unknown to the author, and all incidents are pure invention.

MIRA and the Star Colophon are trademarks used under license and registered in Australia, New Zealand, Philippines, United States Patent and Trademark Office and in other countries.

Visit us at www.mirabooks.com

Printed in U.S.A.

To H.P.R., who survived.

ACKNOWLEDGMENTS

The Historical Society of Saratoga Springs provided invaluable information for my research. Although Vandam Square and Moon Lake Lodge are my inventions, they were very much inspired by their real counterparts in this unique and beautiful historic city. Dramatic liberties have been taken with the town's layout, and fictional characters are, of course, my own invention. Many thanks as always to Joyce, Barb, P.J., Rose Marie, Janine, Lois, Kate and Anjali. Thanks for being first readers, mentors and friends. And finally, thanks to H.P.R., who kept her promise.

"Heaven has no rage like love to hatred turned,
Nor hell a fury like a woman scorned."

—William Congreve, *The Mourning Bride*

One

She wore long sleeves to cover the bruises. Although the July sun burned like hellfire and damnation through the soundless house—even the French voile curtains in the parlor windows didn't dare to stir—she kept herself covered in the very height of fashion.

That, after all, was what people expected of a senator's wife. Or, she thought with a dizzying leap of hope, his *former* wife. But that hope would be fulfilled only if she managed to get what she wanted out of this meeting.

She waited in the summer parlor, where the tall mantelpiece mirror was draped in mourning black. Though she'd lived in the handsome house in Vandam Square for years, a fine edge of terror and panic sharpened her perceptions. She noticed all the elegant details and art treasures in the room as though for the first time—the Italianate plaster wainscoting, the Meissen porcelain vase atop a Sheridan table, the ormolu clock on the mantel, the German-made harp in the corner, a series of boring, expensive pastoral scenes of lakes and forests and fox hunts hanging on the walls.

On a wall all to itself hung the strange new painting

she had chosen on her own, just last season. It was the only thing in the room she didn't find boring, the only thing she had acquired without consulting her husband.

It was a scene called *Woman at Bath* by an obscure French painter named Hilaire Germain Edgar Degas. Unlike the bucolic scenes that graced the halls of the vast mansion, this particular painting of a decidedly unglamorous nude drying her abundant body tended to shock everyone, even though it interested and excited her. In the bold distortions of water and light, she could see something special. The intimate, sensuous portrait depicted a woman comfortable in her own skin, and she felt like a different person looking at that painting. For that reason, she loved it. Because she so dearly wanted to be a different person—someone, anyone else.

There was another reason she loved the strange, light-washed picture.

Her husband hated it.

The only reason he let her keep it was that she'd told him it had been a gift from the Vanderbilts. That wasn't true, of course, but it was the least of the lies she'd told him over the course of their nine-year marriage.

The faint jingle of harness outside the open window startled her, even though she was expecting it. She heard the footsteps of Archie Soames, the butler, as he went to the door. She moved to the window, which was veiled by sheer curtains. The wispy fabric exuded a hot smell, like fresh ironing. Because the curtains diffused the view of the driveway, the arriving vehicle appeared like something out of a dream.

With one finger, she pushed aside the crisp white curtain, bringing the view into sharp focus. The black enameled side of the open carriage bore curlicue letters arranged in an arch over a rising, stylized sun—the symbol of the Hudson Valley Institute for Innovation. A tall man stepped down from the vehicle, and for a moment she forgot how to breathe.

Instinctively, she stepped away from the heat and light of the window. But she couldn't resist watching through a gap in the curtains as he spoke briefly to the driver and then headed up the walkway toward the house. He wore green-tinted celluloid sunglasses, all the rage among cyclists and drivers these days, and his clothes were rumpled, as though he had picked them up from a heap on the floor.

She wasn't prepared for the effect he still had on her, after all this time. Yes, she felt bitter resentment—that was to be expected, given the way he'd treated her. But like a current beneath the surface of a calm lake, she sensed something else. Something as forbidden and as undeniable as the passion she had felt when she first met him, nearly a decade before.

She resisted the urge to push aside the shroud that draped the mantel mirror and study her reflection. Instead, she checked and double checked the fitted bombazine sleeves of her black mourning gown, neatly fastened at the wrists with a row of obsidian buttons. Appearances were everything. It was perhaps the first lesson she could remember learning, drummed into her by a stern-faced nanny dressing her at the age of three for her mother's funeral.

Should she be seated? No, that would wrinkle the gown. She positioned herself on the Persian silk hearth rug in the middle of the parlor, posing like one of the concrete statues in Congress Spring Park. Glaring light from the window made her skin prickle with heat. She wore her copper-colored curls swept up, though a trickle of perspiration rolled down the back of her neck. She tried to arrange her face into an expression of serenity—not out of vanity but habit. Her looks had brought her nothing but trouble. Yet she knew of no other way to present herself.

Besides, some perverse part of her wanted him to feel the same waves of nostalgic longing that were coursing through her now.

With a flourish, Archie opened both parlor doors. "A gentleman to see you, ma'am." The butler's voice rasped with the roughness of a summer cold, and his slight emphasis on the term *gentleman* added a note of skepticism.

"Of course. Thank you."

The butler melted back into the foyer and her visitor strode into the room, removing his tinted spectacles and setting them on a side table. His fathomless eyes were even bluer than memory allowed. He took one look at her, and the expression on his face was everything she had anticipated—curiosity and wonder, shaded with suspicion and perhaps regret.

They stared at each other, the air between them heavy and palpable with memories.

"Helena." He said her name in a low voice that reverberated through her like a lingering caress.

"Hello, Professor Rowan," she said, deliberately using his formal title. "Thank you for coming. Would you like something to drink?" She gestured at the carved mahogany sideboard in the corner, laden with a sweating pitcher of lemonade and a silver bowl of chipped ice.

"Yes, please."

She spooned ice into a crystal goblet, then poured the lemonade. Nerves made her hands unsteady. Had she been mistaken in asking him to come? Perhaps so, but she didn't know what else to do. Like a rabbit caught in a snare, she would turn anywhere, do anything to escape, even if running away wounded her worse than staying put. She would do anything to reclaim her safety, even turn to the one man she thought she would never see again.

Terror was a new sensation to her. It clutched at her spine with icy fingers, pressed at her chest until she couldn't breathe, making her dizzy with its power. She refused to live like this, frozen from the inside out. She wasn't rational; she knew that. Fear kept her from thinking clearly. And in that moment of madness, she had sent for Michael Rowan.

Convincing him to help her was a long shot, but she was desperate. Perhaps it was callous, this imperious summons, but she didn't really care. Years ago, Michael Rowan had used her in the worst possible way, then he'd left without even a by-your-leave. So she should not feel the least bit guilty about using him now.

When she turned, there he stood, only inches from her. Flustered, she pushed the glass into his hand. Lemonade sloshed over the side.

"Oh, I—"

"Not to worry." He set the glass on the silver tray. Good glory, how could such an unkempt man be so appealing? His hair was too long, curling several inches over the back of his collar. He needed a shave. His clothes were a disgrace. And yet there was something about him that mesmerized and haunted her. Regardless of the passage of time, that aspect of him hadn't changed.

As unbidden thoughts nagged at her, he lifted his fingers to his mouth and licked the lemonade from them with a methodical, insolent sensuality she wished she didn't remember.

"Delicious," he said, even as she averted her stare. "Though I daresay a touch of tequila would improve it. You'll recall it improved our spirits one evening, long ago."

She picked up a linen napkin and shoved it at him. How dare he remind her of that? Yet once he planted the seed of remembrance, it took root deep inside. Long ago, he had introduced her to the narcotic liquor called tequila, and later that night, suffused by its numbing heat, she had—

Helena stopped the thought and lifted her chin in disdain. "So is that still your solution for everything, Professor? A dose of tequila?"

"Have you found a better answer?"

"Perhaps I'm too optimistic, but I always assumed you would mature with age." Taking refuge in cold haughtiness, she brushed past him and went to stand in front of the mantel of Carrera marble.

He drank down the lemonade in a long, sensual gulp. Watching him, she noted that his shirt was buttoned wrong and his left hand was stained with smudges of ink. Beneath a frock coat with frayed elbows, he wore his waistcoat inside out. He had not changed one whit.

And yet he had. A part of her was forced to admit that. When she had known him before, he'd been intimidatingly brilliant, unapologetically carnal and artlessly attractive in the way of all men who neither recognize nor cultivate their good looks.

Professor Michael Rowan was all of those things now, but the years had added something else, some indefinable aspect of character that was perhaps a shade darker, a level deeper than the Michael Rowan she had known so briefly and loved so foolishly.

"Yes, well," she said, forcing herself not to dawdle

any longer. "You're probably wondering why I asked you to call."

"So that's what it was." He fished a wrinkled card from his pocket and held it out. "'Mrs. Helena Cabot Barnes desires a meeting with you on Tuesday at three o'clock in the afternoon.' Your secretary has excellent penmanship, although the wording's a bit terse."

Helena hadn't wanted to disclose her purpose to anyone, least of all Edith Vickery, who, like all the hired help, was loyal to her husband. It was possible the secretary had already alerted the senator to the impending visit from Michael. Yet in her panic, Helena hadn't paused to reason things out. "But you came," she reminded him.

"My dear, one ignores a summons from the wife of Senator Troy Barnes at one's peril."

She couldn't help herself. She let out a sarcastic laugh. "Oh, please. Tell me you're worried about political appearances."

He gestured at the window, open to a view of his carriage parked in the shade of the horse chestnut tree in the yard. "My entire enterprise owes itself to your husband's support. Didn't you know that?"

Now it was her turn to be surprised. "So that's how Troy got rid of you. How clever of him." A frightening thought, that. She had always taken full advantage of his spinelessness and arrogance. But the fact that he had found a way to separate her from the man she loved meant he was more aware than she gave him credit for.

"I should think it takes some measure of cleverness to be a United States senator. Isn't he up for reelection soon?"

"This November." Helena turned the subject back

to Michael's worrisome revelation. "So you're saying the Institute is funded thanks to my husband."

"Exactly."

"I thought you had more pride than that, Michael."

He didn't move a muscle, didn't blink. Yet she could feel his bitterness as though he'd slung it at her in icy sheets. "Not everyone has the luxury of pride," he said simply, then appeared to lose interest in the conversation. He turned his attention to the gallery of paintings along the wall.

She bit her lip, careful not to let on he'd thrown her entire plan into jeopardy. She'd assumed he would side with her against Troy, but now, knowing Michael owed his success to her husband, she feared she had made a horrible mistake in deciding to ask for his help. But after what they'd shared, could he refuse her?

She wondered if his memories matched hers, or if time and yearning had caused her to embellish the past with her imagination. They had been living in the nation's capital. Michael was a professor at Georgetown University; she was the daughter of the venerable Senator Franklin Rush Cabot. She had seen no obstacle to loving an impoverished teacher. As a young woman, Helena Cabot had believed in dreams and in the power of the human heart to overcome any obstacle. How could a love like theirs be wrong?

By being one-sided; she knew that now. The moment she had declared her love to Michael, he received an offer to work as head of the Hudson Valley Institute for Innovation.

Now she saw Troy's manipulative hand in her life more clearly than ever. He had contrived to make the professor an offer he couldn't refuse—the Institute. The new knowledge made her hesitate. The palms of her hands grew slick with sweat, but she forced herself to go on, drawing from a wellspring of reckless courage she'd never realized she possessed.

"So," she said in a conversational tone that masked her heartache and apprehension. "You threw me over for the sake of science. Tell me, was it worth it? Did you invent a machine for flying? Find a cure for scarlet fever? Change the world?"

Though he stood with his back turned, she saw his shoulders stiffen, his neck redden. Slowly, he faced her. "If leaving you spared me from that sharp tongue, then I did indeed make the right choice."

He glanced away again, aiming a disinterested stare at the rustic paintings. Then he turned the corner to the facing wall, and she could see his entire body come alert with interest. For a few moments, he was completely engaged by the Degas painting. She expected him to express confusion or distaste the way everyone else did; instead, he said, "This is quite fascinating. Uncanny."

She did not want to feel gratified, particularly in the wake of his sarcasm. She ignored the compliment. "So, you traded my heart for a more efficient centrifugal pump," she said, referring to the Institute's most commercial invention. "All of humanity will be forever grateful."

"What the hell do you want from me?" he demanded. "Did you summon me here hoping I would grovel before you, declare my undying love and eternal regret for what happened, beg your forgiveness and tell you that I have suffered all the tortures of the damned for the past nine years, eight months, twenty-four days and—" he glanced at the clock on the mantel "—six hours and eighteen minutes?"

She was too shocked to do anything but stare.

He laughed harshly at her expression and took a step

toward her. "Yes, I do remember, Helena. I remember to the exact second the moment I lost you. We were on the stair. I kissed you. Do you remember how I kissed you?" Without warning, he reached out and cupped her cheek, his touch so gentle that she nearly lost her composure. "Ah, Helena. What could we have become?"

Unbidden emotions crept over her and through her and inside her—that mouth, those clever, inventive hands... The memories were specific and they cut deep. The first time they had made love, he told her the anatomical names for the parts of her body. He explained the natural impulses of arousal and how they could be stimulated in certain ways. He showed her things that made her soar with bliss or weep with emotion or howl with laughter at the absurdity of him, of life, of everything. But he had never shown her the mysteries of his heart. Instead, he'd walked out of her life the moment she needed him most and, apparently, he was about to do it again.

"Why?" she asked, stepping away from him and willfully severing the moment of connection. "Why would you remember that day so specifically?"

He gazed at her for a very long time. "You know why. That was the day it became clear to me that I would never be the sort of man who could keep you happy."

To cover her true feelings, Helena burst out laughing. "Oh, do tell, Professor. Truly, in your work at the Institute, did you invent such a thing as a balderdash machine?"

"There is no need for one when the world has you in it," he snapped.

They glared at each other in silence for a time. He helped himself to more lemonade.

She was trying to find a way to make her request to him when he asked, ''How is your family, in Georgetown? Your father and sister.''

She frowned. Was he being sociable? *Michael?*

''Abigail married Jamie Calhoun eight years ago January,'' she said. ''He will start the fall legislative session as Speaker of the House of Representatives. They have two extremely interesting children, and they travel the world. At the moment, they are in Egypt, studying astronomy at the observatory on a mountain called el-Qurn.'' She looked down at the floor and swallowed hard. ''Or perhaps not. Perhaps they are on a steamer home by now. I had to send them a telegraph message with some terrible news, but I have no idea if they ever received the wire.''

When he crossed the room and touched her chin and brought her gaze to his, she remembered why she had once loved him so. He had a way of focusing his entire attention on her and her alone, with a total absorption that made her feel she was the center of the world. It was an illusion, of course, and it was not unique to her. He gave the same attentiveness to mathematical equations. Yet his genuine concern had always contrasted with the fawning looks she received from other suitors. Beauty was the single virtue men focused on, but Michael looked beyond her outward appearance. He was the only one who ever had.

Unsettled by his touch, she backed away from him.

''Your father?'' he asked, his gaze sweeping over the somber black dress.

She nodded. Was it only ten days ago that she had taken the steamer to Georgetown to celebrate Independence Day with her father?

''I feared so,'' he confessed, ''when I saw the funeral wreath on the door, the black... Sit down, Helena. Tell me.''

She lowered herself to a dainty settee covered in watered silk, discreetly cradling the injured arm in her lap. For once, she welcomed the stiff support of a boned corset; it was a great help in binding bruised ribs.

He took the wing chair opposite her. Clearing her throat, she said, ''It happened at the July Fourth picnic on the White House lawn. Father was to receive a special medal of commendation for his years of service. It was to have been the greatest day in his career.'' Her father was the famous senior senator of Virginia. He'd begun his career as an idealistic young man; then he'd become a bombastic politician and finally a revered elder statesman. In view of an audience of dignitaries, he'd walked up the red carpet to the dais decked in garlands of carnations and bunting in red, white and blue. He'd leaned heavily on his old brass-headed cane, a gift from the late President Grant. The short walk to the dais had seemed endless, but no one made a sound. Out of respect for the guest of honor, everyone watched in breath-held silence.

Helena had occupied a seat of honor beside her husband, the powerful Senator Barnes from New York. She remembered how handsome and upright Troy had looked that day. How proud to show off his connection to the great gentleman from Virginia.

Her father's speech had been brief. He declared his satisfaction with the way his life had unfolded and with his achievement in politics. He was gratified that his two worthy daughters, Helena and Abigail, had married well and were content.

He had been right about one daughter.

Helena didn't blame him for her unhappiness. She

had made her own choices. His skills as a parent were far less well-honed than his skills on the Senate floor, but he loved his two daughters in his way. He was not an unqualified success in all he did, though he strove long and diligently for the things he believed in. At that moment, as the president awarded him a medal, Helena had felt nothing but love and pride for her father.

She tried to put her thoughts together for Michael Rowan, who sat waiting, ready to listen. When was the last time anyone had actually listened to her?

She knitted her fingers together. "It was almost like a staged spectacle," she said, picturing the red carpet and draped bunting, the uniformed attendants and naval guards standing at attention, her father and the president looking as distinguished as graven images. She could still smell the oppressive, funereal scent of carnations and roses.

"A moment after receiving the medal," she said, "he was shaking hands with the president, and he—" She stopped and shut her eyes, remembering. Her father died with almost operatic dignity, sinking like a great warship, with such formality that for a moment no one reacted; they were not even certain what they were seeing.

Helena herself had shattered the spell. She screamed, "Papa!" and sprang forward, breaking through a garland of ribbons. She vaguely heard—and ignored—Troy's order to quiet down and stay back. He was always so concerned with appearances.

She was soon to learn just how concerned.

"By the time I reached him," she said, "his face had turned a most unnatural color and he was scarcely breathing. We did get to say goodbye," she said. "We had that chance." She would never forget his final words, gasped voicelessly through lips that were already blue. "I think I shall see your mother now," he said. "Keep well." A simple goodbye from a complicated man.

She related this to Rowan with the barest hint of a smile. "He issued directives to the end. It was his way." She drew a long breath, trying to fill the raw, empty hollows inside her. "By the time a doctor arrived, he was gone. I sent a wire to my sister that night."

Her husband had quite a different reaction to the tragedy and its aftermath. Even now, she could scarcely believe what had happened, yet every pain-filled breath she took reminded her of the hidden wounds. How had she lived with this man for nine years without knowing what lurked inside him?

She should have seen it coming; that was so clear from where she was now, looking back. But she'd been blind, perhaps willfully blind to her husband's hidden resentment. Now she realized his hatred had always been there, lurking beneath the surface, and his secret rage had escalated over the years. A slammed door, a thrown vase, a golf club broken in two... It was easy enough to sweep away the odd incident. Once, after drinking too much champagne at a fundraiser, he'd grabbed her, shaken her, but she still hadn't understood, or let herself understand what that temper unleashed could do.

She disclosed none of this to Michael Rowan. She couldn't. That incident was frozen, a separate part of a life that could not possibly belong to her. Yet the terror and desperation she hid inside reminded her that, indeed, this was happening to her.

"My father was laid to rest in a full state funeral," she said. "Because he was a veteran in the war, he was interred at Arlington National Cemetery. The pomp and ceremony all but undid me. However, it was as grand and formal as my father would've liked."

Michael Rowan reacted with a long, contemplative silence, and he was so focused on her that his attention nearly took her apart. She had sat through the endless eulogies. She had heard that the nation had lost a treasure, heard that she should be proud and cherish her memories. She had held a folded flag to her chest. She had listened to condolences until she wanted to scream. But no one had looked at her the way Michael was looking at her now.

Finally, he spoke. "Is that why you wanted me to come? To take your sadness away? I can't do that." He regarded her in a way that made her heart hurt and added, "I never could."

"The grief is mine to bear," she stated, holding her emotions in check. "I would not dishonor my father by refusing the burden." The mantel clock chimed the hour of four, and the sound startled her.

"Then why—"

"I need your assistance in a matter of great importance." The words rushed from her on a wave of desperation.

"Yes?"

"I need your help in divorcing my husband." She held her breath and waited. As the chimes of the clock echoed through the parlor, doubts infested her conviction. She'd made a panic-driven decision. Perhaps she should have thought things through, planned more carefully. But how could one plan for something like this? She stared at Michael, still waiting.

Nothing. He gave her no response whatsoever, but simply sat there like a rock. She was not certain what she had expected, but surely not this great silence.

"Well?" she prodded him.

"I'm trying to figure out what you could possibly expect me to say."

"You could start with a *yes.*"

"I am a man of science," he said, "not the law."

"You are the man who used to be my lover," she needlessly reminded him.

He had the grace to clear his throat, indicating that her remark discomfited him. "I fail to see what this has to do with you divorcing your husband."

She fixed an unwavering gaze on him. He was right. What had she been thinking? She hadn't been thinking at all. She'd simply acted. When all the world turned against her, when she'd lost everything, when even her sister was nowhere to be found, she'd turned to the one person she thought she could trust, praying he would help her. Michael Rowan was a stranger now. This was a huge mistake, but it was too late to unsay the words.

Helena pressed her hands into her lap until her bruised arm throbbed. He was no better than the spineless lawyer she'd consulted in Georgetown. The moment the solicitor had realized who her husband was, he'd declared a divorce impossible and advised her to drop the matter. Helena had left his office, but she'd been more determined than ever. She knew there were women whose husbands beat them regularly, year in and year out. It was hard to believe. Helena had suffered through a single incident; she would tolerate no more. The moment the first blow of his fist had shattered her world, she had vowed to break free. But fulfilling that vow was another matter altogether.

"You are as dense as ever, Michael," she said in exasperation. "You see, getting a divorce is quite difficult for a woman to achieve, and so I must make a powerful case for myself. The fact that you and I were lovers is powerful indeed, wouldn't you say?"

"Powerful," he echoed. "And what does your husband have to say about the matter?"

"He doesn't know, and he mustn't be told. Not yet. He's away on business, so I was hoping that we—you and I—could arrange things before he returns."

"Arrange things," he echoed again, a mocking edge to his voice.

"The divorce case," she stated. "You are the proof that I married Troy under false pretenses, don't you see? I pledged to love him when, in fact, it was you I loved."

He was starting to sweat, to take shallow breaths. His alarm came as no surprise. Her declaration of love years ago had literally sent him fleeing for the hinterlands. Clearly he was just as unsettled by her now.

But making him uncomfortable wasn't her purpose. She needed his cooperation. "Don't worry, Michael. I don't love you anymore, so you're safe. But I truly did, once, and that made me a fraudulent bride."

"And this only occurred to you now, after nine years."

Outside, she heard the sounds of Vandam Square—the clop of hooves in the brick roadway, the voices of children at play. It seemed so strange that the rest of the world carried on, while her own life had taken such an unexpected turn.

Like many political couples, she and Troy lived apart most of their marriage, she in Saratoga Springs, looking after the house, keeping up appearances. She had always preferred Saratoga Springs to the nation's capital. Georgetown was a fishbowl, and she was tired of swimming naked in public. Here, she was generally left alone to go about her business. Troy spent his time in Washington, D.C., or Albany, tending to the nation's business and probably, she now realized, to a bevy of prostitutes.

"No, I knew it all along. Don't you remember how I used to love you, Michael? Don't you—" She caught his thunderous expression and forced herself to stop. This was absurd, she realized, wishing she'd never summoned him. What had she been thinking? What had she hoped to accomplish, bringing him back?

She knew. In her heart, she knew. When her father had died, she'd been left completely on her own, and she'd panicked. Her sister was half a world away, her husband a despised stranger, her acquaintances remote and untrustworthy. Stripped of everything, she'd acted out of instinct, like a wounded animal. And instinct had led her to contact Michael, the only man she'd ever loved, the only man who made her feel safe.

Unfortunately, Michael was still Michael—unwilling to compromise his own heart.

She decided to offer one last attempt. "My point is, bearing false witness is unlawful, and therefore it should be equally unlawful to wed with a lie in one's heart."

"Believe me, if that was the case, half the couples in America would be divorced."

"Yes, but—"

He stood abruptly. "There's nothing to discuss, Helena. Only you would think of calling upon a former lover in order to help you get a divorce. Your madcap logic is as entertaining as ever, but I'm not interested in your schemes."

"It's no scheme, Michael."

"Oh, no? Now that your father's gone, you don't have to behave yourself anymore. Is that it?"

"How dare you."

"How dare *you.* Damn it, Helena, you broke nine years of silence because you finally decided you need me to help you get rid of a boring husband. I'm sorry you've grown tired of the fellow, but it's not my job to help you out of a trap of your own making."

"You encouraged me to marry another," she reminded him.

"I didn't hold a gun to your head, darling. Good day."

She watched him stride to the door, her heart sinking deeper with every step he took. *A trap of your own making.* She had done exactly that. She had welcomed Troy as a suitor, had wed him after much calculation and scheming. She could not have known the true nature of the man she married.

But she could not carry on like this. She had more than herself to consider.

"Michael, wait." She hurried after him as he wrenched open the door to the foyer.

He stopped and turned. "There's nothing more to say." He strode across the entry hall and disappeared out the door.

She felt strangely, terrifyingly light, as though she might float away at any moment. Summer sunshine streamed through the fanlights framing the door. On the hall table, a silver tray overflowed with calling cards, their corners bent to indicate the caller had come to express condolences. She took no solace in the attentive gestures. In all her years of living here, she had made no true friends, only well-heeled acquaintances who considered her important because of whose daughter she was...and who she'd married. It was depressing to realize she had no one to give her a cup of tea and simply let her weep for her loss.

"Mama!" The cry came from the rear of the house,

followed by the slap of running feet on the parquet floor. "Mama, guess what? Just guess! You'll never guess!"

William. Heavens, he wasn't supposed to be back yet from his outing. She'd sent the driver to take him on a turn around the racetrack, hoping the excursion would keep him preoccupied while she changed the course of their lives. Now, the mere sound of her son's voice drove home the folly of what she'd just done. Bringing Michael into this mess would suck William into it, too. Had she even considered that?

Stupid, she thought. Impulsive. Hadn't she learned a thing since her reckless youth?

William ran to the foyer through the back entry. Fair-haired and fresh-faced, he barreled toward her.

Only when he practically collided with her did he stop. The impact of his small form against her bruised body was agonizing but she never let it show, never even flinched. "Slow down, my little dynamo," she cautioned, resting her fingers on the boy's shoulders.

A feeling of gratitude washed through her. He was the reason she woke up each day, took the next breath of air. He was the reason she cared to live at all. And he was the reason she was going to leave her husband.

William was a typical rough-and-tumble boy in many ways, although he had his own unique quirks and attributes. He was grubby and bright and adorable, and he was wearing his shoes on the wrong feet and his shirt buttoned wrong, just like—

"Oh," William said, looking past Helena at the front door. "Hello."

"I forgot my—" Michael began, stepping inside.

Man and boy locked onto each other, steel to a powerful magnet.

William stepped out from behind Helena.

Michael strode across the foyer, pale and tight-lipped.

"Hello," said William again, extending a grimy hand. "How do you do?"

Helena's son was blessed with the gift of ease and charm and his manners were impeccable. He was a handsome lad with a ready smile. A freshly lost tooth punctuated his grin as he placed his sweaty hand in Michael Rowan's.

And his eyes, surely the most charming attribute of her beautiful eight-year-old son, were vivid blue mirrors of his father's.

Two

Michael stood motionless in the foyer of the Barnes mansion, looking at his son for the very first time. Shock swept over him in great, numbing waves. The rational, empirical part of his mind, the part that refused to feel the pain, put together the facts. This boy was his. She had borne his son and given him to another man. All these years, Michael had had a son, and he'd never known.

Yet neither Helena nor the boy could see his inner turbulence. They simply watched him, she with a waiting tension, the child with unabashed curiosity. She covered William's shoulders with her hands as if ready to snatch him out of harm's way.

Somehow, Michael managed to shake his son's extended hand, to acknowledge the well-brought-up greeting. "My name is Michael Rowan."

His hand engulfed the boy's. Small and hot and firm. His son. He was touching his son.

"How do you do, sir?" he said again. "I'm William."

"It's very good to meet you, William." With a false

heartiness he instantly hated, he said, "Aren't you a fine big boy. How old are you?"

"Eight years, one month, sixteen days, eleven hours..." He peered at the parlor clock through the doorway, barely paused before adding, "And six minutes."

"That's very clever," Michael managed to say. "Where did you learn that?"

"I figured it out for myself." The boy danced from foot to foot. "Mama, I have a very important thing to show you. A wonderful thing."

"William, Professor Rowan was just saying good day."

"As a matter of fact," Michael said, hiding the cold fury that was slowly taking hold of him, "I came back to collect my spectacles." He retrieved them from the parlor. "I wouldn't be averse to seeing something wonderful."

"It is." William punched his fist in the air. "Come this way, hurry."

Michael permitted himself a look at Helena as the small boy led them through the house. She didn't flinch at his glare, didn't seem the least bit repentant as she walked away. Behind her, he was engulfed by the light floral fog of her perfume and the quiet silken swish of her elegant black skirts. Only Helena could raise this havoc of emotion in him—love and fury and yearning and bitterness. It had been true years ago, and to his amazement, it still was.

She carried herself with a stiff dignity he didn't remember in the willowy girl he'd once adored, and her face bore delicate lines and faint shadows of maturity that were new to him. Yet she still had sun-shot coppery hair and the sort of creamy skin a man longed to touch. Helena as a young lady had been utterly captivating. Helena in the full flower of womanhood took his breath away, even despite his anger at her deception.

As he walked with the mother of his child across the lush, manicured lawn, Michael muttered in a low voice, "When were you planning to tell me?"

"Tell you what?"

William skipped along, oblivious, in front of them. Beds of foxglove and delphinium lined the walkway, their candy colors a vivid contrast to the emerald lawn. For a moment, the boy had the surreal look of a figure in a painting, even though he was constantly in motion.

"Look, you played me for a fool once," Michael said to Helena, "but I'm a quick study. It won't happen again."

She smiled, her expression brilliant, her gaze trained straight ahead. "I positively will not discuss this in William's presence," she stated.

He couldn't help but admire her brittle self-possession. The belle of Georgetown had become the first lady of Saratoga Springs. He'd read about her from afar, but even the most blatant scandal sheets respected the privacy of a woman of her status.

In his rarefied, self-contained world at the Institute, Michael wasn't supposed to pay attention to the mundane matters discussed in the news, but there was nothing mundane about Helena. According to the social column in *Frank Leslie's Illustrated Newspaper,* she was the most fashionable, most sought-after hostess in the popular resort town. Regular visitors to Saratoga Springs included Vanderbilts, Astors, crown princes of foreign lands, captains of industry and millionaires with shady pasts. Blue-blooded Helena Cabot Barnes was the doyenne of them all.

He could understand why. She was not beautiful—

that was too commonplace a term to describe the full impact of her appearance. She had some indefinable, ethereal quality that went beyond mere beauty. It had to do with the way she carried herself, the intriguing charms that hid inside her gaze and flashed in her smile.

It was an odd feeling, to remember the ways he used to touch her, the liberties he took with that exquisite body, the emotions and sensations he used to feel as he lay with her, never thinking of the past or future. Odder still and infinitely more painful was the discovery he had made today. Their heedless pleasure had resulted in the lively boy who led them along the garden path. Michael was a man of science, yet he now knew himself to be in the presence of a miracle, a mysterious creation, an invention that made itself. He could think of William in no other terms.

Michael marveled at the idea of having a son of his own. He'd never thought of taking a wife and having children. After Helena, marrying another woman and giving her children simply made no sense. All other women had been ruined for him. Meanwhile, she had selfishly kept William for herself and, worse, introduced him to the world as the son of Troy Barnes.

The child had no notion of the hostility snapping between his mother and the man he regarded as a stranger. Michael didn't want to confuse the lad so he tried not to stare, but couldn't help himself. He devoured William with his gaze. His son had Helena's coloring—the creamy fair skin with a saddle of freckles across the bridge of the nose, a profusion of burnished copper hair, a smile that rivaled the sun for brightness.

But other things about the boy did not come from Helena. That was obvious. The eyes were unmistakable. Michael Rowan saw those very same eyes when he looked in the mirror. They were a curiously dark shade of blue, like the sky at twilight.

He had another, more haunting memory of blue eyes. In a miserable backstretch alley behind the famous Thoroughbred racetrack of Saratoga Springs, there used to live a woman with those same eyes—bluer than nature had intended, intense, almost burning. It was one of his earliest memories of his mother—and his last of her.

Oblivious to the shifting shadows of sentiment that lay over Michael, William led them across the expansive yard, stirring a flurry of butterflies from the hip-tall, sun-paled grasses. At the edge of the property, he pointed toward an unpaved bridle path. "See? See? Isn't he wonderful?"

Helena stopped walking and stared. "Oh, William—"

"Chalkeye Hopkins brought him over from the racecourse stables. He said I could keep him for my very own." Hopping from one foot to the other, he said to Michael, "Chalkeye used to be a famous jockey. Now he's the chief trainer of the Barhytes' farm. Come see, Mama. You, too, Professor Rowan."

"Don't you dare go near that beast," Helena yelled, her voice wincingly shrill. "William, do you hear me?"

The boy stopped instantly, but set his jaw at a mutinous angle. "Hector's not a beast. He's going to be my very own horse."

"He's going straight back to the Barhytes'."

"Mama, no! Chalkeye brought him all the way over here, just for me."

"A racehorse is a dangerous, high-strung animal,

dear. This poor creature would never make a good pet."

"Let's have a look," Michael said, brushing past her and ignoring her gasp of outrage. He approached the racehorse. The old jock had tethered it by a cord from its halter to the horseheaded iron hitch post at the end of the path, then wisely disappeared so he wouldn't be forced to take back his "gift." The dull-hided chestnut gelding had a Thoroughbred's beautifully sculptured head, deep chest and slender legs now powdered with dust from the pathway.

Crippled, no doubt, Michael thought, approaching the animal. It rolled back one eye at him, then flattened its ears. A soothing sound came from Michael's throat. He'd had little to do with horses since his youth, yet the old affinity bubbled to the surface, and within seconds, he calmed the horse, stroking it about the muzzle and head.

The years fell away as his hands ran over the hot, thick hide. He'd been younger than William when he went to work for Mr. Dishman, the fodder man who supplied the stables with feed for the sleek, beautiful champions. The horses consumed pound after pound of fortified whole oats, steeped in walnut oil and molasses. The fare was better and more nutritious than the food Michael Rowan and his mother shared each night by the sputtering light of a single kerosene lamp. One day, when he thought no one was looking, he sampled the warm-smelling, glossy grain. It had tasted so rich that he'd scooped it up by handfuls, chewing and swallowing as fast as he could until a high-pitched, chiming laugh had interrupted him. Filled with humiliation, he looked up to find a handsome, strapping boy clinging to the hand of a tall, well-dressed man.

"Look, Father," the lad said. "That boy is eating from the feed trough."

The man had pulled the lad away from the stable row, saying, "That's what comes of idleness and lack of supervision. Come along, Troy."

Word of Michael's transgression must have reached the head stableman, for Michael earned a caning for his greed, and they docked a week's wages to pay for the few stolen mouthfuls. Decades had passed since that day, yet still he had not been able to shed the stink of that alley, the pangs of hunger, the tormenting itch of lice and fleas. It was no coincidence that he thought of Troy now, given their lifelong connection.

"Do you know horses?" William asked, straining forward although Helena held his hand, keeping him at a safe distance.

"A bit, yes. I used to work at the racetrack when I was about your age."

Helena tilted her head to one side. "You never told me that."

There was much he'd never told her; simple abandonment had been kinder. She didn't need to know what his past was like, didn't need those dark images in her head. And he certainly didn't want her pity. Now, though, William changed everything.

"And you never told me—"

"I said, not now," she warned him.

Out of consideration for the boy, he dropped the subject and turned back to the Thoroughbred. Running a hand down the front of each of the horse's cannon bones, Michael felt a telltale warmth and swelling. The common, catastrophic injury had been the end of many a horse's career. This gelding, though pretty, was now as useless for racing as he was for breeding.

"He's got bucked shins," Michael said. "He can't race anymore."

William nodded gravely. "That's what Chalkeye said. Can you fix him?"

"Not for racing, but perhaps for the occasional ride, if he has the temperament for it."

"Hurrah!" The boy's shout caused the horse to shy. Helena immediately reeled her son back in, her full black skirts enveloping him. William dropped his voice and tried to extricate himself from his mother's grasp. "Did you hear that, Mama? The Professor is going to fix Hector." His clear-eyed gaze worshiped Michael as a hero. The look made him feel ten feet tall, made him want to give this boy the whole world.

"Ah, William," Helena said in a gentle voice Michael had never heard before. "He's lovely, but we can't keep him."

His face fell. "But if we don't, the owner will send him off to the knacker's. I know what they do to horses at the knacker's. They bash them in the head and tan their hides for harness leather and boil their bones for glue."

Helena pursed her lips. "Chalkeye invented that story to make you feel sorry for him."

"The boy's not far wrong," Michael said. "Horses that can no longer race or breed can't earn their keep, so they're quickly culled."

She shot him a poisonous look, then softened her expression for William. "I'm afraid this is not a good time to be adopting a horse, sweetheart."

"But Mama, if you make me give him back, he'll die."

"We haven't a proper stable to keep him."

"There are livery and boarding stables down every

alley in this town,'' Michael pointed out, earning another scowl from her.

William twisted his hand free of his mother's and moved over to stand close to Michael. ''Yes, a livery stable would be fine. There's one over on Spring Street, and I can walk there all by myself. Could he live there? Could he?''

''William.'' Love and exasperation strained her voice. ''In the first place, that's too far to walk. In the second place, you don't know the first thing about caring for a horse. You've never even ridden one.''

''You can't mean that,'' Michael said.

She pulled William back against her skirts again and held him there, her hand pressed against his chest to keep him still. ''He's very fragile. Why would I subject him to the dangers of horseback riding?''

''Because he's breathing?'' Michael couldn't keep the sarcasm from his voice. Already he was getting an unhappy picture of what his son's life was like. An overbearing mother, fussing and worrying about him. Judging by the lad's pallor and thinness, Michael guessed he led a sheltered life, away from sunshine and fresh air.

William seemed to bear his mother's overprotectiveness with a sort of weary patience that hinted at long practice. ''I'm not fragile,'' he said, a subtle edge of mutiny in his voice. ''I know what fragile means, and I'm not.''

''Look,'' said Michael, ''I've got a rig from the Institute, so I'll be needing a place to put up for the night. The horse can come with me.''

''See? See?'' Once again, William wrenched himself away from his mother, and the brightness of his smile surpassed even the vivid summer colors of the garden. ''Let's get Hector a bucket of water. I bet he's thirsty." Grabbing Michael's hand, he tugged him toward a pump at the end of the yard.

It was an old-fashioned sweep pump, its rusty maw dripping red sludge. William dragged a bucket from under the rickety wooden deck and positioned it under the spout. Michael primed the pump a few times, then a gush of reddish, bubbly water spewed out into the bucket.

"This spring's called Little Red," William said, clearly proud of his knowledge. "My father's family has boreholes all over town."

Michael gritted his teeth at William's mention of a father. He was well-acquainted with the Barnes success story. The family had made a fortune in banking, and had turned that into an even bigger fortune pumping water from boreholes, bottling the rare, health-giving carbonated drink and selling it to big-city beverage companies for shipping all over the world. It was not a particularly glamorous or prestigious enterprise, but it was a lucrative one. Within a few years, Adam Barnes, a collier's son from Newcastle, became the richest man in town. Making no apology for turning the natural landscape into a veritable sieve, Adam Barnes was also indifferent about the vast forests of firewood the stokers at his bottling factory razed each year, just to produce enough bottles.

William caught the water in the palm of his hand. "You want a drink, Professor?"

The offering startled Michael.

"Quickly," the boy said, "before it all drips away."

Michael bent down and sipped the spring water from his son's cupped hand. The cold water tasted of old roofing nails and salt, and the fizz of the natural carbon added a biting edge to the mineral tang. The town owed its fame to the strange-tasting, bubbly water.

People came from the world over to indulge in its curative powers, but Michael had never developed a taste for it. "Thank you," he said as politely as he could.

When he stepped back, William exploded with laughter. "Made you drink it! Made you drink it!"

Michael grinned. "Very funny. Let's see if Hector likes it any better than I do."

They set the bucket in front of the horse. He lowered his head, sucking greedily. William beamed with pride as he watched the horse drink.

"William, my sweet," Helena said, "I truly think the horse would be happier in a place with a proper pasture and barn."

She seemed genuinely regretful, her agony at disappointing the boy palpable. In just a few moments, Michael had the sense that she was a loving mother, overprotective and not always sure of herself, but her devotion to the boy was unflagging.

None of which exonerated her from what she had done. Keeping her son a secret from Michael and presenting him to another man as his own was, possibly, more unforgivable than his rejection of her love. His son, raised by Troy Barnes, of all people.

Nor did her obvious concern make much of an impression on the boy. He pulled down the corners of his mouth. His chin trembled ominously. "But Mama—"

"Ah. There you are, my dear. I've been looking all over for you."

The three of them froze, then turned in the direction of the garden walkway. Michael heard Helena's small intake of breath, but other than that, she said nothing.

A tall, blond man, with pale whiskers and exceedingly red lips, strode across the lawn toward them. It had been ages since Michael Rowan had seen Troy

Barnes in person, and he discovered that he disliked him as intensely as he ever had.

The senator was as impeccably dressed as a fashion mannequin in a snow-white shirt with a hard collar, a paisley-printed waistcoat of peacock green and morning coat and trousers of a luxurious-looking charcoal fabric. And, not surprisingly, he was drunk. He was not a sloppy drunk, but one who comported himself with exaggerated dignity and fancied no one would notice. He did manage to maintain a certain stiff command which some might mistake for poise. Not Michael, though. Michael knew what a drunk looked like.

"Troy," Helena said at last. "I didn't expect you back from the capital so soon." Her reaction to her husband was restrained and tautly controlled. Michael wondered if Barnes was aware of her unhappiness with their marriage. Probably not. She was a woman of secrets and mysteries. She always had been.

"That's clear enough." Barnes aimed a glare of suspicion at Michael, apparently not recognizing him. "I took the late steamer, only to receive a message that I'm expected in Albany in the morning."

She laid a gentle hand on William's shoulder and took a step forward. The movement placed her slightly in front of the boy. But William broke free of her and ran forward. "Hello, Father," he said, his words slashing at Michael with unexpected force. "I have a horse, Father, and his name is Hector."

As the child greeted Troy Barnes, Helena clenched her hands in front of her, though her expression didn't change. With perfect cordiality, William shook hands with Barnes, but made no further move; nor did the man reach for the boy. The two of them showed the formal restraint characteristic of a well-brought-up lad and his father. William eased away, apparently satisfied that he had performed his filial duty.

Barnes had no reaction to the fact that a strange horse stood on his lawn. This was Saratoga Springs, after all, a town that revolved around horses. In the vicinity of the racetrack, many of the lesser roads were prohibited from being paved. Instead, they were sanded like bridle paths.

He glanced at Michael and then frowned. "Good God Almighty, is that you, Rowan?" he demanded, striding forward with a burst of energy. "Damme, but it's been an age."

"Has it?" Michael shook his hand briefly. Barnes had the firm grip of a skilled politician. He flashed a practiced, toothy smile as meaningless as the grin of a panting dog.

"Indeed, I'd forgotten you even existed," Troy Barnes said, throwing back his head and braying with laughter. "So I see you've acquainted yourself with my wife and son."

Michael gritted his teeth but said nothing.

"Professor Rowan came to express his condolences," Helena said.

Interesting that she would lie, thought Michael. Of course, she was bent on divorcing her husband before her father was even cold in the ground. Nothing she said should surprise him.

"For my part, I would enjoy visiting with you, but I'm afraid I must be going. I'm taking the evening train down to Albany."

Michael watched them closely. Man and wife since their fairy-tale Christmas nuptials in Georgetown nine years before, they displayed neither the veiled boredom of an estranged couple, nor the restrained passion of a man and woman deeply in love, nor even the repressed hostility of two people at odds with each other. Yet he recognized something he could not quite define. Neither love nor hate, but a keen interest and heightened awareness. Barnes eyed his wife as a hound might watch a rabbit, waiting to see which way it would run. But Helena was no nervous rabbit; her self-possession was almost queenly.

"So," Barnes said, cocking out a well-tailored arm for his wife. "Come with me and help me prepare for my journey. You're always so adept at that."

"Of course," she said. "I was just bidding the professor farewell."

She was? Again, interesting.

"William," Barnes called out across the lawn. "We'll be leaving for the station in an hour. You and your mother will come to see me off. Archie will fetch you when it's time."

"Yes, sir." William spoke agreeably enough, but he was clearly more interested in the thirsty racehorse.

"Good day, Senator and Mrs. Barnes," said Michael.

"You must call again when we've time to reacquaint ourselves," Barnes said over his shoulder. He did not wait for a reply, but led his wife straight into the house. They walked without speaking, her hand resting upon his bent arm with excruciating politeness, restraint and good manners.

Was that the way her marriage worked? Michael wondered. He thought she might have flickered a glance back over her shoulder at him, but he probably imagined it. The situation was peculiar indeed. He didn't quite know what to make of the turn of events. It was like one of his experiments at the Institute. All the evidence might be present before him, but he was not yet ready to draw a conclusion.

Except on one account. Feeling as though he had entered a strange new world, he walked across the grass to his son.

In her husband's opulent suite of rooms on the second floor of the mansion, Helena struggled to keep her terror in check. The frantic wingbeats of a caged bird fluttered against her chest. She hadn't expected Troy to return so soon, certainly not in the midst of her visit with Michael, of all things. Now she realized her mistake was even more foolish than she'd originally concluded. To arrange a meeting with Michael here, in this house, and dictating the message to Edith, had been the height of carelessness.

She had been blind to everything save one goal—she was leaving Troy. Getting rid of him. That was the sole thought she had in mind when she sent for Michael. Now she realized she should have anticipated difficulties with her divorce plans, should have worked out the details of the escape more thoroughly, should have been more discreet about it.

But could one plan for the unimaginable? Overnight, her whole world had turned upside down. She and Troy might have gone on treating each other with mutual indifference, as they had for years, except that she'd been betrayed. After the funeral, her father's loyal secretary, a man whose heart she'd once broken, had taken revenge for an old, old slight. She scarcely remembered the man. His name was Carlyle Pickett, and when she was eighteen, she had laughed in his face after he'd declared his undying love. Not her finest moment, surely, but she never could have guessed how long his resentment would fester and what turns it would take. Until that night, she'd had no idea he even possessed the means for revenge. But years ago, he had discovered through his snooping a shocking scandal about her, and had decided to reveal it to her husband. He might not have intended for the outcome to be a beating, but he'd probably be pleased, she thought bitterly.

This new horror, on the heels of losing her father, had left little room for thinking or planning. When she needed to see someone, she invited him to her home. It was as simple as that.

Now she knew nothing would ever be simple. In this, at least, she learned her lesson quickly, but terror and panic had clouded her judgment. She hadn't made any sort of plan for the future. Now she was paying the price for her stupidity. Michael and William had finally met face-to-face—she'd let that happen. She'd always prided herself on being fiercely protective of her son, yet in bringing Michael back, she would plunge William into confusion. Why had she done that? Why? Why hadn't she simply boarded a ship in Chesapeake Bay and sailed away with William forever?

Because she was the daughter of Franklin Rush Cabot. She did not run. She did not hide. She did not give way to fear or despair. Nor would she now.

Michael was not the answer; she should never have thought he could help. Even as the disappointing realization hit her, a part of her mind woke up. She had to do this on her own. She had no tools but her own resources. She would make that be enough.

She sneaked a glance out the screened window in time to see Michael showing William something about the horse. She bit her lip to keep from calling out to them, Be careful, watch those hooves. She stayed silent because she didn't want to draw attention to the situation between them. The tall man she had once loved with everything inside her now hunkered down in front of William, and the two spoke earnestly together. Then Michael took the lead rein and walked the horse in a wide circle while William looked on. They spoke some more, then Michael laughed and ruffled the boy's hair. Well, what had she expected? Everyone loved William, and surely his natural father would be no exception.

Hearing a footstep behind her, she turned swiftly from the window. Her husband emerged from his dressing room, where he'd been selecting items for his journey to Albany. He shut the door behind him with a soft click, and his gaze caught the scene outside the window. Just for a moment, for a fraction of a second, agony etched itself across his face. "I wanted him to be mine," he said softly. "I truly did. So much so that I believed he was."

Helena said nothing. There was simply nothing to say. Fear for William kept her silent.

Troy reached her in two strides, his fists ripping at his detachable boiled collar and cuffs. The starch-stiffened accessories bounced and rolled across the floor, white hoops in a child's game. "It appears you wasted no time before inviting your lover here," he said.

Still, she didn't move a muscle. William, she thought, and it was the only thought in her head. William must never know. If he found out, God knew what damage it would cause, or what it would push Troy to do.

Against her will, she flicked a glance of desperation toward the window.

"Rowan won't rescue you," Troy said, reading her thoughts. "You should know that about him by now. He all but handed you over to me when he had no further use for you nine years ago. I doubt he's changed."

"As I recall," she said, pretending she'd been aware of it all along, "you had a hand in his leaving."

"I never forced him to do a thing." He yanked his shirt one-handed over his head, discarded it with a shake of his hand. "For years you played me for a fool, Helena. I know you're sorry about that, but I'm not ready to hear you apologize yet."

She stood very still, having no intention of apologizing. She had learned to go away for awhile, to find a safe place in the midst of hidden danger. Even now, as he railed at her, she heard his words as a distant, meaningless echo. Almost there. She was almost there. She could draw an invisible curtain—

He stuffed his hand into her hair, gripping it as though it were a coil of hemp. He twisted once, twice, the ugly pressure forcing back her head. "You're very quiet today," he remarked, cutting his eyes toward the window. "And rather cooperative. How much would you endure for your boy?"

She knew there was no answer that would stay his hand. When her father was alive, Pickett had held his silence and Troy hadn't dared to mistreat her in any way. He was too afraid of Senator Cabot. Now that he was gone, Helena had lost her protector, her shield. But she had something more, an aspect of herself that was emerging with surprising sturdiness. She intended to survive. A grim sense of purpose was there, though she did not quite know how to go about escaping him.

"You'll miss me while I'm away, won't you?" he said. "You always do."

She stayed silent. It was the only way she knew to save herself so she could save her son. Her private soul raced desperately away, to a place deep inside, a safe haven.

He stank of sweat and whiskey. "Show me," he said. "Show me how much you'll miss me."

She could do nothing. Her throat ached from the awkward, back-tilted position. Her head throbbed from the rough tug of his hand in her hair.

He released her abruptly, swearing in disgust and impatience. With a swift, fluid motion, he removed his leather belt. It slithered like a black snake through the loops of his charcoal superfine trousers.

"All right," he said. "I've got a better idea. *I'll* show *you.*"

She didn't move. Didn't blink. She was gone, hiding in plain sight.

Three

Michael Rowan couldn't stand unfinished business. Clearly, he and Helena Barnes had much to discuss, but just as clearly, it couldn't be done in the company of her husband. Or her son. *Their* son.

He delivered his horse and rig, along with the injured Thoroughbred, to O'Keeffe's livery, then went to seek lodgings in town. He sent a wire to the Institute, informing his assistant, Miss Runyon, that he would be away for an indefinite period of time. He wasn't leaving Saratoga until he got some answers.

The summer crowds, swelling to the thousands that would fill the town at the height of racing season in August, were beginning to occupy the fashionable spa hotels lining the shady streets of the city. Riotous blooms of flowers surrounded the city's burbling fountains, and millionaires roamed the streets, though none of them paid any attention to the man in rumpled clothing as he walked the streets where, as a boy, he had wrested a meager living. The fact was, Michael Rowan's roots in the community went deeper than any visitor's. No one respected him for having grown up in a backstretch alley, but he knew his way around because of it. He knew the captain of housekeeping at the Montclair Hotel would be able to procure a room even though the hotel was declared full up by the officious, skinny-faced desk clerk.

He took supper at the famous Steeplechase Club, where he recognized local businessmen Hiram Thayer and Perry Todd, and afterward retired to the cigar lounge. Across the room, tourists and gamblers sat around the polished mahogany card tables, sipping cordials and eating potato chips, which were all the rage in Saratoga Springs.

He declined an offer to join a poker game, even though he was good at it, and took a certain grim satisfaction in knowing that these men wouldn't give him the time of day if they realized where he'd come from. But he was too restless to sit through a game of cards. Besides, his skill at cards—he had an uncanny memory and a clear understanding of the odds—rarely endeared him to his opponents.

He decided to relax in the hotel's curative baths. The soaking pools were elaborate mausoleums of marble and cut stone, wet and warm from the burbling, furnace-heated waters. Discovered by Indians long before the coming of the white man, the mineral springs of Saratoga were famed for their healing powers. Enthusiasts claimed the carbonated waters, bubbling up from the earth's churning heart, could cure everything from leprosy to madness, although Michael had never seen evidence of that.

Still, the waters were part of his earliest memories. When he was a boy, he used to sneak into the spa to get warm in the middle of winter. The reputed properties of the mineral water intrigued him, and he convinced himself that no one would be able to distinguish a naked alley boy from the sons of rich tourists. Yet somehow he was always found out and banished from the pools as though his poverty and illegitimacy were communicable diseases that might be spread via the mineral water.

He'd learned the answer his tenth winter when Isaac Reynolds, master of the Russian and Roman baths, was escorting him out, still dripping wet. Michael had wrestled himself free, turned to glare at the Negro attendant. "How do you know I ain't a guest here?" Michael had demanded, standing naked and defiant in the middle of the marble chamber. His young, high-pitched voice echoed down the colonnaded hallway. "I'll have you dismissed for this," he threatened.

"Sure you will." Isaac's voice had been low and good-humored, but firm.

"How do you know I ain't a Rockefeller?"

"Easy, honey." Isaac had propelled Michael toward the changing room to gather up the pitiful mound of ragged clothes stashed under a bench. "See, rich boys don't look like you from behind. Who beats you, boy? Who's been caning you?"

Michael pressed himself back against the wall. The thin red-and-white stripes across his back stung with an unholy heat, as though they were freshly inflicted instead of healed over.

Isaac had given him warm clothes, snatching a new flannel shirt from a peg and pretending to mistake it for Michael's. "Go on with you, now, before you get caught," he said, turning his back.

Seared by shame, Michael had quickly donned the clothes, feeling guilty about the new shirt, but not guilty enough to refuse it. His shame burned even deeper when he discovered a loaf of day-old bread wrapped in his old cloth coat. After that, he had never again tried to sneak into the spa. His sense of wonder about the world had led him to a life of science, where matters were classified according to their properties, where the circumstances of one's birth had nothing to do with one's value. But he'd never forgotten those boyhood days.

This evening he wasn't sneaking; he was a paying guest. Yet somehow, even in the crisp white bathing robe, Turkish slippers and hood, he still felt like an outsider, intruding where he didn't belong.

He was startled, but not surprised, to find Isaac Reynolds still at his post, there at the entrance of the baths. The attendant had changed little over the years. He still looked fit and dignified in his double-breasted livery, and despite the heat and humidity of the baths, he stood at attention, every hair in place.

"Evening, sir," he snapped out. "Is there anything I can do for you, sir?"

Michael took a thick-piled towel from an immaculate stack on the bench. "Well," he said, "I'd appreciate it if you'd refrain from throwing me out this time, Isaac Reynolds."

Reynolds relaxed his military bearing to peer at him. Then he gave a start of recognition. "You don't say. You Hannah Rowan's boy, ain't you?"

"Michael Rowan. Can't verify that I'm a boy any longer, but your memory is impressive."

"Well, howdy-do." A grin eased across Isaac's face. "So you come back to visit us, have you?"

"I'm here on business." He didn't want to explain himself any further, because he had too many questions of his own, questions that would have to wait until he could corner Helena. He took off the robe and hung it on a wooden peg. The scars on his back were still there, though he rarely thought about them. They had hardened over and faded some, like curing wax, but they were still there. The difference was, now he was not ashamed of them.

Nor was he ashamed of the boy he had been, although that, like the scars, was still and would always be a part of him. "That business wouldn't happen to involve handicapping a big race now, would it?" Isaac asked, lifting a salt-and-pepper eyebrow.

"I hope you're the only one who remembers that convenient talent of mine." In fact, his knack for handicapping had helped him escape. With his carefully saved winnings he had found a way out of Saratoga Springs and, more important, a way out of poverty. His endeavors had not made him a rich man but they had bought him something far more valuable—an education.

Michael sank to his neck in the oblong, steaming pool. The heated waters were buoyant and strange-smelling, the dank mineral odor evoking a host of memories—most of them unwanted. He shoved them aside, concentrating on enjoying the bath. The only others present were a group of German tourists, gathered at the other end of the pool. Catching bits of their conversation and applying his rudimentary knowledge of German, Michael guessed that they were engaged in a debate over the merits of Saratoga Springs versus the fabled Baden Baden in the Black Forest of Germany.

"You always did know all the local gossip," he said with unabashed bluntness. He was hungry for answers, and running into Isaac was a stroke of luck. "Tell me what you know of Senator Barnes these days."

"I'm on duty."

"You're not busy." Michael looked pointedly at the Germans lolling and talking at the opposite end. Behind the ornate water bar, the dipper boy sat on a stool, his eyelids drooping with bored fatigue.

"What I knows," said Isaac, lowering himself to a bench beside the pool, "is that he ain't no better than he was as a young'un, stirring up trouble every chance he got."

No better. What man was, after all, better than the boy he had been? Certainly Michael himself could not make that claim with absolute conviction.

"So whom does he cause trouble for these days?" Michael asked.

"Anybody gets in his way, I reckon. Fellow named Elijah Ware ran for his seat last term, and everyone thought he had the election all sewn up, on account of him being such a fair-minded, God-fearing man. But when the final count came in, he lost."

"You're blaming Barnes for winning?"

"Some folks say he stole the election, but nobody could ever prove it."

Michael was startled but not surprised. The local election officials were in the control of the Barnes family.

"Folks are scared to go against him," Isaac concluded. "You know, like they used to be scared of his father. Old man's still alive. Still lives up at that big old house on Oak Hill. I heard tell he's real sick, but just as scary as ever."

Across the white ghosts of steam rising from the surface of the water, Michael's gaze caught and held Isaac's. "Not everyone was afraid of Adam Barnes."

Isaac's stare never wavered. "Leaving here's the best thing you could have done, honey."

"Tell me about his wife and...the boy."

Isaac smiled with genuine fondness. "Now, that was something, wasn't it, him marrying up with a Georgetown Cabot? It was like to marrying royalty, only better, her being a real live American princess. Pure gold. Everybody loves her."

It was the one thing everyone had always agreed on about Helena. When she entered a room, be it the silver-ceilinged East Room of the White House or the scullery of a poorhouse, she dazzled with her presence.

"Yep," Isaac continued, "she gives a party, everybody goes. She says the poor need shoes, and you got Gamblin' Jack Shaunessy hisself making donations. She's been a better asset to that husband of hers than his own private money mint."

Which meant, Michael surmised, Troy Barnes wouldn't be amenable to granting her a divorce.

"And the boy?" he asked, pretending it was an afterthought.

"Fine little fella. They say he's the youngest scholar at Penfield Academy."

Michael knew of the famed boys' school. In the off-season, he and his mother had earned extra income cleaning the building after hours. Sometimes, when the schoolrooms were empty in the evening, he used to sit at one of the sturdy desks, reciting in Latin or reading from one of the heavy leather-bound books that lined the endless shelves. School had always seemed a magical place to him, redolent of chalk and ink and the faint scent of charcoal from the wood-burning stove. Now he pictured William there, in short pants and Eton jacket, carrying a little satchel filled with paper and graphite pencils.

"Puts a shine on his papa," Isaac remarked.

Michael had been robbed before, but never of something that couldn't be restored—time with his natural son. No one would ever be able to give him what he'd lost—the chance to hold William, to watch his first smile, to witness his first discovery of the stars at night or a spider spinning a web. Anger didn't begin to address his sense of loss, so he clenched his fists underwater and hid the feelings boiling inside. "So they're the perfect American family."

Isaac nodded. "You can take that to the bank. I reckon Senator Barnes does."

A long-buried memory emerged from Michael's mind. "Tell me, does Barnes have any other children?"

"No, but not for lack of trying." Isaac showed distaste but no shock. Most men of Barnes's station kept mistresses—but most of them sired children.

The memory crystallized. He knew plenty about Troy Barnes. Far more than anyone, Barnes included, could possibly guess.

Overheated from the steaming water, Michael got out. At the same moment, a bent, robed figure hurried to the Roman steps of the pool, right where Michael stood awaiting his towel. The hood of the stranger's robe fell back, and he found himself confronted by a woman. A very old, but bright-eyed woman who stared at him boldly with a broad smile on her face.

"Well, well," she said, her gaze sliding down, stopping, sliding back up. "I see the quality of your patrons has improved, Isaac. What are you using for bait these days?"

"Jesus," Michael said, snapping out of his shock long enough to jump back into the waist-deep water.

"And a man of faith to boot," said the crone, untying the sash of her robe as she prepared to join him.

At the other end, the Germans erupted with sputters of outrage.

Isaac cursed under his breath, then said, "Now, Miz Nellie. You know you're not supposed to be here."

"I do not know that, Isaac Reynolds. Kindly let me pass."

"Let's go, Nellie." Isaac's voice was gruff and commanding but not cruel. He retied her sash, though she clawed at his hands. "You going to leave under your own steam or do I need to carry you?"

"Stop it, I say. This is a public bath and I am a member of the public. You cannot prohibit me from taking the waters."

With a weary sigh, Isaac took her by the shoulders, turning her away. "Now, Nellie, honey, even you know better than that."

"I demand the right to use this bath." She dug in her heels as he propelled her toward the exit. "The management is going to hear about this."

"They sure is," Isaac muttered.

"I am a professional valetudinarian," she said, trying to wrench herself away.

"We all got to make a living somehow, ma'am."

"Taking the waters is an important part of my regime." At the bar, she balked, then demanded a glass of mineral water from the dipper boy. With a shrug, the boy gave her a glass of the murky, bubbly water, and she turned away without thanking him. Isaac continued to push her toward the marble arched door.

"Say, how about a tip?" the youth demanded.

She turned back. "A tip? Why, here's one. Give women the right to vote in this country."

The Germans muttered among themselves while Michael hurried out of the pool and grabbed a towel before anyone else visually accosted him. By the time Isaac returned from escorting the strange woman out, Michael had donned a robe and was drying his hair.

"What the devil was that all about?"

Isaac shook his head. "Crazy Nellie McQuigg. She

tries to sneak in here every now and then. Never does anyone a lick of harm, but she bothers the tourists."

"Where did she come from?" Michael asked.

"She ain't got no proper home. Sleeps in Congress Spring Park in summer. In winter she sometimes gets herself thrown in jail just to stay warm."

"What about Dr. Hillendahl's Sanitarium?" Michael suggested. The facility was highly regarded as a place for people with certain disturbances to "rest."

"Hillendahl has a strict rule."

"What, that you have to be insane?"

Isaac laughed. "No. She would qualify for that. You got to be able to pay."

Michael thought of the harmless, batty old woman sleeping in the ancient stone block jail in the winter. Then he thought of his mother, so long gone she was a wispy memory, a tenderness inside, a bittersweet ache. "Suppose I paid," he said, despite the fact that he had precious little money to spare.

"You mean it?"

The fees would probably clean him out. "Yes."

"I'll see about it for you."

He should have been tired at the end of the long, strange day but he was curiously alert. When Isaac got off duty, Michael joined him for a hand of low-stakes poker in the basement of the Steeplechase Club, a favorite haunt of the locals. They met up with old George Long, a Mohawk Indian who worked as a bartender at the club, and Regis Ransom, a retired jockey renowned for his flamboyant style of dress and a legendary charm that persisted even as he aged. Michael remembered him as a brash daredevil who specialized in winning on horses others had declared wild or unridable.

In turn, the three older men were among the few in Saratoga Springs who remembered Michael Rowan. He imagined they recalled a dark-haired, blue-eyed little boy whose face was haunted by the gaunt shadows of starvation and whose soul suffered a far greater hunger—for his sick mother to get better, for his father to acknowledge him, for his belly to be full.

George, who was sixty if he was a day, was on his third wife, a girl less than half his age. "Sophie is as beautiful as the summer moon," he said with strapping pride. "She's Canadian," he added as though that explained everything. Setting his cards facedown on the table, he took a small gray-toned photograph from the pocket of his threadbare waistcoat. "My seventh son," he announced. "I was afraid the camera would steal the soul out of his body but it is not so. He still has a soul."

Michael joined the others in admiring the picture of the round-cheeked, round-eyed infant.

"He will keep me alive," George said.

"Were you planning on dying?" Regis asked, fussing with a button on his marigold-colored shirt.

"I'm an old man. It is what old men do. But an old man with a young wife and son... Now there is a man who will live forever."

"You sound pretty sure of yourself," Michael said.

"I'm sure. A boy without his father is a boy who loses his way in the woods again and again." George spoke without sentiment, yet his quiet voice commanded attention. "This you know because your father was not your father. You were lost, as lost as a child stranded on an island surrounded by cold water. You are lost still but I sense you know how to be found."

Michael glared at the old man who had drunk half a bottle of whiskey during the poker game. Yet

George's eyes glowed with a strange understanding that had always made Michael uncomfortable. "You're drunk, old man," he muttered.

"And you are trying not to see," George retorted, picking up his stovepipe hat, getting ready to leave. "But you will. Good night, gentlemen."

Regis and Isaac scratched their heads. "He always talks like that when he's in his cups," Regis said. "Pretends he knows things, like a fortune-teller."

But maybe he did, thought Michael. Maybe old George knew what Michael had only begun to acknowledge. His mind had been made up since the moment he had recognized William. Only now he spoke it aloud to himself.

He was going to be a father to his boy.

Four

The next morning, fiery aches throbbed through Helena, yet even though she was alone, she gritted her teeth against a groan of pain. Similarly, she had not made a sound during Troy's attack. Instinct held her mute. She did not want to put her son at risk. Troy made no attempt to conceal the threat—if she resisted him, William could find himself sent away to school, or worse.

As Troy had gathered his trunks and papers for Albany, Helena lay unmoving upon the bed in the still, overheated bedchamber that smelled of afternoon sunlight and her husband's anger and lust. She'd tried to assess the damage. Ribs bruised again or perhaps cracked this time. Her arm sprained, swollen, nearly twisted out of its socket. His cruelty had escalated from that first incident, and this time, she didn't have the cocoon of numbing shock to protect her. She had known what was happening. And then in the aftermath, as he had so fussily and precisely stowed his papers and organized his clothes for travel, she had been filled with a sense of unreality. Who was this person, this man to whom she'd been married for nine years? A handsome stranger with clean hands he subjected to a weekly manicure. An ambitious statesman, debating great matters. A concerned husband who had only recently discovered his wife's unforgivable deception. Somehow, his stunning good looks, impeccable reputation and his sense that he was the injured party made his cruelty all the more chilling.

In the aftermath, she had managed to drag herself up, to rearrange her hair and clothes, to pull herself together. Michael had gone away; Archie had called William in to get him ready for the ride to the train station. With false docility, she had bade Troy goodbye.

Now she was awake even before the servants. She sat in the morning quiet, gazing out the window at Vandam Square, which had been her home since she married Troy. The cluster of yard-skirted, colossal mansions evoked the aggressive grandeur of mismatched times and places—Tudor England, the Baroque period, the French Renaissance, the Second Empire, Queen Anne's reign. There was even an Italian villa across the way. The profusion of whimsical architecture and dollhouse color had always made her feel like a character in a fairy tale, living in a rainbow kaleidoscope of porticoes, cupolas, bay windows, pillared porches, mansard roofs, arches and lacy gingerbread fretwork.

Watching the bright, artificial world around her, she felt alone, unreachable. She was like the damsel illustrated in William's favorite storybook, trapped in an ornate tower perched on a hill of glass, too slick and treacherous to be scaled.

A trap of your own making. She had taken her duties as a senator's wife seriously, and that meant depriving herself of the quiet honesty of close friends. Their friendships were political alliances. Their acquaintances were made for the sake of social expedience, not comfort or simple companionship. Until now, she hadn't realized the magnitude of what she had given up for the sake of Troy's career.

Looking back, she could see that he quite deliberately arranged things that way. Each time she grew close to someone—usually the wife of a big campaign contributor or cabinet member or fellow senator—he steered her away, cut her off, made it impossible to deepen the connection. He built around her that mountain of glass, and no one could come close.

As sunlight painted the world in a wash of gold, she was seized by a sense of time running out. Of the world closing in. The unseen damage inflicted by Troy was somehow worse than the bruises, because she wasn't certain those things would heal. The harm done when he'd flung her legs apart and thrust himself inside her, when he'd clamped her face between his hands, using them as a vise, when he'd bent low and whispered threats in her ear—all those things etched themselves like a blight upon her soul.

Tormented by the memories, she gave way to her sense of urgency and came to a firm decision. She would not stay under this roof. She'd been a fool to think Michael would help her. As always, he only complicated things more than ever. At least he'd helped to cut through the fog of desperation and clarify her convictions, though. She must do this alone.

Most women would not be grateful for a cowardly husband, but Helena was. She had never loved Troy, and had not liked him in a long time. It was cowardice, not kindness, that had kept his brutal impulses so deeply hidden for so many years. He was absolutely terrified of her father. Franklin Rush Cabot had the power to end a man's career with a single well-timed remark.

Troy's weaknesses were several—pride and greed, and a keen hunger for the approval of his own father. Adam Barnes had always seemed an enigma to Helena. The old man had always shown a special affinity for William, which was ironic, given her son's true paternity. Yet for all of Troy's accomplishments in politics, Adam was less than generous in his praise.

She recalled an experiment conducted many years ago at the navy prison, an edifice overlooking the mouth of the Potomac. Accompanying her father, she had witnessed a demonstration of discipline. They had trained a huge mastiff dog to obey his handler's every command. The trainer showed the dog a stout black stick while an assistant tormented the miserable animal with an electrical shock. Each time the stick appeared, the dog received an agonizing shock of electricity, like a bolt of lightning. Before long the dog cowered at the very sight of the handler's black baton and did not need the shock to remind him that the stick signified pain. And so the navy had boasted an attack dog capable of ripping out his victim's throat, but too terrified of a single stick to make a move. After that, Helena refused to accompany her father on any such demonstrations. But she had never forgotten the lesson.

She realized now that her father had been her invisible shield, her guardian angel, her talisman against Troy Barnes, and she hadn't even known it.

"I'm on my own, Papa," she said under her breath. "I swear to you, I won't fail."

She felt better, having made the declaration. But even so, she was absolutely terrified. Perversely, the terror had cleared her mind. Forcing herself into action, she left the window seat and went to her vast dressing room, large enough to house several families of immigrant poor in some neighborhoods. The repository housed French gowns and precious jewelry, hats and gloves and keepsakes meant for no one's eyes but her own. She surveyed the gowns from Worth and Balmain, the coffers containing priceless bracelets and pendants, enough dancing shoes and slippers for a small-footed, feminine army. She clearly understood what was meant by "an embarrassment of riches."

Reaching up with stiff arms, she moved aside a stack of hat boxes from the Bloomingdale Brothers Notions Shop. Behind them was a plain-looking cabinet, and the sight of it bolstered her courage. She had the power to keep her husband away from her. When she had accidentally discovered that Troy's committee had appropriated four full ballot boxes of votes cast practically in his rival's backyard, she hadn't quite known what to do. She'd kept the ballots with no specific purpose in mind. Instinct alone had compelled her to keep quiet about her discovery, and she had learned to respect her instincts. She needed the evidence now. This was Troy Barnes's Achilles' heel; he'd do anything to protect his seat in Congress. She would use the proof she had in order to keep Troy from thwarting her plans.

Unwilling to wait for a driver to be summoned, she walked the few blocks to the heart of town and went to a public scribe to dictate a letter to be certified, copied and opened only if certain circumstances occurred. After that, she paid a visit to the one man who *could* help her—Mr. Jack Shaunessy, the richest man in town. A gambler with a shady past and vast holdings of real estate, he owed her a favor and didn't ask questions when she convinced him to lease her the property known as Moon Lake Lodge.

* * *

The moment she returned from her errands, Helena went in search of her maid, Daisy Sullivan. Amazonian in size, Daisy claimed she could chop a cord of firewood in ten minutes, but currently she was engaged in a more delicate pursuit. She sat on the Saratoga porch taking the ornate white cuffs off a dark gray gown so Helena could wear it during the second phase of her mourning. Daisy looked up from her work and a silent understanding flashed instantly in her eyes.

"We're leaving," Helena said.

"It's about time," Daisy replied, tucking her sewing scissors into the basket by her chair.

Helena nodded, grateful for Daisy's matter-of-fact acceptance of the decision. Daisy was the only person Helena knew who might remotely understand. When she stood up, her great height filled the sunny porch. In the kitchen, Helena helped herself to a biscuit and handed one to Daisy. "I want to get started before William gets up for the day. Lord knows how I'll explain it to him."

"You worry about one thing at a time, missus."

Helena nodded, forcing down the biscuit. She was too excited to be truly hungry, but she needed to fortify herself for the days to come. "This is the right thing to do," she stated, and it felt good to speak the words aloud. "Actually, Troy's attack woke me up. Made me realize that life is happening while I let the years slip by, that I was fading more and more into the background. You don't get a second chance to relive those years, and I simply didn't let myself understand that. Until he beat me."

"Best you find a way to wake up without getting hit," Daisy said, polishing off a second biscuit.

"I thought Michael Rowan would help," Helena admitted.

"That fellow come to see you from down the Hudson?"

"That would be the one." She held her breath, waiting for Daisy to mention the resemblance between Michael and William, but the maid said nothing. Perhaps the similarity was apparent only to Helena, but those eyes. How could anyone mistake those eyes, as blue as the deepest part of a lake in summer? The more she admonished herself to think no more of Michael Rowan, the more she thought of him. It was absurd. He was part of her past. She should have left him there, in the realm of misty remembrance, shoved away into a corner of memory too sweet to contemplate. If she thought too much of how they had been together, of what he had meant to her, she would fall apart.

He had been cruel in a different way than Troy Barnes had been. Michael Rowan's cruelty didn't stem from rage or express itself in violence. Instead, it was rooted in indifference and the shattering refusal to value the one thing in life she'd found truly precious. In his arms she had discovered what love was. Undeniable, heart-deep passion. Soaring ecstasy. He had shown her things she'd never dared imagine, made her feel a joy that was sweeter than breathing. When they were together, every sunrise was a bright gift, every sunset a benediction and every day a miracle.

He had helped her discover a whole new world. And then he took it all away.

For that she would never forgive him. Still, she owed her greatest blessing to him—William, her son. "I suppose I learned one thing from our meeting," she said to Daisy, leading the way out of the kitchen.

"What's that?"

"That I must do this on my own." A shiver passed through her soul. Yet, at the same time, she felt curiously exhilarated. But the dank chill snaked through her again. What sort of Pandora's box had she opened, letting Michael Rowan discover the truth about his son? She had a habit of acting without thinking, being impulsive, relying too much on others. In the future, she must guard against that part of her nature.

"Let's get started with the packing. There's not much to be done, is there, because everything is still in trunks from Georgetown." She paused at the foot of the grand staircase and made a slow turn. "It's remarkable how little one actually needs, isn't it?"

"Where we going?"

They walked together upstairs, Helena moving gingerly, like an old woman, clutching the stair rail. "To a place called Moon Lake Lodge. It's an old estate at Lake Saratoga, and it was once quite grand, but it hasn't been occupied for some time. It's got acres of parkland around it, a beautiful view of the lake, a huge carriage house with stables, flower gardens and an orchard."

"No tennis courts?"

"Not that I know of." Helena realized she was teasing and managed a short laugh. "I hope you don't mind a ghost or two. It's rumored to be haunted."

"Jesus saves, really?"

"I'm sure it's just a rumor. As I said, it's grand. But it never became a popular resort because of the haunting rumors, and then its owners lost it to gambling debt."

"And now it's yours."

"First thing this morning, I leased it from Jackie Shaunessy. He's a casino owner."

"A gambler?"

"A legitimate businessman who just happens to owe me a favor. So off we go."

"Who's we?"

"You, me and William."

"Sounds like a lot of house for the three of us."

"That's what I thought, too. But we'll adjust."

"Jesus saves. A whole resort."

Helena grinned at her skepticism. "Trust me, this is a good idea."

As they worked together on the packing, she felt grateful for Daisy's silent strength, grateful that at her darkest moment she had found someone who was more than a maid.

In Georgetown, the day everything fell apart, Troy had dismissed Helena's personal maid of eight years. Hazel was a pleasant, opinionated woman who loved the odd bit of gossip and could not resist a juicy tale of scandal. If she'd spotted Helena's injuries, the news would have been all over Georgetown in a matter of hours. Clearly, Troy had been well aware of this. He was trying to take everything from her, trying to strip her down to nothing until she had no defenses, no allies. Yet Helena insisted on replacing Hazel right away. With excruciating slowness, she had dressed herself and gone to the canal district to the hiring fair.

That was where she met Daisy Sullivan. She'd been drawn to the six-foot Negro woman, impressed by her imposing size and naturally regal bearing. Then, as she spoke with Daisy and learned her story, she had looked into those dark, shining eyes and seen a kindred spirit.

Troy tried to object to the new maid, but he was the worst sort of coward. The sort who preyed upon the helpless but feared the powerful. In this case, the powerful meant the opinion makers of the capital. When he raised his objections, she regarded him with a calmness she didn't really feel. "Why, Troy. What will people think of us if I go through life without a lady's maid?"

And so he had let Daisy stay, though he remained convinced she would make off with the family silver. Helena knew it was because he deemed a thief preferable to a maid who told her cronies tales about the things he did to his wife behind closed doors. His capitulation also opened her eyes to her husband's greatest vulnerability—he cared far too much about people's opinions of him. This was going to prove very useful to Helena now.

Daisy stayed. Helena believed with all her heart that Daisy Sullivan was the sole reason she hadn't gone mad.

"Beats you a lot, does he?" Daisy had asked that first night as she helped Helena get ready for bed.

"Once was enough." Helena couldn't believe she could even speak of it aloud. "I have to find a way to keep myself and my son safe."

"Uh-huh. Sometimes they holds it in, then it all comes busting out at once. Usually it's the drink brings it on." She spoke from a well of knowledge Helena was soon to discover. "I used to be a slave long time back, down by Fairfax, when I was just a girl," Daisy explained. "The master, he used me and beat me bad. Got me with child, he did, and he beat that out of me, too. I was only just fourteen at the time. But that was the last time. He didn't beat me no more after that."

"What made him stop?" Helena had asked, both heartbroken and fascinated.

"He died. Concrete garden urn plumb dropped on his fool head. I walked away that day. Never even knew President Lincoln freed the slaves a year before that. I walked right to the city and worked at anything

I could find. Did laundry for twenty years, I did. Then I wound up at the hiring fair on account of the navy closed the laundry works."

"And now here you are." Helena beamed. "And you shall come to Saratoga Springs with me. If you're happy with the arrangement, that is."

"Happy? Huh." It seemed an alien concept to a woman like Daisy. Beaten and abused, old before she emerged from adolescence, she was now fifty years of age or thereabouts and still did not seem to know or care what happiness was.

"It is possible, you know," said Helena. "I am going to find a way to keep my son and myself safe."

Daisy had snorted softly, but with no malice or derision. "I hope you do, ma'am."

The overseeing clerk of the hiring fair had made a record that Daisy Sullivan had been hired by Mrs. Helena Barnes. She carefully and painstakingly drew her signature at the bottom of the document. Then the clerk pushed the form toward Daisy. She gripped the steel-tipped pen in her fist and made a bold X.

As they walked away together, Helena said, "You don't read and write?"

Daisy had chuckled. "Who you reckon might've taught me?"

Helena felt foolish for asking, but Daisy soon put her at her ease. She had gone to the hiring fair hoping to find a competent lady's maid, but she'd found someone who was a treasure beyond price—she'd met a woman who might one day become her friend.

"Daisy," she said, pulling her thoughts back into the present and feeling more hopeful than she had in days, "we're going to be safe at Moon Lake Lodge. We'll find a way. You and I, we're very resourceful."

Daisy stopped working and studied her. She didn't

question Helena's assumption that they had something in common. Although it wasn't apparent, they shared the rare and painful bond of survivors.

They took everything they dared. While Daisy added clothing, jewelry and accessories to the trunks and valises from Georgetown, Helena climbed up on a stool and took down a slightly battered, brass-hinged wooden box. She didn't look inside often, but the box held most of the things that mattered to her. It was a collection of keepsakes, really, little bits and pieces of the past that were somehow part of her. It was quite surprising to discover that the things she wanted to keep were so few in number and small enough to fit in this tabletop box.

Opening the lid, she examined the contents item by item. She lingered over a few choice treasures, including some good pieces of her mother's jewelry. The late Beatrice Cabot had been a great beauty known for her style, and Helena loved the Tiffany emeralds especially. They were green and clear, the color of life.

She had a small, precious collection of family photographs, many of her mother as a young woman, lovely and serene, never knowing she would die in childbirth a year later, and others of her father, sister, brother-in-law, niece and nephew. There were several recent postcards from Abigail. She had addressed them to William, printing the messages in clear block letters so he could read them with ease. He had taught himself to read at the age of four and loved to receive news of the travels of his aunt and family to Turkey and India and places that were no more than green specks on the library globe.

She'd never been a quick learner, never equaled her brilliant sister in the classroom. She used to pretend it didn't matter during the years she and Abigail attended

Miss Madinsky's school together. Alongside the pampered daughters of judges and senators and foreign dignitaries, she would sit with her hands folded atop her desk, her mouth reciting words by rote while her mind wandered a thousand miles away, to distant lands and places in the heart where all fathers were attentive, all lessons were easy and all mothers were alive.

Only as an adult did she understand the price of her inability. To her great shame, Helena had never learned to read. Words on a page had always been indecipherable symbols. As a girl, she got by on charm and pretense. She had learned early on that a brilliant smile, a flattering remark, a pointed question had the power to divert even the sturdiest tutor from his task. As a young woman, she found ways to circumvent her shortcoming. There was always someone—her father's secretary, the housekeeper, her sister—to read things aloud to her because she always managed to be too tired, too busy, too...something. An excuse always came to mind. Soon after William was born, she vowed to learn, and she had even studied old school primers and practiced drawing the letters of the alphabet for hours, but her progress had been sluggish, and by the time she finished deciphering a word, she forgot the words that came before. Sometimes, if she worked very hard, she could decipher simple print, but her efforts always ended in frustration, and eventually she had put away the foolish notion. Wishful thinking could not make a thing come true. She was certainly living, breathing proof of that.

Exasperated with herself, she put away the brass-hinged box and went back to the packing and planning with Daisy.

As she worked in silence, she noticed that she had dropped something on the floor—one of the old photographs. Turning it over, she saw an image of her father in middle age, a strapping, intense man who struck the fear of God in the hearts of his opponents and allies alike in Congress. Yet Helena had never felt anything but tenderness for him, though her affection was often tempered by exasperation.

As she slipped the photograph into a pocket of her Saratoga trunk, it struck her that she had not wept for her loss.

Her father had died, and she had not wept for him. She'd been too busy escaping Troy. She despised him for that. For making it impossible to grieve for her father, impossible to heal from the pain of losing him.

She refused to think about what her husband would do when he discovered his wife had moved to Moon Lake Lodge. Before long, not just Troy Barnes but the whole world would know. And this was only the first step in her quest for independence.

"Daisy," she said, "I have something important to ask you."

"Ma'am?"

"If something, anything, happens to me, you're to look after William, do you understand? Even if you must run away and hide, you must keep him safe from Troy Barnes. Can you do that?"

"Ma'am—"

"Take this." Helena handed her the Tiffany emerald brooch. Then she took out one of the letters she had dictated. "Sell the piece, and then go to the telegraph office and send a message to my sister. Do you remember her name?"

"Abigail Cabot Calhoun. Mrs. James Calhoun."

"That's right. The Butlers of Georgetown will know where she's gone in her travels."

"I reckon I can do that."

Helena was relieved that Daisy didn't argue with her, or try to tell her that nothing was going to happen, that everything would be all right.

Daisy knew better. Helena realized this when her maid went to the gun cabinet and selected a Henry repeating rifle. It was a collector's piece, and one of which Troy was especially proud. In return for legislation Troy had initiated, the manufacturer had made a special presentation to him of a gun with single-digit serial numbers, richly engraved and inscribed, and fitted with a rosewood stock. Seeing it in Daisy's large, competent hands reminded Helena of the true peril they faced.

With a weary expression, Daisy said, "He won't leave you be."

"He must."

"I knows the kind of man he is. He needs his pretty wife and child. He won't let you go. What's he going to do when he figures out you up and left?"

"He'll be wild with fury. But I have no choice. I refuse to live my life on the run, like a fugitive criminal. And I refuse to live in Troy Barnes's house. If I stay here, I'm a sitting duck, aren't I?"

"You got that right. So when's he due back from Albany?"

"Tomorrow evening. And he always goes to his club straight from the station, so that gives us a few more hours. But it's not much time, is it?"

"It's enough."

"He cannot do a thing to stop me. You see, after...yesterday, the answer came to me. In order to be free of him, all I have to do is make him too afraid to come near me."

"How you going to scare a man like that?"

"With a black stick," she murmured, then caught

Daisy's look of confusion. "With what I know, I can control him. He stole the last election."

"And you can prove that?"

Helena indicated the low cabinet. "I have the stolen ballots. Archie was supposed to dispose of them, but I took them."

"Old Archie's in a world of trouble."

Helena gave a taut smile. "I think you care about that even less than I do." She stood up and surveyed the room, then went out the door for a view of the house from the upper gallery. A curious feeling crept through her. This vast house had been her domain for nearly a decade, and she was about to walk away. The last time she'd left home, it had been to marry Troy, because Michael had gotten her with child and then abandoned her.

The curious ambivalence shifted to smoldering anger. Each time, it had been a man who had driven her off in a new direction in her life. But this time, she thought, she would make her own way.

Five

Helena awakened in a strange place, feeling safer than she had in days. Her bedroom faced east, with a bank of windows framing a view of the lake. Watery reflections of light and shadow wavered on the ceiling. A curious feeling welled up inside her, so different from the crushing sense of dread and obligation that had afflicted her since the day after her father's funeral. A place of her own.

The rustic lodge had been built for size and comfort. The furniture was sturdy, practical, comfortable. She suspected the pastoral simplicity of the big lodge explained why no one would buy the place. People came to Saratoga Springs for style, not comfort. Well, she'd had her fill of style. She was ready for something different.

Rising from the bed, she ignored the lingering pain in her injured arm and rib cage and looked out the window. It was a beautiful property with its pristine lakeside setting. As with most places around Saratoga, abundant mineral springs trickled from cracks in heaved-up rock or spilled down from the dark woods. They'd found one with enough effervescence to make breakfast bread without soda, and another that was sweet enough to drink without gagging. The house, outbuildings, forest paths, dock and carriage house were in a sad state of neglect, but she would soon remedy that. She spied William and Daisy walking toward the carriage house, undoubtedly to prepare a stall for Hector the horse. William, bless him, seemed to think they'd moved because of the horse. She had yet to correct the notion.

Helena got dressed on her own, a painful business given her injuries, and went downstairs, following her nose to the speckled enamel coffeepot in Daisy's kitchen. Daisy had already staked out her domain, putting away supplies and utensils, scrubbing the plank counters and the big pine table in the center.

The house had been abandoned except for a litter of kittens. Most of the feral animals dispersed in terror when Helena arrived with William and Daisy Sullivan. Only one remained, a skinny, ginger-colored runt that shrank into a corner and hissed at her. Like all creatures whose hunger was sharper than their wits, the kitten was soon won over with a can of Highland Evaporated Cream.

Humming softly, Helena busied herself with cleaning, straightening, exploring, wrenching open windows with creaking sashes and airing out rooms that hadn't been disturbed in years. It was an awkward business, given her injuries, but curiosity and ambition overcame the aches and pains. The lodge was simply built, its upper storeys housing at least nine bedrooms. The main floor was simple, too, with the kitchen in the back, a dining room furnished with a boardinghouse-style table that seated a good two dozen, and a huge open room with a river rock fireplace and a musty billiard table covered in fading green baize.

While surveying the common room, she spotted an ancient, illustrated calendar lying in the corner. Picking it up, she studied the age-brittle pages. There were captions explaining each picture, but she couldn't read them. She really didn't need to; the pictures were self-explanatory. Dated 1848, the calendar was nearly fifty years old, and it commemorated a famous event—the convention for women's rights in Seneca Falls.

The women in the engraving looked appropriately solemn as they took turns signing the long document. Helena liked the picture so well that she dusted the cobwebs from the page and hung it from a rusty nail in the dining room on an empty, light-washed expanse of wall. She missed her Degas, the woman at bath, the glowing light streaming over her soft flesh, the lush colors forming a nimbus that echoed the shape of shoulder, thigh, belly, breast. This was hardly the same thing. The artistic appeal was minimal but it had its own sort of significance.

There was so much to do and she hadn't accomplished much yet. They'd provisioned the kitchen, made up the beds, removed the dust covers from the furniture. The musty smell of disuse still infested the place. But her idea of making this into a home, filled her with a glorious energy she hadn't felt in a very long while. Perhaps never.

In the late afternoon of their second day at Moon Lake Lodge, she heard a sound, and went to look outside. Michael Rowan came riding up the drive on a dun mare.

The sight of him stirred a discomfiting mixture of joy and dread. There was so much between them—danger, passion, secrets and lies. And a past that would not stay buried.

How had he found her? She'd made no secret of her departure; she hadn't had to. She had the power to ruin Troy, and once he understood that, he'd leave her alone. But she had no way to keep Michael at a distance. And now she knew she must. She'd been a fool to contact him. She wished she could have that day back, that moment of sheer insane panic when she had sent him the message, begging to see him, naively praying he would help her find some way to make her world right again. It was too late now.

Though he eschewed proper riding attire, wearing street clothes and shoes rather than boots, he looked exceptional in the saddle. He rode hatless, his dark hair flowing behind him and his tinted spectacles adding a dashing air of mystery.

Waiting in the foyer, she checked her dress in the shabby age-spotted mirror and made a swift assessment of herself as she waited for him to approach along the overgrown walkway. The misty, pockmarked glass, which ran from plank floor to beamed ceiling, reflected a pale, somber and well-groomed woman with red hair and green eyes. A proper lady in mourning for her father, except for the scrawny slip of ginger clawing up her skirt. The kitten wouldn't go away, so she let it haunt her petticoats as she went to the door.

She realized she was holding her arm. She made herself release it, then opened the door. "Hello, Michael," she said. "Welcome to Moon Lake Lodge."

"And where will I find you tomorrow?" he asked, striding across the foyer. "The Grand Union Hotel? The Claremont? Do you plan on changing residences every day?"

"No. I plan to divorce my husband only once."

"It's taken me a day and a half to figure out where

you went. I called at the livery to get William's horse, and was told it had already been collected."

"Why would you fetch the horse?"

"Because I told him I would."

A flicker of concern unsettled her. "That wasn't necessary. A groom from O'Keeffe's brought it 'round."

"Where's your husband, Helena?"

She sniffed. "In Albany. He'll likely be back on the three o'clock train, but he always goes straight to his club from the station. Why do you ask?" She glanced at the case clock, which she'd wound and set that morning. It was nearly three now.

He studied her with a hard and searching gaze. Then, without warning, he turned away, inspecting the premises. He seemed to fill the cavernous foyer with his presence. He had always been an imposing man; that quality had struck her the first moment she had met him. On an autumn morning nearly ten years earlier, he'd fallen out of a tree onto the buckled brick sidewalk in front of her Georgetown house.

He'd either failed to notice—or perhaps he'd simply ignored the fact—that he had ripped his sleeve wide open and his elbow was bleeding copiously. He'd cared not at all that she had lost her favorite silver filigreed hair comb that day, probably while staggering around on the brickwalk to avoid a collision with him.

With scarcely a glance at her, he'd handed her a coil of wire, saying, "Hold that, will you? I just managed to connect to the trunk line, but I need to extend the copper tubing. Once that's done, the house will be electrified."

It had been one of the oddest moments of her life. A spoiled young debutante, she was accustomed to being the center of attention. He was the first man who was not struck brainless by her looks. Instead, he had employed her as unpaid labor while he rigged electrical wiring—so newfangled that it never actually worked—to his house.

Perversely, she had begun to love him right then, as she stood draped in copper wiring and indignation.

She brushed aside the memory and led the way through an arched doorway into the sitting room. "I hope this unexpected visit means you have reconsidered my request."

"About being named a correspondent in your divorce?" He stripped off his threadbare morning coat with an unceremonious gesture of impatience. "Hardly." His voice cracked like a physical blow, imparting a phantom ache.

Helena perched on the edge of a rickety cane-bottomed chair across from him. "I don't know why I expected otherwise," she said. "You were beastly to me when you left nine years ago, and you are being beastly to me now. If I meet up with you ten years from now, I expect you will still be beastly. If I came upon you as an old man in bed, choking out your final gasp, I suspect you'd spend your last breath being—"

"I know. Beastly."

"You always think you know what I'm going to say."

He circled the room, inspecting the outmoded furnishings, the tattered drapes. The ginger kitten tiptoed toward him, swirled around his ankles, and without seeming conscious of the movement, he scooped up the tiny thing, his hands engulfing it so that it disappeared. A purring sound started up immediately.

Helena was mesmerized by the sight of his big, gentle hands petting the kitten. Against her will, she started to think of times long past, and nearly wept with old, unfulfilled yearnings. "Michael, I—" Her whisper was so faint that she had to swallow past the ache of tears in her throat. She glanced away, not allowing herself to speak further.

"What are you doing here, Helena?" he asked, breaking the spell before she could start again. "What are you doing, alone in this place?"

The questions he would not yet speak rumbled beneath the surface, and she knew it was only a matter of time before he asked about William. Grateful for the reprieve, she said, "I have taken a lease on Moon Lake Lodge and will have the option to buy it. My father left a handsome legacy, as you might expect. But it will be in probate a good while, and so I must live in reduced circumstances. Besides, when I buy this property, I wish to be an unmarried woman. I do not want Troy Barnes to have any claim on it whatsoever."

"So you intend to stay here by yourself."

"With William and Daisy—she's my maid. I recently hired her in Georgetown, and she was pleased to be given this chance to travel north with me."

"Why not simply pick up and return to Georgetown? You grew up there. It's your home."

"It was never my home," she said, her heart flooding with bitter memories. "It was the place we lived because of Father's career, but it was no more a home than a hotel. My sister is off to Lord-knows-where in the middle East. My father is dead. I had no true friends there, not after—" She bit her lip, stopping herself just in time again, stopping herself from blurting the truth: *Not after you left.* Taking a deep breath, she said, "This is a wonderful place, Michael. Can't you see that?"

"I see a large, rambling lodge that will fall to ruin if it's not properly maintained."

"Come, I'll give you a proper tour of the house and grounds." Ignoring his skepticism, she led the way out the front and along a pathway leading to the lake side of the house. Sturdy perennial flowers bloomed amid the weeds, and dragonflies skimmed down toward the water. The fresh smells of summer blossoms spiced the air. "I've known of this place for years. It has an amazing history. The foundation was laid by a Dutch colonial. After the Revolution, it was abandoned until the new century when—"

"Silas Moon bought the property and built a deer lodge." He pointed at the high ceiling. "These hand-hewn open beams were felled and milled right on the property."

"How did you know that?"

"I think you'll find I'm quite familiar with local history."

She promenaded him through winding, overgrown pathways, under huge, spreading trees and down toward the lake where a sagging dock and boat launch gave access to the water. The skinny kitten followed at a distance, occasionally pouncing on a cricket or leaping at a butterfly.

"You see, William has any number of places to run and play. And there's a proper stable for the horse. It's just through there." She pointed in the direction of the old carriage house, then caught his look of surprise.

"So you're letting him keep it after all."

"I'm not heartless, Michael. Only cautious. This is a rather big change for William, and I thought perhaps having a pet would ease the transition."

"So you aim to live here, and while away the hours...doing what?"

"Raising my son. Teaching him to be a good man. After so many years of doing the practical thing, the expected thing, I am doing something decidedly impractical. And it feels right. I won't be criticized by you, Michael."

"I didn't come here to bicker, Helena. I came to discuss my son."

Finally. This was the crux of the matter, of course.

"Your son indeed." The words tasted bitter on her lips. She could feel the color creeping back into her cheeks. Perhaps Michael was good for one thing. She felt alive and vital when he was around, even if it was because he infuriated her. "Your son," she repeated. "He no more belongs to you than this kitten belongs to the tomcat that sired it." She picked up the tawny cat that had been shadowing them. It poured its body through her hands and slithered to the ground, swirling itself around her ankles in an immodest fashion.

"Have you always been this bitter, Helena?" Michael asked. "Or am I only seeing you more clearly now?"

You're not seeing me at all, she thought, but resisted the urge to confess everything.

"You weren't the least bit interested in William when I first told you about him," she said. "I don't understand why you're so keen on claiming him now."

"You never told me—" The color dropped from his face.

She watched the memories dawn on his face. "I see you remember. It was a November afternoon, as I recall," she said, heading back toward the house.

"Damn it, Helena. Do you mean when you came to me with your story about being with child, you were telling the truth?"

"Yes."

She'd allow him that. Being truthful had never been a priority for her. Seating herself across from him, she forced herself to take shallow breaths, because breathing deeply caused her ribs to hurt. "As soon as I suspected I was with child, I went straight to you. I said—"

"You said, 'What if I'm with child?'"

"And you said, 'Ah, pet. Don't try to snare me in that old trap. It won't work. You wouldn't want it to, anyway. I'm not cut out to be anyone's husband, let alone a father.' You see? I remember it word for word." She gave a small laugh and instantly regretted it as a sharp pain stabbed her rib cage. Besides, the topic was not amusing in the least.

"So I took your advice," she concluded. "I did exactly as you instructed."

"You should have told me about William. You should have insisted."

"What would you have done? You walked away from me. I did not want to bring you back with the threat of a child you did not want."

"Christ, Helena, how could you not tell me?"

"I did tell you."

"You posed it as a hypothetical question."

"But your reply was very concrete. And I did have my pride, back then, when I thought pride mattered. I did not want to settle for a man I had trapped. I did my part. I asked you if you'd marry me if I were with child."

"*If* you were. You didn't say you were."

"And you said you wouldn't be shackled by that old trick."

"I thought it was a trick."

"Lord, Michael. The years have only made you more difficult."

"Pardon me, but I just found out I'm a father."

"And it would have made a difference if I'd said I was most definitely with child?"

"Of course."

"There, you see?"

"See what?"

"That is precisely why I was merely being prophetical with you."

"Hypothetical." He corrected her with his old arrogance. "Damn it, but I hate arguing with you. You never answer anything clearly."

"I just did."

"You did not. I no more understand what you just said to me than I understand German opera."

"What's difficult to understand about German opera? It's always the same. Boy meets girl, boy falls in love, girl gets devoured by horrible winged creature with claws."

"Could we please get back to the matter at hand?"

"It's already settled."

"The hell it is. Why did you do it? Why did you deceive me about your pregnancy?"

"Oh. Well. You answered your own question a moment ago. You should listen to yourself better."

"Enlighten me," he said with an excess of patience. "What did I say that I didn't listen to?"

"You said of course it would have made a difference if I had told you I was definitely with child. So that's why I didn't tell you. I didn't want you to stay with me because you felt duty-bound to be a father to the boy you made."

"And yet you married a man you scarcely knew."

"As I said, I have my pride." The irony of it stung.

"Pride. You kept a father and son apart for the sake of pride."

"Why would I choose to live with a man who wed me out of a sense of duty?" she asked. "The prospect was simply too depressing."

"You married Barnes out of expedience," he pointed out.

"And look how that turned out. I can't wait to get rid of him. At the time I believed I was making the best choice for my child. I was terrified of the prospect of him being branded a bastard." Ah, but if only she had known then what she knew now, she would have endured any disgrace, and gladly.

"You say you didn't want to marry me because of what I said, and yet you would deceive a man and marry him for the sake of giving his name to your boy."

"Think what you will."

Michael couldn't seem to sit still, but stood and prowled the room. It was a lovely room, or would be once everything was scrubbed and polished. And he looked curiously at home here, his rumpled appearance suited to the big rustic lodge.

"I didn't believe for a moment you were actually with child," he said. "We were using a device of my own invention to prevent conception."

"And," she couldn't resist saying, "it worked about as well as your other inventions."

He flinched. "Touché, darling. You always were deadly accurate with the verbal dart."

Her comment had pierced him, but the satisfaction was fleeting and followed immediately by guilt. He had always wanted to be regarded as a great inventor like Mr. Bell, whose sister lived right here in Saratoga Springs, or like Mr. Edison, whose Menlo Park laboratory was famous the world over. Yet for all his brilliance, he had never achieved a scientific breakthrough.

"I apologize," she said, chagrined to realize how long her bitterness against him had lingered. "That was uncalled for. Contacting you was an ill-conceived idea. I merely thought you would be willing to help me in my divorce suit. Since you're not, then we have nothing more to discuss."

"There's William." Heaving a sigh, he sat back down. "We're only just beginning. Surely you can see that."

His words had a curious effect on her. Along with a chill of apprehension, she felt a subtle but undeniable flare of… She decided to call it "interest," though she knew it was deeper than that. And, naturally, she had no choice but to deny it.

"I cannot, and you're wrong. I don't know what I was thinking." But she did, of course. Her father was dead, her sister halfway around the world and her husband a monster who beat her senseless. She had been seized by helpless panic. Sending for Michael had been an act of desperation. And now, if she could not convince him to go away, he just might make matters worse.

"Helena," said Michael, "you need to understand something."

She clenched her jaw to keep from screaming. She had heard that phrase all her life, so often that she believed it. Now she knew she should have challenged it. "What, Michael? What don't I understand?"

"This changes everything."

"A brilliant deduction."

"William changes everything."

"I've always thought so."

"For me, I mean."

"And that should matter to me?" she asked.

"I haven't thought of anything but him since I found out what you'd done. I have missed the first eight years of his life, Helena."

She felt a cold chill. What did he mean, missed? Weren't men supposed to stand back and let others raise their children? That was certainly true in the case of her own father, and, thankfully, in Troy's case as well. It was the way of the world—fathers were distant, busy creatures who gave their children the odd moment of attention, then moved on to greater matters once more.

But every so often, when she saw a father and child together, really together, she felt a pang. Some men took their children sailing on Lake Saratoga, or strolled along Broadway hand-in-hand with their little ones, lifting them up for a peek into a toy shop window. From time to time she'd see fathers and children raking leaves, playing baseball, laughing as they made a game of jumping across the horse trolley track. Those little glimpses hinted that there was another way for a man to be a father. She'd just never experienced it before, and she'd certainly never thought it was something that could happen for William.

"Are you saying you want to be a part of his life?" she asked Michael.

He stared at her as though she'd asked the question in a foreign tongue. But then his face changed, softened a little, perhaps, and the shadow of a smile eased across his mouth. "Yes."

A bitter hurt rose in her throat. "The way you were part of my life? If that's your plan, Michael, then you'll understand why I must decline your offer. I would not wish that sort of love on the sturdiest of souls, much less a child."

He was quiet for a long moment. She had nearly forgotten that about him—the stillness. It was an unusual trait. The men in her world had always been loud and bombastic and overbearing. Michael, she now remembered, was given to contemplative silences. It was his great talent, though it tended to make him seem odd and distracted.

"This is different," he said at last.

"What do you mean, different?"

"I want to know William, to be with him."

"For how long?"

"Forever."

She was amazed at the swift ease with which he committed to that. "You only just met him."

"That's not my fault." He jammed his fists into his pockets and paced back and forth. "Where is he, anyway? Where's my son?"

"He went to town with Daisy."

"What does Barnes know?"

Shame unfurled its ugly tendrils through her. When she'd married Troy, she'd told the lie of her life, the lie for which she would spend her entire marriage in atonement—she let Troy believe William was his. He made it easy. William made it easy, arriving—as undersized as an early baby—a full eight months after they married. She was guilty of the worst sort of deception, and perhaps the one she had deceived the most was herself. She'd convinced herself that giving her child the name of a wealthy, respected man was a noble deed. Her father had praised the match. All of Washington society had regarded her and Troy as the perfect couple. Now she understood that her deception carried a price she could never have imagined.

"Until the day of Father's funeral, he believed William was his. We never discussed the fact that I didn't conceive again."

Tense anger ticked in Michael's jaw. "So your whole marriage was a bid for your father's approval. I can't say I'm surprised."

She didn't take offense, because there was truth in his statement. All her life she had sought to please her father, even at the expense of her own heart and soul. Only now could she admit that.

"I assume Barnes didn't take the news well," Michael said.

She took a slow, careful breath, then nodded.

"But does he know it's me?"

He seemed intent on hearing it all. And really, there was no reason not to tell him. "He does now. He knew that we...that I once fancied myself in love with you. We thought we were so clever and discreet, hiding our affair. Half of Georgetown must have known. I suppose anyone who saw the foolish way I looked at you would have guessed. At any rate, Troy was surely aware that you and I were—" She paused, choosing her words with care. "I realize now that your sudden opportunity at the Institute, which caused you to walk away from me, was all his doing." She couldn't resist adding, "Of course, his manipulation never would have worked if you hadn't taken the bait."

"I didn't leave you because of the opportunity at the Institute," he said. "You know that, Helena."

She got up and went to the window so she wouldn't have to look at him or think about what he'd just said. She and Michael had both behaved foolishly. In the wake of his departure, her swift courtship with Troy Barnes had been more of a business negotiation than a romance. She agreed to the marriage as a means to save face and give her child a name.

Troy's political ambitions demanded a high-born wife; her need for respectability demanded a marriage of expediency. It had seemed a sound idea at the time. Now she understood that it had been a mistake from the start, and would have been even if Carlyle Pickett hadn't told her secret to Troy. Before her husband had turned on her physically, he'd abandoned her to a loneliness so cold that it settled deep into her heart like a virus, eating away at her until there was nothing left of the hopeful, laughing girl who had once embraced all of life as a grand adventure.

She had tried to deny her unhappiness, of course, even to herself. She mothered William far more actively than most ladies of her class, caring for him and playing with him, taking sweet delight in his every smile. She ran the house in Vandam Square and pretended all was well...until now. Until her father had died, and her world had broken open. And although she was terrified, she embraced the opportunity.

"So Barnes knows I'm William's father." Michael's voice broke in on her thoughts.

Agitated, she turned back to face him. "Why do men go on so about fatherhood? It's not as though you've ever done a thing for William, other than that one..." She searched for the right word. "Donation."

He stared at her for a long time until she began to wonder if he'd even heard her. Then he ended his silence with a bold declaration that sent shivers coursing through her. "I never should have let you go."

Then why did you?

When Helena realized she'd asked the agonized question aloud, she pressed her hand to her mouth.

He got up, following her to the window. A light

breeze rippled over the lake, and the sugar maples in the yard nodded. His presence caused an unsettled heat to move through her. He stepped close to her, and the turbulence between them intensified. Even now, after so much time had passed and so much had happened, she still felt drawn to him. She had never been able to explain it to herself, but there was something about him—a subtle combination of scent and texture and a strange alchemy—that propelled her toward him, even against her will.

"I can't think straight when we're face-to-face," he said, unknowingly echoing her thoughts. "I never could."

She understood completely, but managed a sniff of disdain. "Then go away."

"I can't do that, either." Without warning, he touched her in the old way, as lightly as a breeze, his finger traveling down the side of her face while he watched it with the fascination of an explorer who had just made a new discovery. "The fact is, Helena, staying together would have been a disaster, and you know it. Do you think for one moment your father would have allowed it?"

"We should have defied him," she whispered.

"You never would have done that," Michael stated, the certainty in his voice unwavering. "Don't pretend any different."

He was right, she realized, with bleak disappointment in the spineless girl she'd been. At that time in her life, her father's approval had meant everything to her. It had been more important than the needs of her own heart, so she had accepted Michael's departure without a whimper of protest.

"There's no point in debating what should or should not have happened in the past. I am more concerned with the here and now. I've decided to change my life. I foolishly thought you would help me in this. But I was wrong. Therefore, we have no further business together.'' She marched through the foyer and out the door, determined to dismiss him.

He followed her out to the yard. ''You're wrong. William is mine. Nine years ago I walked away from you, and it was the biggest mistake of my life. I won't make the same mistake with my son.''

His statement brought on a fresh wave of the shivers. She'd been mistaken, too, in letting him go. But things weren't simple anymore. She and Michael were different people now, with different lives. They couldn't take up where they'd left off, couldn't fling themselves blithely into secret meetings and sensual games of laughter and sighs and late-night adventures. They could never recapture the passion that had brought them together in the first place. Youthful abandon was a thin, false bond. Didn't he understand that? In her disillusionment, she could no longer regard him through the eyes of a girl in the first flush of new love.

He, on the other hand, was much the same as he had always been—sloppily handsome, distracted, fiercely brilliant in some respects and utterly ignorant in others. Yet perhaps there was something different about him now—a harsh, almost bitter determination, a forcefulness.

Which was exactly what she did not need or want in her life at this point.

''And Barnes will simply allow you to set up housekeeping on your own?''

''That again.'' She walked toward the front drive. It curved along the weed-fringed yard, with one branch leading to the carriage house and another to the main road into town.

His horse waited in the shade of an ancient catalpa tree with white blossoms dripping down onto the lawn. "I will not discuss it any further with you, Michael. I'm sorry I disrupted your life by contacting you, but I'm grateful as well. You made something very clear to me. I've never been on my own before. I went from my father's house to my husband's. I shall do this on my own with no help from anyone." It was a frightening prospect, but she felt a renewed surge of resolution. "It's all very liberating, and I'm exhilarated, Michael. I am filled with the conviction to succeed."

"What are you going to tell William?" he asked her. "Are you ever going to tell him the truth?"

She sent him a measuring look. It actually hurt to look at him. She could not do so without remembering how much she had loved him. She would never be rid of this man, she realized, even if she never saw him again. He would always be a part of her. His eyes were William's eyes, his smile William's smile, his hands with their large squarish shape were William's hands.

But even more than that, Michael Rowan lived in her heart, an aching memory, so distant and so tender that it was almost like a dream. Perhaps it was a dream, she reflected, idealized by imperfect remembrance and false hopes. The memory of their love would last forever, like a treasure in a museum, set apart even from the very air, in its vacuum-sealed glass case, preserved against the ravages of time.

She said, "He's very young, and would only be bewildered by all this. I intend to wait until he's older. Goodbye, Michael. You shan't be hearing from me again."

"Don't tell me goodbye," he snapped.

"Why not?"

"Because I'm not leaving."

"Fine. Then I shall." Pivoting on her heel, she turned toward the house. She should have anticipated his next move, but she didn't. Without warning, his hand shot out, captured her wrist and pulled her toward him.

She screamed. She couldn't help herself. The pain was too great. It was an agony so pure that she felt faint, and braced herself against crumbling.

Her scream shocked him into letting go. He gaped at her in confusion. "Helena, what's the matter?"

"Just go," she managed, cradling her arm and edging away from him. "Go, please."

"I can't do that." He took a step toward her.

She wanted to shriek again, to flee, to hide, but she was still reeling from the pain and could scarcely breathe.

Reaching for her, he said, "What's the matter? I won't hurt you."

"Don't touch me." She spoke through gritted teeth. There was a hot sizzle of tears in her eyes, and she blinked hard, trying to see clearly. How dare he make her cry, when she couldn't even cry for her father?

Despite her protest, he moved in close and cradled his hand under her elbow. His touch was so unexpected that she couldn't move or think or breathe. With almost surgical delicacy, he unfastened the buttons of her fitted sleeve. He did so with such gentleness that she barely felt his touch. Or perhaps the pain was already so great that she felt nothing. A sense of dread creeping through her, she submitted with a bleak sense of resignation.

He peeled back the sleeve, inch by inch.

Above them, in the spreading elm tree, a pair of robins squabbled briefly, then sped off in a whir of wings.

Michael stared at her arm, at the grotesque swelling, bruises the color of the blooming foxglove in her garden. "My God. What happened?"

She was used to hearing brusque command in a man's voice. It made her stubborn, resentful. Carefully extracting her injured arm from his grip, she said, "I fell down the stairs. You know how clumsy I've always been, Michael."

It was the wrong thing to say. She understood that as soon as she saw the look on his face. The excuse hadn't fooled him for a moment.

Michael's expression underwent a silent but visible change, a shadow slipping across the sun. "God damn him to hell."

He became a Michael she had never seen before, a Michael she did not know as he stepped away, his features hardening to granite. With deliberate, agitated tugs, he drew on his riding gloves, finger by finger.

The gloves didn't match.

"What are you doing?" she asked, confused by his reaction.

"I have good news for you, Helena."

"That's a very odd thing to say, Michael. Good news?"

"Yes. You don't need to petition for a divorce from Troy Barnes," he stated, swinging himself into the saddle.

His socks didn't match, either.

"What do you mean, I—"

"Because I'm going to make a widow of you."

Six

How do you kill a man with your bare hands?

The question plagued Michael during his wild ride across town. Fury enveloped him in a fog as thick and deep as an alcoholic haze. It made him just as reckless as a bottle of tequila might, only this was a very focused recklessness, almost cleansing in its intensity. He didn't even think about the ride through town. Heedlessly he raced past the Congress Street jail, ignoring the shrill, indignant whistle of a town constable as he clattered down Main Street. He crossed Lake Street, narrowly missing the lumbering trolley car. Then he took a shortcut across Congress Spring Park and several vast estate lawns. For all he knew, he'd run over someone or trampled a prized garden. He didn't care. He didn't care about anything but finding Troy Barnes.

Over the years, he and Barnes had barely spoken a dozen words between them, but Michael knew him. He knew the habits of the spoiled and privileged favored son. Knew his haunts, his tastes, his strengths and weaknesses. He had known Troy as long as he'd known himself, it seemed.

So why hadn't he known Barnes was the sort of coward who hit women? Dear God, did he hit William, too?

The clock tower of the whitewashed Huntington Church tolled four as Michael raced by. He heard the bell faintly under the piston-like rasp of his horse's breathing, the drum of hooves, the swish of blood in his ears. He recalled what Helena had said—Barnes would have already arrived at the D&A railroad station, then headed straight for his gentleman's club.

Michael arrived in only a few moments and strode past the startled doorman. He made some sort of sputtering protest, but Michael ignored him and walked on. The Steeplechase Club was the sort of place a man like Troy Barnes would sit with his cronies and sycophants, sipping whiskey and talking until the men dispersed to go to supper. Some to wives, some to indifferent servants who were paid to be polite.

The club had always smelled, Michael thought, like new leather and old money, fine cigars and mellow whiskey. The smells of wealth and privilege. The smells of men who beat their wives and thought they could get away with it.

The grand salon was fairly quiet this time of day. A tall archway opened to the walnut-paneled main room, richly furnished with leather wing chairs and heavy oak card and gaming tables. Behind a massive, altar-like bar constructed of carved wood and etched mirrors, a lone barman indolently polished glasses with a white linen cloth. A card dealer shuffled his deck, readying a table for faro.

A group of men sat by a picture window with a view of the famous track with its pointed pavilions, the mile oval criss-crossed by pathways. The light of the afternoon sun colored the grassy sections a livid emerald.

The rolling, forested hills shadowed the lake. Layers of blue-gray cigar smoke hovered like shapeless ghosts over the nearly empty room.

The men looked up as Michael burst upon them, yanking off his gloves and hurling them to the floor. He recognized Cornelius Cotter, fat, red-faced and jovial, a corrupt millionaire, which probably made him a favorite of Barnes. He didn't know Barnes's other two companions, didn't care who they were. He made straight for Helena's husband, his hand shooting out, fist curling into the immaculate fabric of the starched shirt. A chair tipped over, thudding hard on the Persian silk carpet. The table wobbled, and several glasses fell over, breaking. The sharp reek of spilled whiskey pervaded the room.

Barnes made a strangled sound of surprise and indignation; the others shrank back. Michael knew he'd have the advantage only for a moment, so he wasted no time.

He hauled Barnes to his feet with one hand. Barnes shoved hard with both forearms, threw Michael off and then rushed him, his head angled downward. They clashed. The wind rushed out of Michael's lungs. An ashtray on a pedestal fell over, knocking into a brass-rimmed spittoon. Barnes recovered quickly and came up fighting, fists flying.

Michael felt the skin split at his cheekbone, felt blood running down the side of his face, heard a ringing in his left ear from a side blow. Yet the pain didn't really touch him. Because he was not here for himself. He was here for Helena.

Flushed and panting, his shirt torn at the throat, Barnes looked astonished that Michael didn't go down. The doorman called out, running to summon a constable, but the few men present quickly slid money across the table, placing bets. Betting was, after all, the chief sport of Saratoga Springs.

Barnes lunged again, upending another table. Michael stepped aside. In that split second, Michael regained his breath. He blocked the blows, swatting at the flying fists as though batting at horseflies. They crashed down the center of the room, past tables set with costly, heavy crystal decanters. Time seemed to stretch out forever. This was taking far longer than he'd anticipated.

"Not so easy as beating a woman, is it, Senator?" Michael said.

"You're a madman," Barnes replied, taking a swing and missing his mark as Michael feinted from side to side, fast learning the rhythm of violence.

"And you're a dead man," Michael replied, driving his shoulder into Barnes's midsection.

Warm, whiskey-scented breath pushed out of Barnes as he went down. A decanter fell over, pouring its harsh contents down upon them both. Michael landed on top of him, forcing the air from Barnes's lungs. With the same motion, he slammed his fist into his opponent's face, and Barnes let out a roar of agony.

Now what now what now what? Michael had not been in a fight since he was a lad. He had always hated it. The initial surge of rage had fueled the first moments of the attack. Now he had the advantage, and he wasn't quite sure what to do with it. Fighting was a dirty business, every blow leaving an indelible taint on his soul.

Barnes writhed beneath him, arching his back to buck him off. Blood poured in streams from his nose, but he fought with desperation. Both fists shot up, catching Michael under the jaw.

Half-blind from the blow, Michael clamped his

hands around Barnes's neck. *How do you kill a man with your bare hands?*

Troy Barnes's chin and neck were slick with blood. His teeth were coated in red. Michael had no idea a man's blood could be so slippery.

"...do something," someone said behind him. "This has gone beyond mere sport."

From his position on the floor, Michael saw white leather spats approaching. It was all he could see from his perspective, but he knew it would be one of Barnes's cronies.

He grabbed the upended decanter and cracked it against the edge of the table. Shards of glass exploded outward in a glittering fountain that stung his eyes, his face, his fingers. He'd hit it too hard, reduced it to nothing. The jagged-edged bottleneck in his hand would have to do.

He pushed the broken edge against Barnes's throat.

The approaching spats froze in their tracks.

"Mother of God," someone said. "He's going to kill Senator Barnes."

Michael looked at the bright crystal pressed against his opponent's throat. How much pressure would he need to apply in order to break through that pale skin, that wildly beating artery so close to the surface? How long would it take a man to die?

The moment felt so weighty and fraught with memories of the past that it was almost...biblical. There was never a time in his life when he hadn't been aware of Troy Barnes. Michael could still see him clearly, clean and scrubbed, riding in an enamel-sided Dorchester cart with his parents, right down the middle of Broadway. They had crossed paths often, growing up in Saratoga Springs.

"Listen," Barnes said, his voice a faint whisper as

though he feared that if he spoke aloud, his vulnerable throat would fall prey to the razor-edged crystal. "Let me up, let's talk about this man-to-man."

"Did you give Helena that option?" Michael snapped out.

"Will you look at that?" the barman remarked. "The senator pissed himself."

Barnes trembled and convulsed. "You're mad, I tell you. Completely mad. Someone, get him away from me."

Michael took no satisfaction in having reduced Barnes to a cowardly victim. He felt no sense of power. He merely felt the grim sense of duty he used to feel when forced to put down a broken horse.

Barnes breathed through clenched teeth. Quick shallow breaths. And then they were both breathing in the same fast, dizzying rhythm. Michael gripped the broken crystal harder. His hand was bleeding. His blood dripped down and mingled with Troy's.

The glass had warmed to his touch, yet glittered, sharp as ice in his hand. No one moved. Even the shifting cloud of cigar smoke seemed to hover, waiting, above their heads.

"Stop."

Helena's voice. How had she found him so quickly? He heard her footsteps, treading lightly on the carpet as she crossed the room to him.

"Don't do it, Michael," she said. Her voice sounded different, more commanding than desperate. He realized that whatever Barnes had done to her, he had not broken her. "Put down that glass. You'll only make things worse."

Whispers erupted from the corner table and money began changing hands again.

"Helena, please..." Barnes was begging her.

In a rustle of skirts, she moved closer. Blood seeped into the hem of her black dress, sucking all light from the dark fabric.

"You are no murderer, Michael," she said. "You're a better man than this."

He wasn't. He wasn't. He wasn't. That was the reason he had left her in the first place.

"Don't do this," she said. "If you think of nothing else, think of William."

William. His son. A boy with copper-colored hair and pottery blue eyes, a boy who was missing one front tooth, a boy who had saved a horse from being put down.

A boy whose father was about to become a murderer.

"Do get up, Michael," Helena snapped. "I want to divorce him, not kill him." Her statement sparked an eruption of speculation.

Then Michael sensed a new presence in the room. He glanced up to see the town constable and two deputies crowding into the doorway, polished hickory truncheons raised to do battle.

Helena held them off with a wave of her hand. "Gentlemen, this will be over in a moment."

"Yes, please," whispered Barnes. "I'll agree to whatever you want—"

"A divorce. On terms to be dictated by me, effective immediately."

"Agreed," he choked out.

"Michael, move away," Helena said. "Let us settle this in private. It's better that way, I swear it."

He stared down at the ruined face of the man he hated. The face of the man who had hurt Helena. Then he looked up at Helena, into her lovely eyes, so filled with terror and hope and dread.

He tossed aside the broken crystal and stood up. His foot slipped a little in the blood.

Troy Barnes clung to the brass bar rail and pulled himself up. He grabbed the barman's white towel and carefully placed it over his nose, and with an ugly sound moved it back into place.

The onlookers murmured and squirmed. Barnes dabbed the blood from his mouth and his chin. "Mr. Brody," he said, "you've come just in time."

Michael was probably the only one in the room who understood why Barnes retained such remarkable self-possession. He tensed, but Troy spoke the next words before he had a chance to react.

"Constable, place this man under arrest for deadly assault. Immediately."

Michael picked up a chair to fend them off, but there were three of them, well-armed and well-trained. Within moments, they had the wrist irons on him and were dragging him outside.

"Mr. Brody, no," Helena said, hurrying after them. "That won't be necessary."

Barnes grabbed her arm—the one he'd injured—and she turned completely white, though she made no sound. Michael roared in rage and frustration.

"You came just in time, my dear," Troy Barnes said. "That maniac nearly slit my throat."

"I should have let him."

"And Brody," Barnes called, "please send for Dr. Hillendahl. My wife is obviously hysterical."

Seven

As she was borne away in an express wagon that reeked of urine and decay, Helena guessed at Troy's plan. He would try to convince people that she was insane. Why else would a woman want to divorce her husband?

It was the ploy of a coward, and she refused to be reduced to despair. She was, after all, the daughter of Franklin Cabot, a man known for his sangfroid during times of adversity and tribulation. Besides, after all she'd endured at Troy's hands, the famous sanitarium of Dr. Hillendahl held no terrors for her.

Her first concern, of course, was William. He must be kept safe at any cost. Daisy had promised on her life to look after Helena's son, come what may. Helena had to trust that.

Since her husband had turned from Dr. Jekyll into Mr. Hyde, she had drawn on strengths she didn't know she possessed. Led by the wagon attendant into the handsome brick hospital facility, she clenched her jaw in frustration. Everyone at the gentleman's club had readily believed Troy's assertion that Michael was a mad scientist and she a hysterical woman, and her protests only served to support the theory. So she had surrendered, intending to regroup and find a way past this new disaster.

She wasn't doing a very good job of carrying out her goals. She had always known that divorce was no simple matter, particularly when the object of the suit was a United States senator.

Once inside the freshly painted residence, she released a sigh of exasperation and studied her surroundings. The doctor's office was comfortable and clean, with personal touches here and there—a delicate German figurine on a shelf containing leather-bound books, a dainty music box on the windowsill. A photograph of a plump, smiling woman holding two apple-cheeked babies hung on the wall alongside important-looking official certificates. Were it not for the express wagon attendant across the room, she might even relax and enjoy the view of Hamilton Park visible out the office window.

She made the attendant nervous, she could tell. He was a big man of mixed origin—perhaps Indian and African, she surmised—and he kept glancing out into the hallway.

"I'm sure Dr. Hillendahl will be here soon," she said.

The attendant shuffled his feet. "I'm real sorry about your arm, ma'am," he said.

"It's not your fault. You couldn't have known it was injured." When he'd taken her arm, she'd passed out from the pain, then awakened in the wagon with a canvas jacket buckled around her. It would have been easy to blame him, but she was saving her accusations for the man responsible. "Where is my husband, by the way?"

"I don't know, ma'am."

She ground her teeth in frustration. He moved fast, a weasel on the run. In a single afternoon, he'd managed to have Michael hauled off to jail and her taken to a women's sanitarium. And then he'd managed to disappear. The coward. That attribute had made him a highly successful politician. He knew the scandal would settle down much quicker if he kept a low profile, letting his staff handle such minor, troublesome details as a wife who wanted to divorce him.

Lord, she thought, how did I get here? What had begun as a rather pleasant afternoon settling into Moon Lake Lodge had exploded into disaster. But how could she have known Michael would show up and discover what Troy had done, and how could she have anticipated his extreme reaction? Even now, she shuddered at the memory of the rage burning in Michael's eyes when he'd vowed to kill her husband.

Finally Dr. Hillendahl arrived. He was a diminutive, almost painfully earnest man, clutching a folio of long paper briefs against his chest. "I'm terribly sorry, madam," he said. "I did not mean to keep you waiting."

With visible relief, the attendant stepped out, closing the door.

Helena sent the doctor her most attractive, unfelt smile, knowing it would take him aback. As the most influential woman in Saratoga Springs, she had her own kind of power. She prayed it would be enough, and took pains to appear perfectly calm, even though she was frantic with worry about William. "I will forgive you if you release me from this preposterous situation. Regardless of what my husband said, it really isn't necessary." She cocked her head, knowing she had him. "Of course, you must hear that from all your patients, don't you, Dr. Hillendahl? However, in this case, you may rest assured, I'm no more dangerous than a lamb.''

His cheeks reddened beneath a generous beard. ''Of course, Mrs. Barnes. If you will please lean forward.''

As he unbuckled the fastenings, she said, ''Do be gentle, please. My arm is injured.''

Moments later, she was free, feeling a blessed cooling breeze from the window and an ugly throb in her forearm, which she held cradled in her lap. She considered telling the doctor the truth about what had happened, but decided against it. It was a sad fact that children were spanked and wives were beaten in common practice. Society would praise Senator Barnes for keeping discipline in his household.

She only hoped the doctor would go along with her plan. ''I am ready for my tour now,'' she said.

''I beg your pardon.''

''My tour of the facility.'' She held her breath, terrified that her scheme would fail.

''But madam, I promised the senator I would admit you as a patient.''

She laughed lightly to cover her fear. ''Dear Troy. He is always so thorough in his research, isn't he?''

Hillendahl leaned against the edge of his desk and regarded her with confusion. ''Research, ma'am?''

''Indeed. You see, my husband is thinking about petitioning Congress for a grant of funds to support your excellent facility.''

She knew instantly she'd hit just the right note. His posture stiffened, his eyes narrowed. ''Funds, you say?''

''Yes. That is why he sent me here. To inspect the place. This facility might qualify to receive a grant of funds.''

"But he said you were suffering from a nervous disorder, and I'm to—"

"Ah, I'm such a terrible actress. I was supposed to pretend to be ill. That way, my husband reasoned that I could inspect the place from the perspective of a patient. But you've caught me out, Dr. Hillendahl. You're too wise to fall for petty tricks, aren't you? You can see clearly that I am no more insane than you are."

He gestured at a framed certificate on the wall. "Well, I did train in Vienna, with Dr. Freud."

"Excellent. Then let's dispense with this charade. You can give me a tour of the facility, and I shall report back to my husband. Come along now. I should like to meet some of the inmates."

"Dear madam, we don't refer to them as inmates but as guests." He led her out of the office and down a corridor lit by clerestory windows along the top of the wall, then held open a set of heavy double doors.

"Ah, *guests.* Are they free to leave here when their holiday is over?"

"No, they—"

"Then they are no more guests, my dear doctor, than the prisoners of Sing Sing are guests of the State of New York. But please, carry on with the tour. I am fascinated."

He led the way into the ward, a glaringly bright, empty room that smelled of boric acid and despair. A half dozen beds with white iron frames lined the walls, and there was a common area of sorts, consisting of a set of wooden benches facing windows too high for a view of anything but a ribbon of blue sky. Several women in plain muslin frocks milled about, greeting Helena with supreme indifference.

Their condition did not shock her. They were clean

and calm, some were even articulate and polite. Yet they seemed...disengaged, as though someone had unmoored them from the world and set them adrift.

There was a pale, chubby young woman who sat on the floor in a corner, her arms folded tightly across her chest, her eyes shut, her body rocking obsessively back and forth, back and forth. Tears rolled steadily down her face.

"Hello, Madeleine. How are you feeling today?" Dr. Hillendahl said, then turned to Helena. "She hasn't spoken since she arrived three days ago."

A curiously sweet, unmistakable smell emanated from the young woman. Helena stopped in her tracks. The front of her robe was covered in a spreading dampness, which confirmed Helena's suspicions. "Where is her baby?" she whispered to Hillendahl.

"Unfortunately, the child was stillborn. It would have been her first."

"Good glory," Helena declared, scandalized. "This woman isn't mad. She's grieving."

"Of course she is. Her husband couldn't bear her silence, her constant tears, and so he brought her to me."

"She doesn't need to be locked up. She needs compassionate friends and family around her. Gradually she will accept what has happened, and she will learn to go on. But not if you keep her isolated from the world."

"Mrs. Barnes, I think I can differentiate between grief and madness."

"Of course you can," Helena said, holding back her resentment. For the right price, he would accept anyone as a patient, or so it seemed. "But add a little common sense to that lofty education. Just because this woman's husband finds it difficult to live with her grief doesn't mean she should be hidden away."

Dropping his voice even lower, he said, "She attempted to injure herself. Surely you'll agree that common sense dictates we keep a close eye on her." He moved on. "This is Miss Claire," he said. "I'm afraid her affliction is not so simple."

Helena peered at the small figure huddled on the bed, the covers pulled up over a bony shoulder, neatly tucked beneath a blank, sallow face punctuated by eyes staring out at nothing.

"Miss Claire, dear, can you hear me?" The doctor bent down and gently touched her arm through the covers. "I've brought someone to meet you. Her name is Mrs. Helena Barnes."

"Helena handbasket," croaked the woman. "Everything is going to Helena handbasket." She moved nothing but her lips.

Helena stepped forward. "Ma'am, it's good to meet you."

The woman kept chanting the meaningless phrase, her eyes glazing over with images Helena couldn't imagine.

Torn by both pity and apprehension, she asked, "Dear, can you hear me? Is there something I can do for you?"

The elderly woman fell into silent tremors.

Dr. Hillendahl took Helena aside. "She is in the advanced stages of syphilis," he whispered. "Do you know what that is?"

Helena nodded somberly, feeling a surge of compassion. "Is there nothing you can do for her?"

He shook his head. "In time she will not be able to talk. She is nearly blind now. Her condition is progressive and irreversible. She used to be a great beauty who presided over an establishment known as the Gilded Lily. Do you know it?"

"Everyone knows about the most famous brothel in Saratoga Springs. The ladies in my Temperance League have told the city fathers again and again to shut it down, but they never do." She had always thought Troy should use his influence to close the place, but he declined. For all she knew, he patronized the place himself.

She felt a renewed respect for the doctor. He was greedy and arrogant, but in this case, his care was well-placed. "You're keeping her comfortable, then."

"Yes."

They moved on to Alice Wilkes, seated on a bench against the lime-washed wall. The young woman greeted her with a tired, wan smile and a breathy whisper. "I would shake hands with you, but you see..." She lifted her shoulders in a sheepish shrug and held out her hands. They were bound in fraying gauze bandages.

"What happened?" Helena asked her.

The girl offered a sly smile but said nothing.

"You've been at it again, haven't you," said Hillendahl, shoving aside the bench.

Helena stifled a gasp. There, on the stark white wall, was a small, light-dappled painting of a forest and river. The illustration, done in a dreamy, rusty color that gave it surprising depth, was skillfully wrought.

"That's remarkable," she said. "You're a talented artist."

Alice gazed lovingly at her creation. "They'll make me scrub it off," she said. "They'll make me scrub and scrub and scrub until it's all gone."

Helena turned to the doctor. "Frankly, this dreary room could use a little livening up. Why not—"

"You don't understand." He lowered his voice. "She marks the walls in her own blood."

Helena felt a tremor of revulsion. So that explained the curious, almost da Vinci-like rust and amber colors.

Mistaking the expression on her face for fear, Hillendahl said, "She's completely harmless to others. There's no need to worry that she'll hurt you."

"Of course she won't hurt me. Doctor," she said, "did it occur to you that she might not resort to painting in blood if you gave her proper paints and paper?"

"We tried that, but the results are the same. All her drawings are..." He gestured at the wall. "Like that. Very disturbing. Not at all like proper art."

"I recall that was the reaction when paintings from the Impressionist school were first exhibited. Perhaps you're housing a visionary, Doctor, and you simply haven't recognized her."

"But—"

"Humor me. Bring her something, at least a sketch pad and a bit of charcoal."

"Thank you for the suggestion, but I believe she is responding to treatment. Mrs. Barnes, we should move on. Alice has work to do."

Helena felt a terrible sense of guilt. What had happened to this young girl? What would it take to bring her world back into balance? And why, Helena wondered, had she herself gone through life without knowing such afflictions existed? Shame descended upon her. While she was planning parties and fund-raisers for the cream of society, women were secretly suffering in places like this. She had garnered the highest praise for organizing a project to replant the urns in Congress Spring Park, but beautifying the city seemed such a paltry enterprise compared to this.

"Mrs. Barnes, are you quite all right?" asked the doctor. "It is not my purpose to make you uncomfortable, but you insisted on seeing—"

"I am indeed uncomfortable, Doctor, and for that I thank you," she said, surveying the room, the damaged women, the sadness and despair that seemed to pervade the place. Perhaps the women here did not need to be institutionalized but understood. What if they were to live among people who cared about them? What if they were given worthy work to do?

Helena herself had never done work of any real worth, but perhaps this disaster was an opportunity in disguise. A chance to do something of importance.

"Nellie Freeman McQuigg," said a spritely voice, breaking in on her racing thoughts. "They've put me here again." The small, gray-haired woman had a demeanor that matched the energy in her voice. "Not that I have any complaints about Dr. Hillendahl, here. He looks after me, lets me come and go as I please and serves the most divine fried chicken in town." She winked a bright eye at the doctor. "He thinks I'm crazy, but harmless."

"Why?" asked Helena.

"Because I have devoted my life to fighting for equal rights for women, and I am a lesbian."

This baffled Helena. "I approve of equal rights, and I have nothing against people from foreign countries," she said.

"But the main reason is that I tend to frighten men."

The diminutive old woman looked utterly harmless. "How?" Helena asked.

"I'm the first board-certified female lawyer in the State of New York. I can't tell you how frightening men find that."

"Yes," said Helena, smiling cautiously as an idea took shape in her mind. "Yes, you can."

Troy Barnes had never liked the house in Vandam Square. It was beautiful, and he did enjoy beautiful things. And it was situated in the most fashionable—albeit most boring—neighborhood of Saratoga Springs. But he much preferred the crackling atmosphere of Washington or Albany, where a man could make things happen rather than make an impression. That was what this house represented, and that was why he disliked it. Father had drummed into him the necessity of putting on appearances, insisting that a fine house was the measure of a man. So, as he had all his life, Troy bowed to the will of his father. Still, he spent as little time here as he reasonably could.

The elegant decor of the parlor should have soothed him, but he prowled the quiet, beautifully appointed room in agitation. And in pain. Shoving aside the mourning shroud over the mantel mirror, he stared at his reflection. Bruised streaks underscored his eyes, giving him the look of a raccoon. His grotesquely swollen nose turned him into a stranger to himself. Jesus, Rowan had all but ruined his face.

Rowan. Troy should have guessed years ago that he'd fathered Helena's brat. In that, Troy now admitted to himself he had been willfully, stupidly ignorant, believing her lies along with the rest of the world. The very air itself used to ignite when Rowan and Helena were together, a situation that caused great consternation for Helena's father. In offering Rowan the Institute, Troy had earned Senator Cabot's gratitude. He had also believed Helena would feel nothing but contempt for a man who would leave her so readily.

Perhaps she had, for a time, but the fact that she'd

turned to him now introduced an unexpected new threat. Troy decided to let the bastard rot in jail. And just for good measure, he'd end all the funding for the Institute as well, throwing Michael Rowan back into poverty where he belonged.

That decided, Troy poured himself a glass of brandy from the crystal decanter at the sideboard. As he tipped back the snifter, he caught a glimpse of the crude French painting Helena admired so much, depicting an oversize woman in a tasteless pose. At best, the thing was eccentric and bizarre. At worst, it was criminally lewd. He ought to have the offensive thing destroyed, but it was a gift from the Vanderbilts, who were not to be offended, ever. Perhaps he'd keep the worthless thing simply because Helena loved it.

He winced as the liquor irrigated a cut in his lip, and tossed the whole drink to the back of his throat. Elsewhere in the house, he heard a door open and shut—probably the housekeeper or Archie making the last rounds of the day. He poured more brandy, but even as the smooth liquor slid through him, his thoughts smoldered around Helena. His wife, his false and beautiful wife.

And then she was there before him, as though summoned by his thoughts. He blinked at the slender silhouette in the doorway, wondering if the brandy had impaired him already. But no, it was her, as somber and flawless as she had been the day he'd married her.

With exaggerated care he set down his glass and covered his surprise. "I'm glad you're back, my dear," he said. "You came to your senses quickly, judging by the fact that Dr. Hillendahl released you." Even as he spoke, his gaze probed the shadows in the hallway behind her.

"I came here alone," she said, answering his unspoken question. "But you mustn't mistake that for a foolish lapse in judgment." Helena stepped into the light. He felt her studying his face, and was appalled to see the faintest tightening of her mouth—a tiny, grim line of satisfaction. Then her gaze settled upon his fist, which had tightened of its own accord. "You're like a wounded dog, aren't you?" she said. "More dangerous when you're in pain and feeling threatened."

Her defiance startled him. Apparently, she needed another lesson. "The only threat I feel is from a wife who has taken leave of her senses. Clearly Hillendahl released you too quickly."

Rather than shrinking back, she held her ground. "To be honest, I found my tour of his facility to be rather enlightening. However, the timing was inconvenient. You won't want to try that again. But that's not what I came to discuss with you, Troy, and well you know it. I came to discuss my future, which begins with a simple directive. You are to take the next train down to Albany, and you mustn't come back. I shall be gone from your life, and you will be glad to let me go."

His face heated and throbbed with the bruises and lacerations he'd suffered. He could feel a strong pulse surging in his neck. "What makes you think I would ever allow you to leave?"

"Because you don't want to lose what is most important to you. And that is your position in the Senate."

Oh, she knew him well, and he resented her for it. All his life, he'd believed he was well-suited for public office because he had excellent judgment about the things that mattered most. He believed in a prosperous America, believed in protecting the interests of the country's large industries. The producers of coal and steel and petroleum, and the railroad and steamship companies contributed to the prosperity of the nation. Those industries in turn kept people employed. Better a humble wage than none at all, he often thought.

Drawing his attention back to Helena, he said, "My position is secure."

"So long as I keep silent about the fact that you stole the election from its rightful winner, Mr. Elijah Ware."

His smile froze, and his guts suddenly turned ice cold. "That old scandal. It's a rumor started by a poor loser."

"It's a fact, and I am in possession of the stolen ballots to prove it."

True alarm sank in like a cold, steel spear. She was bluffing, surely. Yet the way she regarded him, with those cool, apple-green eyes, gave him pause.

"Yes, you gave them to Archie to dispose of," she reminded him. "But he was careless." Almost casually, she lay a familiar, pale-green printed form on the table. "That's just one. I've had them since the election and it would be a shame to have to produce them now, wouldn't it?"

He took a step toward her and saw the battle in her eyes—a war between terror and determination. He'd seen the terror before, but this determination was new and far less pleasurable.

She glanced at his fisted hands. "As you can see, I am in a position to make any number of demands. However, I want nothing from you, nothing but my freedom. Oh, and your absence. You never liked Saratoga Springs in the first place, anyway."

"You were only too happy to claim the position of my wife. You were only too happy to pawn your child off on me.'' It hurt Troy to think of William. How proud the boy had made him. William was bright and handsome and polite. Loss hit Troy like a hammer. He would miss William. He gestured around the room. ''Now you're saying you'd be willing to give all this up?''

She looked as though she were about to laugh. ''Really, Troy. We have never had so honest a conversation, have we? I never truly took pleasure in being your wife. However, I settled for a vaguely satisfactory existence, thinking this was the life I was meant to live. Being married to you was slowly draining my spirit, but the change was so subtle and gradual that I didn't really notice. Now I realize how desperately unhappy I was for so long. I give you due credit for opening my eyes to a painful truth. Of course, I'll never thank you for the manner of the revelation, but suddenly life has possibilities again. I look forward to each new day, and that is something I haven't felt in a long, long time.''

He barely listened to her babbling. Instead, his mind raked over the possibilities. She did possess the stolen ballots—he didn't doubt it for a moment. She was an accomplished liar, but she wasn't lying about this. He knew it in his bones. So the question was, could such a thing ruin him?

The answer was grimly apparent. ''Do you realize what will happen to you if you dare to leave me?''

''I know it's hard for you to fathom that I would endure a scandal rather than stay married to you. But in fact, that is just what I intend to do. And you will allow this. I'm not giving you a choice, Troy. You're too smart to think I'm bluffing. You know I have the ballots, and you know that if anything happens to me, the fact that you stole the election will come to light.

So let's make this simple for the both of us. Take your things and go to Albany and pray this blows over quickly."

"I'll make you regret this," he said quietly, letting a hidden threat underscore the simple words. Even in the dim lamplight, he could see her flesh prickle with a phantom chill. He said no more, for he had plans to make now that she was forcing his hand. She was vulnerable, for all her show of bravado. Her precious son was her key weakness. Troy vowed to take advantage of that.

Barely holding his fury in check, he strode past her and bellowed for Archie, who had some explaining to do.

Eight

The last time Michael had seen Nellie Freeman McQuigg, he'd been naked. As he staggered out of the town jail, he blinked at the woman, then held up a hand to shield his eyes. The glaring sunshine was a shock after the dimness of the cell.

Only moments before he'd been sleeping fitfully, dogged by nightmares about Troy Barnes hurting Helena, turning on William, even. The deputy who'd awakened and discharged him had not been gentle. After spending the night on a mouldering pallet, in a cramped cell that smelled of dank stone and damp earth, Michael was fully clothed but mildly confused. Every bruise and laceration ignited with fresh pain. Now he concentrated on keeping his balance as he stood at the chiseled curb of Congress Street.

"Good morning, Professor Rowan," said Mrs. McQuigg. She stood on the sidewalk, her posture perfectly erect as she waited for him to join her. "I almost didn't recognize you with your clothes on."

Could she be any more odd? he wondered, trying to clear his head.

"You were not very gracious the last time we met,"

she said. "However, your generosity to me in my time of need simply overwhelmed me."

In fact, Michael had cause to regret his impulsive decision to help her. His life had suddenly become extremely complicated.

"And it's a good thing, too, because you need a lawyer now," Nellie McQuigg concluded.

"You're a lawyer?"

"Indeed I am, young man. I have suffered my share of bad luck, but I'm a fine lawyer."

Impatience nudged at him. This was all mildly interesting, but he needed to make sure Helena was safe. "I'm grateful for that, but I must be going. There's someone I need to see."

"Helena and William are both fine," she said, reading his thoughts.

"Where's Barnes?" Michael demanded. "Where is the son of a bitch?"

"Senator Barnes's mother had nothing to do with his behavior. Barnes has gone into retreat—a wise move. He's in Albany, hoping the scandal will blow over. His wife was sent to Dr. Hillendahl's, but she didn't stay long. Helena Barnes is perfectly sane."

He was still trying to clear his aching head. "Why was Helena sent to Hillendahl's?"

"Her husband tried to commit her."

He spat a curse. "I should have killed him."

"I'm pleased that you didn't, for that would have made my job much more difficult. Anyway, as I was saying, she's a very clever woman. She convinced Hillendahl that she was touring the facility, and that is how we met. I sometimes lose my hold on the world, Professor Rowan," she confessed with painful candor. "The doctor knows of no cure for that, but he agreed that I do much better when I have a sense of purpose, and Helena certainly gave me that when she engaged my services."

He blinked in the glare of the summer sun. His head throbbed. Everything throbbed.

Turning to the street, McQuigg grabbed his sleeve. "Come along. Walk with me, and I'll explain as we go."

"Where's my horse?"

"I believe George Long returned it to the livery. Walking never did a man a bit of harm."

"It's forty miles to the Institute."

She walked with a surprisingly quick step as she drew him along a brick sidewalk through the center of town. As always, the summer population of Saratoga Springs was a mixture of Wall Street millionaires, foreign tourists, raffish touts selling tips on racehorses, drifters and harried locals. Carriages, traps and dearborns tangled at every intersection, the drivers squabbling in the heat with ill humor. Nellie McQuigg paraded grandly along the crowded sidewalk, though no one seemed to take note of her.

Over her shoulder, she said, "You're not going to the Institute. You've been given the sack. You're indigent."

He shoved away a lock of hair that had fallen over his sweating brow. This was no surprise, of course. Barnes had enough influence to have him dismissed immediately. Michael wasn't sure how he felt about that. His life's work was there, and now it was over. Yet his discovery of William eclipsed his whole world.

"You should count yourself lucky he didn't send you down to state prison for the rest of your born days."

"He...you mean Troy Barnes."

"Our esteemed senator. Fortunately for you, the local prosecutor is wonderfully incompetent. Willard Bates—do you know him?'' She didn't wait for a reply. ''It was almost unsporting of me to take him on. But I suppose it's poetic justice. He preys on the weak, so why shouldn't I prey on him?''

They passed the Armoury and the casino at the center of town, then skirted Congress Spring Park, where a second-rate brass ensemble blared a regimental piece while clusters of overdressed young ladies promenaded along the walkways.

Speaking over the music, McQuigg said, ''I'm afraid you'll have to pay a rather steep fine. But at least you have your freedom.''

''So I have no home. No job. No money.''

''And no assault charges brought against you. So don't complain.''

''Well...thank you.'' He was still muzzy-headed from the beating and rough treatment after his arrest. ''But how? I broke the man's nose. Nearly slit his throat. I'd do it again, but—''

''Young man, you are never to do it again. Is that understood? I'll be the first to agree with you that a man who hits women deserves to die. But not at your hands. That way lies madness. Trust me, I'm an expert.''

''You still haven't explained why I'm a free man.'' He flexed his injured hand, and one of the split knuckles oozed with fresh blood.

''It was tediously simple. No witnesses.''

''What? There were others present, and the bartender—''

''Is a member of the other political party. As were the patrons, even those playing cards with the senator. They saw nothing. Oh, I suppose they saw Barnes trip and fall on his face. Who knew the poor man was so clumsy when he drinks?''

''Those men lied for me?''

''Heavens, don't even think it. That's not the way I work. I'm not in the business of telling witnesses to lie. But when asked to make a statement, they all described the incident as an accident, not an assault.''

He inspected his hands again. ''I'm glad you're on my side,'' he muttered.

''You should be.'' She inhaled through her nostrils, puffing out her bosom. ''A fine summer day, is it not?''

Michael merely nodded. He had no job or home, but he was free. Barnes had gone down to Albany to lick his wounds and probably nurse his hurt pride. Helena and William were safe. ''I need to get to Moon Lake Lodge.''

''Of course. We must prepare the case.''

''What case?''

''The divorce case. Honestly, for a distinguished professor, you're awfully dense.'' She marched him out of town, across Fishkill Bridge. The landscape shifted from manicured parklands and stately mansions to farms and forests and wild, shady places hung with green gloom. They turned onto a gravel drive dotted with overgrown tufts of grass, and he recalled his sense of grim purpose the last time he'd galloped out of here. The sign designating the property Moon Lake Lodge dangled askew from a rusty wrought-iron gate.

''The carriage house is through there, beyond the trees.'' She showed him where the drive veered away from the main house, disappearing into a stand of trees crowned with the thick foliage of high summer. ''You can stay there for the time being.''

* * *

He trudged down the lane toward the weather-beaten carriage house. A battered weather vane in the shape of a running horse creaked in the breeze, and bees buzzed in an overgrown bed of hollyhocks and foxglove. The pouch-like nests of barn swallows were lined up like barracks under the eaves.

He entered through the carriage-port, stepping from sunshine to shadow and then standing still as his eyes adjusted to the dimness. The building had a broad center aisle with side rooms left and right. It had once been a proper carriage house with a clay surface, a watering trough and generous turnouts to a grassy paddock. A broken racing sulky slumped in a corner, and the names of horses were still visible on the corroded plaques in front of the empty stalls. The first small alcove contained a tack shed, its beams and corners knitted together with strands of cobwebs. Part of the roof had caved in and lay rotting on the floor.

The fresh smell of horse and hay hung in the air. A rustle of movement stirred somewhere. "Hello?" he called.

"Hello, Professor. Remember Hector?" said a high-pitched voice from the far end of the center aisle.

Standing in the middle of the hot, cobwebby barn, Michael saw his son walking toward him from the broken-beamed stalls, one of which was occupied by the lame horse. An emotion he'd never felt before penetrated Michael's pain-fogged brain. His son. He had a son. The boy was lively and handsome. His name was William. He was a complete stranger.

The child gazed up at him. "What happened to your face?"

Michael touched the cut on his cheekbone. "I hurt myself fighting."

William's blue eyes widened. "You were in a fight?"

"Yes. I'm not very good at it."

"Me neither."

"Do you get in fights often?" Michael asked. What he really wanted to know was whether or not William had ever been beaten by the man he called father.

"No. I'm a fast runner. And I'm good at hiding. There are lots of hiding places in the woods and by the lake. The feed's over here." William seemed to accept Michael's arrival without question. His friendly, open manner was both unexpected and refreshing. He went to a fat burlap sack, picked up a metal scoop and filled a bucket. "Where are you going to live, Professor? Mama said you were going to be staying in the barn, so I wondered where you're going to sleep."

Interesting, that Helena had taken charge. Some things had not changed. She'd always been a meddlesome woman, organizing people, pairing them off, putting them together, taking them apart. A pity she hadn't arranged her own life so conveniently.

Ah, but she'd tried, an inner voice reminded him. Nearly a decade ago, she'd put her arms around him, pressed her girlish figure tight against him and tried to convince him to stay with her.

William lugged the bucket across the narrow aisle, scraping it along the packed clay surface.

Michael slid open the stall door, wincing at the squeal it made on its tracks. "I was just wondering about that myself," he said. "There should be quarters upstairs. Perhaps I'll bed down there."

As William placed the grain in front of the horse, Michael hovered close. "Does your mother know you're feeding Hector?"

William shook his head. "She thinks he's dangerous."

"He is."

"I'll be careful."

At the moment, the horse seemed docile, lowering his head to eat. The boy stood back and watched in deep satisfaction.

"Can I ask you something?" Michael said.

"Yes."

"Has your mother told you anything about me?"

"She said you're a professor and you got the sack and you got nowhere to go, so you're staying here for a bit."

For a bit. Michael clenched his jaw. Helena was probably determined to make sure his son remained unimpressed by him, regarding him as a temporary wayfarer just passing through.

"I'm glad," William added.

"Glad?"

"That you're staying for a bit."

Michael grew an inch taller just hearing the words. "Well, I'm glad you're glad."

"That way, you can fix Hector's buckskins."

"Bucked shins."

"Yes. So I'm glad. Let's go see where you're going to sleep." William lunged for the stall door.

The horse started, and Michael stepped quickly between the two of them, calming the Thoroughbred with a low and soothing murmur.

"Damn." Too late, he bit his tongue to keep the curse in. "Never make sudden movements when you're around a horse," Michael said. "Particularly an injured Thoroughbred."

Wide-eyed, William regarded Hector's flattened

ears. "I've never been around a horse before. Damn," he muttered under his breath, trying out the new word.

Helena's overprotectiveness would have to change, he decided. How could she expect William to learn the dangers of the world if she didn't let him face them? "Well, they can be unpredictable. Do you know what that means?"

"No."

Michael held the stall door as they stepped out, then slid it back in place. "You never know what's going to happen next."

"Sometimes that's a good thing, right?" William tilted back his head to look up at him.

Michael's heart constricted with a rush of memories. Something about those blue eyes, wide as pansies, swept away the years, reminding Michael of himself at that age. When he was not much older than William, he'd come home from work to find his mother sitting by the lamp one cold night. The tiny room they shared was even chillier than usual, and the lamp had nearly burnt itself out of fuel. With painful clarity, Michael remembered his mother's eyes. They were wide open and staring and oddly bluer in death than they had been in life.

He wanted William to know he had his grandmother's eyes. He wanted everything with William—to teach the boy, to love him and hold him close, to tuck him in at night, read him stories, ask him riddles and tell him jokes. To keep him safe.

They went around to an outside stairwell that led up to the coachman's quarters. William tugged the bell-pull attached to a discordant bell at the top of the stairs, and it protested with a weary clatter. He ran up the stairs and pushed open the door.

Michael followed more slowly, stepping into the

roomy quarters. Cobwebs crisscrossed the place in spidery swags from beam to beam. William startled a pair of swallows nesting in the rafters. The furnishing consisted of an old table and chairs, a dilapidated workbench, a sagging bed with its mattress plundered by vermin. A vast array of iron tools hung from the walls or lay upon warped shelves. Darts of sunlight streamed through gaps in the roof. A claw-footed desk dominated the center of the room. A long waist-high bench bore a selection of veterinary supplies and instruments, enamel bowls, a mortar and pestle, glass tubing and vessels of varying shapes and sizes. Dust motes spun and flashed through the sunlight, bringing the loft to eerie life. The whole place had a look of abandonment and neglect.

"It's perfect," William said in a voice hushed with awe.

"Yes," Michael agreed. "It's perfect."

"Daisy tells me the loft is unlivable," Helena said later that evening as they sat together at the water's edge. "So I thought it would be perfect for you."

Michael leaned back on an old-fashioned, rickety garden bench and crossed his ankles. "It is perfect."

"It's hardly Menlo Park," she pointed out. "It's got a lame horse living in it."

"Hector? He won't mind. He'll barely know I'm there."

He stared at her for a long, measuring moment, watching the play of blue twilight on her mysterious, exquisite face. Leaning back, he savored the end of a very strange day. He'd cleaned himself up after a fashion and they'd all shared a meal—William, Michael, Nellie, Helena and the maid named Daisy Sullivan. Looking more like a giant oak than a daisy, she'd served a delicious meal of trout fried in butter, potatoes and tomatoes. Afterward, Daisy had taken William off to bed. Michael and Helena had left Nellie on the porch, smoking a pipe and looking at the stars over the lake. From the water's edge, they could see the orange flare of her tobacco as she puffed on it. Out in the lake, a distant tiny island, tufted with trees, rose against the darkening sky.

It was the first time he'd been alone with Helena since discovering what Troy Barnes had done. It seemed impossible that so much had happened since that moment. She had a strange power, like a shaft of sunlight pouring down through the clouds after the darkest storm. Everyone looked at her as though mesmerized; no one was immune. Unlike others, he sensed an uncanny spirit beneath the Madonna beauty—like light trapped within the facets of a prism. From the first moment he'd seen her, he'd felt drawn to discover her inner workings, her inner light. Her beauty alone was not what had attracted him. It was that light, which no other woman possessed.

"Why didn't you tell me of your troubles with Barnes right from the start?" he asked.

"I didn't know whether or not I could trust you. I didn't know if you would care."

He fell into silence. He'd given her little enough reason to believe he could be caring. "You should have told me."

She dismissed the subject with an impatient wave of her hand. "Nellie tells me she's seen a lot of you, Michael. What does she mean by that?"

"She's an odd bird," he said, his face heating as he recalled their encounter in the bathhouse.

Helena leaned forward, peering at him in the waning

light. "Why, Michael Rowan, are you blushing? You are, aren't you?"

He leaned down and picked up a stone, then skipped it across the surface of the water. "Am I?"

She didn't answer for a long time. The peepers came out, invisible voices in the reeds. It was a fine summer evening, he thought, the lake a silver mirror under a soft purple sky, the birds settling secretly in the foliage all around them, the stars winking to life, one by one. He caught Helena's eye, trying to read her expression. She watched him with wary curiosity, not the melting heat he recalled from the days when they had been lovers. What a delight she had been back then, so eager to flout convention and to learn what pleasure was, no matter what the consequences. He wondered what she thought of those consequences now.

In her stark black gown, a crown of copper curls shadowing her pale face, she resembled a fairy queen from another world. Only the shallow breaths she took and the tightly gripped hands in her lap betrayed a coiled tension.

Michael wondered if he made her nervous. Or had Barnes made her frightened of all men?

He cleared his throat. "I didn't thank you for getting me out of jail," he said, just to end the silence.

"It's the least I could do."

"And for providing the carriage house."

Another silence drew out. After a while, he said, "You shouldn't have stopped me from killing him."

"Of course I should have. I will not have my son suffer the stigma of a murder in the family." She bit her lip.

Family. That was a concept that rarely occurred to him.

He realized he was angry—no, furious at her with

an unreasoning sense of accusation. He couldn't abide the idea that she had lived with a man who beat her. Why hadn't she told anyone? Why hadn't she left? He forced himself to temper his anger and give her a chance to explain. "Tell me," he said at last. "I want to know exactly how it was between you and Barnes."

She released her lip; her nervous teeth had made it slightly swollen. Speaking in quiet, measured tones devoid of her customary animation, she said, "Marrying Franklin Cabot's daughter helped his career in the Senate immeasurably. He seemed satisfied with my decision to stay in Saratoga Springs, while he spent most of his time in the capital or in Albany. We both knew ours was no love match but we were...cordial. He lived in his world and I in mine, and we seldom had a thing to do with each other, which suited us both rather well. It was actually quite a convenient arrangement. This sort of marriage is hardly unique."

It sounded like an empty, dreary existence. But she sounded almost wistful for it.

"So when did he first attack you?"

"The night after my father's funeral. You see, Father's secretary, Carlyle Pickett, unfortunately had a keen ear for household gossip, and I had a talkative maid. He knew I was with child when I married Troy. But Pickett never said a word until Father was gone. Then he told Troy."

"Why would he do that?"

She stared at the ground. "When I was very young and very foolish, I treated him unkindly."

Michael needed no further explanation. She'd broken many hearts in her day.

She released a long, unsteady breath. "I suppose Troy might have had his suspicions, but if he did, he never let on. As it happens, he was deathly afraid of my father. Every man in the Senate was. While my father was alive, Troy never hurt me. He was quite clever, really. A bit of a cold fish, but what man isn't?''

Michael winced, but said nothing.

''On the few occasions I saw him,'' she continued, ''I'd hear him berating a servant, breaking something, but I put it out of my mind. All men have tempers, I thought, when I thought about it at all.''

Michael had to hear the rest, had to know. Moment by moment, even if every word hit him like a hammer. ''And after your father died?''

''Pickett's disclosure broke his control. And that night…it started.'' She spoke matter-of-factly, though he could tell she was inches from shattering. ''He attacked me when we got back to the Georgetown house after the service. I didn't even realize what was happening. I thought the first blow was inadvertent.''

A cold guilt gripped his chest. Why? Dear Christ, why had she suffered this? Why Helena? Helena, who loved without caution and regarded the world with a rare and innocent optimism.

''And then,'' she continued, ''I had the strange sensation that the attack could not be real, that it was happening to someone else. Truly, it was something so completely out of the realm of my experience that I simply did not know what to do. I imagine it must be like suffering a great accident. I was dazed.''

''Did he hurt William?'' Michael had to ask.

''No, never. I imagine I would have killed him myself if he touched my son. Besides, the very next day I hired Daisy, then took the next steamer home. I knew immediately that I would have to free myself from Troy. I had no idea how it should be done. It's the sort of thing one hears about, but it is all terribly scandalous. I wasn't quite sure how to get myself divorced so I...I sent for you. You were always good at...solving things."

Her voice wavered only slightly and she did not weep. It would have been better if she had, somehow. Her flat recounting of the horror pounded him with guilt. She'd sent for him, and he'd refused to help her.

He touched her shoulder. "You should have told me right from the start."

She moved away from him as though she couldn't bear his touch. "We've never been good at saying the right things."

"Damn it, Helena—" He stopped himself, knowing this was not what she needed now. "You will divorce him," he said. "We'll find a way."

"I have found a way. His campaign workers stole four boxes of ballots in the last election, and I happen to have those ballots. The scandal would end his career more surely than a divorce. He will not oppose me."

He grinned, even though it strained the cut on his lip. "Excellent work. But worse men than Barnes have survived corruption. He's not going to let you go, Helena. You should know that." Yet already his mind galloped ahead. Although the threat of exposure might not work, Michael could add his own threat to Helena's.

"There are other ways." She spoke softly, with a little catch in her voice. In a rustle of petticoats, she turned on the bench to face him. Through the last of the twilight, she regarded him with a steady, clear-eyed stare that both entranced and unsettled him. "According to Nellie, the chief cause of divorce in this state is adultery."

He forgot to breathe, knowing even before she continued what she was about to say.

"Suppose I was unfaithful to him. Suppose I was an adulterous wife."

Each word struck him like a stone hurled in anger. He couldn't believe what he was hearing, and yet it seemed inevitable. Every cell and every nerve ending in his body felt heated and strained. She was the most beautiful woman on the planet, and she wanted him to make love to her. Memories of their youthful affair had tormented him for years. Now, with a word, he could have her again. Have this new, womanly Helena, this wounded Helena in his arms, her skin bared to him, her body open to his. It was a dream come true, and yet…and yet…

"No," he said.

"No?" Even in the night shadows her luminous eyes glowed with incredulity.

"I won't do it. Damn it, Helena. Is this why you brought me here? Is this why you offered me a place to live?"

"No, but now that you mention it—"

"For Chrissake." He got up and paced along the bank of the lake. "Your reputation would never survive."

"My reputation." She laughed bitterly. "Worrying about my reputation compelled me to marry Troy in the first place, and look how things turned out. Do you think I value that more than I do my life? Or is it your own reputation you're worried about?"

"Hardly. In order to worry about my reputation, I would have to actually have one. I'm thinking of you and of William. If we did this, he'd be forced to go through life with a burden he never asked for. Did Nellie McQuigg advise you in this?"

"Certainly not. She merely asked me if it was a possibility in my case."

"I thought she was a gifted woman of the law, but I was wrong. No responsible lawyer would advise you to do this foolish thing. She herself admits to periods of insanity."

"Perhaps we should go away," she said. "I'll take William abroad."

"Oh, really? What if Barnes decides to claim custody of him? In the eyes of the law, he is the boy's father. He's a damned U.S. senator. If you make him the injured party in a divorce, you give him all the power."

She fell quiet and leaned back against the bench to look out over the water. The moon silvered her face with ghostly light. "So, once again, you refuse to help me."

"I refuse to be party to another crazy scheme." He forced himself to slow down his pacing, then to stop. "But I will help you." He sat down beside her. He had an urge to take her hand, but she held herself close and tight, shoulders hunched forward and arms wrapped around her waist, walling him off. It was the posture of a frightened, wounded woman, not a temptress in search of a lover. While she said one thing, her body indicated another.

"Look," he said, "your friend Nellie McQuigg should be able to put forth a better idea. Tomorrow we'll figure out a way to free you from Barnes without acting out a whole bloody farce. Agreed?"

She watched the rustling reeds, where the occasional firefly winked and disappeared. "Agreed," she said at last. "It's late. I should go."

He offered his hand. She hesitated, then stood without help. "Tell me something," she said as they walked back toward the house and stopped on the front lawn. "Were you even tempted?"

He stopped walking. He would have reached out, turned her to face him, but he didn't dare touch her. He didn't know where she was hurt, didn't know how to hold her.

"Helena, there's something you need to understand. I do want you in my bed. I always have. But when we do come together, it will not be because you want to create a scandal."

She opened her mouth, but only a small, wordless sound came out. Very gently he touched her under the chin and closed her mouth. Her skin felt like heaven, and he would have liked to let his caress linger, but he didn't allow himself that luxury.

"What do you mean, 'when we do'?" she asked.

He studied her for a long moment, watching the play of moonlight and shadow over her face, an alabaster masterpiece that would haunt his dreams tonight and probably many nights to come. He was certain his expression answered her question.

"Good night, Helena," he said, and walked away.

Nine

"What's this white stuff?" William asked, scowling down at his breakfast plate.

"Hominy," said Helena. "It's delicious, so try it."

She and Nellie watched the little boy as they sat together in the bright dining hall of Moon Lake Lodge. The cat lazed in a sunny spot on a window ledge. William was sullen this morning because he'd wanted to play on the dock and she'd forbidden him to go near the water. Daisy had laid out a generous but simple breakfast of buttered hominy, fluffy scrambled eggs and biscuits made with carbonate spring water. William, who was accustomed to sugared graham gems and crisp bacon, regarded his plate with suspicion.

He scooped up a single kernel of hominy. "Looks like a big giant tooth."

"Then put it in your mouth," Nellie said. "That's where teeth belong."

He stuck out his tongue and licked the tidbit. His face screwed up with disgust. "Yuck."

"For heaven's sake," Helena snapped. "Will you just eat it and be grateful you have food to eat at all?"

"I want my graham gems. I want my bacon."

The hurt in his eyes flooded her with guilt. How did you tell a little boy who was used to having everything that he was suddenly poor? There was so much to explain to him, she didn't know where to begin.

"Don't whine." Nellie took a sip of her coffee, then patted her gray braid, which was twisted in a lopsided coronet atop her head. "I cannot abide whining."

"I think you're odd," William burst out.

"I think you're rude. And your suspenders are on backward."

William said, "I like them that way. Your hair is on backward."

"That's it," said Helena. "William, go to your room. You get no breakfast at all today."

"An excellent plan," Nellie concurred. "Before long, he'll be too weak with hunger to be rude to me."

William sent her a smoldering look and left the table, his bare feet slapping loudly on the stairs as he stomped to his room.

"I apologize for my son," Helena said.

"He's just out of sorts because you told him he couldn't go near the lake."

"I don't have time to watch him, and he doesn't know how to swim."

Nellie sipped her coffee and said nothing more.

"He's my son," Helena said defensively. "It's my job to protect him."

"Not to smother him."

"It is so hard to set the proper limits, Nellie."

"Did anyone ever imply that being a mother was easy?" asked Nellie. "Listen, dear. You have asked me to be your legal adviser and advocate. I am more than honored to serve you in that way. But there is something I need."

"What's that?"

"The truth. All of it. From the beginning."

Helena finished her breakfast and pushed her plate aside. "William is not my husband's child," she stated baldly. "He was fathered by Professor Rowan."

"Of course he was." Reaching across the table, Nellie patted her hand.

"You knew?"

"It wasn't a difficult puzzle," she assured her. "Daisy knows, too. They look alike. They even dress the same, like a pair of hooligans."

"And you don't...disapprove?"

"The boy is only eight. Why would we disapprove of a child? And here's another guess. You didn't want to use the baby to keep Rowan, so you didn't tell him you were expecting."

Helena's face flushed. "That's fairly close to the truth. It seemed wrong to hold him to me like that. I did tell him I loved him."

"I'll wager that scared the cornpone out of him."

She nodded. "I thought everyone wanted to be loved, but I was wrong about Michael. I never really knew what he wanted but ultimately I concluded that my love was not the answer for him." She veered her thoughts away from her proposition the previous night. "It's for the best. The way I felt about him—it wasn't the start of a love that lasts."

"No love lasts if you turn your back on it. It's not a garden weed. It won't thrive if neglected. Unless, of course, that's your purpose—to keep it from thriving."

Helena rolled her napkin tightly in her lap. "When I was young, I was often accused of having an excess of emotion. Is it dangerous to feel too much?"

"Some would say it's a danger to your heart. It's bound to get broken."

Helena couldn't resist an ironic smile. "You think that frightens me?"

"Doesn't it?"

"I have survived marriage to Troy Barnes. Do you think anything can scare me after that?" But the fact was, she shivered with feelings that still haunted her, even now, years after she was supposed to have forgotten Michael and moved on. Her love for him had broken open a whole new world, had changed the way she looked at life. And now he was back, a hidden danger in the safe place she was making for herself. "The past doesn't matter now," she said. "All my love is for my son from now on. He is what I must focus on."

"I'm sorry, Mrs. McQuigg," said William, poking out his lower lip as he returned from his room and edged back into the kitchen. "I shouldn't have said you were odd."

"You're right, young man. I am odd, but it's rude to say. I've heard that boys who eat hominy every day for a year can fly like birds." She pushed his breakfast toward him.

"Really?" He sat back down and studied his bowl with new interest.

"There's one way to find out."

He dug in, eating his breakfast so fast, he probably didn't taste a thing.

Helena caught Nellie's eye. "If I catch him jumping off cliffs and flapping his wings, I'll know who to blame."

"Flying is an outstanding idea." Nellie stood up, her face bright with purpose. "But today I must travel by train. I'm off to the station, then, to take the morning omnibus to Albany."

Helena caught her breath, feeling a dizzy hope rise

through her. She knew Nellie's purpose was to meet with Judge Standish about the divorce. They'd been up since dawn, drinking coffee and mulling over the possibilities. Nellie hoped to initiate the petition for divorce immediately. Helena had her doubts. Troy was a powerful man, and she was learning that there was nothing more dangerous than a cowardly man who wielded power.

"Do you have train fare?" Helena asked.

"I'll make do."

"My granddaddy Cabot left us a fortune, but it's in probate," said William.

Startled, Helena frowned at him. "Who told you that?"

He stabbed the last bits of hominy with his fork. "People don't always tell me things. Sometimes I figure them out on my own."

"Where's probate?" asked Nellie, her eyes twinkling with amusement.

William shrugged. "Down in Albany, maybe."

"I shall be back by tomorrow evening, with good news to report," Nellie assured her, and hurried out.

"I really do want to fly one day," William declared. "Damn! I think I will."

She glared at him. "Where did you learn that word?"

His cheeks reddened. "I don't know."

But Helena did. Her son spent every spare moment out in the carriage house with his horse—and Michael. She noticed that, in addition to the backward suspenders, he wore a rumpled shirt with its tail hanging out, and his feet were bare. He *was* dressed like a hooligan. "Well, I don't want to hear it again, please."

"Yes, ma'am." William finished his breakfast with a minimum of fuss. Wandering over to the window, he picked up the kitten. "Mama, who is that lady down there?" He pointed out the window.

"You mean Daisy?"

"It's not Daisy."

Frowning, she stood and looked out the window. Sure enough, in the yard below, a black-haired woman in a ragged pink dress and bare feet ran across the grass, a bundle clutched against her chest.

"Stay here, William," she said, untying her apron.

"But I saw her first," he protested. "I want to go see who it is."

"I said, stay here." She closed the door to the kitchen firmly behind her. Honestly, her son was getting more and more cheeky these days, challenging her at every turn, spouting inappropriate words just to watch their effect on her. She kept feeling afraid she was doing something wrong with him, that a proper mother would keep him well in hand. But as far as mothering went, she made things up as she went along, trying her best but never certain she was getting it right.

Daisy followed her out to the yard. "What you reckon she's up to?"

"I think we'd best find out. She certainly looks harmless enough. Why, she's no more than a girl." Helena put on a polite social smile. "Hello," she called, waving her hand. "Hello, can we help you?"

At that moment, Michael Rowan emerged from the wooded path that led to the carriage house. "Stop thief," he yelled, heading for the girl.

The stranger took one look at him and veered away. Her feet tangled in the tattered petticoats and she fell to the grass, then clumsily tried to pick herself up. The bundle she held spilled open, scattering biscuits and other objects across the grass.

"Stay away from her, Michael," Helena said, aghast. "Can't you see she's frightened?"

He stopped where he was, some feet away, but scowled with ill humor. "Can't you see she's just robbed the carriage house?"

"Please don't be frightened," Helena said, ignoring him and edging closer to the young woman. "Is there something we can help you with?"

Bracing her hands behind her, she crab-walked away. She was filthy. Her straight black hair hung in thick, matted hanks. Her face was streaked with dirt, and her wrists and ankles were covered in insect bites. The dress was faded and ragged at the hem. She reeked of whiskey.

"She's a redskin," Daisy observed in a whisper.

"It appears so." Helena leaned down toward the frightened girl. "Are you hurt, dear? Would you like to come inside?"

The girl curled her knees into her chest, regarded her with bleary eyes.

"Lordy, no," Daisy muttered under her breath. "There's no telling what kind of vermin she'd bring in."

"The poor thing's terrified," Helena said. "We must help her."

"She helped herself to my breakfast," Michael grumbled, bending down to pick up his pocketknife, a few coins and a wad of paper money. As an afterthought, he grabbed a biscuit, brushed it off and took a bite.

"She's ill," Helena said when the young woman began to tremble. She edged even closer and rested the palm of her hand on her forehead. The woman flinched, but submitted.

"No fever," Helena said.

"I bet it's the jimjams," Daisy said.

"What's that?"

"It's the bad sickness that comes over a body when it craves a drink."

Helena's heart constricted. The young woman's age was difficult to determine from a distance, but a certain softness around the dark, wary eyes and a roundness to the chin told her she was only sixteen or seventeen. A slow burn of anger curled through her. Out West, white men destroyed whole Indian tribes by giving them blankets infested with smallpox, to which the natives had little resistance. Here in the civilized east, the whiskey method was less deliberate but just as destructive. The problem was heartbreakingly common in Saratoga Springs in particular. The local Mohawks were encouraged to set up colorful encampments for tourists to gawk at, and the spirits flowed freely.

"Let us help you," she said. "I swear, we promise not to hurt you." She snatched the biscuit from Michael. "Are you hungry, dear?"

"No." The girl spoke for the first time, in a low, tremulous voice. "You got any whiskey?"

"To be honest, we don't."

The girl tried to push herself up. "I need to find me some whiskey."

"Child, that's the last thing you need," Daisy said. "You come on with me now. We got something you'll like better."

"Get back." The girl kicked out, baring her legs to the thighs. Then she collapsed and curled herself into a ball.

Daisy picked her up, earning a pitiful cry of protest but no resistance. Helena exchanged a glance with Michael, who looked a bit sheepish. "I suppose she's harmless enough,'' he said. ''But don't let her near any valuables.''

''Honestly,'' she said in exasperation, but decided that now was not the time to spar with him. Even in the midst of a crisis, their prior conversation hung between them, unacknowledged but far from forgotten. Heavens, what had she been thinking?

She hadn't been thinking. That was the trouble. When it came to Michael Rowan, common sense deserted her every time. She had no idea what was going on in his head as he walked back to the house with them, then held the kitchen door open. William still sat at the table.

''Hello,'' he said. When the girl didn't respond, he said, ''Hello, Professor. Are we going to work on Hector's stall today?''

''That will have to wait,'' Michael said. ''I've got to go down to the Institute to collect my things, but we can get started on fixing the paddock fence before I leave.''

Helena bristled. She was the boy's mother. She would plan his day for him. However, at the moment she found herself quite busy. She and Daisy managed to get the visitor to drink a good quantity of cold buttermilk, but she refused food.

''I need the whiskey,'' she said. ''Need it bad. I'm sick. I need it for medicine.''

''I've got something better,'' Helena said with sudden inspiration. She opened the heavy door of the icebox. It was one of the few modern conveniences she'd found at the lodge—a sturdy wooden cupboard lined with zinc and insulated with cork. When she and Daisy had vacated Vandam Square, they'd helped themselves to a number of choice items for the icebox, including a hundred-pound block of ice from last winter's ice harvest. She rifled around in the frigid cupboard and brought out a steel can.

"What's that?" the girl asked.

"Ice cream," William said. "Hurrah! I can't go yet, Professor. I have to eat my ice cream."

Covering her hands with a tea towel, Helena wrenched open the lid and scooped some into dishes, one for the visitor and one for William. "It was made with last summer's cherries."

The girl poked at it suspiciously with the tip of her spoon. Finally, she took a bite, and a blissful smile transformed her face. She devoured the whole bowl, then asked for more.

William seemed completely unperturbed by the girl's appearance. He simply slid into the chair next to her and dug into the ice cream. Between bites, he said, "I'm William. I am eight. Eight years, seven months, nineteen days..." He craned his neck, looking for a clock, then abandoned his usual recitation. "What's your name?"

"Josephine Goodkind." She polished off the last of the cherry ice cream and looked up expectantly.

"We'll have more after supper," Helena promised.

Josephine eyed the empty can. So did William. The girl already looked markedly better, Helena observed. Blessed with the resilience and natural health of the young, she had thrown off the episode of shaking.

"I got a big tub of hot water out in the back," Daisy said. "I was going to launder the drapes today, but I reckon that can wait. Come on, sugar." She took Josephine's hand. "You come with me. You're going to have a bath, and we'll see about some clean clothes for you."

"Why would I bathe in a tub instead of the springs?" the girl muttered.

"The water's nice and warm in the tub."

"I'll find a warm spring, then."

"In Saratoga?" Helena asked gently. "There's no such thing, dear."

"Shows what you know."

Michael motioned for William to follow him outside. Helena wanted to object, but in truth, she was grateful that Michael would keep the boy occupied while she dealt with her new guest. As they walked away together, Michael stooped and plucked a blade of grass, clamping it between his teeth. William immediately did the same.

A twinge of sentiment squeezed Helena's chest. What sort of father could Michael be if she let him into her son's life? Did she owe it to William to allow him to know Michael?

Daisy adopted a no-nonsense tone with Josephine, pegging out the drapes to enclose the round zinc tub. "You get on into this tub, and we'll get you all clean and pretty. You just sit yourself down, you hear? The warm water will feel good."

Josephine shrugged, but complied without protest. She didn't seem preoccupied with modesty as she let her dress and petticoats fall in a heap. Under this she wore a threadbare shift and drawers, which she also discarded.

As she lowered herself into the warm water, Daisy frowned. "Land sakes, child. Who did that to you?"

Helena saw a line of bruises and scars along her back, rib cage, thighs. Some of the wounds were fresh and livid; others had healed, forming dull ridges.

"You hear me?" Daisy asked. "Who's been at you?"

Josephine crouched in the tub and hugged her knees to her chest. "Fellow who brought me down from Dinaga Falls to the summer camp near town. When he drinks, he gets mean."

"Dear heaven," said Helena, shaken. She was as disappointed in herself as she was angry about the situation. For years she'd been aware of the Mohawk and Caughnawaga encampment of bark wigwams in a pine grove near Circular Street, regarded as a boon for the summer tourists. By day the natives sold handicrafts of deerskin and carved wood, brooms and baskets, smoked sturgeon and eel, and in the evenings they entertained visitors with wild chants and dances. It never occurred to her to look past the colorful displays, or to consider the idea that some, like Josephine, were there against their will.

Daisy handed Josephine a grayish cake of lye soap. "Looks like she came to the right place."

The girl turned the soap over and over in her hands, as though mesmerized. "Said I drank too much of his whiskey."

"You're going to learn to like ice cream better," Helena declared, the decision firm in her mind as soon as she spoke the words. She and Daisy exchanged another glance, and she knew they both concurred.

"My name is Helena," she said, "and this is Daisy. Welcome to Moon Lake Lodge."

Leaving Josephine in Daisy's charge, Helena went in search of William. It was past time for him to have his lunch, and she hadn't seen hide nor hair of him. She knew she'd find him at the carriage house with Michael and his horse. She took a picnic lunch with her, because the boy had to eat, and she was in no mood to argue with him about coming inside for a meal.

Besides, it was a lovely day, the sort of warm summer afternoon that settles in the bones, weather to dream about on endless, dreary winter nights. Hollyhocks and delphinium, grown taller than her, nodded over the pathway between the house and stables, and bees burbled lazily from blossom to blossom. The sky was piercingly blue, staining the lake a dark, intense shade.

As she approached the neglected old carriage house, she heard voices and a rhythmic pounding. She emerged from the path to see William and Michael working side-by-side on the paddock fence, their twin hammers swinging in tandem, their heads bent over their task, the occasional pause as one spoke and the other listened. It was such a companionable scene that she slowed her step and simply watched for a while. When Michael wiped the sweat from his brow, William did the same. When he stripped off his shirt and tossed it on the ground, so did William.

At that point Helena hurried forward, already framing an indignant objection.

Oblivious to her, Michael turned his head and spat on the ground and William imitated him.

Heavenly days. Eight years of training her son to be a gentleman was unraveling before her eyes.

"William," she called out, waving as she walked up the drive. "I've brought you a nice picnic lunch."

He waved his hammer in the air. "We're busy, Mama."

Michael murmured something. William nodded, jumped down from the fence. "I mean, thank you, Mama. We're hungry," he announced.

"I thought you might be," she said, keeping her eyes on her son. If she let her gaze stray to Michael, and his tanned face and sweaty bare chest, she'd be lost, she just knew it. ''You can eat as soon as you wash your hands and put your shirt on.''

William turned to Michael. ''We have to wash our hands and put our shirts on,'' he explained as though Michael needed a translation.

''I think we can manage that.'' Michael took his time at the pump, she noted, sluicing water over himself and then splashing William until the boy howled and ran in circles. Just as her patience was stretched to the limit, they donned their shirts and sat down in the shade. Both he and William ate voraciously—leftover biscuits from breakfast, pieces of baked chicken, wild plums from the grove down by the lake and lemonade, faintly salty with the taste of the mineral water so abundant on the property.

William leaped up in impatience as soon as he finished. ''Can I go finish the scything, Professor?'' he asked.

''Yes,'' said Michael.

''Certainly not,'' said Helena.

They glared at each other. ''He's too little to use a scythe,'' she stated. ''He'll cut his feet off at the ankles.''

''He's been doing it all morning. He's practically an expert.''

''Please,'' William said. ''We've got to mow the paddock so Hector has a place to graze. Just watch me, Mama. I won't cut anything but the grass.''

She narrowed her eyes at Michael. ''If you so much as nick yourself—''

''I won't. Watch, Mama. Just watch.'' He picked up a wooden-handled scythe. The blade was rusty, but a bright gleam showed where it had been recently sharpened. William slung the blade in a small arc, cutting down the grass. His expertise startled her. How quickly he learned, and how happy he seemed. In one morning Michael had given more to William than Troy had in eight years.

Alone with Michael, she felt as nervous and flustered as an untried debutante. A foolish notion, given her history with this man. Twirling a long blade of grass idly in his teeth, he lounged against a tree trunk, his long body dappled by shadow and sunlight. He wore the same clothes he had on when he'd fought Troy and had been hauled off to jail. But being Michael, he didn't seem to notice.

His hair, damp from the pump, had been hastily combed by careless fingers. Two days' worth of whiskers shadowed his face, picking out the strong planes and angles of high cheekbones, firm jaw, squarish chin. A straight dark lock of hair fell over his brow, taunting her, making her itch to brush it out of the way.

Watching him, Helena couldn't believe what she was feeling. He was unkempt and surly. He barely spoke or even looked at her, yet she felt drawn to him. She wanted to trace her hands down his back, inhale—Lord help her—the scent of his sweat and sample the taste of his lips.

Don't, she told herself. Don't. If there was a lesson to be learned from this whole terrible ordeal, it was that there was only one path for her life that made sense anymore. The path of independence. It was a road she had never taken before. She knew it was fraught with peril and hidden obstacles, but at least her destiny would be her own.

"I see you've been busy with my son," she stated. "He's devoted to that horse."

"William has a heart made for devotion," she blurted out, then immediately regretted the words. But there they were, for Michael to accept or misinterpret or ignore. Eager to change the subject, she offered a bit of news. ''Nellie McQuigg has gone to Albany, to ask Judge Standish to issue a divorce decree.''

''After what she did for me, I have great faith in her skills as a lawyer,'' he said.

His confidence calmed her nervousness somewhat. ''I just want this to be done,'' she said.

He sat quietly beside her for a while. Finally he stood up, brushed the grass from his trousers. ''I need to get my things from the Institute.'' He seemed to be on the verge of saying something else, but stopped himself.

Helena felt a renewed conviction as she put away the napkins and lemonade jar. It was absurd even to contemplate his merits as a father. He would be like all others. Absent. But he immediately scattered her calmness, holding out his hand to help her to her feet. She hesitated, then offered her good arm to let him help her up.

''I've been thinking about our discussion the other night,'' he said, finally voicing the thought that had been hovering, unspoken, between them. ''About us becoming lovers.''

She snatched her hand away from his. ''It's a bad idea. I can't think why I even considered it. Your initial reaction was correct. We should not even contemplate it.''

''My initial reaction, if you must know, was a state of arousal so painful I couldn't breathe for a very long time. I'll never stop wanting you like that, Helena. The difference is, I am less apt to act out of impulse now.''

Ten

"It's so very hard to say goodbye, Professor." Michael's laboratory assistant, Daria Runyon, trotted beside him down the cavernous wooden hall of the Hudson Valley Institute for Innovation. She always called him Professor, even in bed.

He wondered when that had begun to irritate him. It grated now, as he cleared out his cluttered office, though he didn't let it show. In all honesty, his disenchantment with the Institute itself exceeded anything he felt for Daria Runyon. And his discovery that the Foundation had seized his admittedly modest life savings caused far more consternation than the loss of his appealing but eminently forgettable assistant.

He had come to the Institute years before with a broken heart and a burning ambition. With the resources of the facility and his own brainpower, he was going to change the world. Humanity already had its Thomas Edison and Alexander Graham Bell, its Samuel Morse and Albert Lister, but there was still so much work to be done. Still so much to be discovered or solved.

Yet, after nine years here, what did he have to show

for himself but a series of obscure patents no one cared about and several books and treatises no one read? He'd come here with such big dreams, so big he'd thought they were worth sacrificing Helena for. One thing she had never known was that his tenure here had been her father's idea, though the actual funding legislation came from Senator Barnes of New York. Franklin Rush Cabot loved his daughter and Michael couldn't fault him for disapproving of an eccentric, penniless professor.

Michael had been a man half-formed and careless, more concerned with scientific puzzles than the mysteries of the human heart. Falling in love with Helena had taken him completely by surprise. He had adored her with all that he was. But back then, and even now, perhaps, that wasn't enough. He was not what she needed. He knew that. So when her father had told him privately that Helena would be better off with a man of good family and vast fortune, Michael was inclined to concur.

He'd thought the Institute would fill the void of loss; he'd envisioned an unparalleled research facility. Now he knew it for what it was—a second-rate laboratory, funded as a political favor and run by men more interested in profit than innovation. While others earned a place in history by inventing seismographs, escalators and the brand-new world-altering internal combustion engine, Michael was charged with upgrading the odd mechanical pump or industrial tubing, or improving on a tin can that opened with a key. He was filled with ideas that would never make a dime. No one wanted to hear about hydrostatic principles or radio wave arc transmission. He couldn't even rival Lewis Waterman's fountain pen.

In his office, his assistant stacked books into a carton, throwing him a narrow-eyed look.

"I shall miss you ever so much," Daria said, her hand brushing his to stir him from his brooding silence. She indicated the broken skin over his knuckles. "Were you in a fight?"

"Yes."

"I've never known you to fight."

She hadn't known him at all, he reflected, nor he her. Like the other women he'd been with since Helena, he kept her at a distance, no matter how deep the physical intimacy. After Helena, he had nothing of worth to give a woman.

He stopped walking for a moment, shifted the large wooden crate he carried and stared down into her small, intense face. Though that intensity masked the fact that her features were plain, her fierce intelligence had held his attention far longer than most of his lovers. But lately he'd had more than enough reason to be thinking of the past.

"Daria, there's something I must ask you before I go."

Her face softened with expectation. "Yes, Professor?"

"Would you, er, could you..."

"Yes? Oh, please, ask me, my dear Professor."

Damn. This was coming out all wrong. "Daria, I must know, before I leave, if there is any possibility that you might be with child."

Her face fell like a failed experiment. "That is what you wish to ask me?"

"Yes. I do apologize for my bluntness, but if there is something I should know before I...before..." He kept trying to think of a less hurtful way to say this.

"Before you leave me forever?" she bit out, the

intensity in her face changing to anger. "You can set your mind at rest, Professor. The answer is no. There is no possible way I can be with child."

He released his breath slowly, trying not to insult her further by seeming too relieved. "Yes. Well, then. In that case, I must be going."

"Of course you must."

"Good day, Miss Runyon." He picked up a loaded crate, trying not to see the way her eyes swam with tears. He continued a few steps down the hall.

"Professor," she called out.

He turned back to her. "Yes?"

She went and stood before him, the tears falling unabashedly now. "Would it have mattered if I'd said yes?"

He thought of Helena on the stair, all those years ago, asking him to love her, asking him to stay. Then his thoughts passed swiftly over all the women he had known and discarded so carelessly over the years, all the tears that had fallen, all the angry words that had flown at him. Damn it. Why did they insist on taking love affairs so seriously? He'd never made any promises, not even to Helena, yet they all seemed to expect something from him, something he simply didn't have in him to give. "I honestly don't know, Miss Runyon," he said.

She pulled back her arm and slapped him across the face. He staggered, trying not to drop the crate on her foot. It was an awkward blow from someone unaccustomed to hitting people, but added to his wounds from the fight, she made her point. Then, pressing her hand to her mouth, she fled.

Michael stood alone in the hallway, his cheek ringing from her slap. Yesterday's beating echoed in the pulses of pain. When had he turned into a cad? Had he always been one? How could he change? He wanted to. For Helena and William, he had to find a way to be a better man. He blinked, shook his head to clear it, then took the crate outside with the rest of his things.

There was not much to his belongings and certainly they were of limited value—the flotsam and jetsam of a life haphazardly lived. There were no family heirlooms because he had no family. No mementos of the past because there was nothing about the past he wanted to keep with him. He had a pair of French percussion dueling pistols from Jamie Calhoun, who had married Helena's sister and offered the antique guns as a gift. Other than that, there was only his work, his books, his journals and his unfulfilled dreams.

And now it was over. Almost, he thought, loading the crate onto a hired dray. As he re-entered the building, he passed the animal research wing. This was not his domain. The studies here were done under the supervision of another group of scientists. The trouble was, no one bothered with the caged creatures except the occasional stable lad brought in when the stench got too bad.

Everyone had gone home for the day. The long barn, lined with metal cages and stalls, was empty except for a collection of noisy captives. This had always seemed an unhappy part of the building to him. Even the domesticated animals were cramped and isolated, mere steps from the broad, rolling riverside meadows and woods that surrounded the Institute.

Michael propped open the wide double doors to the outside. Then he moved methodically through the laboratory, opening cages and stalls, urging the animals to take their leave. He freed a pair of mallard ducks, several turkeys and swine, a litter of baby raccoons, a calf, a flock of chickens and a snapping turtle that tucked itself up into its shell and refused to move. Standing at the top of the livestock ramp, he reflected that some of them were no safer out there in the world than they were in the laboratory, but at least they were out.

He headed off to collect the last of his files. A scratching sound made him hesitate and look around, and upon further investigation he discovered a white mouse with a pink tail and a nervous nose, nesting in a steel box fitted with a water bottle.

Michael tipped the box, urging the mouse to escape. The mouse resisted, bracing its tiny paws against the slanted side. Michael gave him a little tap with his finger, thinking to scare the creature, but ended by having to lift the rodent out onto the floor.

"Go on with you, then," he said. "You're free. Go. Do…whatever it is freed mice do."

The mouse didn't budge.

Michael watched it for a few moments, then sighed heavily. "You wouldn't last five minutes out there," he said. Exasperated, he scooped it up in one hand and set it back in its cage. "Never let it be said that you have an excess of intelligence."

He walked around to the front drive and finished securing his things in the hauling dray he'd hired. Climbing up to the driver's seat, he looked back once.

The Institute sat as imposing as ever, its stone edifice a brooding dark scar in the parklike green landscape. Where once he'd sought inspiration, he now found nothing but frustration.

A few years ago, a portion of the grounds had been turned into a golf course, attracting lawyers and legislators from nearby Albany. It was said that more political deals were made on the Ludlow Links than on the statehouse floor. Michael wasn't much for the game, but as he passed by, he recognized Artemis Witherspoon, an administrator at the Institute. Witherspoon waved at him. Michael stopped on the grass verge beside the first fairway. He respected Witherspoon, an Oxford man who practiced poor science but excelled at managing with efficiency.

"I understand you're to step down," said Witherspoon. "A bad turn all around, old brick."

"I'll be fine."

"It's not you I'm worried about. It's the damned Institute." Witherspoon grinned, displaying yellowed teeth. "You're the only serious scientist I have. With you gone, we'll be lucky to produce a better mousetrap."

"You'll be fine, too," Michael said.

In the distance, an eruption of laughter caught his attention. A large party of golfers had gathered to tee off. Some of them looked vaguely familiar, and all had clearly been drinking.

"Judge Standish, Willard Bates and their entourage of law clerks," Witherspoon explained.

Nellie McQuigg has gone to Albany, to ask Judge Standish to issue a divorce decree. Helena had said so.

"So what are they celebrating?"

"Some odd case or other. I heard a lady lawyer came looking for a divorce for her client, and Standish had her cited for contempt of court instead."

When Michael took his leave, he headed south, rather than north to Saratoga Springs. Leaving the Institute had not posed much of a problem, but his next order of business was not going to be nearly so easy. He was going to Albany, to see Troy Barnes again.

Eleven

Troy Barnes had always found his offices in Albany to be a great convenience. The handsome graystone building, prominently located at the corner of Lexington and Rye, was a place to meet with constituents, contributors and committee members. The adjacent apartment was a refuge from the constant demands of his position. The only place he liked better than Albany was the nation's capital, of course, although summers in the District of Columbia were brutally hot and steamy. Those who could afford it fled to cooler climes—and the most fashionable of all summer retreats was Saratoga Springs. A pity. For lately he wished he could get as far away from Saratoga Springs as possible.

People might call him a coward, but at least they wouldn't call him that to his face. Besides, they were wrong. There was a vast difference between cowardice and caution. He needed to meet with his advisors, to mull over Helena's threat about the purloined ballots and to figure out what to do about her. One thing he knew for certain—he must be cautious. Even without her famous father, she had the power to ruin him. He hated that about her. He hated anyone who knew his vulnerabilities. He always had, so he dedicated himself to being invulnerable.

Troy had known from the time he was very young that he wanted to occupy the seat of power. He loved the way it made him feel, loved the influence it gave him. He liked having influence over peoples' lives. He loved having favor-seekers pandering to him, offering every possible inducement to accommodate their needs. And he was damned good at what he did. He could make the head of a meat-packing company feel like a head of state.

People believed that when he won his seat in the Senate, he had reached the pinnacle of all achievement. But that was stupid. Why stop at the Senate when a cabinet position, or even the presidency itself, wielded so much more power?

He stared down over his bare chest to his naked lap, at the girl who was busily servicing him with her mouth. That was another reason he kept his place in Albany. The private apartment on the third floor was commodious and well-appointed, and the whores of Albany were first-rate.

"That will do, my dear," he said a little while later, and pushed her away. He cleaned himself and donned a robe while the girl tied on her bodice and made a halfhearted attempt to correct the disarray of her blond braids.

Troy took a silver Morgan from his bureau drawer. A dollar should keep her plenty happy for a time. He held the coin out to her. At the abrupt motion of his hand, she flinched, and he grew exasperated. "Take it," he said more insistently.

Realizing it was a coin, not a cuff, the girl snatched it from his grip and tucked it into her apron pocket.

"Thank you," she whispered, then slid her feet into a pair of old scuffed clogs and headed for the door.

He stopped her as she was about to leave. She gazed up at him with large, watchful eyes. Yellow braids framed the schoolgirl softness of her face. Very gently, he grazed his knuckles along the slight swelling that marred her cheekbone.

"You shouldn't have been so defiant, Felicity," he said.

Felicity Bond merely nodded, said, "I'll be back," and ducked out.

He stood at the top of the square stairwell, watching her go with a bemused smile on his face. This one was just about perfect for him, he thought. She kept her legs open and her eyes shut and was extremely grateful for his patronage.

The ideal woman, he thought. Did she exist?

He once believed he had found her in Helena Cabot, all those years ago. She had seemed, on the surface, to be perfect in every way. She was so beautiful that conversation stopped when she entered a room. Everyone thought her warmhearted and generous. She had a reputation for being clever and amusing. On top of that, her father had been the strongest political ally in the entire Congress.

Things should have gone well—a whirlwind courtship, a glittering society wedding. He'd even believed the child was his, despite the fact that none of his mistresses had ever conceived, before or since. He took a fierce pride in the lad's good looks, his cleverness. At odd moments, he even felt a rare warmth, seeing, as from a great distance, the true fulfillment that came from being part of an American family. Yet she always held herself apart from him, and not just physically. He'd known from the start that her heart belonged to another, but he thought eventually he'd win her over.

His failure to do so ignited a slow, smoldering rage in him. But the fury had been a silent, invisible eruption, mercilessly capped by ruthless ambition. From the very start, he'd known beyond doubt something he could not deny. He needed her reputation and influence.

It was an imperfect arrangement. Sometimes he felt so torn between duty and desire that he drank himself senseless. Other times, he took his troubles and his temper elsewhere, to women like Felicity who were grateful for what he had to offer and forgiving of his temper. Although they could never understand the demons that drove him, at least they understood the color of his money.

The death of Franklin Rush Cabot had been a blow in more ways than one. Troy had lost his powerful mentor and would have to work hard to maintain the strategic alliances he'd formed in order to accomplish his business. He might have survived the loss, but for one thing. Pickett's hissed accusation had catapulted Troy into righteous anger. The bright handsome boy, of whom he'd been so proud, was not his after all. Helena had played him for a fool.

Showing her the true meaning of discipline had quieted the demons inside him for a time. He had even felt a rare rush of tenderness for her afterward, as she lay shivering in shock and, he believed, shame at the magnitude of her betrayal. That mortification should have reformed her, brought her to her knees in contrition, but oddly it had the opposite effect. One never knew what to expect from Helena. And he could not have anticipated her next move.

She'd simply hired that hulking new maid and left

Georgetown without so much as a by-your-leave, taking the steamer north. To add insult to injury, she'd dared to walk away from the fine house he'd provided for her.

Stopping in front of the looking glass over the washstand, he inspected his injured nose. It was still swollen and tender, and might never again be the handsome, aquiline nose he'd been born with.

She truly was insane, he realized. Did she really think she could escape him, move out of Vandam Square, set up housekeeping at Moon Lake Lodge and completely dismiss him from her life? Did she believe an old election scandal and a fistfight with her former lover would induce Troy to let her go?

Furious that she'd already slipped free of the asylum, he paced the room, picking up articles of clothing one by one, putting himself back together after that bit of sport with Felicity. A chill slid over him as he contemplated Helena's threat, but he was working on a solution for that. Atop his bureau lay a packet of briefs from Cabot's solicitor in Georgetown. Even dead, the old man was still on Troy's side, leaving Helena's portion of the estate in his control. Still, he didn't feel safe—yet. Thanks to Helena's scheming, he had to meet with his closest staff members to determine just how much of a threat the scandal posed.

He was afraid. If he lost his Senate seat, he'd have nothing. The fear filled him with a burning resentment. It was a fine summer evening, yet he could not enjoy it because of her. He should be savoring the prospect of a pleasant engagement at the city club. Instead, she'd forced him to deal with an issue that he'd thought dead and buried. Worst of all, the scandal would cause him to lose the respect of his father. All his life, Troy had labored to please Adam Barnes, to win his approval. Now he had it, and there was nothing in the world he cherished more. The prospect of losing that terrified him. His only solace lay in the fact that he was Adam Barnes's only legitimate son and, as such, would reap the full benefit of his admiration.

He sat down to buckle his knickers. In a moment, he would ring for his driver. At the sound of footsteps on the stair, he frowned and went to the door.

"Felicity? What did you forget now?" She was forever leaving her things lying around—a tattered apron or faded handkerchief. He leaned over the rail, but couldn't see anyone.

The footsteps quickened, and it wasn't Felicity at all, but Michael Rowan.

"Damn it," Troy said between his teeth. He edged back toward the apartment door. He was looking at a ghost. Vivid memories of the attack, the blood, the rage assaulted him. "Stay back," he warned. "I'll call for help."

"You'll need it," said Rowan, indicating a packet of legal briefs under his arm. "Preferably in the form of a lawyer. I assume you have one on retainer. Although he's probably busy playing golf with Judge Standish."

"You're supposed to be—"

"In jail? So you hoped. The charges were dropped. Case closed."

"But—"

"Lack of witnesses."

Troy didn't need to probe further. For the right sum of money, the sighted could be made blind, the hearing would turn a deaf ear. He had made use of this phenomenon himself many times. In fact, he had planned to arrange things so that Rowan met with an unfortunate accident while in jail, a blow to the head, perhaps. Yet here he stood, healthy as a bull moose.

Troy took another step back. He calculated his chances. Could he overpower Rowan, push him down the stairs?

"Don't try it," Rowan said, reading his thoughts. "As you discovered earlier, I am not averse to fighting." His burning blue eyes never left Troy as he drew an old-fashioned, long-barreled pistol from the folds of his frock coat.

When Troy saw the gun, he allowed himself a sarcastic laugh. Yet at the same time, he gauged the distance to the bureau drawer, where his father's 1862 navy pocket pistol lay, something the old man had given him in a rare lapse of sentiment. But the firearm lay out of reach, and Troy couldn't remember if the gun was loaded. He tossed a dismissive glance at Rowan's weapon. "That's a museum piece, you bloody idiot. It's harmless."

"Is it? Now, that's interesting. I distinctly recall putting a lead ball in the chamber, but perhaps I was wrong." He leveled the barrel at Troy's chest. "Shall we test it, then?"

The cold, watery sensation in his bowels was terror. Troy hated fear, but the fact was, the feeling had been with him all his life, for as long as he could remember.

It had stalked each moment of his boyhood, a sledgehammer shadow that struck without warning and without mercy. The world had terrified him when he was growing up. He'd feared his prosperous father. He'd shrunk from committing the slightest misstep. All his life, Troy had been driven by the need to avoid disappointing him, while at the same time, he longed to lord his superiority over people. And now, standing before him, was the one person to whom Troy's power and position meant nothing.

"Tell me what the hell you want," he said to Rowan.

Rowan followed him into the apartment. He lowered the barrel of the pistol, but he didn't put the gun away, and Troy didn't relax. Not in the least. He was a man of very few vulnerabilities. Unfortunately, Professor Michael Rowan was aware of those Troy possessed.

He took a seat at the table that dominated the room and gestured for Rowan to do the same. He assessed him, and was startled anew that Rowan had been able to best him in a fight. Perhaps the carelessly rumpled clothes concealed a bulky strength, Troy conceded grudgingly. He despised weakness in anyone, particularly himself. That was why, as a boy, he never complained about his father's harsh discipline. His mother didn't either, the stupid cow. She made one too many careless mistakes. She deserved what she got. Deserved the shove that sent her tumbling down the stairs.

When she regained consciousness, she was curiously gone. Her empty stare opened to a soul that had fled. A nursemaid was engaged to keep her clean and fed, until she finally passed away.

"Look, if this is about getting your job at the Institute back, you can forget it."

"I don't want my job back."

The ominous weight of an implied threat pressed at Troy. "Then what is it you're after?"

"Your signature. That's all I require." Laying the pistol carelessly in his lap, he set the case of legal briefs on the table, unbuckled the top and took out a machine-typed contract.

Troy jerked the papers toward him and scanned the

document. An icy fist squeezed his gut. "This is a writ of annulment." He muttered the words as disbelief and denial closed his throat in a stranglehold. This couldn't be happening. He had to stay married to Helena. It was as vital to his career as his family name, as vital to his sense of self as his father's approval. He needed her. She was beautiful and cultured and beloved and admired. Everyone from Saratoga Springs to Washington, D.C., envied him because he had such a perfect wife. He loved being the object of envy. It made him feel important. Powerful. Valued in the eyes of a demanding father he'd strived to please all his life. He would not give her up, not for any price.

His disbelieving gaze scanned down the page. *Willful misrepresentation of physical condition relating to matters essential to the marriage union....*

"It's quite simple," said Rowan. "This petition asserts that Helena Cabot was fraudulently induced to enter into the marriage. A legal order declaring that this marriage never existed will be issued by a judge thirty days from now."

Troy had never felt this level of rage before. He thought he knew rage in all its boiling incarnations. Yet this was new. This feeling was so stunning and so powerful that it literally took his breath away.

"Let me be clear on this," Troy said, fighting to retain his composure. "I am to sign this paper admitting I am st...st..."

"Sterile," Rowan filled in for him. "And you knew that when you married her."

Troy leveled a burning gaze at him. He had kept his condition a secret for years. His shock must have shown on his face, for Rowan offered a grim smile.

"My interest in science has always been keen, ever since I was a boy. Your family physician employed me to run errands and work in his laboratory, and he wasn't known to be discreet."

Troy fumed. William's birth had proved the rumormongers—and even his own self-doubts—all wrong. Troy had been triumphant. He grew inches taller overnight and the sweetest victory of all had been the beaming pride in his father's face when they told him.

Troy stared at Rowan dumbly. The rage came rolling back, churning through him with a vengeance.

"Let me give you another reason," Rowan said, mistaking his silence for understanding. "Shall we start with the fact that you and I are brothers?"

Adam Barnes heard the news from Edith Vickery, who served as Helena's social secretary and, more importantly, as Adam's eyes and ears in the household of his elder son. When Edith brought word of his daughter-in-law's behavior, Adam wrapped his fingers around two canes and walked to the bay window overlooking Bankside Park. He stared out at the vast empire he had spent his life building—the palatial Oak Hill house and grounds, the bottling works on the distant horizon, with slender chimneys like the turrets of a castle, billowing smoke. From this vantage point, he saw nothing but abundance.

There was only one area of his life that was small and skimpy and meaningless. Though the heiress he'd married had a pedigree that could be traced back to the Magna Carta, she hadn't managed to give him more than one son before the accident rendered her useless. His mistresses had proved similarly barren, save one. Hannah Rowan had given him a second son, whom he'd watched from a distance for years. He never thought a time would come when their destinies would intertwine, but now, in the cold autumn of his life, that day had arrived.

Some part of him had always known William could not have been sired by Troy. Adam clearly recalled the nervous family physician breaking the news when Troy was barely grown. "Your son is a victim of a serious fever of the glands. He's young and strong but there will be consequences." The doctor had eyed him mournfully. "Your wife's bedridden condition means you'll have no more heirs, and your son's affliction—well, I'm sorry, Mr. Barnes."

Adam had grown bitter then, and despaired of producing an heir to carry on his name. That was why William was such a miracle.

A sinking disappointment dragged at him, but not for long. Troy was not William's father, but William was still Adam's grandson.

His fury was a silent explosion, invisible even to Edith who had served him so well, in so many ways over the years. The heat of it enclosed his heart and burned, reminding him of his own mortality. He turned back to Edith.

"Send for my lawyers immediately."

Twelve

"Let's read a different book, Mama," William said as he lay back against the pillows of his narrow bed. "I already know this story."

Exhausted after a long day of working on the lodge, Helena summoned the last bit of her patience. "You love *Dick Whittington and His Cat.* And now you have a cat of your own." She indicated the purring, ginger-colored lump burrowed in the crook of William's arm. "Don't you think she'd like to hear the story?"

"Cats can't read," he said. "Only people can read, and I want you to read me a new story."

Her grip tightened on the tattered pages of the old volume she'd memorized. "Look, here's your favorite part. 'Turn again, Whittington, thrice Lord Mayor of London—'"

"We've said that part a hundred times. Let's pick something new." His hand stole beneath the covers, and he pulled out a blue clothbound volume. "The professor said I could borrow this one. Let's read it now."

"Not tonight, William." She could feel her nerves fraying, one by one. The tension of awaiting word from Nellie and the bitter ache of Michael's absence were undoing her.

"He said it's an exciting adventure about a boy who gets kidnapped."

"I'm sure it is." She forced a smile. "I have a wonderful idea. Why don't you read it to me?"

"I like the way you read better. I want to hear the exciting adventure." He thrust the book at her. The kitten shot from the bed and skittered sideways across the room.

"I said *not tonight.*" Her voice lashed out, startling them both.

William pulled himself into a ball under the covers. Helena was instantly filled with remorse. She almost never spoke harshly to him, and he took it like a blow.

"Oh, my dear William," she said. "I didn't mean to be cross with you. It's been a busy day, and I'm too tired to read that great, thick book to you." Tugging the covers down, she smoothed the copper-colored hair back from his forehead. "I'm sorry."

"I'll get the Professor to read it when he comes back."

Such faith her little boy had in the stranger who had suddenly appeared in his life. She hadn't the heart to tell him not to rely on Michael Rowan. "Here, let's just read a little of Dick Whittington, and you'll be fast asleep before you know it."

He made a face. "Never mind. I'll just go to sleep, and maybe the cat will come back and sleep with me."

She bent and kissed him, then turned down the lamp. Filled with troubling thoughts, she walked slowly through the upstairs hall. Josephine slept soundly in her spare little chamber. Daisy was still downstairs working in the kitchen. Helena took an odd comfort in the homey sounds of her putting up utensils and setting out the breakfast things. The tension in her chest uncoiled. Somehow, she would learn to forgive herself for being unable to read her son a bedtime story.

By the time she reached the kitchen, she found herself in possession of an idea. The very thought caused the hair to stand up on the back of her neck. Perhaps the rumors about Moon Lake Lodge were true, then. Perhaps it was haunted. But its whispery ghosts were not to be feared.

Something must have shown on her face, for Daisy paused in the midst of scrubbing the chopping block. "You all right?"

"Indeed I am. I have had the most brilliant idea, Daisy," she said. "Actually, the idea seems to have found me. I was simply minding my own business, putting William to bed, and it occurred to me. Suppose there were other women who have suffered intolerable treatment by men."

"What, you think we're the only ones?" Daisy asked with gentle sarcasm.

"Right here in Saratoga, there are women like us, like Josephine. Women who need...a safe place. Suppose Moon Lake Lodge was that sort of place."

"Is it?"

She felt a ripple of fear. Troy would return soon, and she would have to face him. Shoring up her courage, she declared, "We shall make it so."

"How we going to do that?"

"How can we *not?* It's a question of getting the word out."

"That'll be the easy part," Daisy said. "For me, it's one trip to the farmers market."

Helena understood. The domestic help of the wealthy had a culture and insular society all their own, and no one could penetrate it without their permission. But it was very real. Helena had watched Daisy join that society within days of her arrival in Saratoga Springs. She knew every butcher, costermonger and baker in the neighborhood, learned the names of other cooks and maids as well as the names of their children. News traveled among them faster than any wireless or telephone message—who was ill, whose mistress had gone bankrupt, and no doubt, who suffered at a man's hands.

"Excellent," Helena said. "We must get started first thing in the morning."

Word of Moon Lake Lodge took mere hours to spread. The first time Daisy Sullivan went to the market in Maynard Park, she told several housekeepers and maids about the place. Those women passed the news on to their mistresses, and so it went. By day's end, half of Saratoga Springs seemed to know.

In the early morning, before the mist burned off the lake, Sarah Dalton arrived at the kitchen door. She was a soft-spoken woman with a chilling plea on her lips: "My day maid told me this was a safe place to come..." She wouldn't explain her bruises, but then again, she didn't have to.

Daisy, who had been supervising Helena's first attempt at rolling out the morning biscuits, hurried to welcome her. Mrs. Dalton's lip was split and swollen so large she could barely speak, and her shoulder was dislocated. Daisy had pulled the arm back into place, eliciting a thin scream that made Helena grit her teeth. At the same time, she knew their cause was good.

"I can't stay long," Sarah whispered afterward, holding a piece of ice to her lip. "Just until I'm feeling better. The Good Book says the wife should submit unto the husband.''

''The Good Book doesn't mean you're obligated to submit to cruelty,'' Helena said. ''You can stay as long as you like.''

''I'll have a little rest here. My husband needs me at home.''

Helena bristled. ''Your husband needs to be in jail.''

Sarah's eyes flared wide with panic. ''No, Grady's a good man. He loves me, but sometimes when he drinks, I make a mistake and he gets angry. The Good Book says the rod and reproof give wisdom—that's all Grady wants for me. It's just that I can't do anything right. And he's always so sweet and sorry after. I'll just stay a little while, and go home when I'm stronger.''

Why, dear God, would she ever want to go home to that? Helena wondered.

''Are we ever going back to our house in Vandam Square, Mama?'' William asked as he diligently swabbed the floor of the common room.

She paused, keeping her expression neutral as she considered his blunt inquiry. She should have been prepared for her son's many questions about their changed circumstances, but she wasn't. Perhaps there wasn't any preparing to be done. William's world had altered, but he had yet to realize how dramatically. She took a careful breath, set aside the feather duster she was using, then said, ''I don't think so, dear. Does that make you sad?''

''I used to play with Jimmy Jaeger. He's far away now.''

''That's true. Maybe I can arrange for a visit.''

''Maybe.'' William pushed his scrub brush along

the floor toward her, his bare feet dragging in the soapy water. The long, broad common room, with its timber-beamed ceiling, contained a billiard table, a dartboard on the wall and a set of ninepins piled in a corner. There was a big river rock fireplace, now hung with cobwebs, mismatched chairs around a card table and benches against the wall.

"Moon Lake Lodge could become a wonderful place," Helena said. "It simply needs work."

"Like Old Warren Church," William said.

"A bit." She had headed the committee to renovate the colonial meeting house, a remnant of bygone days, famous for being a shelter for fleeing patriot soldiers during the War for Independence. That project, however, had been conceived of as a genteel pursuit, suitable for a senator's wife. Her part in the work had involved dictating guest lists and invitations to Edith, planning tea menus, ice cream socials and flower arrangements with local hostesses. It was a far cry from this.

"Are you going to have an ice cream social to raise funds?" William asked.

She almost laughed. What she was doing now would cost her all of her social connections and more. She knew that. "I believe we'll do the work on our own. William, do you think you'll like living here?"

"I like having a proper barn for Hector. I like being close to the lake."

"I like those things, too." She darted a glance out the window. Since Nellie had gone down to Albany, Helena had been in a state of breath-held anticipation, waiting for news. She kept looking over her shoulder, afraid Troy would come after her at any moment but prepared to face him if he did. Seeing no one outside, she picked up the feather duster and swatted at a swag of cobwebs in the corner of the fireplace.

"Mama," said William, sliding on hands and knees toward the tall windows facing the lake. "Is Father going to come and live here, too?"

Her hand clenched tightly around the duster. "As you know, he's always so very busy in Albany and in Washington." She could see the confusion clouding his face. Explain and be honest with the boy, she thought. That was the thing to do. But there was little to tell him, until she learned how Nellie had fared in Albany. She fell silent, leaving him to his thoughts for a few minutes, letting him mull over what she was trying so clumsily to explain. The hard work of turning Moon Lake Lodge into their home was a welcome distraction, probably for both of them. The fact was, she regarded this place with a protective fervor she had never felt for a house. The lodge was completely unlike anyplace she'd ever lived. She had grown up in the finest residence on Dumbarton Street in Georgetown, but to her, the splendid colonial mansion held little charm. It had been designed to impress dignitaries rather than to feel homey to a girl. The showy mausoleum in Vandam Square had been Troy's choice. It dripped with ostentation, overpowered the senses with its embarrassment of expensive furnishings and fussed-at gardens.

Moon Lake Lodge was solid and simple, an unobtrusive dwelling in the midst of wooded splendor. To Helena, this place represented something she had always wanted but had never dared to claim for her own.

Freedom.

It had never seemed a terribly important principle to her before. Why should it? Her father took care of her every need as she grew up. Then he handed her off to

Troy. And even though she'd found no great joy in her marriage, she had accepted the fact that, in order to be looked after, she had to put up with a man's foibles and his neglect. It was remarkable how much unhappiness she'd endured simply because she couldn't be bothered to explore other alternatives. Independence had little meaning to her. It seemed a nebulous, unreachable concept promoted by wild-eyed suffragists wearing men's trousers and smoking corncob pipes.

Finally, she understood the power of that concept. Independence. The freedom to think and dream and plan and act all on one's own. A century ago, Americans had fought a bloody war for it. Mothers had sent their farmer sons away to fight against trained soldiers, so dearly held was the cause.

Now that she knew Troy's true nature, she had taken a stand and she would not be swayed. She had always lived a small life, concerning herself with inconsequential things—what to wear, what to serve at a supper party, what to buy William for his birthday. She had never troubled herself with deep issues like personal liberty; she had never made any grand gesture for the sake of a great cause.

But she was doing that at last. Moving away from her husband, making her own way in the world, were only the first steps. She had never thought she'd find washing windows and cleaning cobwebs particularly rousing, but her sense of purpose lent a special weight to the task. Cleaning up this house, making it into a home, had become the most crucial prospect in the world. Some of Helena's high-society friends—those few who still deigned to speak to her—didn't understand yet. They believed she had created a retreat for women as a humanitarian gesture, designed to enhance her husband's reputation during an election year. As a result, a decent sum of donations had been delivered, an irony that did not escape Helena.

She had little time to concern herself with public opinion, however.

Coming to the end of one wall, she shook out her feather duster. In the corner, she noticed a spider spinning a web and watched it for a while. Its slow, methodical work was curiously mesmerizing. The gossamer strands formed an elaborate pattern, attached invisibly to the old plaster wall. With a shrug, she lowered the feather duster.

She tried to go back to work, but knew certain things needed to be said, certain understandings reached. For him, she must explain matters in the most concrete of terms. She didn't know yet if her petition for a divorce would succeed, so she didn't mention it. She could tell William only what she knew to be true—that they would never again go back to their old life. Later would come the even more difficult conversation about her marriage.

William went on working, scrubbing away, going over and over the same spot on the floor. What was he thinking? How much should she tell him? Her son was a thoughtful boy with a great deal of curiosity about the world. Sometimes the things he said startled and amazed her. She burned to know what he was thinking just now.

Taking a deep breath, Helena gave the best explanation she could. "I do want you to know, William, that no matter where we live or with whom, some things will never change. You will always be my little boy, and I will always love you, and we will always be together."

William swivelled around on his knees and attacked

another section of the floor. "All right," he said. He worked with fresh enthusiasm for a while, and Helena let out a slow, silent sigh of relief. One of the great blessings of being eight years old was that one's attention span was mercifully short. They finished their scrubbing and carried the bucket to the washroom at the end of the hall.

"Did you know that in England, the Speaker of the House is not allowed to speak?" asked William.

"I didn't know that. But I'm sure it makes for shorter legislative sessions."

"The Professor told me. He knows lots of things, like the word 'war' in Sanskrit means the desire for more cows."

She glanced at one of the bedroom doors, which had been left slightly ajar. "Keep your voice down. We don't want to wake Mrs. Dalton."

"Is she going to live here with the rest of us?" he whispered, craning his neck to see into the room.

Helena nodded, thinking of her newest guest. "I believe so, yes."

"She has a lot of hurts," he observed.

"She does." Helena helped William pour the water down the drain. "I don't know how long Mrs. Dalton will stay. But we'll take good care of her, and she'll get better."

"When's Mrs. McQuigg coming back?" William asked.

"I don't know."

"When's the Professor coming back?"

"I don't know that, either."

"I miss him."

So do I. She nearly said so aloud.

Thirteen

At sundown, Helena heard the distant whistle of the evening train and went outside, her stomach twisting into a knot of nerves. Stars pricked the sky, so numerous that they seemed to pulse and spin with a life of their own. The sight of them made Helena think of Abigail, and all those late nights her sister used to spend on the rooftop in Georgetown, studying the night sky through the lens of a telescope.

Helena felt a pang of yearning. How she missed her sister. And her father. Even sitting among friends, watching the moon rise over the lake, she had never felt so alone and lost. William was already in bed in his cozy little room on the second floor, reading aloud to Josephine Goodkind from the *Newtown Gazette*. It was Mark Twain's story about a jumping frog, and every few minutes, Helena could hear their laughter through the open window. She drew comfort from the sound, but it also awakened nagging questions that were better left unasked.

Even so, her heart asked them. What would her life have been like if her marriage had been a happy one? Instead of being an only child, William might have had brothers and sisters. Helena cherished her sister Abigail, and could not imagine life without her. She shuddered, contemplating the toll her choices were taking on her child.

When the train whistle sounded again, Daisy walked out to join Helena on the porch. They waited in tense silence. There was no need to voice their questions aloud; they would learn the answers soon enough. Helena forced herself to savor the beauty of her new world. There was an almost magical air about Moon Lake Lodge, as though the property held a sweet secret about to be revealed.

"Why does this place seem so special?" she asked Daisy.

"Maybe it ain't this place." Daisy patted her arm. "What about that professor man? When's he coming back?"

A sudden and unexpected veil of tears clouded her vision. "I don't know. He's so furious with me for never telling him about William."

"He ain't mad about that. He's mad at himself." Daisy tensed. "I think Miz Nellie's back."

Coming up the walk, backlit by deep twilight, Nellie looked brisk and professional. In the black shirtwaist and skirt Helena had given her, books and papers under her arm, she cut a handsome silhouette. But when Helena met her on the porch steps, she saw that Nellie's face was pinched by defeat.

"Well?" she dared to ask, then reminded herself to be patient. "Heavens, where are my manners? Have you had supper yet? Would you like something to eat or drink?"

"Just my rocker and my pipe." Nellie settled down in the scarred old rocking chair, propped her foot on her knee and tamped her pipe against the heel of her kid leather boot. At last, she looked from Helena to Daisy and back again. "My dear, I'm so sorry."

Helena's heart dropped. "Are you sure?"

"Yes, Helena. The judge wouldn't hear of it. Said it couldn't be done."

"So Troy would be within his legal rights if he came and dragged me away from here by the hair."

"That's not going to happen," Daisy said with quiet resolve.

"We'll just have to try something else," Nellie said.

"But what?" Tears pressed at the backs of Helena's eyes, but she refused to let them escape. She would not weep because of Troy Barnes, ever. "I scared him off with the election scandal, but if I act on that, he'll be ruined, and I'll still be married to him."

"I'll have to think on it." But for the first time, Nellie's natural self-assurance appeared to waver. She didn't seem to know where to let her gaze rest, while the old, smoke-blackened pipe in her hand smoldered, forgotten.

"Thank you for trying," Helena made herself say. "It means the world to me."

More murmurs and laughter drifted from upstairs. Nellie frowned. "Company?"

"You could say that," Daisy said. "Two ladies have come to stay."

"Their names are Josephine Goodkind and Sarah Dalton," Helena said. "Josephine's from the Mohawk camp. Sarah—we don't know much about her yet." Somehow, the news about Troy made Helena feel more determined than ever to succeed with these women. "We can help them, Nellie. I know we can. My father left me a healthy legacy, and we shall put it to good use."

"You've had news of your inheritance already?" Nellie asked.

"No. The estate will be in probate for some time." Then a terrible thought struck her. "Troy has no claim on my inheritance, does he?"

"Let's worry about one thing at a time, shall we?" Nellie suggested. An ominous look shadowed her features.

"Let's not worry at all, just for tonight," said Daisy.

They sat quietly until twilight sank into darkness and the peepers sang from the rushes at the edge of the lake.

"Well, no matter how Troy responds to all this, I still have my son," she said, trying to pull herself away from despair. She would learn to make her own way in the world. She would never again depend on a man for help. "And your cherished friendship, and Moon Lake Lodge. Those are riches Troy Barnes can never take from me."

"You got that right, sugar." Daisy bade them both good-night and went inside.

Helena awakened to the sound of hooves drumming on the earth, then crunching over gravel. Pulling on a robe, she hurried to the window and saw a horseman approaching at breakneck speed, the lash of his quirt cracking through the silence of the night. The confused animal toiled along the road leading to the house. Misty light from the summer moon washed over the figure of a tall man.

Michael? It couldn't be. He was not so thin as this midnight visitor, and she simply couldn't imagine him beating a horse for any reason. Dear God, Troy…? She was convinced he would stay away from Saratoga Springs, at least until he devised a way to minimize the damage to his own ambitions. That would take time, and she was counting on using that time to advantage.

Barefoot, she ran downstairs and went to the door just as the visitor began to pound and bellow.

"Sarah!" he roared, a drunken howl filled with passion and hate.

Helena stumbled back, grabbing the newel post at the foot of the rail. Her gaze darted to the stairs, leading to the bedrooms. She prayed William would stay fast asleep in his bed.

Pale and wide-eyed, clutching the throat of her pink nightgown, Sarah appeared at the rail above, paused, then rushed down. The hem of the gown wafted out behind her like a pair of wings as she descended the stairs.

She reached the foyer just as her husband put his fist through the sidelight window, then reached to unbolt the door.

Sarah gasped; Helena was too shocked to scream. She looked down at her right hand and was surprised to find herself holding a brass-tipped parasol, plucked from the hall tree. Though she had never used a weapon, she was prepared to defend herself and those in her care.

The door banged open, and the intruder filled the foyer with the smell of cigar smoke, whiskey, blood and rage. "I come to get you, Sarah," he said. "I come to bring you on home."

Helena edged in front of Sarah, who was breathing in shallow gasps. Helena recognized the thin sound of panic that slipped from between Sarah's parted lips. Helena could even sense the fear, a metallic, sweaty smell.

"The constable's on his way," she said.

"He ain't. You got no wire out to this place."

"We most certainly do," she lied. "We have sent for the police."

"Move aside, woman." He took a step forward. Blood from his hand dripped onto the wooden floor, the drops perfectly round and black. It was so dark, shadowy dark. Helena wondered if he would force her to use the weapon.

"You come with me," he roared, surging toward his wife. "You're coming home where you belong."

"Stay back," Helena warned him. "Don't you touch her."

He didn't seem to hear or see her. He was completely focused on Sarah. "What kind of wife leaves her home, her husband?" he asked. "Don't you know it's a sin? The Good Book says the whole duty of a woman is to cleave to her husband. You come with me now. You belong with me."

"Grady, please calm down." Sarah finally spoke up, her voice shaking with heartbreak. "You've been drinking."

"Sure I been drinking. They put my own brother, my own flesh and blood, in jail tonight, and it's got me mighty upset."

"What's Jasper doing in jail?"

"He beat up some ol' girl who was giving him lip. And that's just what you'll get, if you don't come with me."

So, thought Helena. It was a family trait.

"Now, Grady," Sarah said with a weariness that hinted of long practice, "just go on home and go to bed. I'll come see you after you're all sobered up."

Why on earth would she promise that? Helena wondered. Maybe she was only saying that to get him to leave. But Daisy had warned her that Sarah was the sort who went back, the sort who thought she loved the man who beat her, who desperately wanted to believe his threats and groveling and apologies.

"Sarah, if you don't come with me right now, Lord only knows what I might do to myself. It's your fault, woman. Look what you done to me." He strode forward, grabbing for her.

Helena didn't think; she just moved, swinging the parasol two-handed like a golf club. The silk-wrapped hickory shaft whistled through the air and cracked against his outstretched, bleeding hand. He caught the weapon, wrenched it from her grip and broke it over his knee, barely slowing his steps as he bore down on his wife.

"You come on home now, Sarah, else I'll give you what-for." He shoved Helena aside with a single bear-paw swipe.

Her foot skidded through fresh blood and she fell. Her teeth jarred together and the air rushed out of her.

Grady Dalton lunged for his wife. He backhanded her across the face, the blow so hard that a tooth flew from her mouth and pinged across the floor.

Then he grabbed his wife's arm and hauled her to the door, dragging her through the blood and broken glass. Helena scrambled to her feet.

"Grady, please, no," Sarah whimpered. "My arm—"

"I'll teach you to run off on me." In the doorway he froze, and the look that came over his face changed from rage to confusion to stark, white-eyed terror.

The twin barrels of the Henry rifle were pushed into the soft flesh of his neck. At the stock end of the rifle stood Daisy Sullivan.

"You let her go," Daisy said. "Now."

She was a full head taller than Grady Dalton, and

just as angry. But her rage was as cold and focused as his was hot and uncontrolled.

He opened his hand, freeing Sarah's arm. She stepped back, cradling her shoulder.

"You get on out of here," Daisy ordered.

He ducked his head, stumbled down the porch steps and disappeared into the night.

Helena's first thought was for William. But, amazingly, the racket didn't seem to have awakened him or Josephine.

Picking her way around the broken glass, she went to Sarah. "How badly are you hurt, dear?" she asked in a soft voice.

Sarah touched the tips of her fingers to the edge of her jaw. Then she bent and retrieved the tooth, wiping it with a corner of her nightgown in a matter-of-fact gesture that told Helena it wasn't the first tooth he'd knocked out of her head. Far from it. "I'll be all right. He just gets mean when he drinks, is all."

"Hmm. That ain't all," said Daisy. She held the Henry rifle in one hand, a broom in the other as she swept the broken glass into a pile.

"I'll help you back to bed," Helena said.

She held out her hand, but Sarah didn't see her. She simply stared at the open door and the dark empty road. Tears rolled unchecked from her eyes, and Helena realized that the look on Sarah's face was not one of fear or anger, but of pure, helpless yearning.

"Whatever became of that no-account professor?" Nellie asked, shading her eyes against the hot summer sun.

Helena chopped at the ground with her swan-neck garden hoe. She had been trying specifically *not* to think about him, and each day, she convened a work detail in order to keep everyone busy.

"So you think he's of no account?"

Nellie rubbed the small of her back as though to soothe an ache. "He is today."

They were all outside digging and weeding in the kitchen garden, which had been laid out in oblong plots on the south side of the house. Hopelessly overgrown, it had deteriorated into an exotic wilderness of six-foot stalks of fennel and dill, potatoes gone to seed, rampant and haphazard growths of flowering greens and squash, out of control from years of neglect. It was too late in the summer to hope for much of a crop, but Daisy insisted they could bring some sort of order to the beds.

Slipping off her canvas glove, Helena inspected her hand. Despite her precautions, a fine set of blisters had started. "He went down to collect his things from the Institute. Apparently it's taken him longer than anticipated."

As she surveyed her domain, she used the corner of her apron to blot at her face. Sarah Dalton sat on a blanket in the shade with Alice Wilkes, the troubled artist Helena had met at Dr. Hillendahl's. Helena had encouraged Alice to visit Moon Lake Lodge as soon as she was able, and this morning she'd simply appeared, the bandages gone from her hands and a shy smile on her face. She and Sarah were shelling purple-hull peas, which had thrived in the garden despite the neglect.

"Did he say when he would return?" Nellie asked.

"Ah, Nellie, it wouldn't surprise me if he never came back," she confessed. "The fact is, I have no idea what he's thinking. Perhaps I never knew, even though I—we—"

"Were lovers."

Helena blushed, casting a swift glance at William. The boy was out of earshot at the other end of the garden, she saw with relief. "Michael has always been a puzzling man. He seemed intrigued to learn that William is his son, and he certainly didn't hesitate to defend me against Troy, but—" She stopped, appalled to feel a lump in her throat. In all the time since her father's death, she had not given way to tears, but now, without warning, she felt as though she were drowning in them.

"But what?"

She swallowed hard, tried to compose herself. "He's never been the sort of man to stay around. I've always known that about him. And I've always wondered why that is."

Nellie applied her rake to a pile of plucked weeds. "Why don't you ask him?"

"What?"

She gestured at the long, curved drive leading in from the main road. A flurry of dust erupted, then a shape emerged, resolving itself into the solid form of a man on horseback.

Gradually he slowed his pace, bringing the spirited horse to a canter and then a walk. Michael was in his usual state of disarray, the effect exaggerated by the unshaven state of his face, and road dust settling in the creases of his ill-matched clothes.

Helena felt a little pang of anticipation. *He came back.* Then she reminded herself of her new resolve. She was never going to depend on another soul for anything. Ever. Still, as the proprietress of Moon Lake Lodge, she felt it was her duty to greet him, and she walked to the front curve of the drive, meeting him just as he dismounted and removed his battered hat.

"I'm back," he said, unnecessarily.

"So you are." Helena kept her tone polite and neutral.

From behind the green spectacles, he frowned in curiosity at the newcomers working in the distant garden. "What's going on here?"

His tone made her defensive. This was her enterprise; he had no right to question it. "If you must know, we're making Moon Lake Lodge into a very special sort of resort."

"Special. In what way?"

He always challenged her. Question after question. He always had.

"Well," she said, "Saratoga Springs is famous throughout the world for its healing waters."

"Taking the waters is just an excuse for rich people to spend the summer gambling and betting on horses. And shopping for a rich husband. Don't forget that."

"True. Some of the bigger hotels around town are the busiest marriage markets in the country. But what about women who don't care to make one of Saratoga's famed 'correct acquaintances?'"

"They have no business being here."

"You have no imagination. I do. And I'm willing to concede that I could never rival the opulence of the grand hotels, nor would I want to. Saratoga Springs has all the glittering casinos and burlesque shows, the musicales and fireworks it needs. Moon Lake Lodge will be different. It will be a place for women only, where they can come and be themselves and not have to fuss with their appearance, or their manners or anything of the sort."

"Women live to fuss with such things."

"That's what you think. I will serve mineral water

every morning. The property has a very productive spring."

"That hardly makes it unique. Everyone with a plot of land and a borehole has a spring."

"The ladies who stay with me will simply relax and take the waters and find diversions that fulfill them. We'll have morning tea and conversation and evenings will be for singing and storytelling and for whatever we want them to be." She turned on the weedy lawn so the lake was at her back. "Oh, it is a grand vision, is it not?"

"A resort for women."

"Yes."

"You and your madcap schemes."

"That's your opinion. Although perhaps it's correct. It is a madcap scheme."

"I'm sure it hasn't escaped you that William doesn't fit into your plan to turn this place into some sort of women's colony," he pointed out.

"He's my son. He fits wherever I am. He'll be in heaven here at Moon Lake Lodge." She gestured at the women laboring in the garden. "It will be like having a whole village of mothers." Before he could question her further, she asked, "Where are your things from the Institute?"

"Everything's loaded on a dray and will be delivered later."

"So why didn't you drive the cart yourself?"

"I was in a hurry."

An unbidden thrill shot through Helena, though she tried her best not to feel it. But the fact was, no one had ever hurried home to her before.

"Where's William?" he asked, walking toward the garden.

So much for hurrying home to her, she thought,

pointing to the far end of the garden. William had already spied Michael and was running as fast as he could to greet him.

"Hi, Professor." William gazed at him with shining eyes. "I got the whole yard scythed around Hector's paddock."

"Excellent. Did you rake all the old hay out of his stall?"

"Yes, sir."

Although they barely knew each other, Michael seemed perfectly at ease with the boy. He also seemed quite comfortable as the object of William's hero-worship, Helena observed.

"What shall we do next, Professor?"

Michael considered the question with deep gravity, rubbing his hand over his stubbled chin. "I have an idea." Reaching into his shirt pocket, he took out a small white object. It moved and squirmed.

"Have mercy," said Daisy, who had come to the end of her row. "Is that a mouse?"

He held it out in the palm of his hand.

"You just keep that critter out of my kitchen, that's all I got to say." Shaking her head and muttering under her breath, Daisy went back to work.

Michael placed the little mouse in William's cupped hands. William held him as though he were as fragile as a snowflake, lifting the creature so that boy and mouse were nose-to-nose. Wonder and reverence suffused his face.

"Now then," Michael said, "do you think you can make him a proper box, with a water bottle and a lid so the cat can't get in?"

"A mouse house," William whispered, almost quivering with excitement.

"It will have to be very secure. This is the sort of mouse that can't live on its own in the wild."

"I can make just the thing. We've got everything we need in the carriage house."

"It looks like Socrates," Helena said.

"I'd nearly forgotten Socrates." Michael stood up, a bemused smile playing about his lips. "I used to keep a white mouse at my house in Georgetown," he explained to William.

"I kept him after you left, Michael, because you gave him to me, remember?"

"Actually, I don't."

"I didn't think so." She felt an undeniable pull toward him, and simply didn't understand it. He had treated her shabbily in the past, and she no longer knew him. Yet a terrible yearning that defied all logic drew her to him.

His face lit with a grin, William went to make his mouse house. Michael watched him go, and Helena watched Michael. "It feels wonderful, doesn't it?" she asked softly.

He frowned. "What does?"

"Giving William something he loves. Something that makes him smile like that, walk with that spring in his step."

"How did you know what I was thinking?"

"I can tell by the look on your face. You're an expert at concealing many things, but apparently not your feelings for William."

"Why would you—" He stopped himself as Nellie worked her way across the garden toward him, raking her pile of weeds in front of her. She stopped when she reached him. He darted a look at William, who was heading toward the carriage house. Then, to Nellie, he said, "I'm guessing your news isn't good."

Helena's heart ached at the look of mournful disgust on Nellie's face. Although the defeat belonged to Helena, Nellie took her failure personally. "Judge Standish refused to consider it. He is Troy Barnes's creature, as are all the state judges in Albany. They all seem to belong to the same club."

"I thought that would be the case."

Helena felt a prickle of resentment. He sounded terribly casual and unconcerned as he took off his spectacles, folded them and put them in his shirt pocket.

"So," he said, unfastening the buckle of one of his saddlebags. He took out a folded packet of papers and held them out to her like a waiter offering drinks from a tray. "I had an alternative plan. You'll want to sign this right away."

"What is it?" She didn't touch the papers that were typewritten in small, close lettering, with sealed and embossed writing at the bottom.

Nellie scanned the papers. "Helena, this is your annulment decree. You're no longer married to Troy Barnes. By law, you never were. Your marriage never happened."

Everything stopped. Even the wind seemed to be holding its breath.

Helena swallowed three times, cleared her throat and still she couldn't find her voice. But she could find a smile for him. That was the easy part. It started in her heart and blossomed on her lips, and she was certain she was about to take to the air. She stared at Michael. He had done this.

It was the ultimate gift he could give her—an official paper that took away the Troy years and gave them back to her. She knew then how the slaves of yore must have felt when presented with their manumission papers. So filled with elation that they might float away, yet slightly dazed and disoriented as they wondered what to do next.

From the corner of her eye, she saw William leap at a butterfly. Instantly she realized the consequences; this would make her son illegitimate. There was always a price to pay, she knew, but why did William have to pay for her foolishness?

Nellie asked the question that was burning inside Helena. "How did you manage this?"

"Let's just say Troy Barnes allowed himself to be persuaded." He bowed politely at Nellie and Helena. "You'll want to read over that yourself. I'm off to help William with his new pet, and later I'll have to drop this beast off at O'Keeffe's." Whistling tunelessly between his teeth, he took hold of the reins and led the horse toward the carriage house.

"Wait." Clutching the document to her chest, Helena hurried after him. "I wish you'd tell me how you accomplished all this."

He barely glanced at her, but kept his eyes on the narrow dirt lane. "I didn't hold a broken bottle to his throat this time, I swear it."

Helena tried to sort through her feelings. She wanted her independence, and yet here was Michael, taking charge.

He stood still, stopping the horse behind him. "You're awfully quiet. It's not like you."

"You should have told me your plan," she said.

"We've never been good at consulting one another. Besides, I didn't want to give you false hope, Helena. Contrary to what you think of me, I dislike breaking promises."

"You're right," she conceded. "That *is* contrary to what I think. But I do thank you for what you did." She studied the flickering shadows on the roadway.

Through the trees, she could hear Daisy singing a song. Behind her, the lake lapped at the shore. "I must go to the house in Vandam Square and collect the rest of my things. Then I'll see what can be done at the bank."

"He's probably already contacted your bank."

The chill of doubt that had kept her tense and wakeful for days grew even colder. That possibility, coupled with Nellie's reservations about the Cabot legacy, made the specter of poverty very real. She forced herself to cultivate a spark of defiance. "Even if it does cost all that I have, it's not too high a price to pay."

"I thought you'd say that."

Fourteen

The news burst forth with the force of the summer squall off Lake Saratoga, skirling through the town, leaving everyone drenched in amazement. The marriage of Troy Barnes and Helena Cabot was annulled. They were no longer the premiere golden couple of the Hudson Valley. They were not a couple at all, and legally, they never had been.

The first indication that this was going to be a topic for rampant gossip came when the story was published in *Frank Leslie's Illustrated Newspaper.* All was pure speculation, as Helena refused invitations to comment on the situation. And Troy? Who knew what he was thinking.

Helena really didn't care.

It was a bright summer day, and she knew she'd swelter in her mourning black, but it couldn't be helped. She left off her corset and one petticoat to mitigate what promised to be one of the hottest days of the year. Amazing. Not long ago she could not have conceived of buttoning her own shoes or doing her own hair. Now she did these things without thinking.

"Come along, William," she called as she walked

down the stairs, pausing at the front door to inspect the new pane of glass in the sidelight. Hiring a glazier to replace the window broken by Sarah's husband had seemed an extravagance, but Helena didn't want any reminders of that night. "William, do hurry. We must go into town this morning."

Her son came running, an eager look on his face. Every day was an adventure to him; he never wanted to miss a moment. She aimed a pointed look at his shoes. "Wrong feet again."

He rolled his eyes and plunked down on the bottom stair to switch them. "I don't see why it matters," he grumbled.

"Isn't it uncomfortable?"

"No."

"Well, you should wear them properly anyway. The left one on the left foot and the right one on the right foot. Is that so hard to remember?"

"I can remember all the words of 'Charge of the Light Brigade,'" he declared, jumping up and sliding across the floor in his socked feet. "'Half a league, half a league, half a league onward...' *Charge!*" As he ran, he snatched her new black parasol from the hall tree and ran at her, weapon extended.

Trying to appear unamused, she grabbed it from him. "Your socks don't match."

He looked down. "Match what?"

"Each other. Oh, William. Never mind. Just put your shoes back on and we'll have a nice walk into town."

A moment later, they were strolling away from the house, toward the road into town. As they passed the pathway leading to the stables and paddock, Helena heard a muffled crash. Frowning, she turned in the direction of the carriage house, which Michael Rowan now occupied. Should she go and investigate the noise or mind her own affairs?

With Michael, she could never judge. He had stepped back into her life as abruptly as he had left nine years earlier, and her feeling about that swung erratically from gratitude to resentment to confusion. For some reason, she could not think clearly when he was around.

"Professor Rowan is working on a new pump for the barn," said William. "He designed a self-watering trough for Hector."

She raised the parasol to shield them from the sun and walked in the direction of the main road. "How do you know that?"

"He told me when I went to see him. I visit him every day. And he taught me to snap my fingers, see?" He demonstrated, snapping three times.

"I didn't give you permission to go visiting," she said.

"I didn't ask for permission."

"You should have."

"Why?"

"Because I'm your mother, that's why. I love you and I worry about you and I must always know where you are."

"Why?"

"So I'll know you're safe."

"But can't I be safe when I'm not with you as well as when I am with you?"

"You can. It's just that, when you're with me, I'm able to see that you're safe, and—oh, never mind. I wish you would simply cooperate in this."

"But why?"

"William." She spoke more sharply than she'd intended, and he fell silent, walking along with his shoulders hugged up around his neck. Struggling to keep her composure, she led the way past the crooked gate of the property and turned onto Union Avenue. Although it was early in the day, the roadway was crowded with tradesmen and delivery vans and costermongers' carts lumbering in from the outlying farms. Racing season was nearly upon them, and the big hotels and resorts were getting ready for upwards of fifty thousand summer visitors.

"I'm sorry I snapped at you, William," she said. "The fact is, I wanted you with me today for a special reason."

He lowered his shoulders. "That's all right. What's the special reason?"

She bit her lip, took a deep breath, and began. "It is about my marriage to your—to Troy Barnes."

William walked along the cut stone curb lining the street, arms spread out for balance. "Did you have the divorce?"

Heavens, where had he learned that word? "Do you even know what a divorce is?"

"No," he admitted, keeping his eyes trained on the curb.

"Then where did you learn that word?"

He shrugged.

"Have you ever heard the word annulment?"

"I can spell that. A-n-n-u-l—"

"Yes, yes. You're very clever." She realized she was clutching the parasol in a death grip. "The fact is, my marriage has been annulled. Do you know what that means?"

"You're not married." William wobbled on the curb edge, then regained his balance. "You never were. The marriage was annulled."

"Who told you that?" she demanded, aghast. I'll

kill him, she thought. I'll kill Michael Rowan. He had no right to disclose that before I had a chance. "Did Professor Rowan tell you?"

"I read it in the newspaper," he said.

"Oh, William. I'm so sorry."

The curb narrowed and he lost his concentration, slipping into the gutter. Black rotted leaves, damp from last night's rain, clung to the soles of his shoes.

Helena took his hand and brought him to the sidewalk. "Darling boy," she said, "I'm so sorry you read it in the paper before I could explain." She despised herself in that moment. Her cowardly, worthless self. Always thinking that things would wait their turn or simply disappear if she ignored them for long enough. "Are you terribly upset about it?"

"Don't know. Maybe I'll read some more about it in the paper," he said, making a hopscotch game of the cracks in the sidewalk. They passed the casino, a handsome Georgian building in the center of town, then the Opera House at the Union Hotel, where peacocks, married couples, tourists and husband-hunters strolled across the formal gardens.

"The papers don't always get everything right. Neither do mothers. The fact is, I made a very big mistake in getting married."

"A mistake like when I get an equation wrong in arithmetic?" he asked, hopping on one foot to the next square.

"No—well, in a way, perhaps. When you have a very long division problem and you make a mistake in the very first step, then it will always be wrong no matter what, even if all the other arithmetic is correct after that first bit."

"Because the first step was wrong."

"Exactly. That's what I did. I got the first step

wrong, so after that, nothing else could be right, even though I tried to make it so. As a result, everything went more and more wrong until there was only one way to make it right."

"Annulment." He leaped two-footed to the next sidewalk square. "A-n-n-u-l-m-e-n-t. I told you. I already know about that."

"But I'm not sure you know what it means, dear boy. It's going to have a very big effect on our lives." Saying so aloud gave her a nervous thrill of exhilaration.

"Like we have to walk to town instead of being driven by Mr. Flynn."

"Yes." She realized that he would understand the situation best in the most concrete terms. How this or that affected him directly. "William, would it seem very strange to you if we didn't ever live in the house in Vandam Square, or the Georgetown house?"

He grew sober and thoughtful in a way that made him seem much older than his eight years. She could see that he was thinking, hard.

"Maybe," he finally said. "Do I have to know the exact answer right now?"

"No, of course not. I just don't want you to be sad or confused by anything." He was quiet as they progressed to Congress Spring Park, the colorful hub at the center of town. Fountains and gardens gave it the garish look of a carnival, overdressed in bright colors. They stopped to rest on a bench facing the creek that meandered through the park, creating an oasis from the hectic bandstands and crammed promenades. Swans glided across the lake, weaving random patterns between the statues and fountains.

"If Father was never your husband, does this mean I won't have a father anymore?" asked William.

Her heart constricted even as her mind marveled at his sophisticated logic. Had he ever really had a father? Troy had been a figurehead in his life, hurrying from one meeting or social engagement to another when he was in town—more often out of town—but he was all the boy knew.

"Now, that is a tricky question," she said carefully. "I'm not quite sure how to answer it."

She had never felt right about the fact that William and the rest of the world believed Troy Barnes was his natural father. Some day, she would have to tell him another man had fathered him. But not yet. Not now. William was only just getting used to the idea of the annulment. Besides, she didn't want him to give his heart to his natural father when the future was so uncertain.

Michael claimed he wanted to be a father to William, but she was quite sure he had no idea what that entailed. How could he understand the piercing joy of seeing a child's special smile, the crushing agony a parent feels when a child is hurting, the way a parent's hopes soar for him, the way dreams fashion themselves around him?

All right, she thought. William wanted an answer. "It means you won't be seeing him anymore."

"Ever?"

Oh, she hoped so. But she knew such a different Troy than William knew. "I think so," she said. Then forced herself to add, "Will that make you very sad?"

"You mean like I'm sad over Granddaddy Cabot?"

She bit her lip, finding herself awash in emotion. "Not exactly. From now on, I think it will just be the two of us, and Daisy and our guests at Moon Lake Lodge. You are my dear little boy, my own wee Willie, and that is something that will never change. But it might seem strange to you, to suddenly have only a mother.''

''Can I have all my things?''

''Your things?''

Then she realized her little boy was trying to regain his balance after she had upset it. He simply wanted his things, the familiar comforts of a life that had been just fine up until now. ''Of course you can have your things. We shall have them sent from Vandam Square. You'll have your things, and your mother. Is that all right with you?''

He nodded. ''You know what it's like to have a father because you had Granddaddy Cabot. I know what it's like to have a mother because I have you.''

When he said things like that, she wanted to melt with love. He had always been exactly the child she needed. During the years of her marriage, she occasionally got the idea that he sensed her unhappiness, but in a way that she scarcely understood herself. It was a pervasive ennui that darkened each moment like a shadow on the sun, and William always seemed to know how to bring the brightness back.

''Come here, scamp.'' She gathered him into her arms and rested her chin on the top of his head, closing her eyes and inhaling deeply.

She could feel impatience rising through him. After a moment he squirmed. ''Can I go play now? I see some boys from school.''

''In a minute.''

''You always sniff my hair.''

''I like the way you smell.''

He sniffed at the back of his hand. ''I don't smell like anything.''

She smiled. ''You smell like sunshine and grass.'' Relenting, she released him.

"Now can I go?" William asked. "There's Jimmy over at the ball field. And the boys from school. Please."

Poor little lonely lad. Thinking back to the days before all the trouble, she realized that he had been perfectly content playing baseball and riding bicycles with his friends.

"Go," she said, giving him a gentle shove. "Try not to get dirty."

Whooping like a wild creature, he raced down the bank toward the field. He was such a wonder to her. He always had been, from the moment Dr. Gluck had placed the swaddled, mewing newborn in her arms and she had wept with joy.

Troy, of course, had accepted hearty congratulations and costly baby gifts. People who were eager to seek the favor of Senator Cabot's daughter came from miles around to bestow presents on the baby, and Troy's thanks were profuse and magnanimous, his pride endearing to those who didn't really know him.

Helena had not allowed herself to fret about her deception, and Troy made it easy by keeping his distance. She adored William enough for both parents. For a thousand parents. She swore her little boy would never lack for love. She had entered into the marriage with the sole purpose of giving her child a proud family name and the protection of a vast fortune. With that goal accomplished, she vowed to dedicate herself to her son.

She contentedly settled in Saratoga Springs with William and the genteel, well-heeled residents of Vandam Square, and Troy carried on in the capital with his political cronies and the questionable women who comforted him.

From a distance, she could pick out the Jaeger boy

and several students from Penfield Academy. In the midst of the summer holiday, they were as brown as little savages. A group of somberly clad nannies and fashionable young mothers were clustered on benches under the shade trees, watching over the boys. Helena stood, brushing the wrinkles from her skirt as she prepared to join them.

But before she had taken two steps, something odd happened down on the grassy field. The nannies and mothers gathered up the boys and shepherded them away, hurrying and looking over their shoulders. William stood alone in the middle of the field, scratching his head with one hand, the other hand raised in a halfhearted wave.

"What's a bastard?" he asked when Helena came hurrying over.

She felt her face drain of color, then redden as though someone had slapped both cheeks. "Where did you hear that word?"

"From Bobbie Hurst. He told me his mama says he can't play with me on account of I turned into a bastard."

Shock gave way to fury, and she glared at the retreating playmates and their mothers. These were children he'd grown up with. Gone to school with. They'd celebrated birthdays together, gone sledding in the winter and played baseball in the summer. And now they refused to associate with him. It was all Helena could do to keep herself from losing her temper in front of William. Chills slid down her spine. This was only the beginning.

"That's a terrible word, and you mustn't say it or even think it. The fact is..." Lord, what could she say? How could she fix this? How could she make it right? "The fact is, our house and our family are different now. Some people who don't know any better might treat you differently. You must understand that you are no different at all, even though mean or ignorant people might treat you that way. You have done nothing wrong. Those children and their families are simply mistaken in their thinking. But one thing will never, ever change, and that is that I am your mother and I will love you all your life, forever. And you'll make new friends, lots of them. All right?''

They walked the remaining four blocks to Vandam Square. With a resolute step, she marched up to the front door. She had never before noticed how imposing the mansion was, a great pile of concrete and brick, the entranceway a giant, closed maw. Casting aside the fanciful thought, she tugged firmly on the tasseled bell-pull.

How pathetic, she thought, to lack the key to one's own home. But the fact was, she'd never had one. She had relied on others to do even the simplest of tasks, such as opening the door for her.

No more, she thought. No more.

''There's Mrs. Bradford,'' William called, waving at the house across the way. ''Hello, Mrs. Bradford.''

Helena turned in time to see a front parlor curtain swing back into place as a shadow moved in the window. ''She must not have heard you,'' Helena said.

After what seemed like an eternity, the front door opened. Helena's heart dropped like a stone into an icy well. *''Troy.''*

''Father,'' said William, staring up at him with saucer eyes. ''Mama says we—''

''We've come to collect a few things,'' Helena said, trying to speak over the roar of panic in her ears. It was so loud she was certain he could hear. ''William,'' she said, "why don't you play in the yard, over by the spring pump? I'll call for you in a moment."

He didn't need to be told twice. Perhaps he could sense the tension crackling between them. He was gone in a flash.

Troy scarcely looked at the boy. "And what do you intend collecting this time, Helena?" he inquired. "You and that thieving maid of yours managed to loot a good many things that don't belong to you already."

She was dizzy with fear, but refused to show it. "I don't have time to bicker with you." She brushed past him, stepping into the gleaming marble foyer that echoed with emptiness.

He stepped in front of her. "You're trespassing on these premises."

Her courage was melting fast, but she stiffened her spine. At the same time, she strained to hear whether or not someone else was in the house. He read her searching expression. "We're alone, I assure you."

Vowing not to be so transparent, she forced herself to glare up at him. "We had an understanding, Troy. My silence about the election in exchange for your absence from Saratoga Springs."

"We came to that understanding before you decided to rewrite history."

"Then I am no longer obligated to suppress the evidence of the stolen election?" she asked, surprised and pleased by the steadiness in her voice.

He drew back his hand.

"Don't even think it," she said, her voice growing stronger and steadier as the danger intensified. She did not want to have to use the ballots. As soon as she fired that shot, he would be ruined and she'd be out of ammunition. But bluffing was her only recourse. "You can't afford another scandal, Troy."

A word she'd never heard spoken aloud before exploded from him, but he dropped his arm. "I am leaving on the night steamer for Washington. The probate order came through."

Icy tremors crept through her. He meant to seize her inheritance, just as Nellie feared. But how could she object to anything that would take him several hundred miles away?

He picked up a typewritten, yellowed half sheet from the hall table. "Here's the written order, if you'd like to look it over."

"I don't need to look it over. You wouldn't show it to me if you weren't confident of its contents." She glared at him with open contempt. Yet deep down, she felt equal contempt for herself. What sort of person was she, that she hadn't learned to read? Now she was paying the price of her ignorance. She marched into the summer parlor. The sunny room was spotless as always, the white voile curtains wafting in the warm breeze.

She went straight to the Degas painting, unhooked the wire and lifted the large, framed piece from the wall.

"My dear," Troy said, "don't make it necessary for me to stop you."

That, of course, was all it took. She understood that William was in as much danger as she. Still, she had to try to claim the painting. "You despise this picture. You've said it's worthless."

"But if you love it so much, then it's priceless," he said.

She could see the rage building in him. Suddenly she needed to leave—and quickly. She swished past him to the foyer, her heels tapping across the polished marble floor. Just as she reached the door, his hand slapped flat against it. "We're not finished," he said.

"There's nothing more to say." Oh God, she thought. Oh God oh God. She should have grabbed William and fled the moment she spied Troy.

A knock sounded on the other side of the door, causing both her and Troy to jump. Then the door opened, and William stepped inside. "Mama—"

"Come along, William," she said quickly, almost unable to breathe for relief. "We had best be going."

"We have to go, sir," he said to Troy.

As she took William's hand and stepped outside, she caught a glimpse of Troy's face. Oh, she despised what she saw there. In spite of everything, he adored William, and the hurt was etched upon his features.

With her fringed parasol in hand and her young son at her side, Helena left Vandam Square behind. She felt no sense of victory. She knew this was only a reprieve.

"This is a belated thank you." Helena held out a berry pie. It was the only thing that had turned out right lately, not that she could take credit for baking it. She felt a little nervous, having Michael as a proper visitor in the great room with the river rock fireplace. "I was ungracious before, perhaps because I was so shocked, but that's no excuse. Anyway. Thank you for what you did. Nellie says everything is in order and it's really true, the marriage will be very much annulled, and within thirty days, I'll be free."

"That's why you invited me over?" He eyed her skeptically, as though he did not quite believe her.

She wondered what he saw, looking at her. Did he see the worshipful girl he'd once known, or the frightened but determined woman she had become?

"I can see you dressed for the occasion." She eyed him back, taking in his dusty work boots and well-worn denim jeans and shirt, smudged with oil or tar. Her wry comment helped her avoid answering his question. The fact was, she'd arrived home from her excursion into town in a troubled state. She was emotionally exhausted, and her nerve endings felt unbearably sensitive, forced to the surface by the stress of her ordeal.

"I didn't get you that annulment to earn your gratitude." He strolled across the room toward her, his boots thudding slowly on the plank floor.

"Then why?" Nervous, she set the pie on the table and edged away.

"For William. I did it for him." Keeping his eyes on Helena, he picked up a piece of the berry pie and took a large bite, not seeming to notice or care that the sweet juices drenched his hand. "And maybe," he said, flashing a grin, "just maybe, I did it for this pie. My God, Helena. This is the best thing I ever ate." He studied her for a moment. "Maybe the second-best. Did you make it?"

"Daisy."

"She's a goddess who walks the earth."

"I'll tell her you said so."

He sat down in a ladder-back chair and polished off the wedge of pie, making sounds of pleasure that caused her to blush. Everyone else in the house had retired for the night, but she didn't want them to think...what she was thinking.

She shoved a blue-and-white checkered napkin at him. "You look a mess."

He wiped his hands and mouth. "So. You're a free woman. What will you do with the rest of your life?"

She sat down across from him, curiously relieved to

have him to talk to. "At the moment, I can't conceive of planning a single day, not to mention a life."

"I take it your day was less than pleasant?"

"It was just grand. Let me see…it was so eventful, I must try to remember all the details." As she spoke, she seized the berry pie and dug in with a spoon, eating straight out of the pie plate. She had no intention of telling Michael about her encounter with Troy, because she feared he would lose control again, and wind up in far worse trouble than he already had. She skipped over the visit to Vandam Square. "I went to the bank where they acted as though they'd never heard of me. The manager informed me that Troy had closed our accounts, and at any rate, I have no authorization whatsoever, because I am no longer Mrs. Barnes. I walked out of there without a penny." She feigned a sweet smile. "Aren't you glad you asked?"

"You have berry juice on your chin." Before she could stop him, he blotted it with a napkin. "So you're no longer Mrs. Barnes. Did the world as we know it come to an end?"

"I'm not finished." She ate several more bites of pie, then looked up at Michael. "William spied some of his schoolmates in Congress Spring Park, and he ran off to play with them, just as he has all his life. They taught him a new word when they informed him he's a bastard. You've probably already noticed. William is very bright. It didn't take him long to figure out what a bastard is."

Fury darkened his face, and the word he hissed was not familiar to her, but she could guess at its meaning. "We should leave this place, Helena. Move far away, where no one knows you or Troy Barnes. Go traveling with your sister and her family."

"I would never do that. This is my home, and William's. I will not give Troy Barnes that sort of power over me.'' Belatedly, she noticed his use of *we,* but decided not to challenge it. Staring down at the half-empty pie plate, she said, "I can't believe I ate so much.'' She blotted her lips with the napkin, trying to show a little more delicacy than she'd had wolfing down the pie.

"He won't make it easy for you to stay,'' Michael pointed out.

"He has always underestimated me. This is his revenge,'' she said. "And I'm quite certain it's only the beginning.'' She got up and moved across the room to the long wall, stopping to study the yellowed illustration of the women's rights meeting at Seneca Falls. "Why do men find this so fearsome?''

"I don't. Campaigning for suffrage makes sense to me.''

"But you're—'' She hesitated.

"I'm what?''

"You're... You've always been strange.''

"That's what you admire about me.'' He stood and strolled toward her. His lips quirked upward, and his eyes flashed with unspoken memories.

"The fact that you're strange?''

"It's true. The first time we met, you thought I was strange.''

She realized he was trying to keep her from despairing over the legacy. It was working. "My mistake. I should have realized that a man falling out of a tree on my front sidewalk was not strange at all.''

"The second time we met,'' he reminded her, "you kissed me.''

"Your memory is hazy. You kissed *me.*''

"No, I remember it distinctly. We were in the arbor

in your father's garden, and you pretended to get something in your eye."

"I did get something in my eye."

"You tipped up your face like so." To prove his point, he cupped her cheek in his hand and angled her face upward. "And you said—" he switched to a falsetto voice "—'Oh, good glory, Professor, I've something in my eye.' Remember how closely you made me look? 'Lean closer,' you kept saying. 'Lean closer.'"

His hand imparted a distinct warmth, one that spread through her with a swiftness that left a blush in its wake.

"And of course, you pretended you couldn't see a thing, so you kept leaning closer and closer," she said.

"Until we were so close."

"It was almost like an accident."

"But our mouths touched like so..." He brushed his lips across hers, not pausing, just brushing, teasing. "You tasted so good, Helena," he whispered, his breath going into her. "You tasted like cherries. Now do you remember? Do you?"

"No." Helpless, she could only breathe the word as she tried to lean into his kiss, his warmth. "No..."

He pulled back abruptly, sending her a self-satisfied grin. "Liar. You see. I thought you would remember it that way."

Her lips felt stung and swollen from his teasing. She resented him for that, for the flush of desire sweeping through her. Resented him for reminding her that she had long-buried needs, that he had once brought her to life with a touch of fire.

"We were talking about women's suffrage," she reminded him.

"We were talking about our first kiss. It really was

an outstanding kiss, wasn't it? Do you remember how my tongue—''

''No. I most assuredly do not remember that.'' She turned away, hugging herself across the middle.

''Of course you do.'' He came up behind her and stood close, so close. He didn't touch her but she could feel his nearness, his warm breath on the back of her neck. ''How could you forget the way my tongue explored? That was my favorite part, remember?'' The warm, whispery breath moved to the side of her neck and her ear. ''I flicked it in and out, ran it along the edge of your lips.''

She shuddered. ''You're disgusting.''

''You didn't think so at the time. You were pleasantly surprised. You weren't expecting a kiss like that.''

She pressed her teeth into her lower lip, stifling a gasp. ''I know what you're doing,'' she stated. ''It won't work, Michael.'' She turned to face him. Mistake. Their bodies brushed, her breasts to his chest, her thighs to his.

''Tell me,'' he said, his voice so low she had to strain to hear it. ''Tell me what I'm trying to do.'' As he spoke, he lightly traced the tip of his finger down the side of her neck, over the pulsing artery in her throat and down to her collarbone, finding the sensitive hollow at the base of her throat.

She looked him in the eye to prove he didn't intimidate her. ''You're trying to remind me of what we—how we—'' She paused, seeking a way to make their past seem incidental, irrelevant.

''How we what?'' As if by accident, his hands slipped downward, tracing the inward curve beneath her breasts. ''Go on.''

"You're trying to make me remember how unforgivably foolish we used to be," she forced out.

"If that was foolishness," he said just before he kissed her again, "then it is an underrated virtue."

Just for a moment, she let him. What harm could there be in one kiss? It was a good rationale, she thought. Let him kiss her this once. She would use this moment to prove to herself that there was no special magic in kissing him, no wild pleasure missing from her life.

But as his mouth sank deeper over hers, she forgot to think. She forgot that she didn't love him, didn't want him, didn't even like him. She forgot that she was supposed to be able to walk away from this kiss, secure in the knowledge that she could quite easily subsist without it for the rest of her life.

She forgot everything except...except the slow, hot slide of his lips over hers, the shape of his mouth that evoked so many memories, the berry taste of him awakening her senses and the deft invasion of his tongue and its little flickering motions, a tiny wicked lash that echoed the subtle, private pulsations of a passion she had never been able to forget.

What was she thinking? Her independence was dissolving in a puddle at her feet. She had no more resolve than a dish of mint jelly, and even less sense.

She had to do the impossible, had to free herself. Closing her hands into fists, she pushed against his chest. In spite of her efforts, she longed to lean her cheek into that familiar comfort, but finally, almost weeping with the effort, she pulled her mouth away from his. "No more," she said. "That's enough of this foolishness."

"I was right, wasn't I?" he remarked, smiling down at her as he gently pressed his thumb to her kiss-bruised lips. "It *is* underrated."

Fifteen

Something Michael had said was bothering her. It bothered her so much that she lay awake that night, mulling over his words. Finally, she knew she would not rest another moment until she found out what he'd meant. Tugging on a summer robe of cotton batiste, she lit a lantern. She tiptoed out of the house, traveling swiftly across the lawn, down the lane and past the field adjacent to the carriage house.

The full moon was a rose-colored pearl hovering over the lake. At this time of year, it was oversize, exaggerated, filling half the sky. Against its pinkish glow rose the distant lake island. Josephine had told her the tiny dot of land was known as Goat Island, as settlers long past used to take their goats to graze there in the summer. Now it was populated only by wild tall grasses and lacy-leafed trees that seemed inked against the moonlight.

By the time she reached his quarters in the carriage house, she was breathless and a little apprehensive. But she would not back down. She walked to the outside stairs, passing the bellpull at the bottom. It never occurred to her to announce herself.

"I need to ask you something," she said, pushing open the door and stepping inside. Shadowy shapes littered the cavernous loft. She could make out tables and a desk, and against one wall, a large bed, occupied at the moment with an untidy mound. The quarters smelled curiously of herbs and saddle soap. Thrusting the lantern forward, she said, "Michael?"

He woke with a start, shielding his eyes as he blinked against the glare of the lantern. "What the hell— Christ, Helena, is something wrong?"

"No. Actually, yes."

"What is it? Yes or no?" He sat up in bed, the rumpled sheets pooling around his waist, lamplight streaming over his torso. He looked like a fallen god, sitting there, blinking and rubbing his hand over his stubbled jaw. His chest was shaped by firm muscles, and its pattern of dark hair seemed somehow even more fascinating to her now than it had been years ago.

She paused for a moment, hopelessly flustered. He slept naked. She should have remembered that. He had less personal modesty than Walt Whitman, whose forbidden poems her sister used to read in a whisper late at night, when they were supposed to be asleep. That had been one of the many delicious discoveries she'd made back when she was falling in love with him. He advocated a natural state of man, and he made her want to adopt the habit—not that she'd ever dare, of course.

The sight of Michael's naked body as he rose from the bed made her skin heat, and her mouth went dry. She quickly doused the lantern, but the moonlight was enough. One glance confirmed her suspicions. Yes, she definitely should have remembered this habit of his.

A second glance confirmed another concern.

"Darling, your attention is flattering indeed," he said with a wicked grin, following her gaze.

Her cheeks flamed and she turned sharply away. "You are the most rude, shocking man I have ever met."

"Oh, really? Seems to me Troy Barnes was a lot more rude than I." Bitterness edged his words, and Helena knew that just because he'd procured the annulment didn't mean he'd forgiven her for her deception. He went to the washstand and took a drink of water straight out of the pitcher. A slant of moonlight streamed in through the open window, creating a long, fluid shadow of movement. He offered her a swig, wordlessly tipping the crockery pitcher toward her.

She shook her head and kept her eyes averted. "Would you mind covering yourself?"

"What if I said I would mind?"

"I'd ask you to, anyway."

"Look, you're the one who came barging in here."

She could not keep from stealing glances out of the corner of her eye. Strong legs, slim hips, broad chest. *Heavens.* "Fine," she said, half drowning in desires she had no business feeling. "I'll barge right back out." She turned toward the door.

"Give me a moment." Grumbling, he shuffled around in the dark, found an ancient robe. Then he took his time slipping on the loose garment, using a piece of baling twine to tie it around his waist.

She waited, looking everywhere but at him. His living quarters appeared to be a mismatched collection of odd furnishings, equipment, books and papers. It was as disorderly as his house had been in Georgetown, as disorderly as the man himself.

"Now," he said, motioning her inside. "What's the trouble?"

She edged into the room. "It's something you said earlier."

"I said a lot of things earlier. I did an excellent job describing the way we used to kiss, didn't I? Would you like another demonstration?"

"It's about William," she broke in. "You said you didn't pursue the annulment to earn my gratitude but for the sake of William. What did you mean by that?"

His gaze tracked her as she paced back and forth. "How much coffee did you drink after supper tonight? It's made you a little nervous."

"I am always nervous when it comes to my son," she admitted, stopping to lean against the back of a wooden chair. "What did you mean, for the sake of William?"

"I mean for him to be safe. Troy Barnes beat you in a fit of rage. Who's to say William wouldn't be his next victim?"

"I thought the same thing," she said, relieved to know he didn't have a more complicated motive. "That is why I wasted no time in leaving the house in Vandam Square." She marshaled her nerve and asked the real question that had kept her from sleep. "Just what are your intentions when it comes to William?"

"He's my son. That's what I want, Helena. I want my son. I want to be his father."

Oh, those words. They set her heart on fire, and just for a moment, she savored the very sound of them. What a rarity to hear a man declaring his firm commitment in plain terms. Nearly every man she'd ever met would readily say he wanted children, but those who actually wanted to be fathers... She had never known one. Not even her own.

"You never gave me that chance," he said.

She flinched. "Just remember, you walked away from me, not the other way around."

"Well," he said, crossing his arms and rocking back on his heels. "In that case, I have good news for you. I'm walking back into your life."

Helena laughed, though she felt like weeping in frustration. "You have unfortunate timing, Michael. I don't want you back."

"That's a lie. I remember what you said that day in Georgetown, the day I left. You said—"

"I did love you once. I loved you with all that I was, gave you all that I had of my heart." She smiled wistfully. "It was such a wonderful, exhilarating way to feel. As though I had just drunk a glass of the finest champagne. But perhaps that first girlish flush of love is indeed like drinking champagne. The effect wears off, and all you're left with is a headache."

"What makes you think I didn't love you, Helena?"

"Because you didn't stay."

"Look, we both made some poor choices. Now we have a chance to change that. To make things right."

"Exactly. That's just what I'm doing, Michael. Before now, it never occurred to me that I could live on my own."

"I'm not taking that away from you," he said. "I simply want to be a part of William's life. The boy needs a father."

"He's had a father. And a fat lot of good that's done him."

"Barnes was no father. He was never even worthy of the name. He claimed William for his own because it made him look like a family man, and voters like that." She wondered at the note of intensity in his voice. His manner was curiously measured, as though he were holding something back. She forbade herself to probe further. She had no business getting herself or her son involved with this man. And yet…

She wished she could run from the rush of doubts chasing her. William had always been heartbreakingly hungry for a father. Even when he was tiny, William used to follow Troy around, vying for his attention, his approval. As time went on, her son grew more tentative and cautious. He lowered his expectations, somehow aware that it was better not to hope for too much. She felt grateful that he had never experienced the violent side of Troy, yet at the same time, she wondered what sort of person her son was becoming. Could she give him everything he needed in order to be happy and fulfilled? Or would he always carry around that gnawing sense of emptiness, the feeling that a vital piece of his heart was missing?

Reflecting on her own life, she acknowledged that some things could never be remedied. The lack of a mother had defined her, and she had found no substitute. What would define William? The lack of a father? The difference was, she could never see her mother again. William had a father right here. If she chose to let him into their lives.

What would she have sacrificed for a chance to have her mother reappear, seemingly out of the blue?

"Just what is it you're offering, Michael? One summer of adventure? Companionship until Christmas? I'm not going to let you into his life only to have you abandon him when you get an offer that's more interesting than your current position."

He closed the distance between them, caught her shoulders between his hands. "How about letting me answer the question?"

"Only if you tell me the truth."

"I'm not offering a temporary arrangement. I want

William to know I'm his father, and I want him to know it's forever."

No. He had abandoned her once, and she had barely survived the pain. She couldn't risk inflicting that sort of heartache on her son. "Why should I trust that? Why should William? The man he thought of as a father never had time for him. How will you be different?"

"For one thing, I won't beat his mother."

She pulled away. "You know what I mean. My son has known indifference, and I can tell you, it was not satisfactory. But at least it was consistent."

"He's my son, too. Just because you withheld that information from us doesn't make him any less so."

"Very well. Let's assume we decide to explain this to William. Suppose we tell him that he is your son, and that his mother erroneously thought she was married to another man, who believed he'd fathered the boy. How can William begin to understand, Michael?" She twisted her hands in anguish. "This is my doing. I admit it. I started this deception. But introducing you now will only confuse him."

He captured her nervous hands. "I'll win his trust."

"How?"

"I'll find a way. When shall we tell him?"

"We will not," she said, extracting her hands from his. "Not for a good while. Let's let him get used to the idea that Troy is no longer part of his life. That the old man on Oak Hill, whom he thought of as his grandfather, is not his grandfather. That the house in Vandam Square will never again be the place that he lives."

"Helena, I want him to know who I am. He deserves to know. I deserve for him to know."

"And what about what I deserve? A chance to live a peaceful life, on my own terms."

"I'm not disputing that."

Every instinct she possessed disputed that. Was it possible to surrender William without surrendering herself? "He's a little boy. How can we expect him to understand what happened?"

"He doesn't need to understand the past, only that from now on, I'm his father."

"But you're not married to his mother."

"Then—"

"Don't even think it. I've barely survived one marriage." She searched his face, shadowed by midnight and moonlight and secrets. "All right. We'll tell him someday."

"When? Tonight? Tomorrow?"

"No. I need time to get used to the idea. And so do you."

"I've had time enough. I'm ready."

"William is not," she stated. "He's not a student who will pass through your life in a year. Nor is he a mouse in a maze, to be controlled and studied and monitored on a chart. He's a boy, and despite all that's happened to him, he still understands that a father is supposed to be a father forever. So I won't let you reveal yourself, lavish attention on him until the novelty wears off and then move on to your next laboratory or project or research center."

"Why do you assume I would do that?"

"When have you ever done otherwise?"

"Damn it, Helena, he's eight years old." He stared deep into her eyes. "I have a lot of work to do. I have a lot to make up for."

She stared back, trying, as she had many times in the past, to understand him. She often felt pangs of curiosity about Michael, and this moment was no different. What had made him the man he was, a man who would abandon a woman, then pursue his son with such passion?

She didn't know how to ask him, so she simply went to the door. "You claim you intend to be around forever. So that should mean you have plenty of patience."

"I think you'll find I'm a very patient man." Before she could step out of range, he drew his hand down her arm in a frankly sensual caress. "Is that all you came here for tonight?"

"Yes, it was bothering me."

"Something else is bothering me now." He glanced down. "What are we going to do about this?"

She sniffed with disdain, hiding her shock. "Whatever you've done for the past nine years."

His low, rough laughter reached across the room to her. Then he followed in the wake of the sound, his close presence nearly overwhelming her. "Sweetheart, you don't want to know."

He probably had other women, dozens of them at his beck and call. Women had always been drawn to his unconventional, eccentric ways, his unexpected sweetness, his brilliant mind, his unapologetic sensuality.

She turned to leave, but he stood in the door frame with his arm braced across the exit. He grinned down at her. "It seems a shame to waste a perfectly good—"

"Trust me, Professor," she broke in, furious at finding herself in this awkward position, although she had no one but her foolish self to blame. "There is no shame at all in wasting it."

Sixteen

In August, the temperature soared above ninety and the population of Saratoga Springs swelled to fifty thousand. Racing season had arrived at last, and the excitement in the air was palpable. Anticipation wafted through Broadway and Congress Streets along with the aroma of roasting corn and summer roses. A delicious tension seemed to grip everyone in town, from newly arrived tourists to longtime residents. When the stakes were high and the outcome uncertain, people saw and heard and sensed things with a heightened awareness.

Helena found herself too preoccupied with practical concerns to greet the peak of the season with anything more than a passing interest. "Daisy," she called out, coming into the kitchen. "There's something the matter with the steam boiler. It's not producing enough hot water."

"You think I know about steam boilers?" Daisy extracted a pan of perfect, golden-brown cornbread from the oven.

At the sideboard, Sarah Dalton was honing a sharp edge on a large kitchen knife. "I doubt any of us does.

What about your friend Professor Rowan? He seems awfully good at fixing things."

Hiding a blush, Helena wrapped a tea towel around the hot iron skillet of delicious-smelling bread. "What makes you say that?"

"He's been so helpful around the place, fixing up that old carriage house, looking after William's poor horse. Did you know he created an irrigation system for the kitchen garden?" Sarah followed her to the dining hall.

"He does have his uses," said Nellie, folding back her newspaper.

Helena took her usual seat at the breakfast table. The sunny dining room had become their gathering place each morning. When she'd first come here, the endless heavy table, with seating for sixteen, had seemed ludicrously large. Now, however, she could imagine filling each chair. But the plumbing had become a problem.

"We must do something about the bathing situation," she stated, opening her napkin with a flourish. "With seven of us living here, it's impossible to have enough hot water."

"You should tap into the hot spring," Josephine said matter-of-factly.

"Ain't no such thing as a spring that's hot," said Daisy. "Not in these parts, anyway."

"So you say." Josephine shrugged and concentrated on her breakfast. She and Daisy tolerated each other well enough, but didn't pretend to understand one another. However, they had settled into a productive relationship. Josephine had a great affinity for blackberry jam, and she brought abundant quantities of the wild berries to Daisy for putting up into jars.

Alice sent her a teasing smile. "Honestly, a hot

spring. Everyone knows Saratoga water is fifty degrees Fahrenheit, year 'round."

"You should tube the warm spring, then," Josephine insisted.

"Uh-huh." Daisy rolled her eyes and set the big enameled pot on an iron trivet on the table. "Coffee's ready. And I had to heat the water on the stove, like everybody else in town."

"Perhaps Jo knows something we don't," Sarah said, using the knife to cut the hot cornbread into wedges. With dainty precision, she served everyone, making certain each slice was centered just so on the plate.

Helena watched her thoughtfully, her mind straying from the problem of the water. Of all the women at Moon Lake Lodge, Sarah was the least contented. She was getting lonely and restless; Helena could hear her crying at night.

"Where has William gone?" asked Alice.

"The professor took him fishing early this morning." Nellie murmured the answer from behind her paper.

Helena picked up her cup and took a sip of coffee. She had not decided what to do about Michael's vow to be a father to William. How could she allow it? And how could she forbid it? She could not deny her pleasure in seeing William tag along after the tall, unkempt man, emulating his gestures, even his speech. Yet neither could she quell her apprehension about Michael. She didn't trust him to be careful with William. She feared he would break her son's heart and leave her to pick up the pieces.

Or should she give him a chance? She had changed so much from that self-centered young woman who had married so impetuously and so unwisely. Could Michael have changed, too?

Whether he had or not, she knew she must be cautious. There was something more to Michael's insistence on getting to know his son, something he hadn't spoken of aloud, yet it was a palpable force in the air between them every time they were together. It created an inner turmoil that gave her no rest. He claimed he wanted to be with William, yet the way he'd kissed her proved he expected much more than that.

"Are you all right?" Alice asked. "You look quite flushed, Helena."

She blotted her cheeks with her napkin. "I can't believe it's the first of August already. It seems like any other day to me. In past years, there was so much to do—dinners, dances, opera shows, concerts. The parties were absolutely endless. I used to change my clothes six times some days because I had six different engagements to attend."

Alice sighed. "It must have been heavenly."

"I suppose I did enjoy some aspects of it," Helena admitted. "But it wasn't always fun. So often you'd have to make polite conversation with tiresome people who care nothing for you and for whom you care nothing. And I was never fond of gambling, although some people seemed quite excited by it."

"You must miss so many aspects of your old life," Sarah declared. "Your house in Vandam Square is the most beautiful in town, yet here you are in this rambling old lodge."

Her wistful certainty that a life of luxury was worth any price bothered Helena. "I'm grateful to be here," she said, looking around the table at the five women. "For one reason or another, we all ended up at Moon Lake Lodge. I believe there's a reason for that. It's a reason that is larger than any of us, and we should be able to speak freely here."

"I thought that was what we were doing," said Alice.

"True." Helena gazed at the array of faces that had grown so dear to her, so quickly. Just the sight of them filled her with hope. She adored these impromptu meetings, which had started of their own accord but had become a regular part of their routine. She loved being among women who cared about the things that were in each other's hearts. "I've never had a true confidante," she confessed. "After my sister married and moved away, I had no proper friends."

"How can that be?" Sarah looked confused. "You're the most popular hostess in Saratoga Springs. Everybody loves you. You have as many friends as flowers in your garden."

"For a long time, I believed that. But where are they now?" She thought of the young mothers in the park, shepherding their sons away from William. "Now that I've created a scandal and they can no longer win favors from my husband or my father, where have they gone? Are they sharing a cup of coffee with me, listening to my troubles, my hopes, my dreams? No, they're all getting fitted for dressy gowns and trying to figure out a way to approach Mrs. Vanderbilt at the Grace Ball tonight, or how to finagle an introduction to the Crown Prince of Prussia at the Union Hotel Musicale. That's not friendship. That's convenience. I foolishly confused the two things for quite a number of years."

Nellie glanced up from her crossword puzzle. Ever since she'd mentioned that she enjoyed Mr. Dobbs's Crossword Daily from New York City, a fresh copy mysteriously appeared each day on the doorstep. It was an offering from Michael, who could probably ill afford it, yet would never forget that she was the one who had freed him from jail. "I take it you're no longer confused."

"Exactly. I want this friendship to matter to us all. We are together for a reason. It can't just be happenstance that Daisy came to work for me, or that I met you and Alice at Dr. Hillendahl's, or that Sarah and Josephine came to us in their hour of need. Moon Lake Lodge will always be a haven, a sanctuary, our own safe place. I had a husband all the world admired and respected. And he beat me," she stated boldly. "But because the world admired and respected him, I didn't dare tell anyone. I kept the bruises hidden and my pain inside. Being here with you makes me realize I should have dared." She looked directly at Sarah, who was so prim and proper in her frilled dimity dress, demurely buttoned at the neck and wrists. "The first time he hit me, I was utterly confused, so much so that I felt certain there was some mistake. This man could not have done such a thing. But I had the wounds to prove it. Perhaps I blamed myself. I lay awake wondering what I'd done wrong. The second time he hit me, I knew my own mind. I knew no woman should have to endure that. Ever."

"But my situation is so different," Sarah objected. "Grady will change. I know he will." Her face softened with a smile, and in the morning sunlight, her bruises looked almost beautiful, the colors of a rainbow. "He is always so sweet once he sobers up. He buys me presents, and holds me through the night." She looked at Helena with eyes filled with wistfulness. "So you see, the situation is quite different. Our marriage is not perfect, but I made a vow and I intend to keep it."

"Ain't nothing perfect about what he done that other night," Daisy said. "You got your rights."

"I have the right to love my husband," Sarah said.

"But you're afraid of him, or you wouldn't be here," Nellie softly pointed out.

"This is temporary. I told you, Grady comes from a family where harsh discipline is practiced. It's in his blood. His father was a strict disciplinarian, and apparently his brother is, too. He's prone to dark spells and has a weakness for the drink, but he's a fine man who will change if I show him enough love and patience."

Josephine, the youngest and most unabashedly blunt of the group, snorted with derision.

"Honey, the Lord didn't put you here to reform a bad man," Daisy said. "That ain't your job, and besides, it can't be done."

"Grady will get better. I'm sure by now he's already calmed down so much, and hardly drinks at all anymore. He's close to stopping altogether. It would be disloyal of me to turn my back on him after all the effort he's made." Her utter conviction was made more powerful by the tremulous, fragile smile that curved her mouth. She helped herself to a piece of cornbread and let the steam escape. "I've never wanted anyone but Grady all my life. Have you ever had a dream that strong?"

The plaintive question touched Helena in a sensitive spot. "What woman doesn't dream?" she asked, staring down at the patterned oilcloth covering the table.

"You said that right," Daisy assured her. "Dreams is all I got sometimes."

Sarah's smile deepened. "What do you dream about?"

"I dream about voting in the next election," said Nellie.

"Me, I dream lots of things," Daisy said, leaning forward as she warmed to the topic. "Everything. I wish I could go to a Gospel Sunday, like the ones they have back in Virginia. I wish I had a bunch of yellow silk daffodils to put on my straw bonnet." Daisy slid the half-finished crossword puzzle in front of her. "I wish I could read the paper every morning."

Josephine wrinkled her nose. "Reading's a lot of fuss and bother."

"Not everyone believes that," Nellie said. "Reading set me free—quite literally. I was destined for a life of millwork in Five Points, on Manhattan. Imagine standing at a machine loom, in an unheated factory twelve hours at a stretch, turning out clothes for women who wouldn't give you the time of day if you asked them at high noon. All the girls from my tenement either turned to factory work or to prostitution. Those were the only choices available to a girl with no family, no money, no prospects. So I taught myself to read to keep from dying."

Nellie made sure she had everyone's attention. "I was a little older than William, perhaps ten or eleven, the year of a terrible blizzard. People froze to death in their apartments when they ran out of fuel. I was a little mite of a thing, and I knew how to make myself scarce. I slipped into a building through a basement window and warmed myself by the big central furnace. Eventually I got bored and wandered through the building. It was filled with books, more books than I had ever imagined."

Sarah clasped her hands. "You sneaked into a library."

"Indeed I did. And not just any library. It was the law library of Columbia."

"No wonder you're such a gifted lawyer," Helena said in admiration. "You taught yourself to read the law."

"For all the good it's done," Nellie said, shaking her head. "I swear, the laws against women voting are just as oppressive now as they were when I went to the convention in Seneca Falls." With a mysterious smile, she pointed to the old illustrated calendar on the wall. "Did I ever tell you about that picture?"

"I found it in the house when we first came here," said Helena.

"But did you ever really look at it?" An odd, appealing mischief gleamed in her eye.

Alice Wilkes jumped up and went to study the calendar illustration. "I'd hardly call it fine art, but..." She stopped, leaned toward the picture, looked back at Nellie, then at the picture again. "The caption identifies the ladies—Lucretia Mott, Elizabeth Cady Stanton, Margaret Pryor, Experience Gibbs, Eunice Newton Foote... Why, look at this one. Eleanor Freeman." With a smile of delight, she pointed out a petite woman with large eyes and a generous mouth, wearing a bonnet with a feather and bloomers prominently displayed beneath the hem of her dress. "That's our Nellie!"

Murmuring sounds of amazement, the others moved in to have a closer look.

"I was wondering if someone would notice. It's not a very good likeness, is it?" said Nellie. "The engraving depicts our roll call of honor, when the Declaration of Sentiments was signed."

"What sentiments were declared?" Sarah asked.

"Oh, a number of things. That all men and women

are created equal—that one is my favorite. My, my, could it be nearly fifty years ago? Lordy, but that brings back memories."

"Nellie, that's just marvelous," Helena said. "What other great achievements are you concealing from us?"

Nellie patted her hand. "I survived a thirty-year marriage with Blanton McQuigg. Does that count?"

Helena stared at her in amazement, then reached out and took her hands. They were marked by the knobs and blotches of age, and they contained a curious strength. She wore no wedding ring. "Good glory, did he beat you?"

"No, but he nearly bored me to death." She patted Helena's hand and helped herself to more coffee.

"We should have read the fine print long ago," Alice said, paging through the old calendar.

Helena almost spoke up then. I want to learn to read, too. Let me finally learn. But she disappointed herself bitterly by staying silent.

What was wrong with her? How was it that she could tell these women her husband beat her, yet she could not bring herself to admit she had never learned to read? Perhaps because the violence was not her fault. Unlike Sarah Dalton, Helena was very clear on this point. Yet in the matter of the reading, she was not so certain. As a girl, she had willfully avoided schoolwork. It was something of a game to find ways to get out of reading and writing. She had a headache; she hurt her hand while sewing. Her excuses were as numerous as the marriage proposals that began to arrive as soon as she reached her majority.

Foreign princes, war heroes, millionaires—she'd had her chance with all of them, and her failure to read had never mattered. There had even been the odd moment in time when a marriage with Boyd Butler, the vice president's son, had been an option. But no. Her heart would have none of them because she remained true to the only man she had ever loved—Michael Rowan. From the first moment she met him, he had been the cause of both her deepest joy and her greatest heartbreak.

Yet now, surrounded by friends she held dearer than her own life, she made herself face the past. Michael had abandoned her, true enough. But she was just as much at fault. She had let him go. It would have been a simple matter to send for him, but she hadn't allowed herself that indulgence. Because she knew that, unlike other men, Michael would find out. He didn't desire or admire her because she was a senator's daughter. He didn't regard her as a prize to be won. He actually paid attention to her.

She shut her eyes, thinking of William, reading on his own by the age of four, learning things from newspapers and books because his mother never taught him. And she recalled that, after Troy attacked her, she had wanted to confess everything to her sister in a letter. All her life she'd dictated her correspondence to a scribe or secretary or public letter writer. She couldn't bring herself to do that with this matter. Never had she felt so crippled, so boxed in by her inability.

Yet holding in the truth had caused her nothing but trouble. It was time to try a different way. She took a deep breath and forced herself to look into Nellie's compassionate eyes. And then she heard herself say, "I never learned to read and write, either."

Nellie cocked her head to one side as though she'd misheard. "What?"

"I cannot read. Only my sister knows that about me," she said. "And now you." There. She'd stated the truth. This was the first time she had ever said it aloud. And the world didn't come to an end. Amazing.

Alice gaped in disbelief. "How can that be? You're a great lady, a senator's daughter."

Helena's face burned with shame. "I find it as shocking as you do. For a woman of my background, who had all the advantages my father gave me, it's unthinkable. In Georgetown, I attended all the best schools. I even had private tutors and governesses. And still I managed to grow up never knowing how to read or write. What came so naturally to my younger sister was impossible for me, and eventually, I stopped trying. If I struggle, I can decipher a few words in plain print. I can draw the letters of my name, but that is the extent of my abilities."

"That's quite extraordinary," Nellie said. "To go through life without reading is an amazing accomplishment. You must be very resourceful, my dear."

Helena frowned. "Believe me, I never thought of it in quite that way."

"It takes incredible skill to find a way around reading and writing. Because you see, reading and writing actually make things easier."

"I do wish I could learn," Helena said in a painful rush of honesty. "I wish it so desperately."

"How hard have you tried?" Nellie asked.

She stared at her lap. "The fact is, by the time reading became important to me, I was old enough to be ashamed of myself. So I never asked for help." She lifted her gaze to Nellie. "I guess I'm asking now."

"Good," said Nellie. "It would be an honor to help both you and our dear Daisy. Let us work together for one hour every evening after supper, shall we? You'll be reading in no time."

"How about now?" Alice pulled aside the curtain.

"Isn't that man wearing a Western Union Company uniform?"

Even before she opened the door for the messenger, Helena knew it couldn't be good news. Before her confession, she would have been resigned to the task of sitting up late into the night, struggling over the printed words. But now, the ladies of Moon Lake Lodge knew.

Nellie read the telegram with a deep frown of concern followed by a snort of disgust.

"What is it about?" Helena asked, pacing in agitation.

Everyone sat forward, holding a collective breath.

Nellie smoothed the onionskin paper on the table. "Troy Barnes has gone to the capital and laid claim to your inheritance from your father."

Dear God. She had dreaded this. Without her inheritance, she faced—they all faced—an uncertain future.

She held the edge of the table as she sat back down, like an old woman with aching bones. "Do you think he'll succeed?"

"The estate was left to a Helena Cabot Barnes. He claims it in the name of a wife who no longer exists for him since the annulment."

"Oh, Troy." Helena couldn't help herself. She laughed until the tears came, clutching her middle and bending forward. The women looked at her as though she'd lost her mind, and she forced herself to sober up. "What on earth shall we do?" she asked her friends. "The place is still a wreck. The plumbing is a disaster. We need a miracle."

"We need more than a miracle," Daisy pointed out. "We need money. We already sold your jewels and such to get us this far."

She thought tantalizingly of the fortune in possessions at Vandam Square. Did she dare?

No, she thought. She'd already caused William to be a child of scandal; she would not make him the son of a thief as well. Dabbing at her eyes with a napkin, she said, "Josephine, did you mean it when you said you'd discovered a thermal spring?"

"Which one?" asked Josephine.

"There's more than one?"

Seventeen

"Another summons, Helena?" Michael Rowan lounged in the front doorway of the house and inspected her from head to toe. She felt a blush of awareness just from the touch of his gaze, the look on his face.

"I didn't summon you," she said, resisting the urge to neaten her skirts, to pat a stray lock of hair in place. "I simply asked Josephine to invite you to meet with me about a matter of importance."

"Next time, send someone else. Things go missing when Josephine's around."

She ignored the comment. She knew he hadn't trusted the girl since that unfortunate first day, when poor Josephine had been so ill with the drink. As she studied his face, she wondered what he made of his own situation. He looked unhappy, and what man wouldn't be, jobless and without means? Although a brilliant scientist, Michael had no head for money. That had never bothered him before, though. His discontent seemed deeper than that.

"So what is it now?" His sarcasm bit at her. Things had not been easy between them since their dispute over William. Michael was furious at her refusal to declare him the boy's father, but she also suspected he was furious at her for not simply breaking down in gratitude and begging him to come back into her life. He wanted too much, expected too much, and she was of no mind to give it to him. Still, each night when sleep eluded her, thoughts of him overtook her, no matter how hard she tried to forget the way his arms felt around her, his lips settling over hers…

"Actually, I do need something, Michael."

"Excellent." He pushed out of his negligent pose in the doorway and sauntered into the foyer.

"You look absurd when you saunter," she said.

"You look absurd when you pretend you don't want me."

"Perhaps I do," she retorted. "Perhaps that's why I summoned you."

"In that case…" He crossed the room to her and gently took her in his arms.

Trying to ignore the rush of need that seemed to inundate her every time he touched her, she pressed her hands to his chest, holding him back. "Or perhaps not. I should be more careful in choosing my words."

He backed off, holding his hands palms out to prove he was harmless. "Very well, then. I'll do nothing but listen. Choose away."

"Excellent." She couldn't suppress a grin. "I have had the most brilliant and marvelous idea, and I need your help."

His eyes narrowed in suspicion. "What sort of help?"

She clasped her hands. "We're going to dig a well."

A short laugh escaped him. "I've come down in the world. From your lover and the father of your child to ditch digger."

She resisted the urge to take the bait, forcing herself to stick to the topic at hand. "You know it's not that simple. This will be a very special sort of well."

"Drilling is not my area of expertise."

"I will be plain with you, Michael. I am in dire straits. Remember, I was awaiting news of the legacy from my father. Well, it appears that Troy has laid claim to it. I cannot afford to pay an excavation company to come out and tube the new spring. No one in town will extend me credit." She paced back and forth in the foyer. "I've never been poor before. I don't know how it's done."

"Oh, sweetheart. You want to know what poor is? You came to the right place."

She glanced at him sharply. "You've always lived as a scholar. That's different from abject poverty."

"Always, Helena?"

"Didn't you?"

"It's a long story, and it would bore you senseless. Tell me more about this well. Did the current one run dry?"

"No. We're going to find a very special spring."

"In case you haven't noticed, carbonate springs are as common as dahlias in these parts. But finding water is more than a matter of digging a hole."

She clasped her hands over her heart, which felt light enough to float away. "I know that. And I have the most wondrous discovery to report. It's about Josephine."

"What about Josephine? She smokes and spits and swears and would probably sell her eyeteeth for a bottle of whiskey."

"She has a hidden talent."

"What's that? Picking pockets?"

"Oh, leave go of that, Michael. You mustn't judge

her by that unfortunate first impression. She truly does have a hidden talent. You must come and see."

Though she resented his skepticism, she wasn't surprised by it. He was a man of learning, and the miraculous discovery Josephine had made could not be explained by science. She led him outside and they walked together along the path that headed upward from the lakeshore. At summer's highest, hottest point, the garden was alive with butterflies and hummingbirds and bursting blossoms of sunflower, hollyhock and delphinium. The neglected garden, choked by weeds and battered by harsh weather, was a wonder in its own way. Although no one had cultivated the flowers for ages, the perennials kept coming back, and she imagined they were sturdier and more numerous each summer.

The pathway traversed a slope and led to a wooded area. Lush-leafed firs, hemlocks and maples surrounded the ancient, heaved-up rock formations characteristic of the area.

"Almost there," she said. "Isn't it marvelous the way things turned out?"

"How is it marvelous?"

She narrowed her eyes. Was he amused at her? By her? Should she be offended by his amusement?

"Well, Jo simply came running blindly to Moon Lake Lodge—"

"She came," he reminded her, "to burgle the carriage house."

"And she hadn't a prayer in the world for a decent life," Helena continued, ignoring his comment, "and now all of a sudden she's finding water for us."

"This is Saratoga Springs, Helena," he said. "Finding water is no great feat."

"Moon Lake Lodge has a much richer treasure than

a plain carbonate spring. You'll see.'' The path grew rocky, and the hem of her skirt snagged on a tree root. She stumbled, but he was there, his steadying hand keeping her from falling. She clung to his arm, then realized what she was doing and let go.

She spied Josephine in the clearing the girl had shown her earlier in the day, and waved at her. ''I've brought the Professor to see your wondrous discovery.'' She spread her arms to encompass the wooded area. It was a lovely natural clearing, idyllic in its sylvan beauty. The lush woods formed a natural backdrop to an imposing rock formation. The deeply gouged and creviced sandstone bloomed with wild blueberries, moss, lichen and elderberry trees with roots grasping at the rock. Sunlight dappled the forest floor, illuminating a carpet of moss, low-growing ferns and tiny white flowers shaped like snowflakes.

''What do you think?'' she asked Michael.

''It's a pile of rocks.''

''That's all most people see, isn't it? But there's a secret. There's a powerful hot spring right under there, and I intend to tap into it.''

''A hot spring? There's no such thing in these parts.''

''Of course there is. Josephine says so.''

He walked in a slow circle around the layered, slanting rocks. ''And you found this...how?''

''Jo found it.'' Helena looked left and right, though she knew there couldn't be anyone around, and motioned the girl toward her. ''Show him, Josephine.''

The girl came forth with her obsidian pendulum suspended from a length of supple leather. The bit of black stone was carved into the shape of an arrow, its tip pointing downward.

Michael shook his head. ''So she's a diviner.''

"Indeed she is. She's very skilled, aren't you, Josephine?"

"Never been wrong yet," she said. "I can tell you just where to drill."

Michael paced back and forth, clearly exasperated. "Look, anyone with a rudimentary understanding of science can tell you that finding water is a matter of physics and geology, not some strange, intuitive mysticism."

Helena elbowed him and lowered her voice. "Now, you be nice to her."

"That's not part of the deal."

"It is, too."

"We don't even have a deal."

"Yes, we do, and the deal is that you are going to be civil to everyone at Moon Lake Lodge, including Jo."

He jutted out his chin. "I'm always civil."

"Honestly, sometimes you're just like—" She stopped herself. The resemblance between him and William was quite uncanny, but it wouldn't help her cause to point that out. "Anyway, Josephine feels things beyond the senses. She has found a thermal spring, and I intend to tap into it, with or without your help."

"Some people think it's nonsense."

"Some think it's magic. I would rather believe in magic than in nonsense, wouldn't you?"

"Mama!" William's voice rang through the woods. Then, like a fast-moving sprite, he ran into the clearing, Daisy close at his heels. "Oh, hello, Professor. When do we start, Mama? Daisy said very soon." Making strange, mechanical noises with his mouth, he ran in a circle around the spot where Jo had discovered the hidden spring.

"Well?" Daisy asked, looking from Helena to Michael.

"He's agreed to do it," Helena said brightly, praying she'd read him correctly.

"At least he's good for something," Jo muttered.

"Hurrah!" William jumped into the air, then started running in circles around Michael, who put out his hands and swung him around. "I'll help you lots, won't I?" William said.

Michael grinned at him. "I'm counting on it."

Helena felt a pang of apprehension. Was she letting the fox guard the henhouse here?

The day would come when she would have to reveal to William that Michael was his natural father. Her son had already lost Troy, such as he was. Even losing a negligent, indifferent father had affected the boy in subtle ways. She did not want him to get attached to Michael only to have Michael leave, too.

"Jo was just going to explain about the spring," she said.

"It's a mineral spring," said Josephine, "but different from most around here. It's only about seventy-five feet down, I reckon."

"Down where?"

Watching the arc of her pendulum, she indicated a narrow, shadowy crevice in the rock.

"In seventy-five feet of solid rock?" Michael asked incredulously.

"Yes."

"And you have proof that the spring exists?"

"You'll prove it when you find it," she stated.

"What if I don't find it?"

"You'll find it."

William tugged at Helena's skirt, drawing her aside.

"How come Jo and the Professor are always fussing at each other?"

"I suppose because they constantly disagree about certain things."

"Oh. Like you and Father used to."

Her stomach twisted. "What do you mean?" She lowered her voice. "We never fussed."

"You were always cross with each other. You always made a cross face, like this." He arranged his small features in a stiff, somber expression with a wrinkled brow and the corners of his mouth turned down.

"Have I made a cross face lately?"

"No."

"I'll try to remember that you don't like it."

Alice and Sarah had walked up from the lodge and were standing nearby. Jo and Michael were crouched by the tower of rocks, glaring at each other.

"Don't you smell it?" she demanded.

"Of course I don't smell it. If, as you say, it's seventy-five feet down, how would I smell it?"

"With your nose, fool. This spring is going to be the strongest and richest in all Saratoga Springs. And it's warm. I just know it."

"What do you mean, warm?"

She glared at him, visibly losing patience. "The water'll come out hot."

He burst out laughing. "You're actually quite entertaining, Josephine."

"It's a warm spring. I know it," she stated.

"In the Good Book, it says 'Take the rod...and speak ye unto the rock...and it shall give forth water,'" Sarah pointed out, her awed gaze following the pendulum. "Perhaps Josephine has a gift."

Helena looked at their eager expressions and felt the

weight of the trust they put in this new enterprise. Their faces were like blossoms in the summer garden—bright, turned upward, filled with hopes and dreams. Had she ever looked like that? she wondered. Would she ever look like that again?

"'Thou shalt smite the rock,'" Sarah intoned, "'and there shall come water out of it, that the people may drink.'"

"That's lovely," said Helena. "Let's get started."

"There are a few minor details," he said.

"And what would they be?"

"We need a deep-rock drill for boring. And a steam-powered pump."

"Then we should procure them at once."

"Fine. You come up with the equipment, and I'll get started."

His skeptical look infuriated her. He clearly didn't believe she would be able to find such a thing. Ah, but she most certainly could. The question was, did she dare ask for it?

Since coming to Saratoga as a new bride, Helena had always been faintly afraid of Adam Barnes. The years had not been kind to Troy's father, and he suffered from a host of ailments. Sometimes Helena believed that chief among them was a bad temper, but she had always treated him with respect. Even in his twilight years, he took an active role in cultivating his dynasty of prosperity, first in banking and finally in the coin of the realm—carbonation. Despite his infirmities, Adam was widely admired for still going to the Barnes Bottling Plant every day of the year. He was a decidedly unpleasant old man, but he had something she wanted.

She brought William along because her son was the

sole joy of the old man's life. She had, of course, considered the terrifying possibility that his love for the boy had turned to hatred the moment he'd heard the town gossip—which he undoubtedly had—but Helena had learned to trust her instincts. And Lord only knew why, but Adam had always shown respect and admiration for her.

Hand in hand with William, she stood on the wide Saratoga porch between two six-foot palms in alabaster pots and drew on the bellpull.

A weary-looking maid brought them to the formal parlor. "Hello, Grandfather," William said, showing his usual wide-eyed fascination for the ornate room. Adam had an affinity for unusual clocks, and William adored them. Remembering his manners, he went and stood before the venerable wing-backed chair where his grandfather sat. "How do you do, sir."

The spare, rugged face creased into a smile only William could coax from him. "Very well, thank you. And aren't you looking strong and tall."

"Mama made me wear shoes today."

"She did? Well, I'm honored." Grasping both canes, he prepared to get up.

"Please, do keep your seat." Helena drew a tapestried ottoman next to his chair and sat down, holding her reticule in her lap. A maid arrived with a plate of shortbread and tea.

It made Helena's heart ache to see Adam, surrounded by his fine things, waited on by an army of servants, but at the same time as sick and lonely and friendless as a drifter at the train station. He enjoyed a level of prosperity most men only dreamed of, but he'd paid a high personal price for his good fortune in business. His wife had suffered a tragic accident, falling down a flight of stairs and afterward, lying senseless in the front bedroom of the Oak Hill mansion. Neither Troy nor Adam ever spoke of her, and Helena learned not to ask.

His life should have been an American fairy tale. Instead, it turned into a Gothic nightmare. This was the dark side of prosperity. Was it, she wondered, the hidden cost of not living an authentic life?

Adam Barnes seemed fascinated by William, drawn to him as though by a powerful nostalgia. William went to examine his favorite clock, one from Germany with little carved soldiers that marched in formation every hour.

"I bet I can tell how they know when it's time to come out," William said. With one finger, he unlatched the back to expose the workings.

"William, you mustn't touch," Helena said.

"It's fine. Let him look."

"Just like your father, you are," he remarked with an almost-fond chuckle. "A regular firecracker, he was, always asking questions, always making things."

It didn't sound in the least like Troy, and surely Adam had heard the gossip by now, but Helena said nothing. Her purpose in coming here was to discuss Moon Lake Lodge.

"Sir," she said, "I would like to lease some equipment from you." She pushed a printed document across the table at him. Nellie had stayed up late last night, creating it on a typewriter borrowed from Michael. She had been as specific as she dared to be in drawing up the document, identifying her as a femme sole trader. She prayed he wouldn't question that. "This paper gives me a lease on pumping and drilling equipment, giving you a fair share of any profits I make from my drilling."

He crushed his face into a frown. "Drilling?"

"At Moon Lake Lodge."

"Haven't thought about the old place in years. Why would you want to be out there?"

"Mama's letting me have a horse, sir," William said, saving her from having to lie further. "His name's Hector."

"So you moved to the lake for the sake of a horse."

Helena held her breath. He made the plan sound absurd. But he was sparing her from explaining.

"I suppose it's my duty to safeguard my grandson's future." He looked at her with a startling, penny-bright gleam in his eye, and then, with a trembling hand, signed the agreement.

Eighteen

At the start of the drilling, everyone had gathered around to witness the discovery of the first thermal spring in Saratoga. Several hours later, the sun started to go down and even Josephine, who was so sure of the location, drooped with fatigue and boredom. Eventually they all trickled away—off to bed or to their nightly readings in the lodge.

Michael worked alone, and he preferred it that way. Ignoring the twilight flurry of mosquitoes, he rotated the drill stem and rock-cutting bit, flushing out the cuttings and examining the gravel-size pebbles for signs that he had reached water.

He found the work tedious and backbreaking, but what made it even worse was that the drill belonged to Adam Barnes, a man he'd despised for as long as he'd lived. Michael refused to think of him as a father. Barnes used to visit Michael's mother before she lost her health and her looks. With pathetic eagerness, she would put on her one decent dress and meet him at the LaGrange Supper Room, where he'd buy her a meal and take his pleasure from her later. Barnes neither knew nor cared that Hannah Rowan lived hand-to-mouth in a backstretch alley. He did know—but did not care—that she'd borne him a second son.

Michael took no satisfaction in the old man's misery; he had enough troubles of his own. The summer had jerked him out of a quiet, predictable existence and hurled him into a life he had never imagined. On the day she'd so imperiously summoned him to her parlor, one look at his brother's wife had confirmed it—he had never stopped loving her. Yet the thought brought him no joy, only challenges he wasn't sure he wanted.

Frustrated, he continued to pump cuttings from the borehole, digging deeper, finding nothing, brooding about Helena, drilling downward. All the things he'd concealed from Helena began to fester like an unhealed wound, and he didn't know what he could do or say to make it right, any more than he'd known what to say nine years earlier. He'd wanted so badly to stay with her, but he hadn't allowed himself the luxury. Despite her claims to the contrary, she would not have been able to live in the shadow of her father's disapproval, and he didn't want to force her to choose.

Now the problem had grown worse. He was blood brother to the man she had risked everything to escape. When she found out, she would banish him not just from her life, but from William's.

Unless he could win her trust before she discovered the truth. All this was for her; no other woman in the world could compel him to work his hands raw, digging for some mythical hot spring that existed only in a troubled girl's imagination.

"I know what you're thinking," Helena called, her voice startling him as it emerged from the night-shadowed woods. Clutching the hem of her skirt in one hand and a kerosene lantern in the other, she moved toward the clearing. "You're thinking this is a fool's errand, and that you'll never hit water, and even if you do, there's no way it could be warm."

It was not yet fully dark, and the lamp in her hand bounced like a fairy nimbus as she moved through the woods, up the path to the drilling site. He scowled and rotated the stem and bit yet again.

"Well? Have you nothing to say?" She sounded breathless from her climb up the hill.

"Not anymore. You just told me what I was thinking."

He worked in desultory silence while she made herself quite at home, taking a seat on a flat rock and watching him like a spectator at a golf match. "It's entirely decent of you to continue working. I just know you'll find the spring soon."

"How do you know that?"

"Because I have faith in you, Michael." She said it in utter seriousness, then listened patiently to the rhythmic thud and suck of the steam pump as he worked.

"This is absurd." He stopped the pump, yanked off his canvas glove and inspected the latest blister. Swearing, he examined the hole, squatting down to see in the failing light. "I don't know why I keep—" He stopped talking and peered into the shaft. The level of the flushing water receded, indicating that there was open space in the strata far below. A water-bearing stratum?

He plunged his hand into the cuttings. Something was different. The debris that flushed upward from the hole was coarse and gravelly. Did it feel warm? Immediately he restarted the pump and rotated the stem, bringing up more cuttings.

"What is it?" Helena asked, dropping unceremoniously to her knees beside him. ‘‘You’ve hit water, haven’t you?’’

‘‘I don’t—’’ The earth made a terrible exhalation of sound, and a strange wind blew the hair back from his face. Then gas and grit spewed upward, followed by a jet of water. Stunned, Michael put his hand into the stream. ‘‘It’s warm.’’

‘‘You did it!’’ Her ecstatic yell rang through the woods, echoing across the lake. ‘‘You did it, Michael!’’ She flung her arms around his neck, laughing as she fell against him.

It was a moment of shared rapture, as rare as a falling star, a moment so crystal clear and deeply felt that it branded itself on his soul. A soaring bliss seemed to lift him out of himself, to take him to another place. ‘‘There’s no blood running in my veins,’’ he murmured. ‘‘It’s something else…fine wine.’’

‘‘Thermal water,’’ she corrected him. Her eyes danced, reminding Michael that some things were brighter than nature made the stars. Boldly she pulled his head lower so that their lips met. It was more than a kiss; it was a consuming ecstasy, brushed with soft magic. Then Helena sat back on her heels, beaming at the burbling jet of water.

Michael looked down at the palms of his hands. Surely it was just his imagination, but the blisters had disappeared.

Helena barely slept a wink that night, and the next morning she roused everyone early, leading the way to the new spring. The ladies from the lodge and William hurried to see the small miracle. Michael was there already, tubing and sealing the jetting warm water. Helena couldn’t tell whether or not he’d even gone to bed. He was unshaven, wearing the same muddy clothes he'd worn the day before. He looked weary and ecstatic, and she could tell he was thinking about the way she'd kissed him. She could tell, because she was thinking about it, too.

Josephine filled her hands with the bubbling water and grinned at Michael. "I was right."

"You were right," he admitted.

"He smited the rock," said William. "Look, Mama, he smited the rock, just like Miz Sarah said."

"How marvelous," said Helena. "I shall become a balneologist."

"I can spell that," William said. "B-a-l-n—"

"Yes, yes, but do you know what it is?"

"The science of baths, especially mineral baths," he said.

"Exactly, my clever boy. We have been reading a book about it every night, haven't we?" She, Nellie and Daisy had been giving intense concentration to their lessons, and Helena surprised herself by making progress. Perhaps her success had come about because it mattered so much now. "We shall build a bath. A beautiful one, just like they have in Bath, England. It will be very exclusive—the only naturally heated bath in all of Saratoga Springs."

"Who'll build the bath?"

"We will, of course."

"You'll need building materials and workers," Nellie cautioned. "All that takes money."

"How much?"

"A great deal, I'd say."

"We'll borrow it," Helena said.

"From whom?"

Her stomach clenched. She knew the local banks would no longer accept her business. She thought of Jackie Shaunessy, who had been so generous with the lease on Moon Lake Lodge. But burying herself in debt to a gambler was a bad idea; she felt it in her bones. "We'll find a way to get the money."

"How?" asked Nellie.

She took a deep breath. "We could sell the Degas."

"Goodness, you have a Degas?" Alice said.

Helena nodded. "Last spring a New York City collector offered me a fortune for the painting. Degas had a show at the Salon Auteuil last year, and it's suddenly become fashionable to collect his paintings. So my original is worth a fortune. We could use a fortune now."

"You no longer own the Degas," Michael pointed out.

"Then I'll find a way to reclaim it."

"This is a gambling town," Josephine said. "I'll bet we could find a thief to—"

"Don't even think it," Helena said, cutting her off before William grasped what she was saying.

"You can't sell that picture anyway," Michael said. "You love it too much. We might not need as much up front as you think, at any rate."

"Why not?" William asked, his gaze skipping from one adult to another.

"Remember the fairy tale where the miller's daughter is told to spin straw into gold?"

"Yes—Rumpelstiltskin."

"That's what we'll do. Turn a little bit of money into a lot of money."

"How?"

"Son, this is Saratoga Springs. I'm taking this to the racetrack."

"Will the racetrack give you money?"

"That's it." Still slightly dazed by Michael's insight about the painting, Helena took William by the hand.

"I will not have gambling discussed in my son's presence." As she marched the protesting boy away, she reminded herself that Michael was new to being a parent. He had not spent every waking moment, and many sleepless nights, thinking and worrying and puzzling about William—what was best for him, what should be avoided, what hopes and dreams a parent had for a child. Michael did suffer the occasional momentary lapse in judgment when it came to William. But in general, his instincts regarding the boy were sound. She would be less than honest if she thought otherwise.

Nineteen

Race Day was a proper holiday in Saratoga Springs, and always had been. It encompassed not a single day but an entire week, shouldered by the weeks leading up to the event and weeks following it. In the high summer days of August and early September, the sun was brighter, the flowers more colorful and the air sweeter than anywhere else on earth. As a boy, Michael looked forward to the summer orgy of betting, eating and posturing. Rich folks felt expansive and were generous with the tips. There was always plenty of food left over from the banquets and parties held out at the racetrack pavilion and in the city's hotels, clubs and open-air parks. Once he found an entire picnic, completely untouched. The basket lay abandoned after the horns summoned everyone to the track. He and his mother had feasted for days.

In the jocks' room and chute alley, where the horses and riders waited, he had gleaned more than copper penny tips and leftover crumbs. He learned how to handicap, and how to bet. It was more than a matter of studying the sheets and logs posted, giving the odds and statistics. It was a delicate mingling of science, art and instinct, and he became skilled at it before he was old enough to raise a beard.

He learned to spot when a horse was on, reading its brightness and attitude. He learned to know when a jock was going to throw a race. He learned to measure his confidence and to hedge his bets, and he learned when to take his winnings and walk away.

One thing he had never learned, though, was how to be a fashionable racing patron. This became clear to him when Helena marched into his quarters, carrying a large carpetbag.

"I'm going with you," she announced.

He bristled immediately. "I can do this on my own."

"You need me. And I deserve to be there."

He studied the mutinous set of her chin, and felt a little tug of admiration for her. After what she'd endured from Barnes, she was reluctant to hand everything over to a man. Her stubborn expression did nothing to lessen the impact of her beauty, however. With the morning light gilding her hair, her eyes a vivid green contrast to the silky cream of her skin, she looked like something out of a dream. Each time he looked at her, he recalled in aching detail the way he used to hold her willow-slender body against his, and the way tender, searching kisses had led to deeper intimacies that made his dreams pale in comparison. What an uncomfortable mix of emotions he felt for this woman. The passion and affection were inevitable, but they were tempered by bitterness and regret. He wondered how they were going to go on from here.

"For one thing," she said, "you'll need proper clothing. You simply must dress like a winner if you're going to bet like a winner."

"And how does a winner dress?"

She opened the carpetbag to reveal a collection of men's clothes. "I thought you'd never ask."

"Where the devil did you get this?"

"Brooks Brothers of New York City. They specialize in ready-to-wear. I had Nellie send a wire ordering a few things, and they rushed the order. They thought this was for Troy—I'm sure he will get the bill for it. You're about the same size. Isn't that uncanny?"

Not really, he thought. Discomfited, he drew out a white coat with a pretentious heraldic insignia on the upper pocket and a navy waistcoat made of a finely worsted fabric that slipped through his hands. "I'm not putting this on."

"You'll look marvelous."

"I don't want to look marvelous."

"I've never seen you dressed like a gentleman. You could be so handsome if you tried."

"I don't want to be handsome."

"But you can't help it." She pushed the garments toward him. "Stop complaining. You're more of a baby than William."

"Do you dress him up like an organ grinder's monkey, too?"

"Every Sunday, for church." A shadow fell over her face.

"Helena? What is it?"

"Nothing," she said quickly. Too quickly.

Without taking his eyes from her troubled face, he took the clothing from her and set it aside. "Tell me."

"Sunday services are not quite the same since... Oh, bother it. Would you please dress like a gentleman just this once?"

He saw it then, her need. So simple, so small. And yet so big and all-consuming that it rose before him like an unscalable mountain. Why had he never seen that before? On the surface, the annulment of her marriage was a simple thing. Mistakes were made, remedies acknowledged. Papers were signed. But now she had to deal with the aftermath. With that one dark and fleeting look, he understood the situation from her perspective. Despite what had happened, she had to go back into her world. She had to hold up her head and face the people who had known her as a different person. She had to be the person she was now.

And she didn't want to do it with a man who looked like a ragpicker.

"Leave the damned clothes," he said. "The first race isn't until four o'clock."

"I shouldn't be wearing the gray." Just out of the bath, Helena stood in her sheerest chemise and drawers. She eyed the dress hanging on the front of her armoire while the other ladies gathered around to help her get ready. "I'm still in mourning."

Daisy smoothed her hands down the luminous dove-gray sleeves of the pique silk gown, trimmed with cream-colored piping. "Of course you are, sugar. But it's summer. You're going to the races. Your daddy wouldn't want you going out there looking like an old black crow."

Nellie regarded the black crepe bonnet as though it were a dead bird. "This is ugly and in bad taste. You would do well to discard it."

"I owe my father the tribute of a proper mourning."

"Let that tribute be made of the memories in your heart, dear. Not the gloominess of your gown."

"This is surely the prettiest dress I've ever seen," Sarah said, holding it against Helena. Taking her by the shoulders, she turned her toward the mirror. "This will do just fine."

Helena assessed the image in the glass as though looking at a stranger. Where was the laughing girl in the shocking French gowns, the silk dancing slippers? Where was the belle of Georgetown? Where was the Helena who had looked into the blue eyes of an eccentric young man and seen the whole world in their depths?

She recalled her insistence that Michael dress properly for the races. She, too, must look the part. "All right," she said. "The gray, then."

The music of feminine chatter crescendoed as they happily descended upon her. Cream silk stockings, corset and crinolines went on in a ceremony that was still familiar to her.

As Helena was being primped and preened, Nellie went to the window and looked out. "I wonder how Prince Charming's coming along."

Helena escaped Sarah's comb and Alice's artful tying of bows and joined Nellie at the window. Beside her, Josephine looked out, too. "Who are those people?" she asked, watching three men coming up the drive in a smart two-horse dearborn carriage with curtained sides.

"All the king's horses and all the king's men?" asked Alice.

Practically bouncing with excitement, William hailed them on the drive and pointed the way to the carriage house. Helena couldn't suppress a smile. To her son, this was all a grand adventure. He had no idea her fortunes hung in the balance.

"I think it's that bartender from the Steeplechase Club."

"Appears to be." Nellie confirmed it. "It's George Long, Regis Ransom and Isaac Reynolds. Regis used to be quite the man about town, strutting around in suits from Savile Row.''

Sarah laughed. ''I think the professor had to call for reinforcements.''

Helena turned away, troubled by a nervous flurry in her stomach. ''This is a bad idea.''

''Getting rich in one afternoon?''

''No. You know what I mean. Going to the races with him. He's never been good for me.'' She was deeply uncomfortable with the idea of relying on Michael's expertise. This was to be her time of independence, her moment to stand on her own, yet already she was putting her faith in a man. Not just any man, but Michael Rowan.

''We need his knowledge and expertise,'' Nellie said. ''There's no shame in seeking help when you need it. It's simply wise business.''

''Something tells me it's an invitation to trouble. When Michael is involved, that's usually the case.''

''He got your marriage annulled,'' Alice pointed out.

''All right, he's been good for me one time.''

''He's about to do you another favor,'' said Sarah.

''But I'm beginning to wonder if I should let him.'' She bit her lip, turned away from the window and looked around at her ladies. Their smiling faces turned to her like blossoms to the sun. Only they were infinitely more beautiful to her than flowers. When had she started to think of them as her ladies? Right from the start, she realized. They were living, breathing proof that her cause was good. Her life here made more sense than it ever had before. But this plan was putting it all at risk.

''What do you suppose they're doing over there?''

asked Daisy, arranging the cream lace jabot around her throat. "Why does he need all that help?"

"Like father like son," Nellie said. "It would take three assistants to get William dressed properly, too."

Alice and Sarah exchanged a glance.

"He doesn't know," Helena confessed, her cheeks heating. "William doesn't know. I made Michael promise not to tell him until—unless—we know what the future will bring."

"He won't hear no tales from us," Daisy assured her.

"No use getting the boy's hopes up," Alice agreed.

"Why not?" asked Josephine. "Hope is a good thing."

Sarah looked at her. "Not if you hope for something that might break your heart." She straightened the fashionable peplum of the racing jacket. "You look perfect. Pretty as a picture."

Alice nodded. "I would love for you to sit for a portrait one day."

Helena walked to the door, then paced up and down. "I can't believe I'm doing this. I vowed to be an independent woman, yet as soon as I needed something, I turned to a man."

"That's one way of looking at it," Nellie said.

"I should be ashamed."

"Another way," Nellie added, "is to think of it like this. You have a problem, and you're smart enough to know where to look for the solution."

"Smart." Helen hissed the word like an oath. "If I was smart, I wouldn't be in this situation to begin with. I would never have married Troy. Never."

"It's going to be all right," Nellie insisted.

"You think you're the only one got things to regret?'' Daisy asked. ''Everybody got that. So what you going to do? Answer me that. What you going to do?''

She looked around the room at her friends, all of them damaged and angry and funny and sad and, most of all, filled with hope. Suddenly it was easy to smile at them.

Michael scowled at his image in the shaving mirror, which was fast fogging up with the steam rising from the cramped bathtub. His friends and William were gathered in the loft, helping him get ready, though their help was intrusive and annoying.

''It's disgraceful. You have neither a beard nor are you clean-shaven,'' said Regis, the fussy arbiter of taste and style. He took a seat on a low stool by the tub and slapped the razor back and forth across the strop.

''That's because I don't like beards and I don't like shaving. When it gets to be a bother, I shave.''

Behind him, Isaac snipped away at his hair with a pair of rusty shears. George was sitting by the window, smoking a cheroot and whittling at a piece of antler.

''What the devil are you doing with my hair?'' Michael asked.

''Just hold still, honey,'' Isaac said. ''I'll be finished by and by. When was the last time you visited the barber?''

''Why would I ever visit a barber?''

Regis chuckled. ''I don't believe he's ever been.''

''You've never been to a barber?'' William asked.

''Is that so strange?''

Isaac, Regis and George exchanged a look. William snickered. ''How do you keep your hair cut, then?''

''With scissors. When my hair gets too long, I take the scissors and cut it.''

William drew a lock of his own copper-colored hair down over his forehead. His eyes rolled up, practically crossing as he tried to see. "That's a good idea. I'm going to cut my own hair from now on."

Tilting back his head as Regis applied the razor, Michael felt a rush of gratitude he didn't deserve. There was something about the boy. He found it tremendously satisfying when William looked up to him, emulated him, tried to be with him constantly.

A son. I have a son. The thought came to him at odd moments, like untimely sunshine through dark clouds. The idea made him feel dizzy and disoriented, the way he'd felt when he had experimented with a human-size centrifugal that spun him around until he forgot who he was. *A son.*

He had been watching the boy for days, and he could see his own childhood in William. He could see the burning brightness of innocent interest about the world, could hear the wonder in the young boy's voice as William described the way a dragonfly hovered over the grass or the sound of an echo in a cave. Michael had been a poor boy. He'd watched his mother starve and freeze to death, but for all that, he had been filled with the same sort of marvel and curiosity he saw in William.

He knew what he wanted, and finally he was beginning to understand how to achieve it. He wanted William to know who his father was. A simple concept, yet difficult to achieve, given Helena's doubts. She didn't want to tell William because she didn't trust Michael to stay. She was too fragile to put her faith in any man. She had to recover from the Troy Barnes ordeal, had to relearn trust at her own pace, in her own time, on her own terms. Michael vowed he would be there when she was ready. But the fact that he and Troy were brothers hung like a pall over his hopes.

He'd puzzled over the problem since their quarrel about telling William. Bit by bit, the solution was revealing itself to him. Before he could be a part of William's life, he had to earn Helena's trust. He had to prove himself worthy, but could he?

Nine years ago, he had not been good enough for her or for her family, and he'd walked away. What was different now? Why could he succeed with her now when he hadn't before?

He was going to have to turn himself into the sort of man he should have been long ago. What an idiot he'd been, pretending he had to leave her so she could marry "up." The real reason he had left her was that he was afraid he would fail. She was the only person he had ever dared to love, and he didn't trust himself to do it right. So he took the coward's way out. He left. As she'd said, he was good at leaving.

The real test would be to see if he was any good at staying.

He stood up in the steel tub, slung a towel around his waist and stepped out of the bath. "You want to finish my sarsaparilla and potato chips?" he asked.

William took a swig straight from the bottle. He sat on the workbench, swinging his legs back and forth while watching the proceedings like a spectator at a magic lantern show.

Regis produced something that resembled a crop-spraying pump. Before Michael could duck for cover, he pumped away, engulfing Michael in a fog of scent.

"Me too! Me too!" William jumped down and threw himself into the fog.

Michael choked, rubbed his watering eyes. "What the hell is that?"

"What the hell is that?" echoed William, delighted to be swearing.

"Bay rum," said Regis.

"It's poison." Michael batted at the cloud of fragrance.

"The ladies love it."

Michael waved a hand in front of his face. "Maybe it'll keep the horse flies off."

Isaac brought over the clothes from Brooks Brothers. "You better get a move on. Don't want to miss the start of the races."

Like the ceremonial dressing of a knight of yore, they put him together, piece by piece. Each item passed from Isaac to William to George to Regis, as though to receive each man's approval and benediction for the ordeal to come. Only instead of chain mail, breastplate and gauntlets, this garb consisted of tennis socks, drawers, undervest. Yet his attendants treated the situation with the gravity of a solemn ceremony.

And perhaps that wasn't so far off the mark, Michael thought, and a certain solemnity to the proceedings was appropriate. Helena's world hung in the balance. His success or failure today would determine whether it rose or fell.

He was a knight errant, off on a quest for his ladylove, a quest sung by the troubadours and told around the cover fires of evening. And he was doing so in white pajamas. He glared down at the cream-colored pants, the white spats, the insanely, glaringly white shirt. "This is absurd. No one will take me seriously if I show up at the betting office looking like Wee Willie Winkie."

"I take you serious, Professor," William said loyally.

"You're not finished." Regis clicked his tongue at

him. "Hold out your arms." Regis proved himself quick with needle and thread, tailoring the trousers and jacket so that the fit was perfect. He fit Michael with a waistcoat in navy blue, buttoning it down the front. The blue was a bit better. Not so glaring. But the frock coat was also white, as was the band around the brim of his summer-weight straw hat.

William stood back and planted his hands on his hips. "You look different, Professor. You look good."

"Dapper," Regis said, clasping his hands in elation. "You look positively dapper."

"I've always wanted to be dapper," Michael said wryly. "It has been my main goal in life."

"Speaking of goals," Regis said. "You'd best get a move on. Come on, Isaac. Let's go get the cart ready."

George held out the bit of antler, which he'd carved into the shape of a horseshoe. "It's very powerful," he said.

Michael slipped it into his pocket. "Thank you. I'll take luck where I can find it."

Isaac paused, fished something out of his pocket. "You take this along for luck, too, you hear? It's a pair of Swiss opera glasses I won off some swell in a card game." He stuck the small brass binoculars in Michael's pocket.

"Thanks, Isaac. I'll bring it back to you."

"You do your betting right, you can buy me a new one."

"And take this for luck, also," William piped up. He dug deep in the pocket of his dungarees and produced a tiny velvet parcel. The fabric was instantly familiar and recognizable. Tiffany blue. Was the boy a customer of Tiffany's?

William reverently opened the drawstring of the

bag, emptied the contents into the palm of his grubby hand, then proudly held it out to Michael. "It's the third-best thing I own," he said with hushed reverence. "I think it might be real lucky."

Michael did not want to compromise the gravity of the offering. "Is that your tooth, William?"

"Yes. I've been keeping it since I was six." He put it back in the bag. "You take it now, Professor."

Michael received the gift with unsmiling dignity and put it in his trouser pocket. "I'll look after it for you."

Then Regis bustled forward. "Don't forget the gloves."

"They're white."

"Of course they're white. They're made of the finest buffed kid."

"I'll do without the gloves."

"But every man of fashion wears them."

"Who said I'm a man of fashion?"

"You are today." Regis sniffed in a self-pitying way. "You accepted a talisman from each of us. You must accept the gloves from me."

"Bother it," Michael grumbled, but he slid his hands into the fine white gloves. Then he grabbed his green celluloid spectacles from a shelf and put them on.

"Michael, no," said Regis. "I beg you, please."

"I'm wearing them," Michael said. "All this bright white hurts my eyes." He slid them on, hooking the earpieces around his ears.

William stepped back and surveyed Michael. "I like the glasses. I like them, I do."

"Well, guess what? I have a second pair—in the top desk drawer. Why don't you put them on, William, and then you'll be lucky, too."

"Hurrah!" He ran over and put them on, then admired himself in the shaving mirror.

Regis sputtered as they trooped down the stairs to Isaac and George, who waited with the borrowed open cart and horse. "But they spoil the effect."

"No," William interrupted. "He looks dapper."

"The boy's right," Michael said. "I do look dapper. I look so dapper I could just—"

"Well, now, look at you." Isaac turned with the reins in his hands. He checked out Michael from head to toe, then gave a low whistle. "Dapper," he said.

George echoed, "Dapper."

"I'm sorry I even bothered," said Regis, but he was grinning, too, as Michael got in and clicked his tongue at the horse, heading up the drive to the lodge.

"Don't be too long," Regis called after him. "That carriage might turn into a pumpkin."

Twenty

A stranger came to call.

As Helena peered through the fanlight of the door, she frowned in confusion at the handsome man in navy and white, coming up the walkway.

"Are we expecting someone?" Sarah asked.

"Other than Prince Charming?" Nellie said.

It was Michael Rowan, of course. Only Michael as she'd never seen him before. The room began to feel hot and close. She couldn't take her eyes off him. "I wish you wouldn't keep calling him that. He's not a prince and he is certainly not charming."

"You seem to like him well enough," Alice said, lightly teasing.

Helena pulled the door open as he approached, but she couldn't leave Alice's taunt unanswered. Turning back, she said, "I do not like him well enough. I don't like him one little bit."

She turned back to greet the visitor and found herself staring at a dazzling spectacle. The crisp white shirt was buttoned with gleaming obsidian tacks. The jacket and trousers perfectly outlined his broad chest and slim hips. He looked so splendid, his face shaven clean to reveal the perfection of his features.

He grinned down at her. "Then we are agreed, darling," the stranger said in Michael's voice. "I don't like you, either. But just for this afternoon, we'll have to pretend."

Ignoring her gasp of shock, he held out one gloved hand, palm up. She simply blinked in surprise but made no move. Leaning forward, he gently touched her chin. "Close your mouth, dear. You don't want to let any flies in."

He took her hand and led her to the borrowed conveyance. With a gallant flourish, he helped her up into the open seat, his hands lingering intimately at her waist. Then he climbed up and took the reins. She swayed backward a little as the cart rolled forward, but the whole time she kept sneaking glances at Michael. What had they done to his hair? Its dark waves gleamed beneath the hat, and curled gently against the perfect collar. Her fingers itched to twine themselves in the glossy strands, to run along his smooth cheek and jaw.

Finally, as they pulled out into the roadway, she spoke through dry lips. "You look marvelous."

"Now you know how you've made everyone feel all your life. You're so damned beautiful, it's like looking at a piece of art."

"Now you know how it feels to be stared at like a piece of art. And I do mean that—you look wonderful."

"Thank you." He put on his tinted eyeglasses and studied the road ahead. "And thank you for not saying dapper."

"I mean truly, wondrously marvelous," she reiterated. He had always been attractive to her in his unkempt, almost scruffy manner, heedless of fashion, concerned only with utility. But now that Regis, Isaac and George had cleaned him up and dressed him, the transformation was amazing. He took her breath away. Just looking at him made her giddy.

"You seem shocked."

"I am."

"I wonder if I should be insulted. Was I decidedly not marvelous before?"

"You would never feel insulted over looks," she said with assurance.

"How do you know?"

"Appearances, especially your own, are the last thing that matter to you." She shut her eyes and inhaled. "Glory, you even smell marvelous."

"Careful, dear, any more of this and my head might swell bigger than my fancy new hat." He ran his forefinger around the brim.

"What's the matter?" she asked, noting the red flush on his face.

"I still feel like an organ grinder's monkey."

She sagged back in disappointment. "I only suggested the new clothes because most people enjoy looking stylish. I didn't force you to wear them."

"No, but I wanted to for your sake." He glanced down at her. Behind the spectacles, his eyes were keen and bright with understanding. "I know that to you, appearances do matter."

"Does that make me hopelessly shallow?"

"Hopelessly conventional, perhaps."

They drove along the tree-shaded street with its stone Georgian facades and straight-trunked maple and elm trees. The traffic grew thicker, a colorful congestion of carriages, barouches, hacks and carts. Helena recognized many faces in the fashionable crowd heading toward the racetrack.

Already, several sharp-eyed matrons had recognized her and were whispering behind their lace-gloved hands and ivory-ribbed fans.

"I do not think being conventional is going to work for me anymore," she said, resisting the impulse to close the curtains around the dearborn.

"Then what is going to work?"

They came alongside a gleaming barouche. She locked eyes with Mrs. Elvira Houghton, whose stare glazed over with crystal-hard contempt before cutting away. Helena deliberately held her ground until the matron looked back at her. She knew Mrs. Houghton would not be able to resist. When next she caught her eye, Helena gave the woman a broad wink. She found to her surprise that she didn't really care about being the subject of scandal. She was making a new life for herself now, with friends who didn't judge her worth on the basis of social standing.

"Being brazen," she said in answer to Michael's question. "Perhaps being brazen is going to work now."

Her spirits lifted as the pavilion came into view. Peaked like turrets, the stands surrounding the racing oval resembled a medieval jousting ground, formal and beautiful and intimidating. Well-tended gardens, with mineral springs covered by handsome Doric gazebos, provided a place for walking, picnicking and gossiping. Carriage attendants shouted and whistled, trying to corral the new arrivals in orderly fashion. Parasols in every color of the rainbow sprouted like blossoming sunflowers over the crowd. Servants rushed to and fro, fetching and carrying for the well-heeled visitors.

On a platform at the edge of the carriage park, politicians held forth, using the occasion to address the gathering crowds. "That's Elijah Ware," Helena said, grabbing Michael's sleeve and pointing. "He's making another run for Troy's seat in the Senate." They had just missed the speech, but the crowd offered the cautious approval of polite applause. Yet when Helena walked into their midst, everyone fell silent and stared at her.

Brazen, she thought, fixing a smile in place as she addressed the humble man at the podium. Garbed in plain black broadcloth and accompanied by his homely, earnest-looking wife and four children, he resembled a farmer bringing his goods to market rather than a candidate for national office. "I wish you the very best of luck with your campaign, sir," she called, looking directly at him. Out of the corner of her eye, she could see local newspapermen scribbling frantically. *Senator's Former Wife Supports Rival,* the headlines would probably read. Good, she thought. Let the world know where she stood.

"Come along, Michael. We should get over to the paddock to start handicapping our horses," she said, pulling him toward the racing grounds. Glancing up, she caught him grinning at her. "What?"

"Nothing."

"You're amused because I spoke up for Mr. Ware?"

"Just amused in general."

She wasn't sure how she felt about that. Did she like the fact that she amused him, or did it make her feel insignificant? While she was considering that, she led the way down to the paddock, where owners and trainers were saddling horses. The area was open to the public, for observing the horses prior to a race was a vital step in handicapping. She had no idea what to look for, but she was certain Michael did.

She spied an unexpected, familiar face in the paddock crowd. "Michael, look. Isn't that Julius Calhoun, of Albion? We must go and see him."

"Should I know him?"

"You met him once. Surely you remember Albion." Years ago, they had gone there as guests at the Calhouns' vast Tidewater horse farm. It had been a short visit, but would forever linger in her mind, because during that visit, at midnight while everyone else slept, Michael had made love to her for the first time.

"I remember some things better than others," he said, his hand pressing intimately against the small of her back.

She blushed and walked more quickly to escape his touch. "Julius is..." She had to puzzle over the relationship for a moment. "He is my sister's half nephew by marriage."

"There's no such thing as a half nephew."

"There must be. Julius is the son of my sister's husband's half brother, and therefore he must be Abigail's half nephew, which makes him my half nephew-in-law." She clasped her hands in delight. "Won't he be pleased?"

"How can he not?" Michael muttered.

"Julius," she called, waving a gloved hand. "Yoo-hoo, Julius Calhoun."

The young Negro man scanned the crowd with a frown. Helena remembered him well, and with fondness. His life could not have been easy, but then again, it might have been harder. His grandfather was the formidable Charles Calhoun, master of Albion. His grandmother had been a slave. According to Abigail, old Charles had developed a devoted fondness for Julius and had sent him to a fine private school in Philadelphia, then put him in charge of Albion's breeding program.

Weaving through the throng of jockeys, trainers, grooms, hotwalkers and stable hands, he approached Helena and bowed politely. "Ma'am."

"Do you remember me, Julius? I'm Helena Cabot, your aunt Abigail's sister. And this is Professor Michael Rowan. We're here to bet on the horses."

"Good luck to you, ma'am." Clearly distracted, he glanced over his shoulder at some commotion in the middle of the paddock.

"You're busy," Michael said.

"My best jockey just took a spill. Broke his collarbone, I think." A few moments later, the jockey, in Albion's canary yellow silks, was borne away, moaning, on a stretcher. Helena called after Julius to visit her at Moon Lake Lodge, and he answered with a polite but dismissive wave of his hand.

"Let's have a look at the contenders," Michael said.

The jockeys walked around, stretching and loosening their shoulders and legs. Attendants stood ready with jewel-colored silk jackets and caps. Michael and Helena went to the walking ring to watch the parade of horses. At first glance, the Thoroughbreds looked quite similar. They were uniformly gorgeous, dapple-hided creatures with delicately sculpted heads, deep, powerful chests and muscular legs.

"Just watch a moment," Michael said. "We'll find our champion. Let's pick out the sharpest horse of the lot." He told her he liked the horses who had a pop in their step, who kept their ears flicking in the direction of the track, showing that they were experienced racers. With his typical deep concentration, he seemed to be memorizing and categorizing each animal.

"I like that one, the one with the jockey in pink silks," she stated. "Number nine."

"Like him for what?" Michael said. "The horse is dull and uninterested. He's jerking his head up and down and sweating. The flat ears mean he's frightened and angry."

"Well, of course he is," she said. "How would you behave if you had to race a mile with a man on your back? The poor horse feels the same way. And so he will run the fastest, in order to get it over with."

"Of course."

Ignoring his wry tone, she shaded her eyes to inspect the distant rows of sagging sheds that lined the area beyond the paddock. "There is a whole world back here."

"The horses need care every day of the year, race or no race. The people who look after them live there," said Michael, his voice inexplicably sharp.

"Dear me. I thought they were horse stalls."

"The horse stalls are in better condition," he said.

A strange and solemn fascination drew her down to the backstretch area, a place she'd heard about but never actually seen. In a low quadrangle, screened from the track by trees, she saw a world that had been hidden from her until now. There, huddled in unimaginable squalor, was a row of the meanest hovels ever to blight a landscape. It was a neighborhood of stench and want, populated by children racing around, their bare legs marred by sores, their lips cracked and bellies distended with hunger, their backs striped by frustrated guardians or heartless employers.

From time to time, she used to hear that the city elders were trying to clean up the backstretch by sending the orphans to the Children's Aid Society. They would then be transported by train to families in the West.

A horn sounded the call to the post.

"Are you coming?" Michael sounded impatient, edgy. With one last look over her shoulder, she left the backstretch, passing the long drovers' trailers with high sides, which were parked along the bank that ran the length of the paddock. Champion Thoroughbreds never walked to the racetrack. It simply wasn't done.

She reached for Michael's arm, but he was already walking toward the racetrack for the post parade. Thousands of others did the same, and a high mood seemed to buoy everyone along as they anticipated the first race.

"Stop, thief!"

They were startled by a gruff shout from the middle of the crowd. Instinctively Helena clutched Michael's arm, but they stood too far away to see what was happening. Then a boy in a flat cap and brown trousers darted from the crowd, brushed past Helena and Michael and ducked behind one of the trailers.

"A pickpocket?" Helena asked.

"Most likely. And a smart one at that. The pickings are definitely richer before the betting starts."

A constable wove through the crowd in search of the thief. Astride a tall horse, another scanned the throng. "We'll find the little beggar for you, Mr. Cotter," he called.

"You do that, and I'll have his hide for my collection," yelled Cotter, red-faced with fury.

"He's one of Troy's favorite cronies," Helena said. "Huge contributor to his campaign, and crooked as a country mile."

"In that case, we shouldn't feel obligated to tell them where to find their thief." Michael indicated the horse trailer, which rocked a little from the motion of the boy.

Then, as they watched, the door of the trailer swung open. Out stepped a petite, attractive young woman in a blue gabardine skirt, carrying a fashionable carpetbag. A stylish hat trimmed with realistic-looking birds and flowers perched atop her head.

Catching Helena's astonished look, she smiled engagingly. ''Pardon me,'' she said. ''Is this the way to the betting booth?'' She had a perfect English boarding school accent and perfect ladylike posture. She also had a sheen of sweat on her face and an edge of brown trousers showing beneath the hem of her skirts. And was that a brown cap stuffed down inside the carpetbag?

Before Helena could answer, the constable came plowing through, his cheeks red with exertion. Michael stiffened. ''That's Brody,'' he muttered. ''The one who arrested me.''

Helena put on her most pleasant smile. ''Is something the matter, sir?''

Brody staggered a little as he stared at her. ''Um, no, ma'am. Just...'' He addressed the three of them. ''Anyone seen which way the pickpocket went? Little thief took a sack full of double eagles from Mr. Cotter. He'll hang for this.''

The English girl paled, but she stood perfectly still.

Helena shrugged. ''I'm sorry, officer. We haven't seen a thing.''

''Thank you, folks.'' Apparently, he didn't even recognize Michael in his new clothes.

The English girl watched Brody's retreat. She was quite stunning, with glossy black hair, milk-white skin and deep red lips. Up close, she probably wouldn't make a very convincing boy.

"How do you do?" Helena said, remembering her vow to be brazen. "I am Helena Cabot, and this is Professor Michael Rowan. I take it you're new to the Springs."

"Indeed I am." Her black eyes flashed with delight as she shook hands. "Isabel Fish-Wooten," she said. "Lady adventurer."

"Interesting profession," Michael commented.

"Well, actually, I am that sad cliché, a British noblewoman fallen into genteel poverty—a common affliction in my country. My father sent me to America to marry a millionaire so I can save the ancestral family estate. Isn't that absurd? Besides, my father has the wrong impression of your country. He thinks all Americans are millionaires. Are you?"

Helena and Michael exchanged a glance.

"I know it's not considered polite to ask," Isabel admitted, "but I'm told that here in America people speak freely of such matters. So are you?"

She was a little dynamo, and her energy was infectious. Helena liked her immensely already.

"Not yet," Michael said. Helena could see him biting back a smile.

"So anyway, contrary to my father's belief, they are rather hard to come by. The few I've found here are either married or disgustingly old, older than thirty."

"Disgusting," said Helena sympathetically.

"Well, Mr. Ellis wasn't married or disgusting, but he wouldn't do, either."

"Why not?"

"He's a homosexual."

Michael coughed into his white-gloved hand.

"Besides," continued Isabel Fish-Wooten, "I have come up with my own solution. I don't have to marry a millionaire. I just have to become one." She opened her bag and glanced down at her cache of double eagles, gleaming gold in the sunlight. "I just love America, don't you?"

Within a few minutes, Helena and Isabel were fast friends. Helena invited her to stay at Moon Lake Lodge so long as she promised to reform her thieving ways. Isabel was several years younger than Helena, and full of wild dreams. In addition to becoming a millionaire, she wanted to be a sharpshooter in a wild West show, a riverboat gambler, a pirate queen. She wanted to see the Rocky Mountains, the beautiful shores of California, Honolulu in the Sandwich Isles. There was no doubt in Helena's mind that she would do all those things and more. The extraordinary thing about her was that sense of possibility. That feeling that there was nothing she couldn't do.

Had Helena ever felt that way? She couldn't remember, but she was drawn to Isabel for reminding her.

By the time they reached the betting cage, Michael had grown completely quiet. She watched him studying the information chalked across the tote board, which displayed the odds. She realized she wasn't the only one taking an interest in Michael Rowan. Nearly every woman who noticed him lingered for a second glance, sometimes a third.

Helena was distressed. She did not want to feel attracted to him. She wanted to be independent. She wanted to take advantage of him and then discard him when she had no further need of his assistance. But there was a part of her that would never stop needing Michael Rowan. And she wasn't quite certain what to do about that.

Isabel's method of self-support had its temptations, but Helena was no thief, not even when she felt the stealing was justified. It would be too hard to explain to William.

At the betting booth, Michael placed their bets with a confidence she hadn't seen in him before.

"You did that rather well," she said while they moved into the pavilion. "You seemed to know just what to do."

"I grew up here, Helena."

"A lot of people grew up in Saratoga Springs, but that doesn't mean they know how to bet."

"No, here."

"You mean..." Her voice trailed off and she scanned the dwellings that lay far beyond the track, the world that had been hidden from her until today.

She felt him studying her, and made herself face him. "You're from the backstretch alley?"

"Don't be shocked, darling. I clean up rather nicely."

"But...you're a learned professor. How did you acquire an education?"

"Is it only the wealthy who are smart?"

The bitterness in his tone did not escape her. "No. Dear God, of course not." This revelation explained so much. He had grown up like the children she'd seen earlier. Hungry, wounded children who were occasionally rounded up for the orphan trains. At last, she thought. At last, the truth was rising to the surface.

"Why didn't you ever tell me?"

"You never asked."

"Why didn't you volunteer the information?"

"Because I didn't want you to look at me the way you're looking at me now."

"How am I looking?"

"With eyes full of pity and disgust."

"I'm not."

"You are, but I forgive you."

"You should have told me," she repeated.

"Would it have changed anything?"

"It would have changed everything."

He glared at her. "Come on, the races are about to begin." With cocky insolence, he offered her his arm. They proceeded through the reviewing stands, and whispers rippled through the crowd like wind through a cornfield.

They passed a dark-skinned lad in a turban, bearing a pair of velvet cushions for his master and mistress. The exotic couple, wearing silks of marigold and peacock blue, headed toward the pavilion.

Helena stopped to study them, but Michael seemed distracted.

"You're working out the odds, aren't you?" she asked, nudging him.

"I didn't come here to ogle the foreign dignitaries," he said curtly.

She sniffed. "I find watching people interesting."

"Almost as interesting as they find you."

So he had noticed after all. He realized they were being stared at, talked about. Constantly.

"It doesn't bother me as much as I thought it would," she admitted.

"That's because you're brazen and I'm dapper."

"A winning combination."

"Let's hope so," he muttered under his breath, his grin disappearing.

When they reached the reviewing stand at the homestretch, finding a vantage point to watch the races, she forgot everything but the excitement and anticipation of the contest.

For the first race, a one-mile route, they went down to the rail where the starting gate had been placed in front of the grandstand, giving them a perfect view. Michael handed her a pair of brass opera glasses. "Here, use these. Keep your eye on number four."

She focused on the beautiful animal just as the contenders seemed, in a single concerted effort, to leap free of the gate. They separated quickly, stretching in a thunderous string of muscled speed along the oval in a demonstration of breathtaking power.

Michael stood behind her, pressing close, and heat pulsed through her, forbidden and undeniable, her skin in flames for him. "You're smothering me," she said.

"You like it."

"Hush. I will not debate this with you." She gripped the rail and leaned forward, mesmerized by the raw power and energy of the horses churning up the turf as they thundered down the stretch. "My pink horse is losing," she said, her heart sinking.

"It's supposed to. I put it third in the trifecta."

"What?"

"I bet *against* it winning. Now, watch the number four horse. That's our winner."

She sank into silent awe, taking the opera glasses away. She no longer needed them. The roar of the crowd seemed a distant, muffled rumble, like the boom of waves on the shore. Everything fell away except the two horses in the lead, dueling toward the finish line in a contest so swift and graceful, it was almost like a dance. Her heartbeat seemed to match the drumming of the hooves.

When they crossed the finish line, a shout went up from the crowd, and Helena's voice joined the cheer of victory. She screamed until she was hoarse, until she felt Michael staring at her.

"What?" she asked.

"Do you even know which horse finished first?"

"Actually, no. I was so caught up—" She saw the gleam in his eye. "We did it, didn't we?"

"We need to do it again—for the next seven races."

"We will," she yelled, and there, in full view of all the spectators, she threw her arms around his neck and hugged him hard. It was a wonderful embrace, driven by a natural, undeniable passion and a deep triumph that made her forget, just for a moment, where she was.

But then, as the roar of the crowd abated, she fell back into herself and realized she was doing her cause no favor with this behavior, and she broke away from him. Still, she could not stop smiling, and neither could he.

Twenty-One

They stayed up late to celebrate their victory, sitting around the table and toasting their success with glasses of lemonade and root beer. Everyone made Helena recount again and again how they had played the odds. And they brought another guest to Moon Lake Lodge. Isabel Fish-Wooten, the English lady who had been sent to America to marry a millionaire, had not had any luck with her betting and lost all of her ill-gotten gains.

"That ought to make an honest woman of you," Helena said once Isabel confessed her dilemma after supper.

"Doubtful," Isabel said cheerfully. "But it'll make me more cautious, perhaps. Don't worry. I won't nick your silver and jewels. I did promise to behave, and I do keep my promises. Actually, I have a keen social conscience."

"Admirable," Helena murmured. She patted her sleepy son on the back. "To bed with you, young man."

"No, please, let me stay up," he protested.

"Don't put up a fuss," she said.

"But it's—"

"Your mother said go to bed," Michael broke in. With one motion, he swept the boy up out of his chair and hoisted him onto his back. "I'll take you there myself. You're Sandoval, the greatest jockey that ever lived, and I am Wind-in-Your-Face, the fastest horse on the planet. Away!" With a great clatter, they headed for the stairs.

Helena watched them go, and her heart constricted. A father putting his son to bed was not such an uncommon event. Yet it had never happened for William. Until now.

"I shall retire as well," Isabel said with a delicate yawn. "I cannot tell you how much I appreciate this. I spent last night in—well, that's over now."

"Alice, why don't you show her to her room?" Helena suggested.

One by one, the others drifted off, until only Nellie remained.

Helena tensed, listening to the rough-and-tumble sounds of man and boy upstairs. Feeling Nellie's gaze on her, she said, "Troy Barnes was never much of a father to him."

Nellie snorted. "Barnes had nothing good to offer a son anyway."

"That's true. But it doesn't stop William from yearning for a true father." Helena stood and paced the floor. "Oh, Nellie, I'm so confused. Am I doing a terrible thing, depriving my son of two parents?"

"William is doing just fine. He's bright and loving and interested in the world. You've done a beautiful job, Helena."

"Have I?" She stopped and faced the window, seeing a distorted ghost of her reflection there. "I grew up without a mother, so I had no guide in this, and clearly, I made some wrong turns. All I ever wanted was to give my child two parents. That's why I married Troy."

"You don't need a man. You're strong enough on your own."

"Then why have I made such stupid mistakes?"

"Ah, Helena." Nellie took both her hands, held them fast. "You're a wonderful person who had the bad luck to wind up with a terrible man. But that part of your life is over. Everything will be better now."

"But you see, that is my dilemma. I could raise William alone, or let his natural father be a part of his life."

"Why not do both?" Nellie watched the expression on her face. Helena felt naked and exposed. "You need to ask yourself what your real dilemma is. I think the answer will surprise you."

"I don't know the answer."

"You have to do the work, Helena. Make difficult choices. The things that came easily to you turned out to be not worth having. Troy Barnes, the house in Vandam Square, your social position. The things worth having are harder to attain. The things you would fight for, die for, are precious and few, aren't they?"

Helena nodded. "William. And the life I'm trying to make for us here."

Nellie stood and shuffled to the stairs. "Then that's what matters."

After Nellie left, Helena could still hear Michael in William's room. Michael's deep voice rumbled, then William answered. She could not make out their words, but something vital and good was happening between them. She could hear it in their voices.

But what about the side of Michael she knew? He was secretive about his past. Only today she had learned that he grew up in grinding poverty. He was distracted by scientific problems that were impenetrable to ordinary people. There were places inside him he would never let another person venture.

And he was a lot better at leaving than he was at staying.

His quiet tread on the stairs startled her. She took in a breath, turned to watch him coming toward her. He still wore the fine suit, but he was starting to inhabit it. The crisp neck cloth was gone, the collar hung askew, the tops of his spats flapped as he walked.

"Finally," he said, coming through the doorway to the common room. "He fought sleep every step of the way. Does he do that often?"

She stood up, busied herself tidying the room after their celebration. "Every night. He is afraid he'll miss something." It felt both strange and yet perfectly natural, speaking of William with Michael. What a unique gift this was, discussing her son with someone else who cared about him. Yet it was bittersweet, because it made her think about how different everything would have been if only Michael had listened to her the day he'd left. If only he'd stayed, they might be comfortable as man and wife right now, relaxing in the quiet of a summer evening and talking about their son. The thought sobered her and her smile disappeared.

"Helena." He moved close to her, taking the drinking glass from her hand and setting it down. Then he braced his arm against the wall and gazed down at her. The warmth of his nearness enclosed her, seeped through her.

"Yes?"

"You've raised him well. He's a goodhearted, loving boy."

Her heart soared, because his words echoed Nellie's statement. "He is. I don't claim credit for that."

"You should. The way a boy is raised is far more important than who sired him."

She narrowed her eyes, suspicious of this unexpected comment. "Meaning?"

"Exactly that. William is who he is because of how you've brought him up. It doesn't have anything to do with his breeding. It's the way he's been nurtured. Can you agree with that?"

She thought for a moment, trying to discover the meaning behind his words. He was a puzzle to her; the way he thought and spoke challenged and sometimes frustrated her. He was such a brilliant man, and she was so simple in that respect. Yet for some reason, he never made her feel inadequate.

"I suppose I can," she said at last.

"Don't ever forget you said that."

"Was it that important?"

"You have no idea." He turned away and gathered up a few glasses and bottles. "So. We conquered the races today. Accomplished what we set out to do."

She picked up an oil lamp to light the way to the kitchen. "Good for us."

"I think we're due for a celebration."

Taking the glasses from him, she set them in the sink for washing. "We've already celebrated, the whole lot of us."

"With root beer and mineral lemonade."

"And that was perfectly adequate. I wouldn't dream of drinking hard spirits with Josephine around."

He turned out the lamp, took her hand and led her to the back door. "She's not around now," he whispered.

"I haven't a drop in the house."

"Not in this house," he said, stepping outside and drawing her along behind him. The night should have been inky black but instead, a bright slice of moon, underscored by a shadowy underbelly, gave the air a strange blue water quality, spilling ghostly radiance over the grounds. A breeze whispered across the lake, stirring restless sighs over the tops of the silver birches and sugar maples.

She dug in her heels. "It's late."

"Tomorrow's Sunday."

"I've already toasted your success quite properly, thank you very much." In truth, when she had realized the extent of their winnings today, she'd experienced a moment of intense craving for good champagne. It was one of the few luxuries she missed from her former life.

"Then come along with me and celebrate *im*properly."

She balked and squawked all the way along the lane to the carriage house. When they arrived, Hector grunted once, then fell silent. In the loft quarters, Michael lit a lamp and held the door open for her. She stepped inside and looked around, inspecting the premises. The last time she had come here, she'd been too upset to pay attention to the living quarters, but now the place seemed eerily familiar.

"Amazing," she said. "You've been here just a few weeks and yet your presence completely dominates this place."

"I have no idea what you're talking about."

"You've already written in chalk all over the wall."

"I was making a drilling calculation and couldn't find a piece of paper."

"The bed's unmade," she boldly observed.

"Why bother making it every day? It only gets messed up again each night."

"There's something growing in that jar on the windowsill."

"I'm researching the mineral content from the water."

She shook her head, depressed. "You've not changed a bit, Michael. This is just like your townhouse in Georgetown."

"I liked that house." He stepped close behind her and trailed his hand suggestively down her back. "You liked that house."

She stiffened her spine. "How do you know?"

"Because you were always finding an excuse to visit, even in the middle of the night."

She sniffed at the reminder of her youthful folly. She moved away from him before his touch could ignite memories she was trying to elude. "I don't do those things anymore."

"What? You don't visit your lover in the middle of the night?"

"That's correct."

"You're visiting me."

"You are not my lover."

"That can be changed." His arm reached out, slid around her waist, and he turned her to face him.

Perhaps it was something about the fall of dim light over him or the physical intimacy of his embrace, but just for a fraction of a second, just for the blink of an eye, she thought, *Troy.*

The fleeting thought was more than enough to make her step back with a gasp of alarm.

Instantly, he dropped his arm and turned away. "I promised you a celebration," he said, "and a celebration you'll have.'' He rummaged around in a wooden crate and produced an amber bottle.

''Good glory,'' she said. ''Is that what I think it is?''

He uncorked the bottle, took a swig and his features creased into an expression of pained bliss. ''Still good.''

''Tequila?''

''Either that or kerosene.'' He held out the bottle to her. ''I don't have a proper glass.''

''Even out of a glass, this liquor is improper. I haven't drunk tequila since—'' She stopped. One whiff of the peculiar, exotic liquor made her eyes water and sting.

''Since we were last together,'' he finished for her.

''Yes.''

''So take a drink, Helena. Heaven knows, we earned it today.''

She gripped the angular shape of the bottle, took a deep breath, then lifted it to her mouth. She didn't taste the first sip at all. It was liquid fire, burning across her tongue and down her throat, igniting a bonfire in her belly. She shut her eyes and felt the liquor's hot tendrils spread quickly through her, radiating out along her limbs, bringing hidden parts of her to a state of burning sensitivity.

Too dizzy to open her eyes, she swayed a little, then took another sip. She felt him standing close to her, too close. She just...sensed him there. Everything from the past came rushing back over her, all the little moments and sensations she'd spent years trying to forget. And the hell of it was, he wasn't even touching her...yet.

She raised the bottle a third time, feeding the fire.

''Open your eyes, Helena,'' he said.

''Must I?''

"Yes."

"Why?"

"Because I want you to know for certain I'm not Troy Barnes."

She dragged open her eyelids; already they were weighted by the drink. "I know who you are."

"Good."

"Why is that so important to you?"

"Because I want you to be certain when I—" Michael took her hand, lifted it to his mouth. The warm touch of his breath and then his lips reminded her of how much she wanted, needed. The sight of Michael, cradling her hand with exquisite tenderness, his gaze watching her over her knuckles as he carried them to his lips, fanned the memories to a fever peak. Nine years. It had been nine years since she had been held, caressed, loved.

A sound of helpless yearning escaped her. He slid his splayed hands into her hair, bringing down the pinned-up coils, his fingers getting lost in the thick waves. He lowered his mouth to hers, pressing lightly and tenderly, parting his lips over hers, then moving his tongue with subtle suggestion. She remembered this, oh, God, she remembered the way he used to kiss her. Even the effort to forget made her remember all too vividly.

Helena had convinced herself that she didn't need a man's love, or the intimacy of the marriage bed. And she'd been right. She didn't need just *any* man.

She needed Michael. She always had.

No more thought, no judging, only feeling. Her head tipped back, and his thumbs skimmed over the sensitive skin of her throat. Her mouth opened beneath his and her limbs went slack, relaxing against him as he pulled her close. She let out a soft cry of wonder as unexpected passion came from one of those hidden, burning places inside her.

But finally, common sense took hold. He might not have changed, but she certainly had. She forced herself to accept the melancholy, mature acknowledgment that things between them could never be as they once had been.

For one more bittersweet moment, she lingered, then ended the kiss and pressed her cheek against his chest, curling her fists into the starched white fabric of his shirt, feeling the firmness and warmth of him. She used to make him laugh, long ago, and she had loved to put her ear against his chest and hear the rumble of his mirth.

He wasn't laughing now. His breathing and heartbeat came fast and strong.

"I have to go," she said.

"No, you don't."

"I do."

"Stay with me, Helena. Tonight. All night."

The temptation blazed through her, and it was all she could do to say, "No."

"You want to. You want me to—" Gripping her shoulders, he bent and whispered a reminder that heated her blood even more than the tequila had.

Shaken by the forbidden suggestion, and by the nearly irresistible urge to yield to temptation, she stepped back. "I can't. I'm not that kind of person anymore."

His jaw worked as he clenched his teeth, and he glowered at her. "So what the hell kind of person are you these days?"

"I didn't mean to sound superior. It's just that I am different. I can no longer fling myself into your bed."

"Why not?"

"Because I have responsibilities."

"William, you mean."

"Of course William. And a hundred other things."

"I see. So, at half past midnight, which of those hundred things is keeping you from spending a few hours in mindless pleasure?"

"All of them," she said, hugging her arms protectively around her middle. "All the time."

"Let yourself go, Helena. Just for tonight."

"No."

"Why not?"

"Because there is always a price," she snapped. "There are always consequences."

"Is that what you're afraid of?" he asked with an incredulous laugh. "Consequences? Isn't it a bit late to worry about that now?"

She moved behind a chair, gripping its back. "It's not a question of being afraid. I had a husband who beat me, Michael. Do you think I could ever be afraid of your kisses?"

Stepping toward her, he cupped her cheek in the palm of his hand. "Yes."

She jerked her head away. "Oh, do tell."

"My kisses are more of a threat, Helena. Because there's so much more at risk."

The truth of it hammered at her. Damn him, he always did this. Always managed to drill straight to the truth. She wondered how he did it. Keeping the chair between them, she moved backward toward the door. "Thank you for...everything," she said, feeling awkward. "For the betting and winning, and for the tequila. It's late now. I must go."

"Helena, we're not finished." He crossed the room and grabbed her hand, lifted it to his lips as he had earlier, with that curious combination of chivalry and raw lust.

She pulled her hand from his grasp. "Let me go."

"You don't want to go."

She edged closer to the door. "It's not a question of wanting, either."

"What else is there?"

Now *that* sounded like the old Michael, the man who had taught her to seek pleasure without a thought for consequences. And it gave her the strength to remember the deeper commitment she had made.

"Well. I'm certainly glad you asked. There is everything else in the world, Michael. Everything that lasts. Everything that matters."

"Why must that exclude letting me hold you in my arms, letting me take you to bed?"

"Because when you do that, nothing else matters." She gasped, appalled at herself. Her mortification, perversely, gave her the strength to walk out the door without looking back. She didn't wait to hear his reply as she clattered down the stairs. He called after her, but she didn't slow her steps. She wanted to put as much distance between them as she possibly could. Yet even as she hurried across the yard and down the lane, his touch seemed to linger on her skin, as though a soft warm breeze she couldn't escape caressed her.

There's so much more at risk.

She didn't want him to be right, but she couldn't deny it. Bruises and broken bones were painful, but the pain went away when the wounds healed. There were only so many ways Troy could hurt her. He could never penetrate that last bastion of the sacrosanct self, could never harm the most vulnerable part of her.

The real danger lay ahead, she thought, her soul haunted by what had nearly happened between her and Michael.

Twenty-Two

Michael couldn't remember when he'd spent a more restless night. She tormented him. Haunted him. Lust alone didn't begin to explain the way he wanted her. He wanted to engulf his soul in her, to fuse himself to her, with a need so powerful it hurt. The lusts of his youth, powerful as they had been, were pale ghosts of the bright passion that consumed him now. It wasn't a question of desire, but one of necessity. That, and a complete certainty that she reciprocated his feelings. He didn't love her because he needed her. If anything, that caused him to resent her as a man resents any woman who exerts so powerful an influence over his will. No, his affliction was far worse than that.

He needed her because he loved her. There was a world of difference in the distinction, but little enough consolation.

Unshaven and out-of-sorts, he trudged to the drilling site. Although it was still early morning, everyone was already hard at work, and he stood there for a moment, just watching. Around the hot springs, an algae bloom had appeared, painting the rocks with unnaturally bright colors. In the emerald shade of morning, the site had an eerie, otherworldly look to it. Yet the remarkable beauty of the mineral spring didn't make him any less irritable as he headed down the slope to join the workers.

The laborers were as unusual as Moon Lake Lodge itself. The women wore canvas overalls or dungarees, with hobnail boots, thick gloves and oversize smocks. And then, incongruously, sunbonnets. Not just any bonnets, but bird and fruit-infested creations that Alice had created, hats that would make an Astor or Vanderbilt proud.

"Hiya, Professor." Already filthy from digging, his bare feet covered in mud, William raced across the clearing to greet him. "You're late."

"So I am. I'd best get to work." As always, Michael's heart lifted at the sight of the boy, the sound of his voice. That was one of many startling things about having a child—the pure, unreasoning joy of knowing he was alive and in the world. No one had ever told Michael it was like that. Had it been so for his mother? He couldn't remember. But perhaps he could. Even in the most desperate days of poverty, she had always been able to summon a smile for her son. He could still remember the way her midnight-blue eyes shone when he came in from chores, or jumped out of bed in the morning. The knowledge that he'd brought her joy comforted him years after he had resigned himself to the loss of his mother. And the lesson was learned, oddly enough, from the grandson Hannah Rowan would never know.

He ruffled William's hair and picked up his leather apron, heavy with tools. Across the clearing, at the site of the bathhouse, Helena sent him a cool glance and a neutral wave, then carried on working.

So that was the way things were going to be, he

thought peevishly. He'd pushed her too far last night, hoped for too much, and now she had stepped back. Two steps or more.

Unlike men, the lady workers chattered the whole time, as though the lively conversation fueled their labor. Yet despite the constant talk, they worked as hard as men, hauling loads uphill, mixing concrete and mortar, consulting the well driller's diagrams and excavating the oblong pool for the main bath.

Daisy and Josephine had proved to be invaluable when it came to finding day laborers. They seemed to have a connection to nearly every working woman in town and had brought many of them to Moon Lake Lodge with the promise of a fair wage and a hearty midday meal. Some of the workers brought children along, and with undisguised relief, Isabel Fish-Wooten abandoned the backbreaking labor, set aside her shovel and gloves and appointed herself caretaker of the little ones. William delighted in playing with them, although Michael's laboratory and Hector's paddock had an irresistible allure for him and just as frequently, he could be found there.

Daisy led the workers in Negro spirituals. It was a little incongruous, seeing an English noblewoman, a group of American beauties, a Mohawk Indian and the first lady lawyer in the state all singing "Massah's in the Cold Cold Ground." Yet the singing gave them a certain rhythm and a unification of purpose that seemed to make the work go smoothly.

During his years at the Institute, Michael had never seen his scientists and technicians work with that level of diligence. Of course, the nature of their pursuit was quite different. Perhaps some esprit de corps would have made a difference. Perhaps they would have achieved the sort of breakthrough science practiced by

Edison's team at Menlo Park. For the first time, it occurred to him that he could have approached the staff at the Institute in a different way. He should have engaged their hearts as well as their minds in the business at hand. Maybe that would have elevated the work to a vocation. But it didn't matter now. The Institute was behind him. What lay ahead was an infinitely more complex task, fraught with peril. Tubing a spring and building a bathhouse seemed easy compared to the real struggle—winning her back.

In the midst of the day's work, the sound of a gunshot brought Helena to her feet on a surge of panic. She had never run so fast in her life, tearing across the yard and down to the lake. The shots rang out again, three, four and five times, each one stinging her with terror.

She burst into the clearing at the lakeshore in time to hear Isabel say, "Pull!"

The clay disc catapulted into the air. The rusty shotgun in Isabel's hands exploded and the clay pigeon shattered in a cloud of earth-colored dust. William, who was standing behind Isabel, jumped into the air. "Six in a row!" he yelled. "Good show, Miss Isabel." Then he spied Helena. "Mama, did you see? Miss Isabel got six hits in a row. The Professor and I fixed the catapult, didn't we, Professor?"

Too angry to speak for a moment, she grabbed William's hand. "Is it too much to ask that you keep my son away from deadly weapons?"

Isabel set aside the gun, chamber emptied and barrel down. "He was in no danger. I'm a crack shot. However, if you prefer, I can find some other place to practice."

"I do prefer," Helena said.

"But Mama—"

Michael came over. "You're finished?" he asked Isabel.

"We both are. I told Helena we would find a shooting range somewhere else." She beamed. "It's better that way. I can shoot for money, bringing me closer to the fortune I must earn."

"Where did you find a shotgun, Isabel?" Helena asked, suddenly suspicious.

"It was all in the carriage house—the shotgun, cartridges, clay discs and the launch," Michael answered for her. But he didn't look at Isabel. His gaze clung to Helena, challenging her. Taking apart her convictions, one by one.

She couldn't do this, not now. "We should get back to work. We've still got several hours before dark."

"What's it like, having an admirer?" Alice whispered to Daisy, elbowing her.

Helena paused in her work, suppressing a grin as Daisy waved Alice away like a bee at a picnic. "The lady doth protest too much," she couldn't help murmuring.

One bright morning, responding to Helena's invitation, Julius Calhoun had arrived. The young horseman from Virginia only pretended to listen closely to Michael's explanation of the layout of the project. Anyone could see that his real interest was Daisy Sullivan. Each time she paused in her labors, he hurried over to offer her a drink of water. Each time she struggled with a wheelbarrow or tree stump, he appeared at her side, ready to help.

"Get on with you, girl. I got no admirer." Glowering at Alice, Daisy stabbed her spade at the ground.

The yellow flower Julius had stuck in the brim of her hat nodded in the breeze.

"Do too. Julius Calhoun, the one Helena knows from down in Virginia, has been after you all day."

"Fool boy's young enough to be my...younger brother."

"Old enough to be your lover," Alice said, clearly savoring the scandalous idea.

"You get on out of here, girl," Daisy grumbled. "I got work to do."

"And I know someone who'll be glad to help." Helena nodded cheerfully at Julius, who was helping to unload a delivery of tubing pipes.

"Huh. You got your own kind of admirer," Daisy said.

"Ah, yes. The kind that ignores me." She darted a glance at Michael, who was with the drillers, laying out the excavation line for the tube that would pipe the water to the reservoir. He'd barely spoken to her since the shooting incident, and she refused to be the one to break the silence. She'd done nothing wrong, after all. It was his fault they were so awkward with one another. He wanted the sort of physical intimacy they'd shared long ago, and couldn't understand why she needed something else altogether. In her youth, passion for him had consumed her like wildfire, had burned her common sense to ash. She was different now, but he didn't seem to understand that. He still believed there was an ardent girl inside her, hidden away somewhere, and that he could find her again simply by reminding her of how deeply she used to feel, how much she used to love him.

Pushing aside the troubling thought, she went to look over Alice's sketches for the bathhouse fresco. The girl's dreamy fragility kept her from being of much use when it came to digging and building, but her artistic talent would have a chance to flourish once the open-air structure was complete. Rather than the predictable spouting fish and mythical water nymphs, Alice had chosen to drench the wall in a wash of color, depicting a light-dappled garden in the style of the French Impressionists.

"Mama, who's that man?" William asked, pointing at the gravel drive. Now that a path had been cleared leading to the building site, the main drive was visible through the trees.

Instantly alert, Helena shaded her eyes. Sure enough, a visitor was approaching. As she scanned the area, her mouth twitched with wry irony. Not long ago, receiving visitors meant polishing the tea service and awaiting the delivery of a calling card. Nowadays, it meant wiping the dirt from her hands and the sweat from her face.

As the clop of hooves grew louder, everyone froze, clutching tools as they watched the man coming up the drive. He drove a smart little trap harnessed to a horse with polished hooves and a whimsical bouquet of daisies secured to its forelock.

Sarah Dalton caught her breath. "It's Grady."

He looked completely different from the raging stranger who had slammed his way into the house in the middle of the night. This Grady Dalton had been freshly barbered and was nattily dressed, his shoes brushed to a high sheen. With a sob of pure joy, Sarah ran down to meet him. Michael and Julius exchanged a glance, then edged closer to her. Helena and the others followed more slowly, holding themselves at a respectful distance.

"Whoa." Mr. Dalton jerked the pretty horse to a halt. It was a fine chestnut Morgan, and it danced a little nervously before settling down. Julius murmured under his breath to Michael. Sarah's husband secured the reins and stepped down from the pristine trap. He held one hand palm up to Sarah, the other held a bouquet of sweet peas.

He had eyes for no one but his wife. "Come home, dearest." His voice was soft with emotion.

"Oh, Grady." She reached back to untie her smock.

"Don't you do it, girl," Daisy warned. "He gets a few swallows of whiskey in him, he'll be back to beating on you."

Something glinted, fast as a blink, in his eyes. It was so quickly gone, it might have been a trick of the light. Except it wasn't. Helena knew that. She could tell Daisy knew it, too.

Grady Dalton ignored them both. "Things will be different from now on, you'll see, dearest. Please. I've put in a new sink and painted the house yellow, and your dahlias are blooming."

Sarah all but melted into a puddle at his feet. "Grady, did you really?"

"I'd do anything for you. Give me a chance to prove my love to you. Please."

"Sarah, wait." Helena stepped forward, but she didn't know what else to say. She couldn't—wouldn't—keep Sarah here against her will. Yet at the same time, it felt all wrong to see her friend so heart-struck and willing to submit to this man.

"You made a vow to me, Sarah," her husband reminded her. "You swore before the Lord God that you'd be my wife, in sickness and in health, until death do us part."

"Oh, Grady, I know." Turning briefly to Helena, she said with utter confidence, "I'll be fine." Love and wonder shone from her eyes, and the old bruise on her jaw had faded to a pretty shadow of color. "Thank you for everything, Helena," she added, already walking toward him. "I'm going home with my husband now." Then, with a cry of joy, she flung herself into his arms. He treated her with tender gallantry as he helped her to her seat, and spared no further word for the ladies of Moon Lake Lodge.

The picture they made as they drove together down the lane was purely romantic. The elm trees arched overhead, letting golden dapples of sunshine fall through the canopy of summer leaves. His arm slid around her slender form, and she leaned her cheek delicately on his shoulder. They looked for all the world like a pair of newlyweds, setting off on their life together.

As the trap turned onto the main drive, the Morgan balked a little. Grady Dalton corrected it with an efficient cut of the quirt, and the horse obediently moved out into traffic.

Helena released a sigh. She felt no sense of nostalgia for the life of a married lady. None at all. Nor was she fooled for a single moment by Grady Dalton.

She felt curiously isolated in that moment, though she was surrounded by people and, in the distance, children laughed and played on the lawn. Being an independent woman had unanticipated pressures. She did not shy from them, but sometimes, late in the night, she ached so deeply with loneliness that she felt physically ill.

She was no stranger to solitude. Her husband had never been good company and she had learned to occupy herself with other pursuits. But despite her new friendships and new responsibilities, she sometimes felt the piercing need for something more. Inexorably, her gaze drifted to Michael, who stood at a distance, watching the Daltons leave. Even in old denim jeans and a shirt with the sleeves torn out, he appealed to her in the most elemental way possible, creating a tumult of resistance and desire inside her.

As though he felt her gaze, he turned to her, and she quickly looked away, ducking her head to hide an untimely blush.

Something was building between them, something as dangerous as it was inevitable. And despite the heat of the late-afternoon sun, she shivered.

Twenty-Three

They argued for half a day about the hole, continuing the quarrel until sunset, after everyone had stopped work and gone in to supper. Helena and Michael remained in the clearing, which glowed gold with the colors of the sinking sun. It was the most beautiful spot on earth, she decided, but could take no pleasure in the sight. Not this evening. Michael was making it impossible.

Helena envisioned the thermal pool as a neo-Roman masterpiece, reminiscent of the ancient historic facility in Vaison-la-Romaine, in the south of France. Her father had taken her and her sister there when they were girls, and she had never forgotten the formal splendor of the majestic pools, open to the sky, with classical arched seats around them, sheltered by a colonnade.

Michael believed the manmade bath should reflect the Napahock Mohawk tradition of the people who first discovered the sacred Place of Many Waters. He wanted the reservoir to be constructed of river rock, set into the curve of the slope as though it had been formed by the hand of nature. He envisioned a simple roof supported by lodge poles, open to the surrounding woods.

"The enterprise is mine," Helena said, pacing up and down the building site. "I want a Roman bath."

"Then go to Rome." He did not look up from his surveyor's level, laid across the top of the reservoir.

"I can bring Rome here."

"I'm in charge of the work," he said. "I say we use the stone we have."

"Fine. I'll find someone else to build it."

"Fine. I'll dismiss the masonry workers I engaged yesterday." He straightened up, rubbing the small of his back.

They glared at each other while Helena tried to decide why she was arguing with him, why she constantly found reason to quarrel several times a day. It was a form of self-defense, she decided. A way to keep a necessary distance between them. Already she'd made the mistake of letting him come too close. When he kissed her, he gained power over her. He took away her free will, turned her into a weak and needy creature who believed life without him was utter misery. After all her hard work, she refused to succumb to sentiment.

"Do what you must," she said through clenched teeth.

Hooking his thumbs into his back pockets, he paced back and forth. "It's a damned hole in the ground. Why are you making such a commotion over it?"

"Why are you being so overbearing?"

"I'm not. My design is practical. It costs the least and involves the least amount of work. It has the added bonus of paying homage to the Mohawk, who were here before the white man ever touched these waters."

She hesitated, scanning the work site. The newly tapped thermal spring sang into the silence as it spilled over rocks to the reservoir. Josephine said the water music came from the lost souls of people trapped beneath the earth, hoping that healing others would set them free. Wisps of steam rose, then scattered before a light breeze. "All my life, men have dictated their will to me. They've told me what is best, what is right, what is proper, what is expected. Never once did anyone ever ask me what I wanted."

Michael stopped pacing and stood before her. "You're wrong."

"What?"

"Either you're lying or you're being willfully obtuse."

"What do you mean?"

"I asked you, Helena."

"Asked me what?"

"I asked you what you wanted."

"You did not. Name one time."

"Every time we made love, I asked you." He fixed her with a stare that seemed to see straight through her. "I know you remember. Or perhaps not. Shall I remind you? I asked you how you wanted to be held, where you wanted me to kiss you, to put my hand, my finger, my tongue…remember? And you said—"

"I know what I said." Her cheeks burned. She had been so young, so filled with insane desire. So convinced that she could fulfill her cravings without paying the price.

"And then when I offered to put my mouth there, you said…"

"I *remember.*" She could not bear to hear anymore. But her own ecstatic cries echoed back across the years to her. *I want… I want… I want…* Heavens. How had the conversation deteriorated to this?

"All right," she said peevishly. "You've made your

foolish point. If you insist on turning my thermal bath into a primitive waterhole, then I won't stop you."

"Fine."

"Fine."

She whirled away, flouncing off blindly down the slope, intent on returning to the lodge, finding her ladies and joining Daisy and Nellie for the nightly lesson in reading. The current text was Dr. Steele's excruciatingly boring discourse on mineral baths, but Helena vowed to give it her full attention in order to keep her mind off the fact that Michael Rowan had been right about one thing.

All those years ago, he had asked her what she wanted. And all those years ago, he had given her exactly that.

But there was one flaw in his logic. Despite the delights of the flesh he had bestowed upon her with unbounded generosity, he had withheld the one thing that would have made all the difference.

His heart.

"William, stop fidgeting and eat your hominy," Helena said in exasperation. "We've got a busy day ahead of us, so we mustn't dawdle over breakfast." She darted a nervous glance at the case clock on the wall, then at Nellie, who seemed perfectly content and unhurried as she sipped her coffee.

"Do as your mama say, boy," Daisy advised, giving him another helping of eggs. "Lordy, but you done shot up like a Virginia pole bean."

Despite her impatience this morning, Helena felt a wave of affection. Daisy was right. William was growing and flourishing this summer, as beautifully as the garden they were slowly reclaiming from the wild. Almost overnight, it seemed, he had grown pounds heavier, inches taller. He looked like a different boy, with his skin turned dark from the sun and his hair touched with gold.

Perched halfway off his chair, he scooped the hominy into a mound, poking a hole in the center with his thumb. "This is High Rock Spring," he explained in a scholarly tone that was eerily familiar. "The mineral deposits give it a chronicle structure."

"Conical," said Michael, walking into the dining room. "Finish your breakfast. We've got work to do."

William shoveled in several large bites of hominy and scrambled eggs.

Nellie didn't glance up from her paper. "Good morning to you, too."

"Have you abandoned the courtesy of knocking?" Helena asked. She hoped her cool voice masked her reaction to seeing him.

"I knocked, but there was so much chattering going on that no one heard. However..." Pointing his toe with mock formality, he executed a mincing bow. "Good morning, dear ladies. I came to beg you for the favor of your company, digging a ditch today." He went around the table, taking each one's hand and lifting it to his lips in a foppish kiss, causing William to fall off his chair with idiotic laughter.

"My, my," said Isabel, flushing with pleasure. "Are you quite certain you're not a millionaire?"

"And if I was?"

"I'd marry you immediately."

"What's so busy about today?" asked Josephine, clearly less enchanted than Isabel as she wiped her just-kissed hand on her shirttail.

Helena and Nellie exchanged a glance. "We have an appointment with Mayor Dashell and the Township Water Board."

"We should leave soon." Nellie folded her paper and got up.

Michael prodded William with his foot. "Come on, Dr. Watson. You've got a horse to feed."

"Wear your boots in the paddock," Helena admonished him as she went to the foyer. "I don't want you getting stepped on."

"How will boots prevent him from getting stepped on?" Michael asked, following her.

"Don't annoy me this morning, Michael. I have much to do." She shooed William upstairs to find his boots, then rummaged in the hall tree for her black parasol. With so many residents at Moon Lake Lodge, the umbrella stand was filling up. She came across her old parasol, the one with the broken shaft. "I keep meaning to throw this out. He destroyed it, you know. Grady Dalton broke it."

"I didn't know."

She recalled that Michael had been away in Albany that night…finding a way to free her from her husband. She shoved the parasol aside and selected another. "I see her sometimes."

"Who?" asked Michael.

"Sarah Dalton. When I'm doing errands in town, I sometimes encounter her. But she never seems to have a moment to visit with me. I worry about her, Michael."

"Why?"

"Because I…I think I make her uncomfortable with my concern. Michael, I don't believe he has stopped hurting her. Yet she claims she's never been happier, and that since she found out she's expecting a baby, Grady has been the model husband."

"But you don't believe her."

"She wears dresses with long sleeves and high collars."

He frowned. "That's significant?"

"I suppose a man wouldn't see the connection."

"What connection?"

"It's the end of summer, and it's ninety degrees in the shade," she said. "Yet Sarah covers herself with long sleeves and high collars, and bonnets with brims so deep you can hardly see her face. She has something to hide, I'm certain of it."

His scowl deepened. "Why didn't you say so before? The bastard. I'll pay him a visit myself."

Helena shook her head. "What good would it do if she denies that he hurts her?" She tried to put Sarah out of her mind, but couldn't keep from worrying. How much did you owe a friend? she wondered. How hard should she fight to prove the man Sarah adored was dangerous? And what if she was wrong?

"I shall visit her myself," she said. "I'll invite her back to Moon Lake Lodge."

Helena and Nellie were early for their appointment to obtain the permit for the spring, so they decided to pay Sarah Dalton a visit on the way. They crossed through the Lower Village, a tidy, modest neighborhood south of town. Tree-shaded houses slumbered beneath the afternoon sun. The Daltons lived in a yellow house with white trim and bright bursts of dahlias blooming along the walkway.

Everything appeared to be in order, yet it was odd for the windows to be shut and the curtains drawn on such a hot day. As she knocked at the freshly painted front door, Helena felt a chill of apprehension. "I feel like an intruder."

Slow footsteps sounded within, then the door opened slightly.

"Sarah?" Nellie said. "We've come for a visit, dear. May we come in?"

"I'll join you on the porch," she said, slipping out and shutting the door quickly behind her. Yet she was not so quick that Helena failed to notice the stench of cigar smoke and whiskey inside. When Sarah stepped into the sunlight, she moved with a cautious hesitation Helena recognized. Her heart sank as she drew her friend to the wicker settee on the porch, and the three of them sat down.

"Tell us what's the matter, Sarah."

She said nothing at first, but took out a handkerchief embroidered in her fine needlework, and pressed it briefly to her cheeks. "Grady's having one of his spells. His brother was unjustly convicted—"

"Of what?" Nellie demanded.

Sarah hesitated, then said, "Assaulting a woman. But it wasn't his fault. She started the trouble, and he was sent up for disciplining her."

"None of this is your fault," Helena said. "Yet you're the one who's been hurt."

"He's just having one of his spells."

"Then you must come back to Moon Lake Lodge," Helena said. Yes, that was the thing, to get her away and then convince her to keep herself safe from her husband.

"Oh, but he needs me."

Helena was startled and dismayed to feel a flash of anger at Sarah. "Look, you're risking not just yourself, but the baby as well. I know you wouldn't want that."

"Do it for the baby, Sarah," Nellie urged her.

She crushed the handkerchief into a ball in her hand. "Maybe...I'll come along later."

''Come now. We'll all go together. We'll just walk away,'' Helena said.

''Sarah,'' her husband bellowed from within. ''You come back inside now.''

''I'll come on my own, as I did last time,'' Sarah said, speaking with gratifying conviction. ''There are some things I must attend to before I...leave.''

''But—''

''I insist,'' Sarah said, lifting her delicate chin. ''Now, please excuse me.'' She stuffed the handkerchief into her apron pocket and slipped back inside.

Helena and Nellie looked at one another. ''Now what?'' Helena asked.

''It's difficult. One doesn't want to push too hard, and yet—''

''You're worried, too, aren't you?''

''I am,'' said Nellie. ''She is a grown woman, though, and she made her wishes clear. Why don't we finish taking care of our business, then come back and see if she's ready to go.''

It was not an ideal arrangement, but Helena agreed, and they proceeded to the center of town where the summer crowds filled the sidewalks and squares. A wrought iron fence and rows of urns gave a stately look to Congress Spring Park. It was a grand place of sculptured figures, shaded glades, arbors and walkways populated by ambitious gents and fashionable ladies seeking that all-important ''correct acquaintance.'' Tourists and health-seekers clustered around the pavilions covering the springs, and Helena could not help but note that the formal white-washed structures looked...pretentious.

The tiny circular railway, packed with children and sight-seers, lumbered past the rustic Deer Lodge, and she felt a familiar twist of anxiety. William used to love riding the railway and feeding the tame deer from his hand, yet she had taken him away from the familiar pleasures of ordinary friendships. Now he ran like a hooligan with the workers' children.

Coming along the sidewalk toward them was the headmaster of William's school. Helena stopped to greet him. "How do you do, Mr. Peabody? This is my dear friend, Mrs. Nellie Freeman McQuigg."

"Yes, er, how do you do?" He was a tall, athletic-looking man with a salt-and-pepper mustache, side whiskers that reached deep along his jowls and a beard that nearly succeeded in hiding a decidedly weak chin.

"Mr. Peabody is headmaster of Penfield Academy," Helena explained.

"I'm familiar with the school," Nellie said. "It's very famous, Mr. Peabody. It has a fabulous reputation. Of course, it would be a better institution if you allowed girls to attend."

"Er, indeed." Dressed in a pinstripe suit, he looked quite uncomfortable, as though the summer heat was getting to him.

Helena tried to ignore a flicker of foreboding. "Sir, I want to thank you for your letter of commendation about William." Three months earlier, she had received a note on the school's letterhead and had asked William to read it aloud, praying it was not bad news. She needn't have worried. Everyone loved William. And he was doing beautifully in school. "It meant the world to me. I'm very proud of my son."

The headmaster's gaze shifted, taking in the strolling tourists in the park. Then he cleared his throat. "Yes, er, you're quite welcome indeed, Mrs., er, Miss…"

For a headmaster, he wasn't very articulate. "William is looking forward to his classes in the fall,'' she said with a smile.

He made a choking sound, cleared his throat again. ''Didn't you receive my recent letter, ma'am?''

She shook her head, and the flicker of foreboding rose to a nervous flutter in her chest. Although she had known Mr. Peabody for years, his manner now seemed chilly and almost furtive. ''I'm afraid it must have been delivered to my former home.''

''Ah. I'm sorry to hear that. Madam, I'm afraid we won't be able to accommodate William in the future.''

She frowned, and the flutter intensified. ''I beg your pardon.''

''We just don't feel Penfield Academy is the appropriate place for William, and in my letter I suggested you make other arrangements for your son.''

Nellie made a harrumphing sound.

''What do you mean, Penfield is not appropriate?'' Helena demanded, although she knew, God, she knew, but she wanted to make him say it. ''William loves Penfield. Hasn't my son been an exemplary student?''

A bead of sweat rolled down his temple and disappeared into his side whiskers. ''He has. But we have to consider what's best for the student body as a whole.''

''I heard no protest from you when we made a large contribution to the school each year.''

''The generosity of your contributions has always been appreciated. However, in light of recent events, the Board of Directors has determined that William's presence at the school would be disruptive—''

''Recent events,'' she cut in. ''Can you be more specific?'' Say it, you unctuous windbag.

''To be blunt, Madam, the change in your circumstances has created a great moral alarm, and therefore we cannot accommodate William in future years.''

''I see. And what about the proposed construction of Cabot Hall? Surely you received word that a portion of my father's legacy was to be donated for a new science lab at Penfield.'' Though Troy had laid claim to her father's fortune, she was quite certain Mr. Peabody didn't know that, and she wasn't about to tell him.

''Well, of course, we will have no choice but to honor the esteemed Senator Cabot's wishes—''

''Heavens, I should think not,'' Helena said with exaggerated distress. ''Because, you see, I am a Cabot. The donation of Cabot money is sure to have a bad effect on the morals of your students. After all, you must keep up appearances. I shall see to the problem immediately,'' she said, smiling graciously. ''In fact,'' she added, gesturing at Nellie, ''my solicitor and I are on our way to conduct some business right now. I shall see to it that the legacy is diverted to a place more concerned with education than social status.''

They left him sputtering on the sidewalk and proceeded to Broadway. ''Can I do that?'' Helena asked Nellie in a whisper.

''Not since you forfeited your inheritance. But the important thing is, he believed it.''

Armed with a permit, Helena and Nellie returned to Sarah Dalton's house. The tranquil scene they'd encountered earlier had exploded into noise and confusion. A police wagon hitched to a Shire horse stood in the middle of the block, and a group of constables and civilians gathered around the yellow house.

''Dear God.'' Nellie strode forward with a speed that belied her age.

Helena walked even faster, yet she couldn't say a word. Every instinct inside her pulsed with raw dread.

"We'd best find out what's going on." Nellie's face was grim.

Neighbors pressed close to the fence in front of the house, trampling dahlias underfoot, craning their necks for a view and whispering amongst themselves. Despite the noise of speculation, the buzzing of flies and bees could be heard. Helena spied a delicate white handkerchief in the grass along the walkway. Picking it up, she recognized Sarah's fine piquet stitching, and her heart seized. She and Nellie jostled a path through the cluster of neighbors and authorities.

Two patrolmen rushed out of the house. The older one held a bloody kitchen knife between his thumb and forefinger. At the sight of it, the onlookers gasped and whispered. The younger man held a beefy fist to his mouth, and his face was pasty white. He staggered down the porch steps and grabbed on to the picket fence a few feet from Nellie. She took the handkerchief from Helena and thrust it at him. "We are friends of Mrs. Dalton," she said. "What happened here?"

"Ma'am, I'm sorry. I'm so sorry."

Helena clutched at Nellie and stumbled back. They clung to each other, and Helena whispered, "Nellie, he killed her, he—"

"Oh, dear heaven." Nellie stared at the front door of the house. There was Grady Dalton, between two more constables, his wrists shackled and his eyes downcast. Blood spattered his face and hair, covered his hands and clothes and shoes.

The ashen-faced patrolman shook his head. "It's a bad business, I tell you."

Grady Dalton was put into the patrol wagon and carted away. Helena stared after it, cold with shock.

"Nellie," she said, "did I do this? Did she die because I convinced her to leave him?"

"Absolutely not," Nellie said. "Don't even think it."

Twenty-Four

"What are you doing?" asked William, perched on a three-legged stool by a long, cluttered table in Michael's laboratory.

"Titrating this water sample for minerals." He held up a corked beaker. As distractions went, it wasn't much, but it would have to do. Since the news of the murder of Sarah Dalton had stunned the whole town, everyone at Moon Lake Lodge had been subdued. Defeated, even.

Michael hadn't known the young woman well, and yet he had. She possessed that pale, submissive quality that some women affected when confronted by domineering men. He recognized it, because he'd seen it in his own mother, every day of his boyhood.

William studied the tangle of tubes and beakers with gratifying interest. "Why?" he asked at length.

"So I can see if this compound contains cobalt."

"Why?"

"Because it's important." He made a notation in his lab book.

"Why?"

"Because if I don't figure it out, then..." He hesitated, but opted for honesty. "Because I want your mother to know the mineral content of her springs."

"Why?"

"Because it would make her happy, and she deserves to be happy, and if you ask me why, I'll titrate *you.*"

William gripped the edge of the stool. Michael could see him gauging the distance to the open door. Then the boy looked him in the eye and asked, *"Why?"*

As soon as he spoke, he vaulted off the stool and raced for the door. Gales of laughter streamed in his wake.

Michael set down his book and bolted after him. The boy was quick as a minnow, darting across the carriage house yard and down the path toward the lake. From the corner of his eye, Michael could see the workers pause and look up, but they were used to the boy and his antics, and they were getting used to Michael's participation as well.

Michael allowed the boy to elude him for a short while. The fact was, he loved the sound of William's laughter and the sight of him tearing around the property like a woodsprite. To William, the world was a series of endless wonders: a spider spinning a web, a trout lazing in the shallows, Hector pacing around the paddock to exercise his healing legs.

The boy sped out onto the dock, where Michael had begun assembling a boat launch operated by a hand crank. The contraption had yet to work properly, but he scarcely had time to work on anything except the hot spring these days. Waving his arms in taunting fashion, William lured him to the dock. Then, as Michael watched, one of the wooden planks gave way and the boy plunged in. Michael was startled but not alarmed. The day was hot, the water cool and the boy could do worse than go for a swim.

William took his time breaking the surface. A stream of lazy bubbles floated to the top. This was all part of his game, Michael thought, the little scamp. He'd probably swum under the dock and was hiding there to give Michael a scare. Except...

Michael ran faster than he'd ever run in his life, faster than worry, faster than fear. He dove off the end of the dock and surged downward with powerful strokes. A blur of sunlit water streamed past. Shadowy weeds waved along the pebbled bottom, and a submerged tree branch created a confusing tangle of shadows. He swam toward a violently moving object on the bottom, grasping at what appeared to be a fallen limb from the tree.

It was no branch but William, flailing and struggling with jerky, panicked movements. Michael grabbed his hand and struck for the surface. William exploded with a fit of coughing, then inhaled greedily as he clung to Michael.

He said nothing; he couldn't. His heart pumped like an overheated piston, and he sucked air as though he, too, had nearly drowned. He put his arm around William, swam for shore and hauled them both out. For a moment, he simply stood in the shadows, holding his son. The boy was all angular limbs and shivering flesh, his matted hair dark red in the sunlight, narrow shoulders and knock knees outlined by wet clothes. "There now," Michael said in a calming voice. "You're all right now. Don't be afraid, my William."

Thank God. Thank God he was all right. A wave of affection broke over Michael, and inside him something began to shine. It was not just that William was his son, or even that he was Helena's child. The overwhelming, bright heat of emotion was something far more powerful. It was love for a child, a boy he'd never known until this summer. William didn't know it yet, but he was at the center of Michael's world. It struck Michael that he would do anything for this child, suffer any torment, die for him. It was not a comfortable feeling but he welcomed it, glowed with it, and he knew it would burn inside him all the rest of his days.

"Did you hurt yourself?" Michael asked.

William's color was returning fast, though his lips were still edged in blue. "No," he said in his scratchy little-boy voice. "Nothing hurts. And I wasn't afraid, I swear it, Professor. It was sort of fun, once I got up to the surface."

"I was scared," Michael said, feeling raw and exposed.

"Please don't tell my mama." William's instinct to protect Helena was as strong as hers to protect him. "She's already real upset over Mrs. Dalton, and I don't want to worry her."

"What did she tell you about Mrs. Dalton?"

"That her husband was a bad man who hurt her, and then she died." Trouble brewed in William's eyes. "Why did that man hurt Mrs. Dalton, Professor?"

"Some men are just plain bad. I can't explain it. Hitting a woman or a kid is just about the worst thing a man can do. I'd never do it myself, and I have no respect for any man who would."

"Same here," said William, apparently satisfied with the answer. "Besides, it can be real dangerous, getting a lady mad at you." William's teeth chattered.

"That's a fact." Michael removed his boots and socks, setting them on the warm stones beside the lake. Then he peeled off the boy's wet shirt and dungarees, draping them over a blooming acacia bush to dry them in the sun. William laid out the contents of his pockets—a slingshot and a little box, two copper coins, a fish hook, his green-tinted spectacles and three smooth stones.

"Do you know how to swim?" Michael asked.

William solemnly shook his head.

"Most boys your age know how to swim."

The skinny shoulders lifted in a shrug. "Mama says it's dangerous."

Michael set his jaw. "Not knowing how to swim—now, *that's* dangerous."

William nodded. An expression of yearning flickered in his face as he stared out at the clear, cool water.

"Would you like to learn to swim?" Michael asked.

The boy nodded again, then looked up with imploring eyes. "Can you teach me?"

Twenty-Five

Helena decided that Michael had been right about the river rocks, not that she would ever admit it. The man's pride didn't need encouragement, that was for certain. But she was willing to concede that making the thermal pool resemble a natural feature of the woods had been the right choice. The bath was becoming an enchanted place, touched by sunlight and shade, painted with intense colors from the surrounding woods and mineral bloom on the rocks. In the wake of Sarah's tragedy, the oasis in the clearing took on a special significance for all the ladies of Moon Lake Lodge. They were more dedicated than ever to finishing the project and making room for more guests.

Sitting with Nellie beside the stone-lined tank, Helena gratefully drank a glass of lemonade and used a corner of her apron to wipe the sweat from her brow. On the opposite bank, the workers took a break from their labors. She noticed that Julius and Daisy had taken to stealing away by themselves, walking through the woods or wandering down to the lakeshore. They made an incongruous pair. Daisy was his superior in both age and height, yet they seemed completely compatible, as though they'd known each other for years.

Although they had Virginia roots and their race in common, the similarities ended there. Julius was the product of wealth and privilege, while Daisy's nightmare of slavery was a past she struggled every day to overcome. Even so, they were constantly drawn to each other.

"It's coming along beautifully," Nellie commented. "The thermal pool will be ready before you know it."

"And not a moment too soon," Helena murmured.

"What's that?"

Helena hesitated. She hadn't meant to disclose her troubles, but she could already see the understanding in Nellie's eyes.

"Bill collectors?" Nellie deduced.

"Our winnings from the races are spent. Now the racing season is over, and I certainly don't want to resort to casino gambling. Once we're established, benefactors will step forward, but until then, we must be prepared for sacrifice. I learned fund-raising at my father's knee, and I'm good at it. Everything will be all right. I have to believe that, Nellie."

She surveyed the area. Isabel played with the workers' children on the lawn at the edge of the vast woods. Alice worked with feverish passion on her mural for the pavilion. Josephine was marking off water levels with a collection of smooth, round stones she had found for this purpose.

A mixture of gratitude and wonder filled Helena. She suddenly felt as though she were brimming with blessings. "Sometimes I can't believe what we've built."

Nellie patted her hand, but said nothing. She was tackling one of her "episodes," Helena knew, for Nellie had warned her of a bad spell coming on—perhaps triggered by shock over Sarah. Leaving her to her private troubles, Helena watched the children at play. Isabel was trying to teach them a game called cricket, which was all the rage in England and Europe. Following the herd of children with her gaze, she sharpened her scrutiny. "Excuse me, Nellie," she said, getting up. She hurried over to Isabel. "Where's William?"

Isabel pointed in the direction of the carriage house. "He went to see the professor some while ago. They were going to perform some tests on the water."

"I saw them running down to the lake," said a little girl. "They were having a game. I heard them splashing in the water."

Despite the heat and the dirt-streaked sweat streaming down her face, Helena felt a clammy chill. It was not like her to lose track of William, not like her at all. She had always been the most attentive of mothers, rarely letting William out of her sight unless she knew precisely where he would be. She approved only of safe activities—school or dancing lessons, walks in the park, perhaps a ride in a sulky. But with Michael around, she had relaxed her vigilance in a way she never had before. Her son found a constant fascination with the professor, and she allowed them to spend a great deal of time together, as though to mitigate the fact that she kept putting off explaining everything to William. Still, she should not have surrendered control.

As she headed down the dirt path to the lake, tension squeezed her chest tighter and tighter until she found it difficult to breathe. Michael didn't realize William was afraid of the water. What if…

She didn't permit herself to finish the thought, but picked up her skirts and started to run. The first sign of trouble was a shirt. William's shirt lay stretched over a bush, crisply dry and bleached in the sun. Next to that she found his dungarees. His pocket treasures were all lined up on the ground.

Good glory. Was the child naked and dead in the lake?

Her breath caught on a sob that turned to a gasp when she spied Michael's castoff clothes and boots on the lakeshore. She shaded her eyes and looked out, her gaze searching the water.

There. Two figures floundered in the distance. They had swum halfway out to Goat Island.

"Curse you, Michael Rowan," she said with a leap of horror in her chest. At the same time, she felt the tension uncoil. William was with Michael. He was safe.

When had she started to think of Michael as a safe haven for William? It was absurd, really. Michael was a careless man, he admitted that freely. He neglected people, forgot them, didn't trust himself with them, walked away from them. Wasn't that what he had told her when he'd left?

Yet William had a magical effect on him. He made Michael a different man, a man who was attentive, mature, caring. William transformed him into—Helena couldn't stifle the thought—a father.

She cupped her hands around her mouth. "William!" She called his name at least ten times before they decided to acknowledge her. Then, side-by-side, they swam toward her.

Swimming. William was swimming—clumsily but effectively, and with joy. It was such an alien concept that for a moment she just stood there, blinking like an owl. Though the idea of her son in the water frightened her, she could not deny a surge of pride. Then, insanely, she felt a rush of tears down her cheeks.

Michael had taught his son to swim.

He had taught her to swim as well, long ago, at midnight in Chesapeake Bay. He'd been appalled when she admitted she didn't know how to swim, and had insisted on teaching her. They had just become lovers and everything about each other was brand-new, a miracle. She had found him endlessly fascinating, from the way he designed a windproof candle holder to his habit of wearing his shirts inside out. That sense of wonder still lingered inside her, but she kept that part of herself hidden.

Hurrying to the end of the dock, she passed the iron boat lift—an innovation of Michael's that didn't seem to work—and stood at the top of the ladder.

"William! Young man, you come out of that lake at once."

He played like an otter, showing off by switching from front to back, splashing and laughing as though he'd been born swimming. "Look at me, Mama," he said even though she hadn't taken her eyes off him. "Look how I can swim. The professor's going to teach me to swim clear out to Goat Island."

As they neared the dock, she discovered she could not retreat. The heel of her shoe had lodged between the planks and did not want to let go. With as much dignity as she could summon, she composed her face into a stern expression. "You frightened me," she said. "Get out of the water this instant."

"But Mama."

"Now." With an angry jerk of her leg, she freed her foot.

He gripped the ladder and climbed up. By the time

he reached the third rung, she realized he was buck naked. She was just assimilating that realization when a new one hit her.

So was Michael.

Twenty-Six

With a furtive movement, William's hand stole across the table and snatched a handful of sugar lumps from the bowl.

"Oh, no you don't," Daisy said, seizing his wrist. "We only got one sugar loaf left in the pantry."

"If you must steal, for Lord's sake don't get caught," cautioned Isabel.

"But I need it," he said, his gaze darting around the dinner table. "The lemonade's too sour," he added.

"You ain't going to feed my sugar to that no-account horse." She took back the sugar and replaced it in the bowl.

"It's for the lemonade," William said, his voice edged by desperation.

Daisy took hold of his hand, turned it palm up. "Boy, what've you been up to?" she demanded.

"Nothing."

"You got more calluses than a field hand in July." She frowned. "Or a jockey working leather."

He snatched his hand away and scowled at Daisy.

Comprehension dawned unpleasantly on Helena. "William, do you have something to tell us?"

He poked out his lower lip. "No, ma'am."

He didn't have to say another word. She knew exactly what was going on. She hurled her napkin onto the table. "William, I want you to go to your room."

"But Mama."

"Now, William."

He moved with slow deliberation, taking his time as he put on his tinted spectacles. Helena didn't allow him to wear them at the table, but he insisted on wearing them at all other times, indoors and out.

"Ladies, will you please excuse me? This won't take long."

"Bet it will," said Daisy, exchanging a glance with Isabel.

Helena ignored them and hurried out of the dining room. This was the last straw. The swimming had only been the beginning.

She was losing control of her son, and it was all her fault. She had allowed herself to be consumed by the bath project, spending nearly every waking moment on the rustic pavilion and wooded grounds. Meanwhile, William ran wild. He spent his time with Michael and his cronies, George, Isaac and Regis, learning to swear and spit and play poker and scratch himself in inappropriate places. And those were only the lessons she knew about. What else were they subjecting her son to?

Most of his steps away from her were barely noticeable, but taken as a whole, the change was dramatic. He was like a sturdy young tree, growing his own way, resistant to any propping or pruning she might attempt. Apprehension and pride warred within her. He was still so little, so fragile. How could she let him run free? Yet at the same time, she took reluctant pride in his accomplishments and, occasionally, a fond pleasure in seeing him forge a bond with one of his many mentors.

He found lots of them at Moon Lake Lodge. On any given day, she might find him tracking wild animals in the woods with Josephine, painting a picture with Alice or working a puzzle with Nellie. She was less than pleased to discover that Isaac Reynolds had taught her son to play poker or that George Long had him whittling wood with a sharp knife. Regis Ransom tried to teach him the proper way to dress, but gave up in exasperation and took William driving in his two-wheeled sulky instead. That day, Helena had spent the entire afternoon in tense impatience, terrified that they would get in an accident. Yet when they had returned, rolling up the drive with William at the reins, a tentative pride took hold of her.

As often as not, she would find him in Michael Rowan's laboratory, the white mouse perched on his shoulder, a pair of eyeglasses balanced on his nose as he watched Michael work. William's face always reflected an admiration not far removed from worship. At such moments, she yearned to reel her son back in, to warn him not to give his heart so freely. When Michael left—and despite his claims to the contrary, she believed that he would—William would experience a wound of abandonment that might never heal.

But what could she do? Forbid him to see Michael?

This was good for her and William, she told herself again and again. She understood the importance of independence. She had to let go, even when it frightened her, even when it felt wrong. Except in the matter of the horse. She drew the line at the horse, and Michael knew it.

Seething, she marched down the lane and across the yard to Michael's house. On the way, she passed the wooded area surrounding the bath and pavilion, with its flower garden. The concrete had finished curing, and tonight they would pipe in the water for the first time.

This should be a time of celebration, for they were poised on the brink of success. But Michael had ruined it.

She yanked one time on the bellpull outside the carriage house, but did not pause or give him time to answer. Bunching her skirts up over her knees, she stomped up the stairs and marched in.

The cronies were sitting around a table, playing cards, smoking cigars and drinking beer. And their numbers were increasing, she observed. They had added Julius Calhoun to their cadre of mongrels and scoundrels. The handsome, dark-skinned Virginian fit right in with them, as debauched as the others, leaning back with his feet hooked around the chair legs as he studied his cards.

Startled by her arrival, the men bumbled as they stood up, knocking over a chair or two in their haste.

"To what do I owe the pleasure?" Michael asked, removing his eyeglasses.

She silently cursed him again. Even in a dissolute state, wearing a work shirt open at the throat and ancient denim jeans, he managed to look roguish and falsely innocent as he smiled at her.

She glared at them all through a layered fog of cigar smoke. "I take no pleasure in this visit. You've been teaching William to ride a horse."

"No, ma'am," said Julius. "That'd be me."

"It doesn't matter who is teaching him. What matters is that he's been riding a horse."

Michael's mouth quirked in a half smile. "And?"

"And I forbid it. I thought that was understood. William is too young and frail to ride. Particularly on a Thoroughbred trained for racing."

"Julius is the best trainer in the country, and Hector's legs need the exercise. I'm merely taking advantage of a rare opportunity. The boy's doing fine."

"So was that jockey we saw at the racetrack, right up until he was carried out of the arena. I want this to stop." She swept her imperious gaze over the other men, who cowered appropriately. "This and all the other unseemly things you've been teaching him."

"I just remembered something I have to do," Regis said, edging toward the door.

"We all got something to do," Isaac said. "Don't we, boys?"

After they had slunk away, Michael leaned his hip against the table, raffish and unrepentant. "Unseemly. You mean like swimming."

"Yes."

"He loves to swim. And he's good at it."

"He could drown."

"Sweetheart, he'd be more likely to drown if he *didn't* know how to swim. Look, lightning could strike him dead during an electrical storm. Forbidding him from normal boyish activities is not going to protect him from all the hazards of life, Helena. Nor is it going to endanger him unreasonably."

"I'm protecting him."

"You're smothering him."

"You're taking risks with him."

"What's riskier, Helena? Letting him grow to manhood with no notion of what the world has in store for him?" He gestured at the little cage filled with shavings. "This mouse has to live his life in a box because he never learned to survive in the wild. Is that what you want for William?''

''What if I do? At least he's safe from harm.''

''And safe from challenge and accomplishment and joy and, yes, tragedy and danger and all the things that make life such a rich adventure. Now, what else would you like to discuss?''

She paused, then thought of another grievance to air. ''Pugilism. What can you be thinking, teaching my son to fight with his fists?''

''It's a sport we're learning together,'' Michael said. ''It teaches quickness and strategy.''

''It teaches him to settle problems with his fists.''

''Sometimes that works.''

''It certainly worked for Sarah Dalton's husband, didn't it?''

''Teaching William to box is not going to turn him into a violent man. Training in this sport will teach him self-control and respect for his opponent.''

''And sailing,'' she accused, listing another complaint. ''You taught him to sail a catboat.''

''He is an excellent sailor. If I taught him to play golf, Helena, I suspect you'd disapprove of that, too.''

''I disapprove of you exposing my son to things without my knowledge.''

''That's because if I tell you what I'm going to teach him, you forbid me to do it.''

''Exactly.''

''What the hell would you have me do, Helena? Teach him petit point? Painting on glass? Oh wait, no, he might cut himself.''

''Don't you see, you're making him impossibly rambunctious. He refuses to stay inside. He eats like a horse. He's brown as a gypsy and he wants to be outside all day.''

"You've described a normal, healthy boy. What is wrong with that?"

"You may not let him ride that horse."

"He's going to learn to ride."

"Over my dead body."

"Why must you object to everything?" he asked.

"Because I'm afraid," she blurted out. Instantly she knew she'd revealed too much of herself. Trying to regroup, she said, "Michael, you have a brilliant mind. You could teach him the great ideas of physics and mathematics."

"And I shall. But not when he's eight years old. Right now he simply needs to learn reading and writing. You can teach him that."

She took a deep breath, preparing to leap. It was time Michael knew. Perhaps then he would understand why she felt so protective of William. She had put off telling him for far too long. Still, she hesitated. Clearly he already thought she was an inadequate mother. If she admitted her secret failing, that would only crystallize his conviction. "No, I can't," she said quietly. "I can't teach him."

"Why not?"

"I never learned to read."

He regarded her with surprising calm, lifting one eyebrow. "You never told me that."

"It's not something I'm proud of. But I'm telling you now because…because it's wrong to deceive you about it."

"You didn't deceive me. You simply never told me. There's a difference."

She looked at him sharply. "Not in my mind. I want you to know this because perhaps it will help you to understand how crucial every aspect of raising William is to me. I had a father who raised an illiterate daughter and never knew it. I won't be that sort of parent."

"Of course you won't." He helped himself to some potato chips from the table and offered her the bowl.

Confused, she shook her head. "Aren't you shocked? Scandalized? Disgusted?"

"Hardly."

"But I just told you I can't read."

He shrugged. "I never learned to speak French or do needlepoint."

"That's not the same, that's—"

"Helena." He wiped his hands on his pants, then rested his palms lightly on her shoulders. "You are wise in ways no book can teach you. That's your gift. Most of us have to read and memorize the rules. But you already have them. Right here." Leaning forward, he lightly kissed her brow.

She was too stunned to speak for a moment. Then, pulling away, she turned and left.

That night, Helena couldn't sleep. She went over and over the confrontation with Michael. His reaction had amazed her. He didn't judge her, didn't criticize. Perhaps, she thought, he simply didn't care. Scowling at the notion, she flipped her pillow over and willed herself to stop thinking of him at all. But then other concerns intruded. A hundred invisible worries and agitations pressed at her like the moist heat of the summer night. Abandoning all hope of sleep, she paced back and forth in front of the window, her thin gown wafting out in the wake of her bare feet, her hair in a braid that lay heavily against her back.

Things were going well, she told herself. Even as the household slept, the spa was filling. Soon she would preside over the dedication of the facility.

Excitement then. That was what kept her awake, her skin warm and tingling strangely. Her hands were restless, itching to grasp on to something, to pull back the veil of night and bring the dawn quickly. She paused at the window, looked out at the unrelieved darkness. The moon had turned away and would not show its face. The stars bathed the lake and grounds in the faintest wash of white, outlining the shapes of trees. She looked in the direction of the bathhouse, trying to see through the darkness but failing—it lay too deep in the woods. Yet something drew her eye. A flicker of light. Perhaps it was the reflection of a star, winking on the water. But no. This was more ominous.

A prowler?

The heat dispersed, changed to a clammy chill that crawled in cold droplets down her spine. Yet she did not hesitate. This was her home, her enterprise. She would defend it with her life if need be. Not even stopping for a robe or wrap, she hurried downstairs and grabbed the rifle. Her shooting was rusty but the prowler didn't need to know that.

Letting herself out the back, she raced across the yard, wetting her feet in the dew. Despite the darkness, she knew the way and would have known it with her eyes shut. She'd made the trip hundreds of times, from the initial drilling to the laying out of the large pool to the design of the pavilion covering it. The building consisted of a simple shelter with a roof on four poles and canvas shades that could be lowered for foul weather.

As she neared the spa, she saw the flicker of light again, confirming her suspicion. Someone was there. The intruder had a small candle lantern and moved unhurriedly along the bank from the tubed source down to the pool.

The night was quiet but for the constant musical trickle of water. The reminder of the old Mohawk legend should have sent shivery fear through Helena, but the possibility of vandalism fired her righteous indignation.

She felt faintly ridiculous. What, exactly, did one say to a prowler? *Halt, who goes there?* sounded a bit theatrical. Taking a deep breath, she stepped forward and said, "What are you doing?" Her voice echoed over the peaceful dribble of the water. The intruder jerked violently, startled. With his arms windmilling through the night air, he lost his balance and plunged into the pool. The lantern fell on its side, the glass chimney breaking and the flame sputtering out.

She heard a waterlogged curse and hurried to the pool. "Michael? Is that you?"

"No," he grumbled. "It's the creature of the Northern woods."

She leaned the gun against a lodgepole. The dark was nearly impenetrable but she could make out a shiny flicker of stars reflected on the water and his inky shape in the middle of the pool.

"What are you doing?"

"I came to check the water level and to make sure there are no leaks. Now, it seems, I am taking a bath." He moved to the edge of the pool and reached an arm toward her. "Help me out."

Without thinking, she took his hand. Too late, she realized her mistake. He needed no more than an easy tug to pull her into the water.

There was no time to call out. She barely had a moment to hold her breath as she plunged into the warm, bubbly water. She came up sputtering. "Curse you, Michael Rowan. You will never grow up."

"That's part of my charm," he said, holding her by the shoulders.

"Charm? You? Don't be absurd. You have no charm."

"You're probably right. But you love me anyway."

"I do not love you."

"You do, Helena," he said softly, in a whisper that caressed her ear. "You always have."

And then he kissed her in the way only he could, not just with his lips but with his whole being, surrounding and engulfing her in a consuming embrace. Any protest or hesitation drifted away, unexamined, unspoken.

How did he know? she wondered. She had been so careful to hold back her true feelings, to keep them hidden, buried beneath a thousand doubts. She turned her head, freeing her lips to speak. "I never said I loved you."

"Ah, Helena." She could hear the smile in his voice. His hand covered hers, which clutched helplessly at the wet fabric of his shirt. "You're saying it now."

She couldn't find her voice to deny the charge. She took a dizzying pleasure in touching him, clinging to him, feeling his arms around her. She always had. To deny it now would seem not just preposterous but petty and immature. She did so anyway. "I am saying nothing of the sort. You think you know me, Michael. You've always thought that, but whatever you choose to believe is wrong. I am my own person. It's taken me a while to achieve that but I have, at last."

"Loving me doesn't mean surrendering your independence," he said. "You know that."

She said nothing, not even when he removed her nightgown and dropped it in a sodden heap on the flagstones. Instantly the sensation of thermal, carbonated water drifting over her bare skin took her breath away. The fact was, she wanted to be immersed, to feel the bubbly earth-heated spring water on her skin. The bubbles clung and brushed over her, and she reached for him, discovering without surprise that he, too, had shed his clothes.

Her resentment drained away. She had tried to deny passion but he'd been relentless for weeks, probing deep, finding hidden rivers of latent desire, bringing them to the surface almost against her will. Almost. She wanted him, she always had, even when she believed he was lost to her.

He pulled her against him. She went, not just willingly but with a sense that they had been building to this moment for weeks, ever since she had summoned him to her sterile formal parlor in Vandam Square.

With the carbonated water surrounding them, he felt both strange and familiar. She wanted to know him again, to relearn every inch of him, as she had long ago. She wanted to rediscover the mysteries of him. But the girl she had been knew one Michael Rowan. The woman she was now knew him differently, understood him in a deeper sense. Years ago she had been blind to his flaws, oblivious of his limitations. Now she understood them all too well. But right now, not a single one mattered.

Flattening her hands against his chest, she ran them slowly downward, feeling bubbles fly free in their wake. I wanted this, she thought. I dreamed of this.

''So did I, love,'' he whispered, and only then did she realize she'd whispered the admission.

After that, there was no more to say. Words could add neither meaning nor clarity to an event that had become the inevitable conclusion of all the weeks of working together, bickering and teasing, arguing, making each other laugh, challenging each other, hurting each other's feelings. Keeping each other awake at night.

The dancing waters transported them to a different world, a place of wishes and dreams, delicately veiled and separate from the past or the future. She was entirely alone with this man. Nothing else intruded. Doubts and worries trickled away into nothingness and a powerful inertia drew them to one another.

As though her hands had made a secret pact with her heart, she touched him everywhere. She explored the damp strands of his hair, the rugged contours of his face. Then she drew his head down and tipped her face up to receive his kiss, feeling only tenderness from him, letting herself surge upward into his embrace. She pulled him closer, as close as she could, melding herself to him while a raft of bubbles rose around them and floated downstream.

Her hands slipped across his shoulders, down his back, splaying over him. The summer's labors had hardened and defined his muscles, and his leanness startled her and made her hunger more urgent, sharper.

He changed the kiss, slanting the angle, probing deeply with his tongue, seeking the final surrender of all her secrets. Didn't he know she had no secrets from him anymore? She had given him every part of herself, not even holding back her one unspeakable shame. He made it cease to matter; he was the only person who had ever been able to do that.

Nothing mattered but the way he was holding her, kissing her, touching her. The brush of his hands was as gentle and evocative as the bubbles skimming over her flesh. Closer, she thought, hold me closer. Don't let go.

He lavished attention over every inch of her, his caresses lingering in forbidden places, allowing no time for protest. Not that she would stop him now. She acknowledged how vast the gaping wound of loneliness in her was. She had kept it filled by staying busy, but she had never stopped needing him.

There were places inside her that belonged to him and no other. They had simply lain deep, slumbering, waiting for him. Now all the hidden longings sprang to life with a speed and intensity that was so passionate it almost hurt.

As though sensing her delicious torment, he stroked her with a lingering slowness that both calmed and excited her. She floated, buoyed by a raft of sensations carrying her along, bringing her closer to fulfillment, yet not close enough.

He answered the pleas she dared not ask, still stroking slowly, drawing the tension taut, bringing her need to a peak until she trembled against him, grasping, urging. ''Now,'' she pleaded against his mouth. ''Now, please.''

''Soon,'' he said, sliding her against the slanting ledge of the pool. ''No need to hurry, after all this time.'' He slid his mouth down her body, throat and breasts and belly, dipping his head briefly, firing her with tormenting flickers of his tongue before coming up for air. Then his hands slipped down, deft fingers pressing. She boldly answered him in kind, teasing and tormenting, and his involuntary gasp echoed her desperate need.

She brought herself against him, using the buoyancy of the water to ease herself upward with a gentle motion. She slid her legs around him, clasping as, with a single graceful effort, he slipped inside her, filling and surrounding her. They surged together with a subtle rhythm, and the elegiac pace swept them up, together, closer than the water to their skin. The waves of sensation built, intensified, and she leaned her head back, all modesty gone as he bent forward to kiss and suckle, even mark her with small gentle bites. The warm water sluiced with their quickening rhythm, and the waves swept her higher, higher, then brought her crashing down, against him. She clung to him in a state of helpless, shattering ecstasy, falling, plunging down, until she was replete, until she was home.

With lush generosity, he kept on, the rhythm steady until she felt the heated jolt that snapped through him. His mouth lingered against hers while spasms shuddered through him and their mouths softened damply against each other. The motion of the water carried them, lapping between their spent bodies.

Helena was weightless, floating, engulfed. He had taken her to a place from which she never wanted to return. She relaxed completely, cradling her cheek against his chest, listening to the vibrant rhythm of his heart and the ceaseless trickle of water from the spring. She felt cleansed, reborn. This was the essence of life, no less than that. She realized at last what had been happening to her this summer. She was falling in love with him all over again, only this time it was not with the star-struck abandon of a girl, but with a woman's clear-eyed passion.

He stroked her with lazy, loving motions of his hands, and pressed small kisses to her brow, temple, the top of her head.

"I thought you were a prowler," she said.

"If that's the way you treat a prowler, then expect an increase in criminal activity around here."

"Michael," she said, too vulnerable to hold back.

"This is only for you. In nine years, that has never changed."

"I won't lie and say I've been a monk," he admitted. "But there is something I've never given anyone but you."

She pulled back, saw the starlight gleaming in his eyes. "What's that?"

"My love."

It was the last thing she'd expected to hear from him, yet the only thing she'd ever wanted. But how could she trust him when his actions contradicted every word? "You never loved me in the first place."

"You're so wrong." He must have discerned her stunned expression despite the darkness. "I loved you then, and I love you now. That's the way it's always been."

"Even long ago?"

"Even long ago."

"Then we have a problem."

"Now what?"

"If you loved me but left me in spite of that, then it means love is not enough. If love can't hold you, what will?"

"Everything is different now."

"William."

"And...other things. I'm a different man, Helena. I left because I didn't believe I could give you the sort of life that would make you happy."

"And now?"

"I'll never be good enough, but I'll be as good as I can."

She clung to his shoulders, wishing the darkness would lift so she could see his face. "Why would you think that?" she whispered.

"Why would I not? Christ, I'm eaten up with guilt

about what happened with Troy. I have to live with that every day. What have I done all my life but fail? I fancied myself a great inventor, yet I've never managed—''

''You've managed to make life easier for us at every turn here,'' she reminded him. ''Perhaps you've won no prizes or patents, but if not for you, there would be no spa. I can't grant you a patent for that, but I'll always be grateful.''

He took her face between his hands, stroking his thumbs along her temples, her cheekbones. ''You still don't understand. Loving you is like loving a star. I can't get close enough.''

''You're wrong. You were wrong then, and you're wrong now.''

''Am I?''

She tried to reply the way he wanted her to, but couldn't make the final leap. So much had happened, so much pain and betrayal. She'd won her independence and she didn't know if she could surrender that to him, to anyone. By making love to her, he upset the balance, made her feel too much, too intensely, like hot water on a sunburn. She had no judgment now and did not trust herself to make the right choice.

''I'm back, Helena. I'm back, and I'm staying. But I need more from you than gratitude.''

Twenty-Seven

It wasn't hard to avoid him the next day. Moon Lake Lodge was a hive of activity as they readied the property for the official dedication. Yet she couldn't keep from thinking about them, about what had happened at the spa and what it meant. In their youth, forbidden intimacy used to be such a natural and joyous component of their relationship. Now it complicated everything. When they made love, there were things she wouldn't and couldn't hide from him. Like the fact that she loved him, always had and always would. But she could not give up what she had wrested for herself here. She needed to figure out who she was when she wasn't Franklin Rush Cabot's daughter or Senator Barnes's wife. She needed to be herself on her own.

Suppertime found them all famished from working. Daisy had fixed a big ham and made her famous spa-water biscuits. They drank their customary lemonade, and at the end of the meal, Michael offered to supervise William's bath.

"I don't need a bath."

"True," Michael agreed. "But it's something men

do in order to keep their womenfolk from yelling at them."

William clearly liked being included in the company of men, and readily followed Michael upstairs.

Nellie proposed a toast. "To Helena, the first lady of Moon Lake Lodge. Helena, you came here with next to nothing, and see what you've built."

"What we've built, all of us." Emotion brimmed in her as she regarded her friends. Tipping her glass, she paid tribute to each. "Daisy, you helped me survive when my world cracked open. Nellie, your nightly teachings touch me with brilliance. Josephine, your special gift created a miracle here. Alice, your talent has brought beauty into our lives, and Isabel, your youth and spirit remind us every day of why we carry on." Melancholy swept over her, and she knew the others were thinking of the glaring absence at the supper table. "I do miss Sarah. Oh, my, I wish—"

"We all wish it," Nellie assured her. "We all wish we could have saved her. But the fact is, some women love the men who are cruel to them, and the love and cruelty combine to do terrible things."

"You can't be saving everybody," Daisy added.

At the far end of the table, Isabel and Josephine were holding a whispered conversation. "We have a presentation to make," Isabel announced. With a gamin smile, she jumped up and led Josephine to the stillroom off the kitchen. They returned a moment later with a tall, draped object which they propped on a chair.

Even before they unveiled the gift, Helena knew. Her mouth dropped open and her heart sped up. "Dear heaven, you didn't."

Isabel withdrew the drape with a flourish, and Helena found herself staring at the only thing she missed from her former life—her beloved Degas.

"Let's read a different book, Mama," William said, feeling warm and tired as he lay back against the pillows of his narrow bed. "I already know this story." He waited, watching her face. Oftentimes she chose Dick Whittington or Paul Bunyon, stories she'd been telling him for years. She sometimes got cross when he wanted something new, but lately she didn't seem cross at all. She sang a lot these days, even though her singing made the cat hide under the porch and Miss Daisy pull a face and hold her hands over her ears.

Mama didn't get cross this time. She sat down on the low stool by the bed. Alexandra the cat sidled into the room and leaped on quiet feet onto the covers. "What book would you like to read?"

He put out his hand to let the cat lick him with her raspy tongue. His other hand stole beneath the covers, and he pulled out a thick book. "The professor loaned me another one. Let's read it now."

When he mentioned the Professor, Mama's face looked a little different, softer, and her eyes turned toward the open window, where the stars were coming out. Tonight after William's bath, he'd heard her telling the Professor how Miss Isabel had gone to a lot of trouble to bring Mama's favorite painting from Vandam Square, and was it really hers to keep.

The Professor had said, "Who else could love it like you do, Helena?"

William hid a smile beneath the edge of the sheet. Mama liked the Professor, maybe even more than William did, but something inside him knew they shouldn't talk about it, not yet, anyway. It was like seeing a rainbow. You didn't want to look too hard or all the colors would melt away.

She turned back to William. "All right, but only for a few minutes. We have a big day tomorrow. What is this one about?"

"*From the Earth to the Moon* by J..." He frowned at the unfamiliar name.

Mama tilted the page toward the light. "Jules Verne. It sounds like a book your Aunt Abigail would like—anything involving the moon and the stars. I have a wonderful idea. Why don't you read it to me?"

William bit the inside of his cheek to keep from whining, but the whine came out anyway. "I like the way you read better."

It used to make her cross when he said that, but since she'd been studying with Mrs. McQuigg every night, she didn't mind so much. Tonight she took the book from him and turned up the lamp. When Mama read a new book, she concentrated very hard and spoke slowly. "'Chapter 1—The Gun Club. During the War of the Reb...Rebellion, a new and in...fluential club was established in the city of Baltimore in the State of Maryland....'"

William snuggled up with the cat and shut his eyes. Sometimes Mama had to stop when she came to words like "mechanician" or "*sine qua non,*" but he didn't mind one little bit.

Twenty-Eight

''Hell's bells, Isaac, I don't understand what more the woman wants from me,'' Michael said as they readied themselves for the dedication of the spa. ''I told her I loved her. I said I wanted to be with her forever. I told her—''

''Telling is one thing,'' Isaac said, ruthlessly straightening Michael's cravat. ''You got to prove it. Else you'll lose her again.''

God. Losing her now would be a form of dying. The night at the hot spring had taken him far beyond dreams. He thought when he'd pulled her into the pool that he would rediscover the girl he had once loved with such abandon. Instead, as she always managed to do, she'd surprised him. That girl was gone. She'd been melted into the crucible of adulthood. She had emerged a woman whose poise and strength did not quite mask the vulnerability he was always able to find. Her stubborn independence and need made for a potent combination. He took pure delight in excavating the emotions and appetites she had so carefully buried.

Michael took over the tying of the cravat. ''Here. I can do it.''

"Since when?"

"Since I've been practicing. She admires a man who dresses well, so that's what I'll have to do from now on."

"You don't say."

"I'm trying to prove myself, damn it," he said. "Every day. But my best is never enough."

"Maybe that's because you're leaving something out."

Michael knew exactly what he meant, but that didn't make it any easier. She equated silence with deception, which made him wonder if she could forgive him for the things he hadn't told her.

When he'd made love to her, Helena had been emotional and insatiable and...honest. She wanted to love him but she wasn't ready yet. They had struck a delicate balance, but it was a false equilibrium. All during the previous day, she'd avoided him. He had kept his distance, not wanting to push her, not wanting to take the hardest step of all.

"So have you told her?" Isaac asked.

Michael flinched. Did he have ears to hear his thoughts? "I will," he said. "Soon." But when? He'd asked himself over and over again. Was there ever a good time to tell her that the man she feared and despised above all others was his brother?

"Today," he said with hard-won conviction. "I'll tell her today." He would do anything for her, he realized. Even leave, if that was what she wanted.

Troy Barnes felt strange being back in Saratoga Springs, and stranger still in this house, this empty, soulless mausoleum. He had dismissed Archie for his unforgivable error in handing Helena the damning evidence that could end his career, so there had been no one to greet him when he'd arrived a short time ago. The halls echoed with the lonely sighs of the end of summer. If the housekeeper was around, she was keeping to herself. Perhaps she, too, had left along with the rest of the staff. Without Helena here to run the house and pay the wages, they had all disappeared.

This house used to be Helena's domain. When she had lived here, fresh flower arrangements graced every table, baking smells emanated from the kitchen and William could often be heard shouting or singing somewhere, in that incessant way of his.

And, as always, Troy would feel pushed aside, relegated to the fringes of a family to which he'd never belonged. The two of them had never needed him, and he knew now that the disparity had upset the balance from the very start.

Needing her too much—that was at the core of the trouble. The bitch had taken shameless advantage of the imbalance, sailing through life with no regard for her husband. When he'd discovered the truth about William, he realized she had never needed anything from him but a name for her brat. Beyond that, she had no further use for him.

There was only so much a man could tolerate. He'd done his best to take his darker needs elsewhere, to mill girls and prostitutes and the occasional abandoned waif, like Felicity Bond.

She was the reason he'd returned to Saratoga Springs today. The foolish girl had run from him two days ago, sobbing in pain. Ordinarily her babyish crying subsided readily enough, and she would accept a gift of bonbons or ribbons of silk with dewy-eyed relief and a faintly pathetic gratitude. But last night, with surprising gumption, she had escaped.

He had waited too long, expecting her to come groveling back. When she didn't, he grew concerned. Searching through her meager belongings for clues, he came across two leads. The first was a pamphlet describing the activities of the Children's Aid Society, which sent orphans to live with farm families in the West. He doubted Felicity would choose that sort of life. She was a lazy slut of a girl who preferred working flat on her back.

The second clue had set his temper on fire. Thrust away in the pocket of her apron—the one she always wore when going to the farmers market—was a small handbill printed on cheap foolscap.

That was when he knew. That was when he loaded his father's old-fashioned navy pocket pistol and headed to Saratoga.

All summer he'd heard rumblings that Helena and her lady tenants were filling the heads of impressionable girls with lies and encouraging disobedience among proper wives. There was even a scandal already. Some poor man's overwrought wife had become so rebellious that she'd been killed. If the woman had known her place, that never would have happened.

And now Felicity. It was risky, he knew, but he had never been a man to back down from a challenge. If he let Helena win on this point, he would be forever lost to her stronger force.

He didn't know why he had stopped at the house in Vandam Square before going to fetch Felicity. Perhaps to ascertain…what? He walked through the deserted rooms, hot and musty in their abandonment. The mirrors were still draped in funeral shrouds. That worthless French painting had been removed and there was a dark rectangular shadow on the wall where the offensive thing had hung. He suspected Helena had plundered other items that didn't belong to her. Apparently her true nature was coming out. He would add theft to the other charges he intended to level at her.

He was a stranger here, as he was everywhere he went. All his life, he had heard the censorious voice of his father, pointing out his every inadequacy, beating decency and respect into him at every turn. That voice was never silent. It howled at him even when he slept. It was only silent when he was in complete command of his world, his life…his wife. But she had slipped away, holding the ax of disclosure over his head. She had to be stopped. William was the key, of course. She would do anything to keep the boy safe.

Bloated with rage, about to explode, he went to his sun-heated, stuffy dressing room and put on a fresh cravat and groomed his hair. Then he went outside to his hired driver. "Come for me at four o'clock this afternoon," he said. "I'll be going to Moon Lake Lodge."

An unexpected visitor interrupted breakfast. Helena saw a familiar rig drive up, and she darted a look of alarm at Nellie. Together, they went to the front door and waited.

"What do you suppose he wants?" Nellie asked, watching two attendants helping him down from his carriage.

"I leased the drilling equipment from him," Helena said. "But there's no money to pay."

"Adam Barnes can afford to wait."

Helena nodded, struggling for composure. Why today, of all days? They were going to dedicate the spa today. Everyone of importance was coming this afternoon for the event. Already the kitchen was a hive of activity as Daisy and the others prepared the refreshments. She turned to Nellie. "I'll deal with him. You go help the others."

Helena stepped out on the porch and watched her former father-in-law coming up the walk, supporting himself with two stout canes.

"Hello, Adam," she said as his footman helped him up the porch steps. "If this is about the drilling pump—"

"Never mind that. I hear you found a warm spring. Is that true?"

"It is. I'd be happy to show it to you if you like. I know I owe you a fee for the drill."

He waved a gnarled hand, then lowered himself laboriously to a chair on the porch. "Never mind that."

She sat across from him, concealing her surprise as she said, "Why are you here, Adam?"

"Mama." William ran out onto the porch, banging the door behind him. "Mama, can I— Oh. Hello, sir."

"Hello to you, young man," said Adam, his face creasing into a grimace of a smile. "How do you like living out here by the lake?"

"I like it fine, sir. Would you like to see my horse? His name is Hector and he is in the carriage house."

"Maybe later, son."

William shifted from one foot to the other. "Can I go, Mama? Miss Isabel promised to play a game with me."

She nodded distractedly, eager to conclude her business with Adam. She faced him directly. "Why have you come, Adam?"

"I'm too old to mince words. I want you to know that I don't approve of your doings here, but I intend to make certain my grandson's future is secure. I've changed my will to make him my principle heir."

Helena held in a laugh of hysteria. "He's not your

grandson, Adam. The rumors you've undoubtedly heard are true."

"William is Michael Rowan's boy, isn't he?"

Her mouth dropped open. Dear God, how did he know? And how was he acquainted with Michael, of all people?

"Then he's still my flesh and blood."

"But that can't—" She stopped, nearly choking as comprehension dawned.

He looked at her with a startling, penny-bright gleam in his eye and then, with a trembling hand, motioned for his assistant to hand her a thick envelope. He said something, but she couldn't hear his words through the madly rushing pulse in her ears. He left, leaving her standing there, battered by wave after wave of shock.

It was then that she finally understood. The last of Michael's mysteries broke free and she saw the facts gleaming, piercing, brighter than the sun. The stark truth radiated like a beacon.

Michael and Troy were brothers.

She felt sick with betrayal. Why hadn't Michael told her?

Helena went storming off to the carriage house. She found Michael wearing a long-tailed shirt and nothing else. Standing in front of his shaving mirror, he struggled with the button tacks on his white shirt.

"Adam Barnes just came to see me," she said, and knew by his reaction that she didn't have to explain further.

Michael's hands dropped to his sides, the color draining from his face. "I've been trying to find a way to tell you."

"I was just beginning to trust you," she said, a hitch in her voice betraying her fury and disillusionment.

"You'd think, after all I've endured, that I'd know better."

He took a step toward her, and she stepped back, holding her hands in front of her chest like a shield. Dear God, why hadn't she seen it before? He was so like Troy—big and burly and handsome, powerful, sharp-witted and...frightening.

"I'm not the sort of man my brother is," he said, reading the fear in her expression. "That's why I didn't want to tell you."

She thought of herself and Abigail, of how much they had in common and how their values were so similar. Then she thought about Jasper and Grady Dalton, violent blood brothers. Finally, she thought of Michael himself, and the fury that percolated from beneath his surface and overflowed the day he'd attacked Troy barefisted, beating him within an inch of his life.

"I'm nothing like Troy," he said, "and you damned well know it. I had no idea he was like that, or I would never have left. I thought your marriage to him would work out well for you. Jesus, Helena, don't you think I'm eaten up with guilt over that?"

She didn't trust the desperation that haunted his face. She could never trust a thing about him. "We're both secret keepers, Michael. We don't know any other way to be. And we could never be happy together. It's time we admitted that, don't you think? Let's just part ways before any real damage gets done."

Twenty-Nine

Helena had never been more nervous in her life—not at her coming-out ball in Georgetown, certainly not at her wedding. She'd been numb that day, resigned, convinced that she was doing the right thing. Her father had been so proud, all her friends had congratulated her on making a brilliant match. And Troy…Troy had looked wonderful in his traditional white tie and tails, and he'd treated her with a gallantry that had given her hope that their marriage would be, if not a passionate love match, at least founded on mutual respect and civility. She had clung to that illusion for years, pretending that all was well, believing that the life she had made with her child was enough.

Yet even then, she'd known there would be a price to pay for her duplicity. Now, finally, that part of her life was behind her. She'd created a new world here, in the company of a group of extraordinary women, in a place of magical beauty and healing.

Standing in front of the looking glass that afternoon, she regarded her somber black gown with resignation. Today of all days, she yearned to wear sunny yellow and brilliant white, a gown that reflected her defiant mood. She had an urge to rebel against a world where men made the rules, men lied and hid things. Restless with indecision, she went to the window of her bedroom to watch the guests arrive. Her gaze fixed on a stranger with yellow braids and wearing a blue dress. She didn't recognize the young woman, but that was not surprising. It seemed half the population of Saratoga Springs had come to see the wonder discovered at Moon Lake Lodge.

On the bedside table lay a folded onionskin paper. It was a wire from her sister, sent from Cairo. Heartsick over the news of their father's death, Abigail promised that she, Jamie and the children would come right away. Helena had read the words herself, slowly and painstakingly. Perhaps she would never be a brilliant woman of letters, but she was making progress in her evening lessons with Nellie. She would need her new skill, Helena realized. Everything was different now.

If she didn't allow herself to think about Michael, she might convince herself that everything was perfect. Daisy had prepared trays of biscuits, huge bowls of her berry jam, gallons of lemonade and tea. Late-summer asters and roses filled the garden around the spa. A patch of Sarah Dalton's favorite dahlias, transplanted from the garden of her house, occupied a special place.

The scene around the spa was a bouquet of color, with women in their summer dresses, children playing on the lawn and even the gentlemen of the mayor's entourage looking jovial and respectful. There were some in Saratoga Springs who would never visit. They considered her scandalous. But others—she had underestimated their tolerance. She wasn't sure how Nellie and Isabel had convinced the mayor and Mr. Elijah

Ware that this was an important civic event but there they were, shaking hands and greeting people. She was perhaps a latter-day Madame Jumel, who, despite her criminal intimacy with Aaron Burr, had become a leading lady of the city many years before. People did love intrigue.

But something was missing. In the middle of her good fortune and hope for the future, Helena still felt hollow. Incomplete.

A knock sounded at the door. Daisy, perhaps. But Daisy knew Helena no longer needed the services of a maid. "Come in," she called, turning just as the door opened.

Helena stared. She could not believe her eyes, and her heart nearly burst as she flew across the room. "Abigail," she said, and enfolded her longed-for sister in her arms. Oh, dear heaven, it was Abigail. She was more than a sister; they had been each other's refuge while growing up, and now she was back. The closest companion of Helena's heart, Abigail loved without reservation, accepted without question. As they held each other, the years of separation melted away.

Small and slight, dark and quick, Abigail was the antithesis of her sister, yet their hearts and minds worked as one. Abigail made a sound of bittersweet joy, and Helena pulled back, still clinging to her sister's hands. "You're here. I simply cannot believe you're here at last." They cried together then, each thinking what neither would say aloud. With their father gone, they were orphans, adrift in the world, and no matter what their age, they suffered from irretrievable loss.

Abigail pulled herself together first, snuffling unceremoniously into a wrinkled handkerchief. "Your wire was weeks old by the time it reached me, and then the trans-Mediterranean packet was delayed, and—oh, bother it. I must know what is happening. Heavens, you've left Vandam Square, and there's been the most scurrilous talk—''

''Which is probably all true. Come sit with me and I'll explain. Oh, Abigail,'' she said, ''everything wonderful and terrible has been happening.'' It all came out in a flood of talk and tears, the devastating loss of their father, Troy's ugly rage when he found out about William, the terror and exhilaration of her escape, the brilliant sense of purpose she felt about Moon Lake Lodge.

''I can't believe what Troy did to you.'' Anger flashed in Abigail's eyes. ''I always thought him a bit of a cold fish, but to strike you— It's beyond imagining.''

''It's worse. He laid claim to my share of Papa's legacy.''

''He won't get away with that.'' Abigail gave a superior sniff. ''My husband is Speaker of the House. He'll straighten things out before you know it.''

''I know Jamie will help me.'' Helena took a deep breath. ''But there's something else. Michael Rowan is back. He's here, Abigail, and that's the most wonderful and terrible thing of all. Everything between us has changed, and nothing's changed. I love him, Abigail. I always have.''

''Then why is it terrible?'' Abigail asked, organizing the clutter on the bedside table with endearing precision. She could always think better when things were in order.

''Because I can still love him. Which goes to show you, there must be something wrong with me.''

Abigail sent her a look of bemusement. ''How can it be wrong?''

Helena took a deep breath. "He never told me that his father is Adam Barnes."

Abigail blinked in astonishment. "No."

"Yes. I had to learn the truth from Adam himself. How can I feel this way about Troy's blood brother, about a man who abandoned me?"

"Ah, Helena." Abigail paused in her straightening. "In the first place, he's Troy's half brother, and was raised to be a different sort of man. In the second place, he didn't abandon you. Don't you see? It makes sense now. He was trying to protect you from the stigma of marrying beneath you. Leaving you was the best way he knew how to love you."

"No." But the chilling truth and its significance devastated her. She could scarcely bear to admit it, but finally, with Abigail holding up the mirror, she realized that shame and guilt and pride had cost her years with the man she loved. She'd been vain and proud and too insecure to risk displeasing her powerful father by marrying beneath her. As a frivolous belle, she would never have been able to abide the ostracism of her peers. Michael had known her better than she'd known herself. In his heart, he had believed she'd be better off with a wealthy, famous husband. Unwilling to be the cause of her misery, he had stepped aside, never knowing a worse fate awaited her.

She had married Troy to avoid scandal. Now she realized scandal held no terror for her. She and Michael deserved to be happy together.

Such a simple concept. What would have happened if she'd allowed herself to believe in the strength of their love? Her heart broke for all the years they'd missed and all the troubles they'd suffered. She was still paying the price of her pride and his doubts, and so was Michael.

"You're a different person now." Abigail stood and went to the window. She had a bad foot that had given her trouble all her life, but her characteristic limp didn't slow her down one bit. "Look what you've done, all on your own."

Helena could only nod to acknowledge the truth of it. She *was* different. She could forgive where before she condemned. She could accept without judging. She could love without fear.

She jumped up from the bed and joined Abigail at the window. A crowd had already gathered on the lawn, and more guests were streaming up the pathway toward the spa. "You fill me with hope, Abigail."

"The right sort of love changes a person. Surely you recall how miserable I used to be, and I was determined to remain so until Jamie walked into my life."

"But he didn't turn around and walk out."

"No, I did that. And nearly lost him because of it."

Helena's hungry gaze sought Michael out. This took no effort at all. She was always aware of him, the way one is aware of the position of the sun. He wore the fine suit of clothes she had given him, she noted, hat and all, and she hadn't even asked him to dress nicely. Could he have thought it up all on his own? Michael?

After their encounter in the thermal pool, she had been forced to acknowledge the changes and upheavals taking place inside her, inside them both. They were silent, invisible, like the secret strata of water deep beneath the surface of Saratoga Springs. *Michael.* He was the only man in her life who had treated her like a real person, not a trophy. He knew the geography of her heart better than she did. The knowledge that Troy was his brother had been a shock, but now she knew it had no power over her, over the way she felt.

As she watched, William ran to him.

"Can that be my nephew?" Abigail asked, wonder in her voice. "Goodness, what have you been feeding him? He's huge—and so handsome and filled with energy."

"He's had a remarkable summer," Helena said. "He and Michael are so natural together, so easy. It's as if they've known each other forever."

Abigail fixed her with a knowing look. "That's as it should be."

Helena knew she had to take the next step. She used to believe she would have to surrender her independence in order to give her love to a man. But being independent didn't have to mean living without love. She'd only been using that as an excuse. The fact was, she'd been afraid. During her years with Troy, she hadn't lived an authentic life, hadn't known how to love her son without smothering him, didn't realize it was possible to love a man without surrendering herself. In the confines of a loveless marriage, she'd taught herself to be emotionally self-reliant and distrustful of men. Finding Michael again, learning what love could be, had taught her a far greater lesson. He had left her once, and what followed was nine years of unhappiness. She had blamed him for that. Now she was finally able to admit that her happiness or lack thereof was not something to be bestowed or taken away at any man's whim. It was all up to her and no other.

"Abigail, I said some terrible things to him this morning. I ordered him to leave."

"Then you must explain that you spoke in haste."

"Yes." She unfastened the sleeve buttons of her drab black gown. "Social correctness be damned," she said. "I'm going to wear my yellow taffeta."

Abigail beamed at her. "I'll help you dress."

They chattered away as she got ready for the ceremony. She even donned her new high-heeled shoes, the tall, ivory-colored beauties with mother-of-pearl buttons to mid-calf. It took them a good ten minutes with the button hook, but the shoes made her feel tall and confident, and Lord knew she needed that now.

Then she and her sister went downstairs and outside to welcome her guests. The sign designating the property Moon Lake Lodge, which had once dangled askew from a rusty wrought-iron gate, now hung straight, the ornate iron freshly painted with black enamel. Michael, she thought. He was always fixing things—anything from a broken sign to a ruined racehorse to a shy little boy…to a woman whose sham marriage had gone sour. A foolish, frightened woman who had told him they could never be happy together.

But he did more than fix things. He was an inventor. He saw things in new ways and made them better than they were.

Her brother-in-law, Jamie Calhoun, grinned from ear to ear as he bent to kiss her cheek. "I'd give you a bear hug," he said into her ear, "but you need no help from me. You've already scandalized the entire eastern seaboard all on your own."

"So kind of you to remind me," she said, but could summon no indignation. Not now, not when everything was so clear to her. "Where are my niece and nephew?"

He gestured at the broad lawn between the lodge and the woods. "Maria and Leo are already off playing with Cousin William." His handsome face sobered. "Are you all right, Helena?"

She smiled up at him. She'd always liked her brother-in-law, whose irrepressible joie de vivre had rescued Abigail from the life of a cloistered scholar.

He exuded the confidence of a man who loved truly, with his whole heart. That was what she dreamed of with Michael, and she prayed it was not too late.

"She's going to be fine," Abigail said, joining her husband. "We all are. Now, go and see to your guests."

Helena greeted people as she made her way to the table that had been set up on the lawn. She saw curiosity, but no malice, on their faces. They wished her well. They did.

"Extraordinary," Mayor Dashell said as he stood beside a beaming Jack Shaunessy. "You've discovered yet another wonder in Saratoga."

"Actually, it was found by Josephine Goodkind, one of my guests."

"I wish you all the best. This is an historic day for our city."

A photographer from the paper took their picture. Edging between the guests, she tried to find her way to Michael.

He stood alone at the edge of the crowd, and her breath caught at the sight of him. He was unraveling already, his cravat loose and his waistcoat open. Yet he always looked dear to her, and she realized, with a certainty as deep as her heart, that he always would.

As though he sensed her watching him, he looked across the crowd at her and their gazes locked. She felt everything then, the love and fear and joy and surrender. She wondered if her heart shone in her eyes. Surely he understood that her bitter words of dismissal this morning had sprung from confusion and panic. Now she was calm and full of hope. She could not blame Michael for the accident of his birth any more than she'd blame William. She managed to move close enough to brush her shoulder against him. "I need to speak with you," she said. "In private."

His face was neutral, betraying nothing. "When?"

"This evening, after the dedication."

"Fine. Down on the dock, then."

She nodded. The dock would do. It was quiet and private.

"What is this about, Helena?"

"Miss Cabot, can you answer some questions for the *Albany Recorder?*" a reporter called, pushing toward her.

"Are you ready for the dedication photograph?" the photographer said.

She sent a desperate look at Michael. There was too much to say, so she said nothing more. She merely gave him a soft, intimate smile, then moved off to begin the ceremony. Later, she thought. Later she would tell him…everything.

"Are you ready?" The photographer repeated his question.

"Yes," she said, still looking at Michael. "I'm ready."

She did not get close to him again as the afternoon went on. Isabel took all the children away with her, because they had grown restless with the grown-up socializing. Imprinted like ducks behind their mother, they followed her some distance away to play on the lawn. It was just as well, Helena thought. What she was about to say was not for the ears of innocents.

Taking her place in front of the pavilion, she prepared to make her statement. Nellie tapped a spoon against a bottle to call for attention, and the noise gradually subsided.

An overwhelming feeling of purpose rolled over Helena. She was suddenly conscious of every detail of the moment. The late-summer breeze sharpened by the first hint of autumn. The rustle of leaves and the coo of wild doves. The scent of flowers and fecund aroma of freshly turned soil. And, always, the unceasing song of the spring water trickling from some warm secret heart deep in the earth.

Swallowing hard, she gestured at Julius, who signaled Josephine and Alice to raise the canvas shades that concealed the bathhouse. Moist clouds of steam escaped, rolling off the surface of the thermal pool and curling skyward. Gasps of wonder escaped from everyone. The crowd shifted closer and people craned their necks to see.

Helena smiled. ''I didn't believe it at first, either. A warm spring, at Saratoga? Who had ever heard of such a thing?'' She paused. ''But then again, who had ever heard of a group of women working together to make a place like Moon Lake Lodge?'' She scanned the faces of those who had started with her—Daisy, Nellie, Josephine, Alice and now her beloved sister, Abigail.

''How very dear you are to me, all of you. There was a time when I fancied myself the most important woman in Saratoga Springs.'' She indicated the reporter in the front row. ''Mr. Leslie, I believe you once printed that in your paper.'' A ripple of reserved amusement rustled through her listeners. ''And while I was flattered, I must be honest and say that simply being the daughter or wife of a certain man does not qualify a woman for any sort of admiration. Honor those like Nellie McQuigg, who has worked for decades for the rights of women. Like Daisy Sullivan, who survived slavery, or Alice Wilkes, whose magnificent art graces this site, or Josephine Goodkind, who understands the land and told us where to find this miraculous spring. Most of all, let us acknowledge the one woman who cannot be here today for this beautiful event." She gathered in a deep breath. "I didn't know Sarah Dalton long, but I knew her well."

The mention of the scandal-tainted name caused a wave of whispering, as Helena had anticipated. "I knew what it was like to be a young bride, so eager to please, so determined to make life a happy and meaningful adventure. I knew what it was like to create a lovely home and garden, to attend church services, to cultivate the admiration of friends and neighbors. I knew the joy of expecting a child. And I also knew the terror of having a husband who beats you."

The crowd erupted. She suspected a good number of them now believed she was insane, but she would never again lie or hide the truth. "There is one great mystery to which Sarah Dalton knows the answer and I do not. I pray no other woman will ever find out what it is like to die at her own husband's hand."

For a moment, no one stirred. Faces froze in expressions of shock, grief, outrage, disbelief, curiosity. And, in the face of the girl with the blond braids, Helena saw a sort of relieved recognition.

Then came the whispers, murmurs, throat-clearings. A few indignant denials but even more righteous exclamations of anger burst out here and there. Good. Let people talk about it, argue about it. Anything but silence.

"And so it is in grief but also in hope that we dedicate this place to Sarah Dalton today, that we may carry the lessons of her beauty, her suffering and her ultimate redemption. In remembering her tragedy, let us dedicate ourselves to the sanctity and safety of all women."

Then Nellie said, ''Hear, hear.'' The dam burst after that, and everyone started talking at once.

Helena lifted a hand to signal for silence. ''While women are at the heart of this enterprise, certain men are equally important. A dear comfort to them, I'm sure. I thought I would have to turn my back on men in order to be an independent woman. But I proved myself wrong. The world is filled with good men, and I would like to thank some of them. Mr. Jackie Shaunessy was kind enough to offer me a lease on Moon Lake Lodge. Other significant contributions came from Julius Calhoun, Dr. Hillendahl, Mayor Dashell and Mr. Elijah Ware. My son William gave me reason to keep myself safe. I honor the memory of my late father, Senator Franklin Rush Cabot, who taught me that one person, man or woman, can make a difference. And finally, I must thank Dr. Michael Rowan, whose labors and services have meant more to me than words can ever say.''

Applause and a babble of conversation thundered through the air. Her heart full, Helena left the dais and invited everyone to dip their hands in the wondrous water, to converse and question and gossip. She found the girl with the braids and welcomed her.

''We've not met,'' Helena said. ''Have we?''

''No, but please, may I stay?'' The girl cradled her arm in a too-familiar way. ''My name is Felicity Bond.''

Thirty

William was afraid of the outhouse. It was dark and full of spiderwebs and you had to hold your breath till your eyes watered. In the main house, there were two real flush commodes with water closets, but it was a long walk just to do a minute's business. William didn't want to miss a moment of the cricket game they'd started up while the adults talked endlessly about the new spa. His cousins had come to visit and he was excited about that, but he didn't want them to know the outhouse scared him, so he decided to head for the woods.

Mama often told him he shouldn't go wandering in the woods. He might get lost. She always found something to worry about. But Mama was busy with her company right now. She'd never know if he slipped away for a minute. Besides, the Professor never minded, and he never told.

While the other children raced and played, and the grown-ups drank tea and made speeches, William walked past the spooky old outhouse and went into the forest. He liked calling it a forest. It made him feel brave.

The shouts of the other children faded behind him. Miss Isabel played with them, showing them new games and teaching them words their mothers probably didn't want them to know. Miss Isabel was wonderfully naughty for a grown-up. She was, in fact, his third-favorite grown-up.

Mama was first, of course, because she was his mother and, as the Professor explained, a boy puts his mother first, always. In fact, the Professor was his second-favorite grown-up.

Lots of things in William's life had changed over the summer and the Professor was a part of that. Most of the changes were good. William had a horse and a cat and a mouse, and he lived by the lake. But he no longer played with his usual friends, and Mama told him he wouldn't be going to his usual school. That made him feel different and a little funny in his gut. When Mama told him about the school, she got two round spots of color on her cheeks the way she did when something made her cross, and William understood that the change was on account of he was now a Bastard. Mama didn't let him say that word but she couldn't stop him from thinking it.

When he looked in the mirror, he still saw the same boy—a round head, red hair, blue eyes and more than forty-one freckles. But now that it was a fact that his mother and father had never actually been married, William knew that made him different.

He felt different at Moon Lake Lodge, but in a good way. Braver, stronger, like he could do more things. Before, he was good at reading the train schedule or playing scales on the piano, being able to identify a fish fork, finding the Netherlands on a map or locating the planets using Aunt Abigail's star chart. This summer, no one had seemed to care about those lessons.

He could do new things now, like climb the hickory tree in front of the lodge, lickety split. He could swim, too, and row the dory and sail the catboat. Also—Mama didn't know this yet—the Professor had rigged a rope swing, and he could fling himself far out over the water and then just let go. Best of all, there was Hector, the finest horse in the whole world. Hector followed William wherever he went. He was like a big dog. Even when William hid, Hector could sniff him out.

The Professor had taught William to whistle, and he did so now, walking through the forest. His favorite tune was a drinking song. Mama didn't like that one. But she was far away with all the important people who came to look at the spa. In fact, everybody was far away. That was why William was startled when he stepped out of the wooded shadows and encountered a man.

Just for a heartbeat, he felt confusion, but that was quickly followed by a leap of surprise. ''Hello.''

''Hello, William,'' Father said, a calm smile on his face. ''I'm so happy to see you again.''

William didn't reply. He tried to figure out if he was happy, too.

''How would you like to show me around?'' Father asked a question but William knew it was a command. ''I understand you have a horse.''

''Yes, and a cat and a mouse and two boats and—''

''I should like to see that first,'' said Father. ''The boat.''

William glanced in the direction of the crowd in the distance. ''I should tell Mama—''

''She knows,'' Father assured him. ''She agrees that

you're grown up enough to show me around. Come along, boy. There is so much to see."

"Yes, sir." Turning away from the lodge, William led the way to the lake.

Michael hurried to his quarters to prepare for his meeting with Helena. He wouldn't have bothered at all, except that Regis, Isaac, George and Julius had convinced him that a lady appreciated a fresh splash of bay rum and some sort of offering or gift. He did have something to give her, something she would never expect from him. It was an ornamental comb that had fallen from her hair the day they'd met. It was the only item of sentimental value he'd ever had—until William had given him his tooth the day of the races.

He slipped the silver filigreed comb into his pocket and went to the washstand to make liberal use of the bay rum. As he set down the bottle, he was surprised to discover that his hand was shaking. Bracing his fists on the edge of the stand, he stared into the old, scarred shaving mirror.

Afraid. He was afraid. This mattered too much to him. What he felt for Helena and William was huge and overwhelming, and the idea of losing them was devastating. Yet the possibility was very real. Everything he'd ever attempted in his life had ended in failure. For a scientist, that wasn't such a bad thing, because he learned from each failure. But there was no science involved now, and nothing to be gained from failure but heartache.

He studied his image, trying to decipher the character buried in the familiar, squarish features. How much did a father own his son? What aspects of the Barnes nature lived inside him? Ruthless ambition?

Greed? Pride? Violence? Or did his character belong solely to him?

He wondered if William would ever stand before a mirror and ponder the same things.

Pushing away from the washstand, he attempted to straighten his cravat as he hurried out the door and down the stairs. Who had invented such a thing as the boiled collar and cravat, anyway? The infernal things had no use that he could see.

On his way to the path leading to the lake, he passed several groups of departing visitors. Beyond a casual wave or nod of the head, he didn't stop to greet anyone, for he was in a hurry. Even so, he felt a shining pride in Helena for what she had accomplished today. She had defied the rules and social conventions that had governed her life, and this was the result. Every person of note in town had come to see her and hear what she had to say.

One straggler caught his eye, a young woman with long yellow hair and a drooping blue dress. She moved almost furtively, throwing glances over her shoulder as she kept to the edge of the path that bordered the thick woods.

Despite his haste, he paused when he reached her. "Miss, are you lost?"

She looked up at him and gasped, feinting back a little. "No, sir. I was just I'll be on my way now." Her face was paper white, her thin wrist bruised. She had that look, deep in her eyes, the one he recognized because it haunted his dreams.

"Miss," he said, "if you'll go to the lodge, the ladies there will look after you."

"Everything's fine, sir, just fine." She scuttled away, clearly distrustful of him. This stranger was part of the same silent sisterhood of powerless women his mother had belonged to. He hadn't been able to save his mother. The thought struck him hard as he strode toward the lake.

This was one appointment he wasn't going to miss. Even if Helena's purpose was to dismiss him from her life, he would not be late. Her failed trust in him, her shock and fear, were justified. He had lied to her. He didn't want his relationship to Troy to matter, but that was foolish. Whenever she looked at him, she would see Troy. Like it or not, Michael shared certain traits with his brother—a breadth in the shoulders, perhaps, or an angle of the gaze. Subtle resemblances that had gone unnoticed until the truth came out. Forevermore, Helena would see shadows in Michael—shadows of the man who had threatened her, beaten her, violated her.

Yet she was giving him this chance. He pondered the meaning of her public speech today. Had it been a declaration of independence that left no room for him? Or a treatise on tolerance to indicate the door was still open? He had to convince her that his character was his own and no other's, that she possessed his heart more surely than Barnes possessed any part of him.

He reached the dock and paced, his heels thumping on the uneven planks and his mind racing. The colors of early evening were deep and intense. The wind rippled over the lake with increasing agitation, its sharpness signaling the leading edge of a squall. Distant Goat Island lay in shadow. He noticed a scattering of boaters on the lake, taking advantage of the last light of day. Not far from the dock, a man rowed a dory with powerful strokes. A pair of herons browsed in the long reeds at the water's edge.

She hadn't arrived yet. Perhaps she wasn't coming.

Restless, he retraced his steps up the path, into the gloomy woods. No one was in sight. She wasn't coming, he thought again. Yet she had requested this meeting, he reminded himself, she—

He heard a hollow thump against the dock and hurried down to investigate. A man emerged from a rowboat hastily tethered to the end of the rickety wooden structure, Michael's non-functional boat lift looming over his tall frame.

Michael made a strangled sound in his throat as he recognized Troy Barnes. Feeling as though his nerves had been torched, Michael strode to the end of the dock, but stopped short when Barnes aimed an old-fashioned pistol at his chest.

Michael raised both hands, palms out. "Put that away, Troy." His mind raced as he tried to figure out a way to defuse the situation. Helena would be here at any moment, and Troy was as taut as a coiled spring, his finger jumpy against the trigger. Michael didn't doubt he would fire if pushed, and he didn't need much pushing.

"I think not," Troy replied, his grip firm on the gun. "You've proved it many times in the past—you are not a man to be trusted."

Michael started to sweat. He did not want Barnes armed and dangerous when Helena arrived. Her appearance would light the fuse of Barnes's smoldering temper. Positioning himself between the footpath and the end of the dock, Michael knew he would die to protect her. It was a hell of a way to prove his love, but if it came to that, it was a sacrifice he was willing to make.

"Tell me what you want," he said as evenly as he could. "I'm sure we can come to some agreement without anyone getting hurt." He realized it was presumptuous to assume Troy wanted to avoid hurting anyone, but perhaps the suggestion would appeal to some latent, hidden sense of decency that might yet live inside his brother.

"You can't really think I'd give them up," Troy said.

You never had them in the first place. Michael didn't let himself say it aloud. "Put the gun away and we'll talk about it." He edged imperceptibly toward Troy, hoping his brother wouldn't notice his gradual approach. It was all he could do to resist the urge to look around and make sure Helena had not yet arrived.

"He's changed his will, you know. He's cut me off."

So that's what all this was about. A father's regard. It meant the world to Troy Barnes. He clearly could not understand that it meant less than nothing to Michael. "I don't want anything from the old man. I never have. I'll tell him so myself, right now. Come with me and we can tell him together."

"You lie. You came back here to get into Father's good graces. All your life, you've wanted him to claim you."

Confusion flickered through Michael. Nothing could be further from the truth. He'd never wanted a thing from Adam Barnes. "Look, Troy, I'll speak to you about your father and anything else you like. But you have to stop waving that gun around. What would your constituents think?"

"That I'm man enough to reclaim what's mine."

"You'll never survive this, Troy. There's simply no point. Voters tend to get nervous when their elected officials threaten people with guns."

"Public sentiment is with me and always will be. Not with an adulteress, her lover and their bastard."

He peeled his lips back in a mocking grin. ''Your mother was a backstretch whore who got lucky,'' he said. ''But the truth is, you'll never rise above that. You'll always be the flea-bitten ne'er-do-well eating horse fodder from a trough. He only changed his will because of the boy.'' Ice glazed Troy Barnes's stare. ''But what if there was no boy?''

Michael's blood caught fire, even as he battled the explosive rage that had lived inside him forever. It took everything he had to keep from reacting when instinct urged him to choke the truth from his brother. ''We should sort this out like men of reason,'' he forced himself to say. ''Let's go see your father.''

''So you can show him how you took everything from me?''

Michael understood something clearly in that moment. Troy Barnes was a stranger to him in every sense of the word, their father notwithstanding. Michael was nothing like this proud, pathetic and dangerous man. But as liberating as that notion was, he was still trapped by the gun pointed at him and by the threat to William.

The last time he'd confronted Troy, Michael had allowed rage to possess him. He was a different man now. He allowed himself to possess the rage, and that made all the difference. Rather than attacking suddenly and blindly, he measured his chances. If he harmed Troy, he might be putting William in jeopardy. Yet if he didn't seize the gun, Helena might show up to disaster.

It was a risk, but Michael held out his hand. His fingers hovered in the air only inches from the barrel of the gun. ''Put it away, Troy. Let's go see Father.''

It was the first time he had ever called Adam Barnes by that name—and the word stuck in his craw—but it had the desired effect on Troy. Fury flashed in his eyes and snapped like an electrical charge through his body, down his limbs. Michael seized the split second of opportunity to lunge for Troy's gun hand.

The pistol flew in a high arc, then dropped into the tall grass fringing the lake.

Barnes's fist shot out, connecting with Michael's jaw. The force of it knocked him backward. He lost his footing and fell to the planks, landing with a teeth-jarring thud.

Still seeing stars, Michael made a grab for Troy, missed. He managed to scramble to his feet, righting himself just in time to see an oar swinging straight for his head.

Lightning exploded in his skull. He fell back, toppling over the edge of the dock, his arms wheeling in the air. The expected splash never came. He landed awkwardly in the boat, the wind rushing out of him. Unable to breathe, he grasped the side of the boat, struggled to get up. The oar descended again and the pain turned to red fire that roared through his head and overtook him. He sank back, his fury and terror blurring into helplessness. Then he felt himself drifting away, gone somewhere deep in the dark.

''Have you seen William?'' Helena asked Daisy.

''He's off playing with Isabel and the other little ones. They'll be hungry for their supper soon.'' Daisy balanced a tray of used glasses on her hip and headed for the lodge.

Helena surveyed the dwindling crowd. The food and drink had disappeared at a remarkable rate. She'd accepted a gratifying sum in donations and offered everyone a chance to test the waters, but even as her guests left, she knew her day was far from over. In fact, the most important event, for her at least, still awaited.

The giddy nerves of this morning did not compare to the riots of emotion that possessed her now. Addressing the past in public had laid old fears to rest. But baring her soul to Michael was a larger matter in every way. She was about to make herself vulnerable again, to offer her love and expect nothing in return. That was the difference. That was what she had discovered at the end of the long road she had traveled. She'd once believed loving someone entitled her to being loved back. Now she understood that it was a gift given freely, or not at all.

She saw the sun sinking over the lake and knew it was time.

She walked through the house to make certain all was in order. The women were busy clearing up after the guests. Jamie and Abigail went to gather the children in for supper.

Satisfied that all was well, Helena practically ran to the dock, her skirts brushing over the low-growing ferns, along the darkly wooded trail leading to the lake. He hadn't arrived yet, so she walked to the end of the dock and looked out over the water, now glazed by the setting sun. It was a sea of beaten gold, rare and precious, bright and shifting, a fleeting beauty she wanted to clasp in her heart forever.

The breeze was light, blowing at her skirts with gentle insistence. She heard footsteps on the path and turned, her pulse racing. The lowering sun lit him from behind, obscuring his features. The golden rays outlined his tall, broad silhouette, his correct posture, his perfectly cropped hair.

She froze. Everything seemed to stop—even her heart.

"Troy," she said, dragging her voice out of the icy depths. He was so upright and well-groomed and handsome, this man she had married so impulsively. This man who had betrayed her. This man who had beaten her.

"Hello, my dear. You staged quite an event here today, quite an event, indeed. You were always good at that sort of thing. Such a touching display, baring your soul like that."

It horrified her that he'd been lurking, unobserved, listening to her speech. Yet a part of her felt gratified. Not so long ago, she would have been afraid to speak her mind in front of him.

They were completely alone, the two of them, out of earshot from the lodge and screened from sight by the thick woods. Out on the water, a few boaters lingered in the last light of day, but they were too far away to hear her shout. She was unarmed, unprepared, yet she felt curiously unafraid.

The bony skeleton of Michael's boat lift threw its angular shadow across the planks of the dock. He had installed the contraption of pulleys and gears and cables, but the thing had never once worked right.

"You're not welcome here, Troy," she said, "but of course you know that."

He laughed with silky amusement. "That won't stop me."

Michael, she thought, glancing around frantically. The westering sun hammered at her face, tormented her eyes. The breeze picked up, shoving a bank of bloodstained clouds across the sky.

"He's not coming," he said, guessing her thoughts. "I doubt you'll be seeing him again. I've always been able to best him to my will, ever since we were boys." He grinned at the expression on her face. "Ah, so you finally found out that Rowan and I are brothers. I'm surprised it took you this long.''

She hadn't wanted to see it, hadn't wanted to know that the man she loved shared a bond of blood with the man she despised. ''An accident of birth,'' she stated.

''But a convenient one, no? No one knew the truth about that brat you passed off as mine. Not even me, until Pickett finally told me the truth.''

She knew then where his greatest vulnerability lay. ''Someone knows, Troy. Your father.''

Fury chased across his features. ''Father will never claim the son of a backstretch whore as his own.''

She allowed herself a tight smile. ''You should ask him some day.''

''How dare you speak to me like that.''

Ah, she recognized that voice. That black lash of imperious command. She had heard it before, but it didn't frighten her the way it used to. He no longer had that power over her.

The wind intensified, blowing a bank of thunderclouds across the sun. The breeze carried the taste and smell of rain.

She watched him walk toward her on the dock. The old Helena would have simply borne the punishment. But no more. Drawing deep from the well within, she looked him in the eye. She saw him clearly now, every detail of his brutally handsome face, hard mouth and eyes that opened to a soul that had never known a moment's peace.

''I think you've said enough for one day,'' he stated.

She realized what the effect of her earlier speech at the dedication had been. She had ruined Troy Barnes without ever bringing up the matter of the stolen election, and he seemed to know that. She had belittled him by pointing out what Troy had probably always understood—that Michael was the better man, and always had been. She no longer had any leverage with Troy, and perhaps, judging by the murderous expression on his face, he intended to silence her forever.

She squared her shoulders, stood her ground and said, "I must be going now."

"I think not."

"Step aside, Troy. You will not harm me. You are the worst sort of coward, and you will not."

And with that, she reached down and pulled the lever of the boat lift. The iron beam swung out and knocked him backward into the lake. He made a satisfying splash as a fount of water erupted, sprinkling the hem of her dress.

"Hmm," she said, shaking out her skirt. "I shall have to change for supper, then." She pivoted around, only to discover that the narrow heel of her high button dress shoe had lodged between the planks of the dock. Tugging hard, she tried to free her foot, but failed. She hiked back her skirts and began wrestling with the buttons, a difficult operation without a buttonhook.

She could hear Troy struggling and gasping in the lake and felt a grim satisfaction. She couldn't recall whether or not he knew how to swim. She didn't really care.

Her nail broke as she unhooked the first button. This was impossible. And quite absurd. She was stuck to the dock by the heel of her shoe. Before she managed to free her foot, she heard a great, wet slogging sound. Troy Barnes emerged from the water.

She tried prying her foot from the boot. Sweat ran in rivers down her back.

"What's your hurry?" he said, moving toward her, his wet hair plastered to his skull, his clothes streaming. "I suppose you think Rowan will come to the rescue, but that's a vain hope. If that blow to the head didn't kill him, he'll be off searching for the boy."

He finally managed to scare her. As she straightened up, everything drained out of her. "Troy, what did you do? I beg you, I'll do anything you ask, retract the annulment, hand over the damned ballots, anything."

"Of course you will. I'm counting on it."

She should have known that simple surrender would never satisfy him. He backhanded her across the face, snapping her head to one side. Her cheek flamed with pain. He raised his hand for another blow. She knew then. Could see it in his eyes. He would not stop until he killed her.

She twisted frantically. He shoved her hard, and the blow freed her trapped foot. She started to run. His fist gripped her flying skirts, and he tugged her back, wrestling her into a deadly embrace, his thumbs digging into her throat.

She fought, but he would not let go. Defeat tasted so bitter in her mouth, particularly after her day of triumph. To lose everything like this choked her with frustration.

Then a great crack of thunder split the air, followed by a wet slapping sound.

Troy made a terrible noise and his grip fell away. Helena sank to the dock. She searched herself for wounds, her ears ringing.

As her hearing returned, she detected a gurgling sound, followed by choking. Troy couldn't speak.

Helena scrambled up, frantic now. Outlined by the last light of day was the new girl, Felicity, holding an old-fashioned navy pistol.

Thirty-One

A loud pop startled William. He knew what that noise was. It was the sound of a gun going off. The report shimmered across the water from somewhere far away.

William wished he hadn't let Father bring him here. Father had taken him out in the boat, and he'd told William to go ashore at Goat Island and wait. Wait for what? Father hadn't explained. He said he'd be back shortly, but that was a long time ago. William hiked from one side of the island to another and back again, but even before he did that, he knew the truth.

Father wasn't coming back. He'd never intended to. He was playing a mean trick on William.

And now the wind was up, stirring whitecaps across the lake, and the sun was going down, and it was getting cold. William paced back and forth on the bank, feeling the prickers scratch at his legs. With the pop of the gunshot echoing in his ears, he ran into the water's edge in time to see Mama in her yellow dress and another lady in a blue dress go running up the bank. He called out to them, but the wind was too loud and they were hurrying away too fast. They disappeared without a backward glance.

William cupped his hands around his mouth and called out at least ten more times, but no one came. The dock was deserted now except for something that looked like a dark heap of sail cloth. His throat ached and he squatted down in the reeds and poked out his bottom lip. He was cross with Mama for running away and not hearing him. He was cross at Father for the stupid game. And he was cross because he knew it would be dark soon, and he positively did not want to spend the night alone out here.

He walked all the way around the island, trying to picture the herd of goats that used to graze here. How had they returned to the mainland when they were done? The Professor had told him the shortest distance between two points was a straight line.

It looked very far. William had never swum so far before. He wasn't really afraid, he just didn't want to. Josephine said there were ghosts deep in the earth, and they came to the surface through the springs. But William knew they weren't bad ghosts. They came to help and heal people.

Maybe they would help him now.

He took off his shoes and socks, hurrying. He was wearing his good shoes because of the dedication today, but he could swim better with bare feet. He didn't take off his shirt, though. He knew he was going to need it. The Professor said it was important to learn water survival, and he had shown him a way to make a float in the water out of a shirt. It was the only time the Professor was fussy about dressing.

William put all his pocket treasures into one of his shoes, and waded into the water. It felt chilly, but he didn't mind. He would rather be in cold water than alone on an island. Taking a deep breath, he plunged in and struck out for the shore. He was a good swimmer, he'd been practicing all summer, but his heart was pumping hard as he entered the deep water where his feet couldn't feel the bottom anymore. Then he did the thing the Professor had taught him. He fastened the shirt's collar button and opened the next one down. Taking a deep breath, he bent forward, held open the gap in the shirt and blew with all his might.

Maybe the spirit people were helping him, because a gust of wind helped inflate the wet fabric. He held the shirt tightly in his fist to form a bubble of air. The cloth bubble buoyed him, just as it had when he'd practiced it with the Professor. He kicked toward the shore. A straight line, he reminded himself, the shortest distance between two points. The bubble deflated gradually, but he wasn't worried. He knew the wind would fill it up again and again for as many times as he needed it. But it seemed so very far to swim.

He made himself concentrate on the things waiting for him there. Mama. She would scold because she always did when he did something brave, but she'd be happy to see him. And lately, she was letting him do more brave things than ever before. The Professor wouldn't scold at all. He almost never showed his temper. He was never grumpy like Grandfather Barnes. He never acted impatient like Father did. The only time William had seen the Professor angry was when he talked about Mrs. Dalton's husband and other men who hit people and were just plain mean.

For a long time now, he'd had a secret wish. William called him Professor Rowan, but inside he had another name for him. Papa.

He was tired and the shoreline was still so far away but he kept on, thinking about getting warm by the kitchen stove and the hot cup of cream with honey Daisy would give him and his visiting cousins. His legs kept wanting to slow down but he knew he mustn't. He thought of the lost Mohawks whose spirits ran beneath the surface, and he wished they would give him a little more help because he was so tired. Maybe he could rest a little, but each time he tried, a wave sloshed over him and made him choke. He filled the shirt again and kept on, listening to his own loud breathing. But he was so tired. He just wanted to stop. He quit thinking about everything except how tired he was. Maybe he wouldn't make it after all. Maybe the spirit people had another plan for him. Maybe they were taking him someplace else.

He wanted to sleep. He knew he should refill the bubble, but his arms were too heavy to raise yet another time. He floated for a while, turning on his back to look at the clouds of evening. Rolling dark thunderheads piled up over the lake. The Professor had once told him why storm clouds were dark, but William couldn't remember the explanation.

He just wanted to float, to sleep and not think at all. A peaceful feeling slipped over him, and he was going away somewhere, slowly and gently, as if he were drifting in a dream. But then something grabbed his arm, yanked at him. He gasped, sucking in water, choking it up. The spirit people— No. He heard a voice saying his name. It was the Professor's voice. The Professor was bringing him home.

He clung fast, and was amazed to see how close to the shore he'd gotten all on his own. But now he let the Professor do the rest of the swimming and held on tight even after they reached dry ground. Then the Professor was hugging and kissing him all over his head, and maybe he was even crying a little but William couldn't tell.

"It wasn't my fault, really," William said, when he

could catch his breath. ''He took me out in the boat and—''

''I know, son,'' the Professor said. ''I was so worried.''

''I'm sorry I worried you.''

''I looked all over—''

''And you found me. I heard a gun go off. What happened to your head?''

''There was some trouble, but it's over,'' said the Professor. ''I got hit in the head with an oar, and when I came to, I discovered I was adrift in the dory. That's when I spotted you.''

''That's lucky. I'm lucky you found me.''

''I know, son,'' said the Professor. His voice was low and rough. ''I know. I'm lucky, too.''

Thirty-Two

In an agony of panic, Helena searched for her son. Troy had been cryptic, but it was clear he'd done something terrible. In the aftermath of the shooting, she had taken the gun from the hysterical Felicity Bond and hauled the girl to the lodge. Nellie was charged with calming Felicity and summoning the authorities.

Helena had babbled out her terror to the others, and everyone had joined the search. Even now, she could hear voices calling in the woods around the spring and the lodge, along the pathways to the lake and carriage house and roadway. Her voice was hoarse and ragged from screaming for William, and fear iced her nerves, numbing her to scratching branches and sharp rocks.

Through the trees, she saw a lantern bobbing toward her. ''It's me,'' called Daisy. ''It's all right now, Helena. They're both back at the lodge.''

Helena stopped breathing, then found her voice. ''William and Michael.''

''Uh-huh. They had a scare, but everything's fine.'' Daisy took her hand and they ran together to the house. Helena was still lost in a fog of numbness and burgeoning relief as she heard Daisy explain that Michael had rescued William from the lake and brought him home.

She burst inside and raced up the stairs. Nellie, Abigail and some of the others were clustered in the doorway to William's room, but they fell back and melted away at Helena's approach. She moved to step inside, but something about the sight of Michael and their son made her hesitate.

William's clothes were in a wet heap on the floor. Michael had wrapped him in blankets and was holding him close on the bed. A low flame of gaslight washed the room in deep shades of gold.

"Did I ruin Mama's dedication?" William asked.

"Everything will be fine, once she knows you're safe and sound. That's all that matters." Michael cupped his hand over the boy's head. "There's something I need to tell you."

"All right."

"Your mother and I, we— Well, it's like this. I might not be able to stay on at Moon Lake Lodge, but I'll find a place to live so we can see each other every day."

William's chin trembled. He squeezed his eyes shut. "I want you to live here. I love you."

"I love you, too, son, and I'll love you no matter where I go."

Helena caught her breath on a sob, and stepped into the room. She rushed to the bed and took William in her arms. She felt Michael stiffen with uncertainty as he moved aside.

"Mama," William said, bursting into tears. "The Professor found me and he saved me, but now he says he's going away."

"I heard him say that."

"He thinks we don't need him anymore."

"Well." Helena pursed her lips in her no-nonsense way, conquering her tears as she sank down on the bed. "He has made a career out of being wrong." She dried William's tears, tucked the covers around him and looked straight at Michael, his poor, battered face so dear she nearly wept again. "He can't leave. We won't let him."

"We won't," William agreed, yawning and burrowing down into the covers.

"We must convince the professor to stay here and marry me," Helena said, her gaze steady and strong.

And Michael's face transformed into the cocksure expression she loved so well. "How about you let me do the asking?"

"That's the best idea ever," William said, his eyelids drooping.

Michael tucked him in and whispered goodnight, then led Helena out of the room, to her own private chamber. She nearly collapsed in his arms. "I was so afraid," she whispered.

"Did he hurt you?"

With trembling fingers, she lightly touched the swelling at his temple. "Not like this. Are you going to be all right?"

"I am now."

Footsteps and rumblings from below indicated that the constable had arrived. Soon they would have to go down and give their statements.

Michael shut his eyes as a shudder went through him, and raw emotion roughened his voice. "God, I thought I'd lost you." He took her into his arms, his wet clothes dampening hers, his mouth covering hers.

Ah, this was what she'd wanted all along—his love,

his understanding, his forgiveness. She pulled back and whispered, "How can you think of going away?"

"You said we should part ways—"

"I spoke out of anger and fear and shock, Michael. Now I'm speaking from the heart. I love you. Stay with me, please. Stay with us. I know I'm difficult and temperamental, but I've learned so much. I'll never stop learning, and I'll always be grateful for this new chance we've been given. We can be happy together. We know how to do that."

Even in the faint light from the hallway, his smile enchanted her. "Yes," he said. "Yes, we do." He stepped back and took something from his pocket. "I believe this is yours."

Helena frowned and held it up to the light. "This is my silver hair comb, isn't it? I lost it the day we met."

He took it from her and tucked it awkwardly but adoringly into her hair. "No, my love. It was never lost."

Author's Note

Dear Reader,

Saratoga Springs in the Gilded Age was a special world, an appropriate setting for the unusual romance of Helena and Michael. Eventually, however, the unregulated tapping of mineral springs nearly depleted the area of its rare treasure. By the early 1900s, the State of New York shut down all but nineteen of the springs, and today visitors can still enjoy them. In addition to being the premier resort in America, this beautiful city was indeed the birthplace of the potato chip, created and served by Native American chef George Crum at the real Moon Lake Lodge.

Although Helena and Michael are on their way to wedded bliss, Isabel Fish Wooton's travels are far from over. A dangerous voyage in the company of thieves brings her together with Blue Calhoun, the troubled son from *The Horsemaster's Daughter*. Now a successful physician, Blue finds himself struggling with an unthinkable tragedy, a family crisis and suddenly, an unconventional lady adventurer who turns his life upside-down. Isabel, with her light fingers and big heart, might be just what the doctor ordered.

Please look for Blue and Isabel's story in August 2003, from MIRA Books. And watch for my first contemporary hardcover release, *Home Before Dark*, coming April 2003.

Happy reading,
Susan Wiggs
www.susanwiggs.com

New York Times
Bestselling Author

DEBBIE MACOMBER

204 Rosewood Lane

Grace Sherman
204 Rosewood Lane
Cedar Cove, Washington

Dear Reader,

If you've been to Cedar Cove before we've probably met. I've lived in this town all my life and raised two daughters here. But my husband and I—well, about six months ago, he disappeared. Just…disappeared.

My hometown, my family and friends, bring me comfort during this difficult time. And I'm continually reminded that life can and does go on. For instance, my best friend's daughter impulsively got married a little while ago. My own daughter Kelly recently had a baby. And my older daughter, Maryellen, is seeing a new man, but for some reason she won't tell me who it is.

But that's only the beginning…. Just come on over and we'll talk!

Grace

"Popular romance writer Macomber has a gift for evoking the emotions that are at the heart of the genre's popularity."
—Publishers Weekly

On sale September 2002
wherever paperbacks are sold!

Visit us at www.mirabooks.com

MDM929

Meet Jennifer Blake's newest Louisiana Gentleman

WADE

Wade Benedict has a job to do: infiltrate a treacherous land and bring Chloe Madison home. The problem is, this stubborn, angry and courageous woman doesn't want to be saved. Committed to the dangerous world of an underground rebellion, she won't abandon her cause—even though her own life is at stake.

But Chloe has met her match in Wade, a man as honorable and determined as she. And when deadly danger stalks them all the way to Turn-Coupe, Louisiana, together they must face a battle that can only be won by the indomitable will of family... and of love.

JENNIFER BLAKE

"Blake's trademark...sultry, deep-south charm."
—*Library Journal* on *Kane*

Available the first week of September 2002 wherever paperbacks are sold!

Visit us at www.mirabooks.com

MJB898

Till death us do part

On her wedding night, seventeen-year-old Anna Langtry stole her husband's car and fled into the darkness, racing toward freedom. She felt only desperation to escape the nightmare of her Colorado home—an isolated rural community that condoned her forced polygamous marriage to become one man's third wife.

Fifteen years later she is pulled back to the past she left behind as she tries to help her parolee, Joe Mackenzie, look for justice in a community of dangerous secrets and deadly schemes.

THE THIRD WIFE

Available the first week of September 2002 wherever paperbacks are sold!

Visit us at www.mirabooks.com

MJC931

MIRA®

A novel of psychological suspense,
from bestselling author

MEG O'BRIEN

CRIMSON RAIN

Paul and Gina Bradley wanted the perfect family. When they discovered they could not have children of their own, they adopted twin girls, intent on giving them a good home. But something was terribly wrong with one of the twins, and after a terrifying event, Paul and Gina returned five-year-old Angela to the orphanage, assured she would get excellent psychiatric care.

Now, sixteen years later, the Bradley family is crumbling. Paul and Gina have drifted apart. Their daughter, Rachel, is acting like a stranger. But when Rachel disappears, Paul and Gina are forced to pull together—for the sake of their family, for their very survival. Because someone has released a vengeful fury on the Bradleys.

"An absorbing suspense thriller that never eases up until the reader completes the final pages."
—*Midwest Book Review* on *Gathering Lies*

Available the first week of September 2002 wherever paperbacks are sold!

Visit us at www.mirabooks.com

MMO93

It takes one to know one....

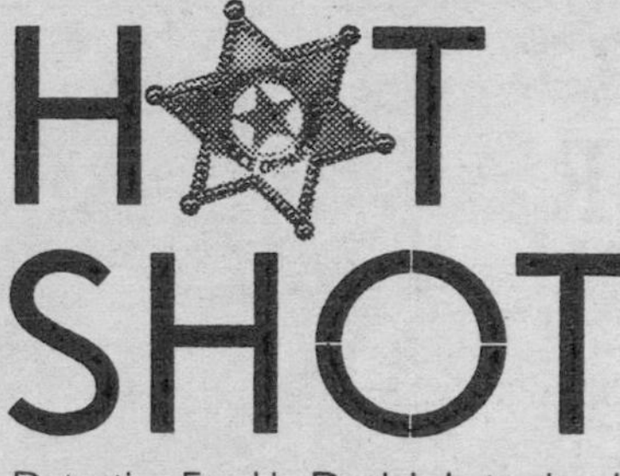

SHOT

Detective Frankie Daniels hates her life—well, what's left of it. After a romance with the wrong man goes bad, the tough Atlanta police detective finds herself "transferred" to Nowhere, USA. Purdyville, South Carolina, is tantamount to a sentence of death by boredom for the street-smart, chain-smoking cop.

When Frankie arrives to find her rental home in flames, she proceeds to chew out one of the locals—only to realize she's just told off her new boss, the annoyingly gorgeous and smug Sheriff Matt Webber. But Matt is more intrigued than angry at his new deputy. Underneath that tough-cookie exterior, Matt's pretty sure Frankie's got a soft spot.... He just hopes it's for *him.*

Charlotte Hughes

"In a tale rife with humor and emotion, Ms. Hughes demonstrates a great flair for storytelling. With well-crafted characters and delightful banter, this is just plain fun!"
—*Romantic Times* on *A New Attitude*

Available the first week of September 2002 wherever paperbacks are sold!

Visit us at www.mirabooks.com

MCHU941

Had she survived by fate, coincidence or just luck?

KEEPER OF THE BRIDE

If Nina Cormier's wedding had taken place, she would be dead by now. But after the bride was left at the altar, the church stood empty when the bomb went off. It wasn't until a stranger tried to run her off the road, however, that she realized someone wanted *her* dead.

But who? That's what Detective Sam Navarro needs to find out...fast. As a nightmare unfolds around them both, Sam and Nina decipher the stunning truth. Now they're at the mercy of a brilliant madman who plays for keeps....

"Tess Gerritsen...throws one twist after another until the excitement is almost unbearable."
—*San Jose Mercury News*

Available the first week of September 2002 wherever paperbacks are sold!

Visit us at www.mirabooks.com

MTG935

MIRABooks.com

We've got the lowdown on your favorite author!

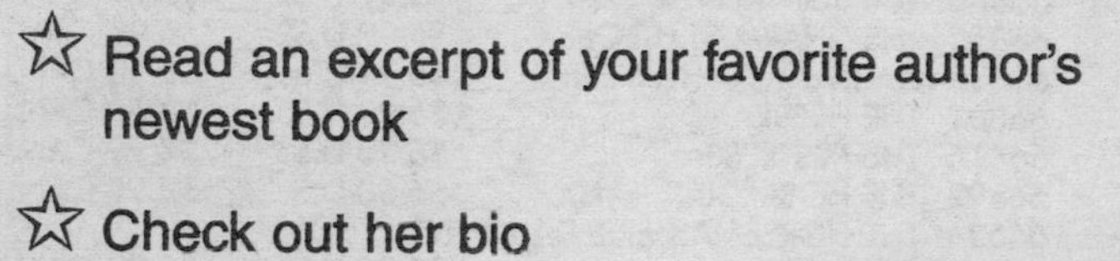

☆ Read an excerpt of your favorite author's newest book

☆ Check out her bio

☆ Talk to her in our Discussion Forums

☆ Read interviews, diaries, and more

☆ Find her current besteller, and even her backlist titles

All this and more available at

www.MiraBooks.com

MEAUT1R2

SUSAN WIGGS

66880	THE LIGHTKEEPER	___ $5.99 U.S.	___ $6.99 CAN.
66855	THE CHARM SCHOOL	___ $5.99 U.S.	___ $6.99 CAN.
66837	HALFWAY TO HEAVEN	___ $6.99 U.S.	___ $8.50 CAN.
66801	THE FIREBRAND	___ $6.99 U.S.	___ $8.50 CAN.
66610	THE MISTRESS	___ $6.50 U.S.	___ $7.99 CAN.
66592	THE HOSTAGE	___ $6.50 U.S.	___ $7.99 CAN.
66534	THE HORSEMASTER'S DAUGHTER	___ $5.99 U.S.	___ $6.99 CAN.
66459	THE DRIFTER	___ $5.99 U.S.	___ $6.99 CAN.
66449	THAT SUMMER PLACE	___ $6.99 U.S.	___ $7.99 CAN.

(*limited quantities available*)

TOTAL AMOUNT $________
POSTAGE & HANDLING $________
($1.00 for one book; 50¢ for each additional)
APPLICABLE TAXES* $________
TOTAL PAYABLE $________
(check or money order—please do not send cash)

To order, complete this form and send it, along with a check or money order for the total above, payable to MIRA Books®, to: **In the U.S.:** 3010 Walden Avenue, P.O. Box 9077, Buffalo, NY 14269-9077; **In Canada:** P.O. Box 636, Fort Erie, Ontario L2A 5X3.

Name:________________
Address:________________ City:________________
State/Prov.:________________ Zip/Postal Code:________________
Account Number (if applicable):________________
075 CSAS

*New York residents remit applicable sales taxes.
Canadian residents remit applicable GST and provincial taxes.

MIRA®

Visit us at www.mirabooks.com

MSW0902BL